To: Pam

May you flu... ...

high on the Dou...

Melody S...

MW01154662

# ON THE *Wings* OF A DOVE

## MELODY S. DEAL

**BALBOA.**
PRESS

A DIVISION OF HAY HOUSE

Balboa Press books may be ordered through booksellers or by contacting:

Balboa Press
A Division of Hay House
1663 Liberty Drive
Bloomington, IN 47403
www.balboapress.com
1 (877) 407-4847

Because of the dynamic nature of the Internet, any web addresses or links contained in this book may have changed since publication and may no longer be valid. The views expressed in this work are solely those of the author and do not necessarily reflect the views of the publisher, and the publisher hereby disclaims any responsibility for them.

This is a work of fiction. All of the characters, names, incidents, organizations, and dialogue in this novel are either the products of the author's imagination or are used fictitiously.

Any people depicted in stock imagery provided by Thinkstock are models, and such images are being used for illustrative purposes only.
Certain stock imagery © Thinkstock.

Print information available on the last page.

ISBN: 978-1-5043-4424-1 (sc)
ISBN: 978-1-5043-4423-4 (e)

Balboa Press rev. date: 11/17/2015

# Contents

For my children,
Yancey, Adam, Dustin and Katy,

# Acknowledgements

Warm thanks to Maxine, who inspired me to write Sarah's story, to my husband Robert for supporting and encouraging me through my writing madness, to Alice, Connie, John, Pat, and Shel who mentored me and kept me on track, to my mother, Bonnie and my father, Joe, whose parenting skills mirrored that of Sarah, to friends and family who believed in me, and most significantly, to God, my rock and my redeemer who sustains me.

# Chapter 1

"Ma, Ma, come quick," Josh screamed as he burst through the kitchen door. The nine year old, near exhaustion after running in the stifling heat collapsed to his knees gasping for air. The freckles that usually populated the boy's face were lost in a mask of red flush.

Sarah dipped the corner hem of her long apron in the bucket of water on the dry sink and began to bathe her son's face. "Calm down. Take a deep breath and tell me what's happened."

"It's Pa. He's taken sick or somethin'. He fell off the hay wagon and he's just layin' there in the field a mumblin'. Abe sent me to fetch you."

"Which field?"

"The one farthest over, next to Thompson's pond."

Sarah grabbed a wooden apple crate that she kept by the kitchen cupboard and ran out on the back porch. "Zeke, come climb up on this apple crate and start ringing the dinner bell. Don't stop until Josh takes over."

Zeke was digging in his dirt pile under the shade of their large maple tree. "That don't make no sense, Ma. It ain't supper time."

"Now Ezekiel, now!"

Zeke knew that when his ma called him Ezekiel he'd best be fast to respond. He dropped his shovel and ran. After climbing atop the wooden crate he grabbed the rope and started pulling.

The hearing of a dinner bell at any hour other than customary meal times equaled the sounding of an alarm in the rural community. Although the details weren't specific, the message was clear. Come quick, help is needed. Sarah hoped her neighbors would hear the frantic mid-afternoon ringing and respond.

Sarah grabbed her sun bonnet. *What do I need to take? Water!* She snatched up the bucket of drinking water and sprinted out the door.

Before Sarah took off she dispensed orders to Josh. "Stick your head under the pump and cool off. Take turns with Zeke ringing that bell until help comes. Tend to your baby sister when she wakes up from her nap and stay out of the sun."

With their team of horses out in the hayfield, Sarah had no choice

1

but to cover the distance on foot. When the water started to slosh out of the bucket she was forced to slow her pace. Her apron and long skirt kept getting tangled between her legs. She stopped long enough to gather up her skirt and petticoat and tucked them in her waistband.

Sweat soaked Sarah's hair and streams of wetness ran down her back. She stumbled frequently on clods of earth and crop stubble lying in the field. Lashes of fear whipped painfully at her heart. She'd told Henry when he and the boys came in for dinner at noon that it had grown too hot for them to continue field work. She'd pleaded with her husband to do chores around the barn and leave the hay until the next morning when it would be cooler.

In her mind she replayed the scene that had taken place. The children were gathered at the table and she was standing at the sink. Henry, with his long legs on a six foot two frame had crossed the distance between the table and her in one stride. He'd wrapped his arms around her waist, nuzzled her neck and said, "It's the last field of hay. I want to go to bed tonight knowing that I have all of it cut. We'll be careful and rest if we get too hot. I promise to save myself plenty of energy to sashay you around the dance floor at the social tonight."

With a throaty voice, he'd whispered in her ear. "I'd better get out of here while I still can."

Sarah had felt her own yearning, leaned back and whispered. "Yes, you'd better go. Some of our children are getting old enough to catch on to these shenanigans."

"I'm goin' with you, Pa," Luke had said with his mouth still full of food. "Tommy Wilson helps his Pa and he ain't even as big as me. I've never got to go and I just heard you tell Ma this is the last field. I won't get me another chance to cut hay this summer."

In an attempt to intercede, Sarah said, "Henry, he's only seven and I think he's too young to be working in the hayfield. Especially today with it being so hot and humid."

"Sarah, I understand your concern," Henry had responded. "I did say he could help and a promise is a promise. Luke, roll down your shirt sleeves and grab your straw hat."

Henry had motioned to Abe his eleven-year-old and Josh his

nine-year-old to come stand beside him and Luke. "Boys, let's show your Ma that we Whitcomes are tough."

Sarah giggled as her handsome husband and stair-step boys flexed their muscles and collectively gave a low growl, "Gerrrr."

"What about me, Pa? I'm gettin' big," Four-year-old Zeke had cried out as he jumped off his chair.

Scooping him up in his arms Henry had said, "Now if you was to go, who's gonna dig up that ground out yonder under the maple tree? You stay here and get that done and next year we'll talk about you helpin' with the hay. Besides, we need someone to stay back and protect these women."

He'd put the boy down then leaned over the high chair and kissed his thirteen month old daughter. "Hathaway, how about you take a long nap today. I don't want your ma all wore out tonight." After winking at Sarah he'd left for the field, his boys in tow, scurrying to keep up with his long strides.

\*\*\*

Remembering the sweetness of those moments brought tears to Sarah's eyes. *Dear Lord, let him be all right.*

Abe and Luke saw their mother running toward them. Jumping and waving their arms they yelled. "Hurry Ma, somethin's bad wrong with Pa."

Sarah reached the wagon and dropped to her knees by her husband's side. He lay unconscious on the hay-strewn ground. The smell of the newly cut crop, once a pleasant scent, now sickened her and she felt her stomach lurch.

Henry's splotchy complexion confirmed her worst fear, heatstroke. She'd seen that same discoloration of the skin on their neighbor when he lay limp and unconscious in his field the summer before. Harley Seamore was forty-three. He never woke up.

Sarah slapped her husband's cheeks. "Henry, Henry talk to me!" Getting no response she ordered. "Boys, help me drag him into the shade of the wagon."

Sarah lifted Henry's arms while Abe and Luke each grabbed a leg. Working together they were able to scoot him to the spot that provided sun shield. Sarah tore Henry's shirt open. She ripped off her apron, wet it and began to bathe her husband's face and chest. Getting no response she barked orders. "Luke, take your pa's hat and fan his face. Abe, pull his boots and socks off."

A team and wagon could be heard approaching. Sarah looked up to see their neighbor Jeb Carter and his grown son Julib barreling toward them. The dust from the parched earth billowed up as the wheels made ruts in the hard packed soil.

Sarah whispered, "Praise God."

Henry Whitcome was a big man and weighed nearly 250 pounds. Sarah had been in doubt that she and her two sons could lift him without help.

Jeb reined his team to a halt. "We heard the bell and came as fast as we could. Dropped my missus off at your house. Josh told us where to come."

"Heatstroke," Sarah called out. "Help me get him back to the house."

Struggling against the heavy limp weight, the pair managed to place Henry in their wagon, then hop up on its seat.

Sarah barked orders as she scrambled into the wagon's bed and cradled her husband's body. "Jeb, drop us off, then go fetch Doc Adams. Abe, you and Luke drive our team back to the farm. Rub the horses down good and give them a little water. No oats until they've cooled off."

Abe and Luke stood side by side watching their pa being taken away. "Will he be alright?" Luke asked, reaching over and taking his oldest brother's hand.

Abe released from the grip, wrapped his arm around his young brother's shoulder and pulled him close. "Sure, he'll be fine. Now don't you worry none."

Luke looked up just as a tear spilled from Abe's eye. He watched it as it traced a path through the dirt on his brother's face, down across his cheek, pausing just at the cleft of his chin before it dropped to the parched soil.

The seven-year-old resisted the urge to reach up and wipe it away. He thought Abe might be embarrassed if he knew he'd seen him cry. Instead Luke shoved his hands deep in the pockets of his bib overalls. "I sure hope when Pa wakes up he don't remember Ma a slappin' him like that."

# Chapter 2

Sarah sat in her kitchen sipping her morning cup of coffee. The quiet before sunrise, before the house came alive, had once been a relaxing time for her. Now she felt anxious about the family's future. It had been two months since Henry's heatstroke and the debilitating effects lingered.

Doc Adams' diagnosis of Henry's condition played over and over in her mind. "Henry's general health seems good. However, I've got little hope that his faculties will come back to him. I think his mind is permanently afflicted."

Accepting that Henry might not make a recovery, keeping up with chores as mother of five and seeing to the needs of the farm weighed heavy on Sarah's shoulders.

*Heavenly Father, I know the scriptures say you won't send more our way than we can handle with your help. I'm claiming that promise, Lord.* Sarah began to softly hum the refrain from *I Need Thee Every Hour*, one of her favorite hymns.

She was thankful that the corn and beans had been harvested and sold at market before Henry's heatstroke. With the help of neighbors, the remainder of the hay had been baled and stored for feed.

It was already mid-September and winter was approaching. No fieldwork meant the workload around the farm would lessen. The pace would slow and chores would center more on the livestock and building maintenance. Sarah felt that she and the two older boys could handle feeding the animals, chopping firewood and taking care of most routine repairs. Barring any other major troubles, they'd make it through the next few months without outside help. She'd use the time to figure out what to do and make a plan before spring planting time.

Henry was unable to dress or bathe himself. He now preferred the use of a spoon over a fork and eating was an arduous task for him. His attempts to fondle Sarah made it difficult to care for him and his sexual overtures were a growing concern.

Sarah knew from the blank look in his eyes that his advances weren't coming from any lingering bond they had once shared as husband and wife. They were random and aggressive and left her feeling violated. She tried to be discreet when she pushed his hands away. The younger children appeared to be oblivious, but not Abe. She knew from the look on his face that he understood and that his father's actions embarrassed and angered him.

A couple of times she felt the boy was on the verge of intervening on her behalf. Sarah sensed that he was beginning to assume the role as guardian for the family. He was too young for that to happen.

Sarah needed a respite from the worry. She let her mind be transported to thirteen years prior, July 4, 1890 and the first time she'd met Henry.

Sarah was at a town hall dance with her brother Jack and his wife Becky. She'd been reluctant to go but had allowed herself to be coaxed. She was twenty and much older than most of the single girls in their community. Her unmarried status was by choice. There'd been many suitors, but none had held her interest.

Sarah was tall and slender, with auburn hair that glistened in the sunlight. She had striking, chiseled features and long lashes on large, brown expressive eyes. She didn't like pretense and wouldn't feign shyness to appear more feminine.

Being introduced to Sarah was a memorable encounter. It was her habit to look at others with an intensity that was more like an embrace than mere eye contact. She was energetic and intelligent and LaFontaine, Indiana had no eligible men who could hold Sarah's interest for long.

Sarah was sipping her lemonade, when she noticed the silhouette of a man standing in the building's entrance, hat in hand. Eventually he strode from the shadow into the light. The day's waning rays of sunlight reflected from the hall's west bank of windows and shone across his figure. He was tall, taller than Sarah. He appeared to be six foot two or three and broad at the shoulders. Sarah thought him to be handsome despite his unruly blond hair. It appeared that Sarah wasn't the only one to think this. She noticed that several women gasped slightly when they looked at the man. There was no gasp from Sarah Riley. It wasn't her nature to let her composure falter.

Sarah was standing next to her bother when the man walked toward them. As he neared, a warm sensation unlike any she'd ever experienced washed over her.

Jack extended his hand. "Welcome. Glad you could come."

"Glad I could make it," the man responded.

"Henry," Jack said. "This is my wife, Rebecca, and my sister, Sarah. Ladies, meet Henry Whitcome."

Henry nodded and bowed slightly toward both women, then looked at Sarah. "Pleased to meet you Miss Riley."

"Call me Sarah," She replied as she held him with her eyes.

\*\*\*

The sound of the children's footsteps coming down the stairs snapped Sarah out of her daydreaming. She quickly dished up oatmeal and set the steaming bowls on the table alongside a pitcher of milk and a plate of biscuits.

Luke entered the kitchen first. "Good mornin', Ma." He and Sarah hugged.

Josh came in next. After looking at the table he teased, "Oatmeal! I was hopin' for pancakes today." He too gave his mother a morning hug. "It's ok, I like your oatmeal."

Sarah smiled and gave the boy's cheek a gentle pinch. "You'd better, or you'll go to school hungry."

Abe came in from doing morning chores. "Ma, today it's my turn to fill up the wood box at school. I have to get there early. I didn't get Moon Blossom milked yet. What should I do?"

Sarah was busy filling glasses with milk. "Don't worry about it, son. Just leave her for me. We'll get a plan for getting morning work done without your Pa's help figured out soon."

Sarah's three oldest boys, Abe, Josh, and Luke, had been back in school for two weeks. Signs that the fall season was in full swing were evident and it now frosted most nights.

Day broke with a brightness that shone briefly on the roofs of the barn and woodshed. The reflection of the sun against the buildings' frozen crusted bonnets gave the illusion of millions of sparkling diamonds. They appeared to dance about but came to a rest when the rays of light moved to the maple tree, setting the leaves ablaze in brilliant shades of orange and yellow.

Zeke, still groggy with sleep, came staggering into the kitchen. The four-year-old pointed, "Look, Ma, the barn's roof has sugar all over it."

Since the start of school the tyke had gotten up for breakfast with his older brothers in hopes that it would be the day he'd grown big enough to go too.

Luke was excited about his first year at school. His continuous yammering, with details of playing marbles in the dirt at recess with his new friends, only made it harder for Zeke to adjust.

Midway through breakfast Luke laughed. "Ma, look at Zeke! He's done fell asleep at the table again."

Abe jumped up from his chair. "I got him, Ma."

Sarah's heart felt full as she watched Abe wipe the oatmeal from the small boy's face and gently lift and carry him back to his bed.

After the boys left for school Sarah got Henry up and dressed and served him his breakfast. While he ate she headed for the barn. She hoped to get the remainder of the milking done before Zeke and Hathaway woke.

She found Moon Blossom tied in a stall fidgeting, waiting to be relieved of her burden. Sarah winced when she saw the cow's engorged udder. "Sorry, old gal. I've often felt the same way when I was breast feeding."

After sitting down on the three-legged stool, Sarah began her much practiced art of manipulating the cow's teats to extract the creamy richness. The relief the milking brought seemed to soothe and calm the cow and both Moon Blossom and Sarah relaxed into the rhythm of the process.

Sarah's first inkling that she and cow weren't alone in the barn was a prickling sensation on the back of her neck. Glancing up, she saw the shadow of a figure moving up behind her. She looked over her shoulder just as Henry grabbed her about her waist, pulled her off of the milking stool and on to the barn floor.

Sarah struggled, but Henry managed to pin her down with the weight of his large frame. She felt pain as his hands groped her body. Henry pulled her long skirt up above her thighs. He jerked her bloomers down below her knees. Sarah felt hay stubble prickle and scratch at the bare skin on her legs, buttocks and thighs. "Stop. Stop, Henry." She was strong, but no match for a man Henry's size. Sarah cried out. "Dear God in heaven, send me help."

After leaving for school an uneasy feeling had nagged at Abe. *Did I leave the lantern lit in the barn? Is it Ma? She looked tired and worried. Is that what's botherin' me?*

The boys had gone about a quarter mile down the road when Abe abruptly stopped. "Josh, I need you to take my place fillin' the wood box this mornin'. I've got to go check on somethin' at the farm."

Josh whined. "It ain't my turn. You'll be late for school."

Abe pleaded. "Josh, please. You can have my piece of pie tonight."

"Alight, but you gotta take my turn fillin' the wood box next week," Josh bargained.

Abe took off running and yelled over his shoulder, "Done deal."

Abe was nearing the fork in their lane when he heard his mother's voice coming from the direction of the barn, screaming for help. Veering right he ran full bore, skidding to a stop at the barn's door.

His eyes strained to adjust from the bright sun to the dim darkness of the barn's interior. A wide beam of light intruding through a crack in the roof illuminated two bodies awash in swarming dust particles, struggling on the floor. *It's Ma. What's happenin'? Who's on top of her? It's Pa! I shouldn't be lookin'. Ma's screamin'. He's hurtin' her.*

Abe grabbed the back of his father's shirt. Using strength that tore at his young muscles, he yanked him off of his mother. "Nooooooo!"

Sarah pulled her clothes together and got to her feet. Abe was standing over his father with clenched fists. The boy's chest was heaving and tears were streaming down his cheeks.

Sarah took ahold of Abe's arm and pulled him back a few steps. "Just let him be for a bit. Let him be."

"Ma, did he... did he, hurt you?"

"No...uh, no. You stopped him."

Henry lay on the barn floor looking up at his wife and son. The expression on his face was one of confusion, as if he had no understanding of what had just occurred.

Abe looked at his mother. "What do we do now?"

"We help him up and take him to the house."

"How can you help him after what he just did?"

"Abe, he's your father. He's not in his right mind. He doesn't know what he did."

Together they got Henry to his feet. Sarah nearly broke down when she saw the look of anguish on her son's face. He had witnessed the man, once the family's protector, become his mother's predator.

After brushing the hay and dirt from Henry's clothing, they walked him to the house and to his makeshift bed they'd set up for him in the parlor. Sarah removed his shoes and shirt and coaxed him to lie down. Henry appeared to be exhausted and quickly fell into a deep sleep.

Anxious to collect herself Sarah said, "Abe, go finish milking Moon Blossom. When you're done come back to the house and we'll talk."

With trembling hands Sarah smoothed down the front of her apron. She pulled her shoulders back, lifted her head high and went to get the baby who was awake and fussing.

After walking a few steps Sarah felt dizzy. Her gait faltered and the knot in her pompadour slipped. She reached up but it was too late. Her heavy mane broke free and dropped, jerking her neck when it landed below her waist. Sarah's hand fell limp to her side. *There's no point, it's destroyed beyond fixing.*

# Chapter 3

Sarah put a piece of apple pie and a glass of milk on the kitchen table in front of her son and sat down. "Abe, I'm sorry you saw what happened in the barn. What caused you to come back when you did?"

"I just had a bad feelin' that somethin' was wrong. I didn't know if I'd left a lantern lit in the barn…the thought that you might be sick went through my mind. I don't know, somethin' just pulled at me to come home, and quick." Abe took a long drink of milk.

"I was in trouble and cried out to God for help. I'll always believe He heard me and sent you." Sarah leaned over and kissed the boy on the cheek.

"Ma, it's gonna be hard to not be mad at Pa for what he tried to do to you. You may think I ain't old enough to know, but I know." The boy's face turned beet red. "Pa wasn't lovin' on you, Ma…he was hurtin' you."

Sarah patted her son's hand. "Abe, your father's brain was damaged when he had that heatstroke. We have to make allowances for him."

"He was hurtin' you, Ma. I can't make no allowances for that," Abe said as he shoveled in his last bite of pie.

Hathaway was sitting in her high chair eating a cookie. Her mixture of gumming and munching away at the treat had created a lot of crumbs. She traced her tiny fingers through the mess and then in one fell swoop, brushed them off on to the floor.

Sarah got up and fetched the broom. "Should I be mad at Hathaway for making this mess and causing me more work?"

"Of course not, she's just a baby. She doesn't know any better," responded Abe.

Sarah started sweeping up the crumbs. "That's what I think too. I also think that your father doesn't know any better right now either. We can hope and pray that he gets well. In the meantime, we have to understand and forgive him when he does something that we don't like."

"I can try, but he ain't no baby," the boy said rubbing his sore bicep.

Sarah put her arm around Abe and pulled him up for a hug. "Now go on to school for the rest of the day. Tell the teacher you're late because I needed you to help me with something here at the farm. Let's keep the details private."

When the boy didn't budge, Sarah asked. "Are you worried about leaving me here alone with your pa?"

"Yes," Abe whispered.

"He's sound asleep and I think he will be for several hours. I know now that I have to be more mindful of what he might do. Please try not to worry. This is for me to work out." Sarah took Abe by the elbow and gently encouraged him out the door.

\*\*\*

Sarah was popping pans of bread in the oven to bake when she heard a horse and buggy coming up their lane. She looked out and recognized the rig. It was Doc Adams.

Five years ago when LaFontaine's doctor for over fifty years died, the small rural community feared they'd have trouble finding a replacement. They felt blessed when Ben and Beth Adams moved to the community and decided to make it their home.

The first time she and Henry met the young couple, Sarah knew they were special people. They became good friends to her family. She and Henry grieved with Doc when Beth died giving birth to their first child. The baby was stillborn.

Sarah opened the door to greet Ben before he knocked. "Good morning. I'm surprised to see you out this way today,"

"A two year old a mile from here has the croup. Since I was close, I thought I'd come by to look in on Henry," Ben said as he stepped in to the kitchen taking off his hat.

The air was permeated with the delicious smell of baking bread. Ben pulled in a deep breath. "I never appreciated the scent of yeast loaf in the oven when it was a routine occurrence at my home. Now that Beth is gone I realize those seemingly little day-to-day pleasures weren't really so small."

"I bake bread three days a week and I never grow tired of the smell. Sit down. The loaves will be ready in a few minutes and I'll cut you big slab. For now, how about some coffee?" Sarah went to her cupboard to get a cup.

"Sarah that sounds like just what this doctor should order." Ben said with a smile, taking a seat at the table.

"You said you paid a call on a sick baby close to here. Was it the

Slawson's baby, Gabriel?" Sarah asked with concern, placing Doc's coffee on the table.

"Yes."

"How ill is he? Is he going to be alright? Do they need anything?"

Now don't go taking on worry over the Slawson's child. He's sick, but he's strong. He'll weather through this cough. You've enough to worry about."

Sarah took a seat at the table. "That's true Ben, but I certainly can take time to lift Gabriel up in prayer. Does Millie have family to help her?"

"Yes, her mother is there. I'm sure your prayers will be appreciated." As Ben blew on the rich brown liquid to cool it he looked over his cup at Sarah. She was nervously picking at the pocket on her apron. He reached over and patted her on the arm. "How's Henry been the past couple of weeks? Any changes in his behavior?"

Doc's caring touch broke her resolve to keep Henry's assault a secret. Sarah's voice trembled as she told him what had taken place in the barn that morning.

"Oh Sarah. I'm so sorry that happened," Ben used his handkerchief to take a swipe at tears that threatened to spill from his eyes. "I'm sorry for you, I'm sorry that Abe witnessed it and I'm broken hearted for Henry."

Placing the linen in his inside jacket pocket he said, "Sarah, you know how much Henry loved you and the children. In his right mind he would never hurt you."

"I know that Doc. It comforts me to hear you say it. I don't want the sweet man Henry was to be forgotten." Sarah whispered.

"I won't forget him, he was a good friend to me." Ben leaned in toward Sarah. "I've talked with Doctor Mathews over at Lagro about Henry's lingering symptoms. He's treated several patients with heatstroke and he's in agreement that Henry's memory should have recovered by now. Based on Doc Mathew's experience he predicts Henry will get worse and harder to handle. We're advising you to not hold a lot of hope that his mind will heal."

Sarah clutched her friend's arm. "Doc it's only been two months, aren't you giving up on Henry too soon?"

"When a heatstroke occurs, it's due to the body's temperature rising to a dangerous degree. That causes the brain to swell and exhaustion to occur. Once the body cools to a normal temperature and has a chance to rest sufficiently, normal function will return if irreparable damage hasn't taken place. It's my opinion that Henry's brain has had enough time to rest and recover if it was going to," Doc said.

"Ben, are you saying I should give up *all* hope?"

"What I'm saying Sarah, as your doctor and your friend, is that you have five young ones to think about as well as yourself. If Abe hadn't come back home this morning when he did, you might have been seriously hurt. I'm recommending to you again that you consider having Henry placed in the mental hospital over at Logansport. They can provide him with the care and supervision he needs."

"So your recommending I send him away and let someone else take care of him. The children and I should go on with life like he doesn't exist."

"Sarah, I know this is hard for you. If Henry can stay calm for long periods of time, the hospital might allow him to come home for short visits."

Ben had first suggested hospitalization when he visited Henry two weeks earlier. Sarah hoped the need to make a decision like this wouldn't come. "I respect your advice Doc and I don't take my responsibilities for Henry and our children lightly. I know a decision about his care has to be made soon. I'll be talking with the Lord this afternoon on the subject. I need to know that He's in agreement when I make a plan," Sarah said.

Ben wasn't surprised that Sarah told him she needed to first consult with the Lord. Over the years that he'd known her, he'd heard her talk about her relationship with God as if it was personal. Ben's wife Beth talked about God and prayed. He felt he'd understood Beth's reverence for The Creator. But this "communication" Sarah seemed to have with God was different. She referred to The Lord and I this, The Lord and I that… like they had a friendship.

It seemed as if Sarah truly sought to live her life daily in God's will. While Doc had tremendous respect for her, he couldn't fathom surrendering one's will to that extent.

Beth had wanted him to come to a fuller understanding, a greater acceptance of God. He'd thought he might one day, but the chance of that died with Beth and the baby. Ben didn't doubt that there was a God. He'd continue to go to church when it suited him, but he wouldn't put trust in a God who would take his family from him.

Ben looked across the table at Sarah's lovely face. *I wonder how she'll reconcile God's will with the reality that the man she loved is gone. Her husband, the father of her children isn't coming back to her.* "I'm going to go check on Henry. Is he sleeping in the parlor?"

"Yes, thanks Ben."

When the doctor returned to the kitchen he said, "He seems to be in a really deep sleep. I didn't try to wake him." Ben handed Sarah a small bottle of liquid. "This is Laudanum, give him a couple of spoons full if he tries roaming around at night. You need your rest and he needs watching when he's awake."

"Thanks. Bread's done…want a piece?"

"Smells mighty tempting but I've got more calls to make and need to get on my way."

Sarah handed Ben a loaf wrapped in a linen towel. "I expected as much. Here's some for later."

"Thank you Sarah. Contact me when you've made your decision. I'll be glad to help any way I can."

Doc Adams climbed in his buggy and gently placed the loaf of bread, still warm, on the seat next to him. Since becoming a widower, the suppers he prepared for himself had been sparse. Sarah's bread would be a welcome addition to his evening meal. As he headed down the road he mentally ticked off his remaining stops before his day ended and he would return to his lonely house. He searched his mind for a pleasant thought to ward off the melancholy that was threatening to set in. The scene that day at Sarah's table came to mind. Her lovely face…his hand reaching out…resting on her arm to comfort her. *Whoa…was my advice to Sarah to hospitalize Henry medically appropriate, not borne out of my affection for her?*

His doubts subsided as he recalled his close friendship with Henry as well as with Sarah. Those memories were dear to him. The pain of losing his sweet Beth still stung. His confidence in his diagnosis of Henry's mental health was solid.

\*\*\*

That afternoon while Zeke was busy playing with his farm animals and Hathaway and Henry continued to nap, Sarah knelt by the side of her bed and poured her heart out to God.

"Lord, thank you for answering my prayer this morning and sending Abe to help me in my time of need. Father I pray that he be able to remember Henry as the wonderful, loving husband and father he has always been. Lord I don't understand why Henry has to suffer lingering effects of the heatstroke. I ask again that he be healed and made whole. In the meantime Lord, we have a decision to make about Henry's care. Heavenly Father I come to you asking for your divine guidance to know if sending him to the mental hospital for care is what is best for Henry and my family. Lord I need a sign from you, a sign so clear that I will have no doubt about being in your will. Should I admit Henry to the mental hospital?"

As Sarah prayed, a peace that surely does pass all understanding washed over her body. She was filled with calmness.

Luke's call, "I'm hungry Ma," followed by Zeke's, "me too," brought Sarah to her feet. The call meant that the boys were home from school. The two older ones would be in the barn doing chores and she had a meal to cook. Hathaway was awake and standing in her crib. Sarah picked her up as she left the room.

"Quiet boys, your Pa is resting," Sarah chided as she walked into the kitchen. "I'll have supper ready in about an hour. Grab yourselves and Hathaway a cookie to tide you over." She handed the baby over to Luke.

"Ah…Ma…she's wet," the boy complained.

"Yes, I know. You can go put a dry diaper on her or peel potatoes. You get to choose," Sarah said with a smile.

Hathaway wailed as her brother held her at arm's length on their way to get her dry britches.

\*\*\*

"Supper's almost ready," Sarah said to the boys who were playing Jacks in the corner of the kitchen. "Go ring the bell so Abe and Josh will come from the barn. Then you fellows get washed up at the pump. Luke, please help Zeke get his face and patty cakes clean."

The-four-year old bounced the small ball and snatched up three of the six metal spirals before it descended and touched the floor. "Score! Luke, Luke, I got 'threesies.' See Ma, I'm gettin' big. I don't need no one to help me wash up."

"Well, now that you mention it, you do seem taller." Sarah winked at Luke. "Priming the pump takes a lot of muscle, how about you help your brother. Two working together is always better than one."

Luke put his arm around his younger brother's shoulder and started ushering him toward the door. "I'll make sure he gets clean Ma." Looking back at his mother he said, "Supper sure smells good."

"Luke, come here." Sarah said with her arms widespread. She enfolded her son in a loving embrace. "What a nice thing to say about my cooking." The child's face beamed, obviously basking in the warmth of his mother's individual attention.

At seven, Luke wasn't as tall as Abe or Josh had been at that age. Sarah wondered if he would grow to a tall man like his father. There was no denying that he was a beautiful child with his large dark expressive eyes with lashes any girl would envy. She knew he would be handsome and his gentle spirit would assuredly make him a kind man.

*I'm blessed to have such sweet children.* As the screen door banged shut, Sarah reached down, gathered the baby up in her arms and gave her a hug. She put the child in her high chair and pulled it up to the table.

The sounding bell alerted Henry it was meal time and he tentatively entered the kitchen. Sarah took his hand and led him to his place at the head of the table. Luke and Zeke came in and took their seats. Abe and Josh entered and filled the last two vacant chairs.

The children as if by rote, turned toward their father in expectation of his prayer followed by the signal that supper could begin. The face staring back at them looked bewildered and confused. Most days were like that now. Henry's eyes darted from one child to another, then to his wife. He seemed fearful and Sarah wondered if he remembered the incident in the barn that morning and if on any level he understood what he had done.

Supper at the Whitcomes' had always been an important time for strengthening bonds and nurturing the family's heartstrings. Talking, laughing, and telling stories was encouraged, especially by Henry. When one of the boy's yarns raveled too far from truth or believability, he would good-naturedly wind them in, just enough for teaching boundaries. Now he sat silent at the table. Supper together was a strain. The children didn't want to talk.

Sarah missed hearing her husband's heartfelt prayers before each meal. She called on her oldest to pray. "Abe would you please say grace for us tonight?"

"Yes Ma'am. Lord, thank you for this food that we are about to eat and for the one that prepared it. Amen." The boy looked toward his mother for her nod of approval.

"Thank you son. You may pass the meat." Sarah said.

As she spoke, a movement in Sarah's peripheral vision caught her attention. *A flutter of white, what was that? Wings...a chicken?* She turned toward the window to look. Sitting on the sill was a white bird. Sarah blinked, then squinted. *It isn't a chicken. It's a bird...a white dove.* Sarah rose from her chair and slowly crossed the room. As she moved Sarah could hear her children's voices asking for food to be passed and milk to be poured. They seemed far way, secondary to the beckoning of the bird who was looking at her.

*A white dove...is it real? I've never seen one.* The bird was pristine. An aura of light appeared to surround it. Sarah touched the portion of the windowpane where its body pressed. She jerked her hand back. *Hot! No..., not actually hot.* She touched the window again. *It's more like an energy, a drawing in...as if the dove is touching me through the glass.* The bird didn't move. Sarah let her hand linger, savoring the comfort.

Suddenly a powerful wave of understanding washed over Sarah. She had prayed that day for a sign. God had responded, sending the same sign He'd given to Noah as he waited on the ark for the water to recede. God had sent this dove. Without removing her hand she slid to her knees. In a whisper she prayed, "Thank you Lord."

# Chapter 4

A mere six yards from Sarah's bedroom window, the farm's faithful Leghorn assumed his fence post position and crowed. Sarah's eyes fluttered open. With her head peaking from under her blanket, she looked toward the window. She didn't really expect to see a dove perched on her windowsill, but felt compelled to look. *I wonder if I'll ever again experience the manifestation of God like I did last night when the dove came. I asked Him for a sign that admitting Henry to the mental hospital was in accordance with His will. It never occurred to me to be specific like Gideon was when he asked God to wet the fleece with dew, while keeping the ground around it dry. As it turned out, it wasn't necessary. When that dove appeared, I knew God was giving His affirmation.*

Sarah put on her housecoat and walked to the kitchen. The late September mornings were cool, but not enough so that she needed slippers. Sarah enjoyed the feeling of her bare feet on the kitchen's cool, linoleum covered floor. On Saturdays, when the boys slept an hour later, she allowed herself the luxury of drinking her first morning cup of coffee while still in her night clothes.

Sarah opened the cook stove's fire box door using a hot pad and tossed in a piece of blue spruce. With the stove lid handle she lifted the back right hand burner plate and stoked the embers for direct heat. Then she slid the coffee pot she'd readied the night before to that spot and waited for it to brew.

After filling her cup, Sarah lifted it so she could savor the rich aroma. She began thinking through her plans for Henry's care and the day's related tasks. *As soon as the morning chores are done I'll load everyone up and head to town. First stop, Doc Adams. I'll give him the go ahead to make arrangements at Logansport Mental Hospital and see if he'll look after Henry for the day. Then on to Jack's farm to leave the children with Rebecca.*

The day dawned clear and they hadn't had rain for a week. With dry roads and barring any unforeseen problems, Sarah could make the round trip to and from Ma and Pa Whitcome's homestead in three to four hours. Henry's parents needed to be told about the hospitalization. It was hard news to deliver and it was going to be difficult for them to hear. Sarah needed to go alone.

Sarah had Henry dressed and sitting at the table when Abe and Josh entered the kitchen tucking in shirts and pulling up suspenders. They'd do chores after a quick breakfast. Luke and Zeke trailed behind, rubbing sleep from their eyes, still in their nightshirts.

Before the heatstroke Zeke and Henry had a morning routine. The tyke would pad to his pa who'd lift him to his lap. Using the boy's nightshirt, he'd tuck in the child's feet and snuggle him close. Thus they'd sit while Henry drank his coffee. No words needed to be exchanged, it was how it was for them.

Zeke, groggy from sleep, forgot that his pa's lap no longer held an open invitation. Henry pushed him off. The thud was loud as the boy hit the floor. "Wawaaaaa."

Sarah ran to Zeke and scooped him up into her arms. Abe jumped to his feet, fists clinched and started toward his father.

Sarah stepped in front of Abe. "Stop!" Sarah nodded toward the rocker in the corner of the kitchen. "Grab that afghan and wrap Zeke up. Hold him and rock until he gets settled."

Sarah knew having the two brothers cuddle would calm them both. By the time she'd finished cooking the eggs, Abe's soothing pats to Zeke's back and the tyke's return gesture to the back of his big brother's neck, morphed to a wiggle worm. Both, extremely ticklish boys were transformed from gloom to giggles.

Henry was sullen. Holding his coffee mug in one hand, brushing at his lap with the other as if to sweep away the leavings of something unwanted. The baby, hungry and impatient for her breakfast, was raising a ruckus while Josh and Luke sat quietly.

"Josh, please cut up a pancake for Hathaway while I dish up the sausage." Sarah asked. "Make the pieces small so she doesn't choke."

"Ok, Ma." The boy said, moving to the task.

"Hathaway, stop a bangin' that spoon on your highchair tray and quit that yammerin'. I'm a cuttin' as fast as I can." Josh tossed a piece of flapjack to the baby. "For the love of Pete, you're as bad as a yippin' dog."

"Josh Whitcome, don't use such language in this house," Sarah scolded.

"Well Ma, she does sound like a yippin' dog the way she's a howlin' for food." The nine-year-old said in defense.

"The dog reference was an unkind thing to say. But that's not what I was referring to. It's your 'for the love of Pete' comment that I won't tolerate."

"Why? What's wrong with sayin' that?"

"It is a reference to the apostle Peter and just a clever way some folks think they can blaspheme. To me it's the same as taking God's name in vain," Sarah explained.

"Gosh, Ma. I didn't know that," Josh said red faced.

Sarah set the plate of sausage on the table and ruffled the boy's hair. "Now you do."

\*\*\*

Sarah helped Henry climb up on wagon's seat. The boys piled in to its bed. Sarah handed Hathaway up to Abe, then climbed aboard and took the reins.

"Stop your cryin'," Abe said to the baby who had started to wiggle and wail. "If I don't hold on to you, you'll bounce around like a ball."

"Let's try singin' a song, she might like that," Luke suggested.

"Good idea." Sarah called, "giddy up," then sang out in her clear soprano voice. "She'll be comin' around the mountain when she comes, she'll be comin' around the mountain…"

Henry didn't participate in the singing with his family. He sat hunched shouldered, head down, with his hands fisted at his sides. He remained thus when Sarah reined in at Doc Adam's house, the front of which served as his office.

Sarah tethered the team at the hitching post. "You children stay put. I'm dropping off your Pa, then I'll take you on to Uncle Jack's place." Sarah helped Henry down from the wagon and held his hand as she led him to the door and knocked.

"Sarah…Henry…uh, come in." Ben said stepping aside to allow them passage.

"Thank you Ben," Sarah ushered her husband in, directing him to take a seat.

Ben saw the determined look in Sarah's face. "What brings you here this morning, Sarah?"

"I've decided to take your advice about having Henry admitted to the hospital." Sarah whispered. "I was hoping you would look after him while I ride out to tell his parents."

"Certainly." Ben reached out and took Sarah's hand in his. "What about the children?"

"I'll drop them off to stay at Jack's place. I'll make it quick and come for Henry by late afternoon."

Ben had moved to Henry's side and was helping him take off his coat. "Take your time. The two of us will get along just fine, won't we my friend?"

"When...how long before we...uh, know..." Sarah stumbled over saying it aloud.

"Directly the two of us will take a walk over to visit Jeb. We can use the telephone at the Sheriff's office to contact the...uh... facility. Likely I'll have a date and some plans for you when you come by later to pick him up." Ben smiled opening the door for Sarah.

***

As Sarah drove the team down the familiar country roads that would take her to Henry's home place she reflected back to the first time she'd made the trip. *How long had it been, thirteen or fourteen years? Henry and I'd been courting for nearly two months before he took me to meet his parents.*

*Since the Whitcomes didn't live in our community, I knew little of them, except for what Henry had shared and that wasn't much beyond that they were hard working farmers.*

*We reached the crest of a hill and the team and wagon were about to make its downward descent when Henry pointed, drawing my attention to the farm that lay in the valley below us. My breath caught in my throat as I took in the beauty before me. In all of Wabash County I'd never seen such rich looking soil. The furrows in the fields that lay below us were perfectly straight. The dark rich color of the soil, contrasting off of the acres and acres of green corn stalks and golden-yellow wheat, gave the appearance of a painted farm-scape.*

*At the center of the scene before me was a two-story farmhouse and barn.*

*Both were painted a brilliant white with red tin roofs. A white split-rail fence outlined the perimeter of the homestead. The house was surrounded by lush green grass where huge maple trees rooted, making a canopy of shade over the home's front porch. As we drew nearer, I could see that adjacent to the house, there was a vegetable garden fringed with flowers. All meticulously maintained.*

*Being a bit of a green thumb myself, I was pleased to discover that gardening would be a common thread between me and Ma Whitcome. I hoped a thread through which we might weave a friendship, if my relationship with Henry went where I hoped it would.*

*Henry's parents were gracious and welcoming to me that day. The meal Ma Whitcome served was delicious. On the surface it appeared the Whitcomes had everything. Yet, when we left, I had a feeling something wasn't as it should be with the family. After thinking about it, I realized a couple of things.*

*Mrs. Whitcome seemed to assume a subservient role to Mr. Whitcome. That certainly wasn't how it was between my parents. It wasn't how I thought a marriage should be. I believed couples should work in tandem with one another like a good team of horses. If one or the other lagged behind, it made for tough pulling down life's road. I knew I didn't want that type of relationship in my marriage. I hoped Henry and I would be of like accord on that subject.*

*The second thing I noticed was that Ma and Pa Whitcome didn't seem to be joyful. They didn't laugh or joke. When Ma showed me her flowers it was with a sense of pride for having grown them. When we walked past the Hollyhocks, Emma swatted at the tiny humming birds that buzzed about, attempting to swoop down to drink nectar from the deep-throated blooms. The pride they took in their hard work seemed to be the only thing close to what I'd call joy that either of them showed.*

Sarah was young but even then, she thought that to sustain life's knocks and bumps one had to be able to experience joy. Now she knew that to be true. Joy wasn't something big a person works toward. Joy comes in the small everyday things. Joy could be easily experienced if one's heart stayed open and receptive. If a person tied their happiness to only one thing in life, and that one thing was lost or taken, where did that leave them?

Sarah had grown up in a family where the bible was read aloud nightly. Many of the scriptures her parents shared with her and Jack centered on praising God and being joyful. Sarah knew it was right and appropriate to experience joy even in the midst of extreme heartache. Sarah believed so much in the importance of living a joyous life that, she believed for her, it was a sin to do otherwise.

Sarah reined the team to a stop at the crest of the hill. As she had all those years before, she paused to soak in the beauty before her. Harvest was over. There were no longer crops in the fields. The scene before her was still breathtaking. The trees, with leaves in hues of orange and yellow surrounded the house and barn. The structures' brilliant whiteness, juxtaposed against autumn's glorious pallet, set the vista aglow.

Before starting the descent down the hill to the homestead, Sarah whispered, "Lord, in your love hear my prayer for strength today for us all."

Henry was Jonas and Emma's only child. His debilitating heatstroke was devastating for them. Although Doc Adams told them the likelihood of Henry getting well wasn't good, they'd refused to accept talk of anything but a full recovery for him. Sarah hoped they could come to realize that Henry's hospitalization was best not just for him, but for her and the children too.

"Come, in child! What brings you all the way over here …are you alone?" Emma Whitcome greeted as she opened the door.

"Yes, I've come alone." Sarah pulled her mother-in-law in to her arms and held her tight.

Emma pulled away. "What is it? Has something more happened to Henry?" Emma called out toward the back of the house. "Jonas…Jonas… Sarah is here. She's come alone."

Jonas walked briskly into the parlor. "What's happened? Is it Henry?"

Sarah put her hands up, palms out. "Henry is alright. If we could sit down I'll tell you what has happened and why I'm here."

"You must be tuckered out driving the team all the way here," Emma said. "Would you like a cup of coffee and a piece of pie?"

"Yes, thank you, Ma Whitcome." Sarah responded as they moved toward the kitchen.

\*\*\*

Jonas pushed back from the table, crossed his legs and folded his arms. "I've listened to your story, Sarah, and I think you're overly concerned. A man has certain…uh…needs and expectations of a wife. I don't want to offend, but perhaps Henry is just a comin' to himself…don't ya know. Wantin' to resume his role as your husband and such. The incident in the barn… likely it weren't more than just that."

Sarah's reply was kind but firm. "Pa Whitcome, Henry and I have been married for nearly fourteen years. We've always enjoyed a most loving, affectionate relationship. What occurred in the barn yesterday was in no way related to that. He was attempting to violate me. Abe came in on the scene. Abe saw, he knew. Henry's sick. I think he's a danger to me and to the children."

"Nonsense! That was just one occurrence." Jonas took a drink from his coffee cup.

"Has anything else happened, Sarah?" Emma inquired.

Sarah told them about the incident at breakfast when Henry had knocked Zeke off his lap on to the floor and that there had been several times when he had grabbed at her in front of the children. She tried to convey to them how dire she felt the circumstances were. From there she laid out her plans for having him placed at the Logansport Mental Hospital. She told them she'd sought God's will in her decision and shared the sign of the white dove that had appeared the night before.

The elder Whitcomes attended the little Methodist church at Jalapa somewhat regularly. Although she had never heard either of them speak of their personal faith in God, they had never shied away when she openly spoke of hers and how she confided in the Lord to direct her life. She had anticipated full understanding when she shared with them that she had prayed for a sign that her plan for Henry's care was in accordance with God's will.

Jonas brought his fist down on the table hard, the fork on Sarah's empty pie plate bounced. "Hogwash with God's will! Ain't no bird on a windowsill gonna determine the fate of my son. My boy just needs a bit more rest and he'll come back to himself. We don't want him going to no mental hospital. He needs to stay on the farm with you and the children." He shook his finger at Sarah. "Mark my word, you'll be sorry if you go against us on this."

"Jonas, surely you can appreciate my concern…"

The man stood, towering over the table and the two seated women.

"I've spoke my piece. Now you best get on back home and tend to your children and husband and put these foolish notions from your mind."

Sarah made eye contact with Emma, and gave her a look that pleaded for her support.

Emma Whitcome wrung her hands, her voice a whisper as she spoke. "You best go on home now, Sarah, like you was told."

Tears streamed down Sarah's cheeks as she took the reins and turned the team toward her farm. At the crest of the hill Sarah pulled the wagon to the side of the road and looked over her shoulder. Did the scene look different because the sun was lower in the sky and the once bright white house was now in a different light? Whatever the reason, the Whitcome's homestead now appeared cloaked in darkness.

*"Mark my word, you'll be sorry."* Sarah's face flushed hot as Jonas' words came back to her. She snapped the reins three times and the team took off rapid pace.

*Henry Whitcome, your threats might work on Emma, but they won't work on me. I'll not be kowtowing to you over Henry's care, or for any reason.* When her face no longer felt hot, Sarah tugged back gently on the reins. "Hup, hup, whoa."

The team responded, slowing to an even-paced walk. "Easssyy, easssyy, ... sorry old fellers." Sarah lifted her face toward heaven and prayed. "I know, there's no point in getting mad. It isn't going to change anything. Lord, bring comfort to Ma and Pa Whitcome. Give them the courage to face Henry's condition for what it truly is. Heavenly Father, my faith in you and the sign you gave me is solid. I'm going to carry forward with our plan for Henry's care."

# Chapter 5

Sarah and the children were strolling the family's pumpkin patch that lay behind and to the west of their house. The sun was shining brightly and the welcome heat of it penetrated Sarah's sweater as she walked. The musty smell rising from the pumpkins brought back childhood memories for Sarah of autumns on her parents' farm. Harvest, the gathering and nestling in, and preparing for winter had been a favorite time for Sarah. Remembering gave her a sense of peace.

"Abe, Josh, come and load those four large pumpkins at the edge of the patch in to the wagon for us. They're nice and big and will make great jack-o-lanterns. You each can have one to carve. Halloween is coming in a week. We can't celebrate it without a few jack-o-lanterns."

"Ma, four ain't enough, we need five", said Zeke as he came walking toward her, struggling to carry a pumpkin that was almost as big as he was. The boy plopped the large orange orb at her feet. "You was forgettin' about Hathaway, wasn't ya, Ma?"

"Well I certainly was." Sarah said.

"See I brung one just her size." Zeke gestured toward his baby sister who had toddled over and was trying to sit on the pumpkin.

"How thoughtful, Zeke." Sarah said.

"I'll find one for you, Ma, then everyone in our family will have their own pumpkin to carve." The boy grinned and took off running.

As they drove the horses and wagon from the pumpkin patch to the house Sarah took note that there had been no mention of a pumpkin for Henry. *Have the children forgotten their father already?* It had been four weeks since she'd admitted him to the mental hospital. Sarah winced as she relived the day.

\*\*\*

*My Ma and Pa arrived early that morning. Ma was to stay at the farm and care for the children, Pa to travel with me and Doc Adams to take Henry to the hospital in Logansport.*

*I'd never been to such a place. Doc assured me that in the past decade methods used to treat the mentally ill had greatly improved. Logansport's Northern Indiana State Hospital for the Insane was considered the best at providing modern care. It was built in '88 to handle overcrowding in Indiana's only other mental hospital, located in the state capital, Indianapolis.*

*I appreciated Ben giving me the information. With Logansport being a state hospital and us state residents, there would be no charge for Henry's care. I didn't feel I had any choice.*

*We traveled by train, making stops in Wabash and Peru before arriving in Logansport. The trip took about an hour and a half. Henry contented himself with watching the scenery from his window-side seat. The rhythmic clacking of the train's wheels seemed to sooth him and he appeared the most contented I'd seen him since the heatstroke.*

*Two men wearing white smock-like jackets, greeted us when we got off of the train in Logansport. They introduced themselves as attendants who'd be helping to care for Henry. They said the hospital had sent them to pick us up. The larger of the two explained that he would ride inside the buggy with Henry, Doc and me. He directed Pa to ride up top with the other fellow for the short mile trip to the facility.*

*Inside the buggy the attendant sat next to Henry and attempted to engage him in conversation. Although Henry didn't respond, the man continued talking to him, explaining the sights we passed. The man had a hint of an Irish accent with a pleasant cadence to his words and he spoke to Henry as if he was the only one in the carriage. I guess he was trying to make friends with him. Henry got fixated on the attendant's mouth, at times moving his own lips as the man spoke. It seemed such a curious thing for Henry to do.*

*The entrance to the facility's grounds was flanked on each side with a row of large maple trees whose branches still had a smattering of fall leaves. The branches bowed low making a canopy along the approach to the complex. It was as if they were forming a protective shield over my Henry as he entered.*

*The landscape was meticulously manicured with a black wrought iron security fence that looked more decorative than a guard against escape. The hospital was built of red brick in a Victorian style. It was a sprawling, three-storied structure. There was a long row of windows across the front of the first and second levels. The third had several dormers, each with windows. I was pleased to see that Henry would live where he could get plenty of light. He'd need light to lift his spirits and bring healing. The hospital's black slate roof sported five chimneys. I'd never seen a building that big. It looked more like a stately mansion than a facility to care for the mentally ill.*

*As the horses were reined in and the attendant jumped down to tether them, the gravity of what was about to occur overwhelmed me. A deep groan escaped my throat before I could stifle it. My groan scared Pa.*

*They took us and Henry to a room where there were people dressed in regular clothing. Some were walking about mumbling to themselves. Some sat staring off into space. Several just gazed out the tall windows. It was a nice view of the front lawn, except for the metal caging covering the glass. I asked if they were patients. The big attendant said yes. The smaller one said they referred to them as residents, not patients.*

*Doc, Pa, and I were given a tour. They showed us the room that would be Henry's. They said he'd sleep there alone for the first several weeks. Later, if he tolerated being around others, he might be assigned a roommate.*

*The doctor told us we should give Henry at least two months with them before making any contact or coming to visit. They wanted him to have a chance to make the transition and settle in.*

*When it was time for us to leave, I wrapped my arms around Henry. I held him in an embrace that I hoped would convey to him how much I still loved him and cherished our memories. I kissed his handsome face and told him to work hard to get well and come home. He made no response. We left.*

*I wasn't naïve enough to think that all that went on behind the door we had just closed was as pleasant and serene as what we'd been shown. Although I was explicit that no drastic or irreversible measures be used without my prior consent, I didn't know exactly what treatments would be in store for my Henry. For much of the train ride home I wept, cradled in Pa's arms.*

\*\*\*

It had been almost a month since Henry was admitted to the hospital. Initially the boys asked a few questions about where their pa had been taken, then not again. With his departure had gone the blanket of doom and sadness that shrouded their home since Henry's stroke. Gone was the frightened stranger, the lost soul, who sat at their table and ate meals with them. Gone too was the threat of inappropriate sexual advances that made Sarah on edge and jumpy. The stranger was gone, but Sarah vowed to keep the memory of Henry, the loving father they had once had, alive for her children.

Joy returned to the Whitcome's home. Sarah marveled at how much strength she drew from her children's happiness. Their meals together were once again a time of sharing what had happened during the day, a time of teasing one another and laughing together. Sarah's heart was still sick and grieving over the loss of her mate. Her children's laughter was the medicine she needed.

Halloween, October 31, 1903, fell on a Saturday. The sky was clear and the temperature warmed to nearly 45 degrees at mid-day. Sarah's morning was spent baking pies for the party at the town hall that night. With that out of the way her attention turned to helping the children put together the costumes they were going to wear.

Luke with his red unruly hair sticking out from under one of Henry's old straw hats, made an impressive looking scarecrow. Zeke wanted to be a hound dog. Sarah made long ears out of pieces from an old wool coat and fastened a rope for a tail to his pants. With mittens on his hands, a coal-blackened nose and a lot of imagination, it worked.

Abe and Josh dressed as ghosts. They began terrorizing the little ones as soon as they pulled the flour sacks with cut-out eye holes over their heads. Hathaway screamed and wet her britches. Luke and Zeke begged for more.

Hathaway's disposition brightened when she looked in the mirror at her get-up. Her hair was parted down the middle into two tiny ponytails reaching to the sky. Her nose was also coal-blackened and whisker lines were drawn on her cheeks. She clapped her tiny hands in approval.

Zeke looked at his sister with a quizzical expression on his face. "What is she, Ma?"

Sarah hugged her. "She's our little pet."

Late afternoon Sarah and her five goblins of various heights loaded themselves and the pies in the wagon and headed to town for a night of fun. Sarah had concern that some of the town folk might think it unseemly that she come to the party without Henry. She knew there were those who sided with her in-laws in their belief that she should have tried harder to keep him at home.

Her worries were quickly relieved. Several neighbors came out to greet her and the children and to help them from the wagon. Sarah's boys ran off to play with their pals and she and the baby joined a circle of family and friends that had formed near the stage.

A mixed crew of locals, with stringed instruments, was playing *On the Banks of the Wabash, Far Away.* The group's rendition of the song, published the year before, was down-home quality. Sarah stood for a few minutes and watched. Two men strummed guitars and two drew their bows back and forth across fiddles. All tapped their feet, keeping time with the melody while they grinned ear to ear. The collective age of the four of them Sarah guessed would total near 300. When the song was finished, she clapped the loudest.

The mood in the town hall was light and cheerful. Sarah allowed herself to relax and enjoy the respite from her burdens. Although she had many invitations to dance, Sarah declined all except for those extended by her father, Jack and her boys. Seeing all the couples dancing together caused her to miss Henry even more. She shook the feelings aside and accepted Doc's invitation to join him, Jeb Carter and Jeb's wife outside for a breath of fresh air. This was her life, at least for now. She and her children needed the community of others and she was glad they'd come.

\*\*\*

The weather the following Monday morning was beautiful. The boys were off at school and Zeke was outside digging in the dirt. Hathaway sat in the corner of the kitchen contently playing with wooden blocks. Five loaves of bread were browning to perfection in the oven and Sarah thought the aroma was divine. She hummed one of her favorite hymns *It is Well With My Soul,* as she swept the kitchen floor.

Her humming was interrupted when Zeke entered the kitchen and let the back door bang shut. "Ma, they's a wagon comin' up the lane. It looks like Granny and Grandpa Whitcome's rig, they have someone with them. Wonder who it is?"

The broom froze mid-air in Sarah's hands. A chill moved down her spine. She didn't have to wonder who they had brought with them, she knew. It was Henry. She'd written to her in laws about admitting him to the hospital in Logansport. She'd explained the facility's request that the family give him a couple of months to settle in before they visited. There'd been no response from them. None until today.

A wave of anger washed over Sarah. Her head felt hot and the heat spread down through her body with such intensity that she had to hold tight to the broom to keep from throwing it across the room.

Sarah wasn't just angry that Henry's parents had taken him from the hospital, she was furious. The majority of her rage was directed toward Jonas.

*Jonas Whitcome, you selfish, sanctimonious, old goat. What gives you the right to bring Henry home before he's healed? If you really believe all he needs is a little more time, why didn't you offer to keep him with you and Emma until he gets well. How dare you pretend that you care more for Henry as his father, than I do as his wife! The heatstroke caused the loss of the son you knew. I've lost my best friend, my confidante, my children's father and my lover. I've been walking around with a gaping hole in my soul since he became ill. Admitting him to the asylum was extremely hard for me to do. I'm just now beginning to move forward.*

Tears filled Sarah's eyes and her body began to tremble. Unable to hide her anguish Sarah cried out, "Lord, give me strength!" Zeke saw his mother trembling and misunderstood her cry for strength. Thinking that she was about to fall, he ran to her and wrapped his little arms around her legs. "It's ok, Ma, I won't let ya fall."

Sarah forced herself to calm down and regain her composure. "Don't worry, Zeke, I won't fall," she said as she removed herself from his grasp and gently leaned the broom against the wall.

She picked up Hathaway, grabbed a shawl and wrapped it around the baby. She took Zeke's hand and they walked out to face the Whitcomes and the one they had brought with them.

Jonas Whitcome's greeting as he jumped down from the wagon and tethered the horses to the hitching post was, "I brung him home. This is where he belongs."

Sarah didn't hear him. Her eyes were on Henry. He sat intently looking out toward the barn and the fields beyond. Sarah's heart pounded. *Does this mean he recognizes the farm? Does he know this is his home? Do I dare hope he is remembering who he is? Will he know the children and me when he turns and looks at us?*

When Henry turned her direction she saw that it wasn't to be. What faced her was the shell of what had been her husband, the same shell that she had delivered to the mental asylum a month before. Henry's eyes met hers without any recognition, then they darted about with the same fear they'd held on the day he left.

Zeke was now behind her with his head buried in the folds of her long skirt. Sarah reached back, and stroked his head. "It's all right son. Don't be frightened."

Sarah could see the weariness on Henry and Ma Whitcome's faces. She couldn't bring herself to look at Jonas. She knew he too must be tired. Traveling to and from Logansport by horse and wagon would have been grueling.

Drawing from God's grace she said, "You all best come on in and get warmed. We've got fresh bread about ready to come out of the oven and I've plenty of coffee on the back burner."

Sarah's love for her husband and his parents was still strong. She wouldn't disrespect the memory of the relationship they had shared by arguing with Pa Whitcome.

Sarah believed the driving force behind Jonas' actions was not love, it was selfish pride. He had lived his life with the philosophy that if you worked hard, you could make things come out right. He saw accepting Henry's illness as a personal failure. Therefore he would deny the seriousness of the situation and choose instead to believe that by bringing him home, all would right itself.

The look of pain on Emma's face showed Sarah that she wasn't in agreement with her husband's decision.

Sarah knew that she couldn't allow the children, Henry, his parents or herself to go through this experience again. Her resolve was firm. She would take Henry back to the hospital, but not until she had taken legal steps to assure that his parent's would have no authority to take him out again.

The elder Whitcomes declined Sarah's invitation to spend the night. After a short visit with the older boys when they came home from school, they prepared to leave. Henry followed after them mumbling something that sounded like… "go home".

Thinking he wanted to go with them to his childhood home, Jonas said, "Henry you don't live with us anymore, this is your home."

In a low, menacing tone Henry said, "No, red brick house!"

Jonas whipped his head toward Sarah as if he'd been slapped. The look he gave her was one of disdain. He climbed up in the wagon next to his wife, took the reins and started the team forward. He drove off leaving his son, now in a state of agitation, standing in the cold with his fists clenched.

Henry ignored Sarah's requests for him to come back in the house with her. She called out to Abe, "Fetch your pa's coat."

"Ma, he seems so angry. Please don't try to put his coat on him now," Abe said.

"I won't." Sarah laid the warm garment on the ground where Henry could see it. She too thought it best to give him some space and time to calm down.

Now alone, Henry began pacing back and forth between the house and the woodshed. Sarah assigned Luke the task of watching him from the kitchen window with instructions to alert her if he started to wander off. Abe and Josh went to do evening chores, giving wide berth as they walked passed their pa. Sarah started cooking their supper.

\*\*\*

At dusk a much subdued Henry gave in to cold, exhaustion and hunger. At Sarah's bidding, he joined the people unknown to him at the table.

That night there was no sharing of the day's events, no teasing or laughter. The stranger was back and the joy was gone.

# Chapter 6

Sarah walked the kitchen floor, rubbing at the kinks in her lower back with her left hand while she sipped from the cup of coffee she carried in her right hand. It was her third cup that morning and still she struggled to become fully alert. She'd had a nearly sleepless night.

The evening before, Sarah set up sleeping accommodations for Henry in the parlor just like he'd used during the period between the heatstroke and being admitted to the hospital. She'd hoped the setting would be familiar to him and bring him comfort.

Henry's agitation, as a result of being taken from the facility and brought to the farm, had subsided some by nightfall, but wasn't gone. He still appeared fearful and confused. His continuous pacing seemed to have drained his energy, making him less resistant to cooperating. He'd nodded off during supper and putting him to bed for the night hadn't been a problem.

Sarah was concerned that Henry might try to leave the house while she slept. To guard against that happening she made a bed for herself on the floor just outside of the parlor door. The pine boards were unforgiving and she'd been startled awake each time the old farmhouse creaked and moaned.

Sarah felt an urgency to re-admit Henry to the hospital, but knew she needed to take legal action to prevent his parents from taking him out again without her consent.

On the first Tuesday of each month, the Wabash based law firm of Hawkins and Pickering sent a lawyer to LaFontaine. Using a small room in the back of Parker's Dry Goods, they would set up office just for the day. Sarah wanted to take advantage of the opportunity to prevent a twelve mile trek into Wabash.

When the sun was fully up, Sarah decided to make the short journey into LaFontaine. She'd take Henry and her two youngest, Zeke and Hathaway, with her. With the good weather they could easily get to town, take care of business and get back home before the older boys got out of school.

Henry slept late that morning. The children had left for school when he came to the kitchen for breakfast. Sarah set a cup of hot coffee on the table and gestured for him to take a seat. "Henry, I need to take the team and wagon into town this morning so I can run some errands. I thought you might enjoy going to the barbershop for a shave and haircut while I shop. Nobel Simon does such a nice job of cutting your hair and he's been asking about you."

Her plan was to drop Henry off for a haircut and shave and to ask Noble if Henry might stay and visit. She'd take Zeke and Hathaway with her to see the lawyer.

Henry gave no response to Sarah's suggestion. Instead he looked at her with pleading eyes, "Red brick house."

Sarah placed her hand over her husband's. "You want to go back. I wish you could tell me what makes you comfortable there. I'd try to do that for you here at home." She lovingly patted his hand. "I promise, I'll take you to the red brick house soon."

They encountered several of their neighbors while traveling to town. Sarah thought, *why are so many people going to LaFontaine on a Tuesday? November 3rd, Election Day... I should've remembered. Even though it's just a local election, folks make a big event of it.*

Jeb Carter, friend and neighbor, was running for Town Marshal. Jeb and his oldest boy Julib had helped her with Henry the day of his heatstroke. *Jeb campaigned like he really wants the job. Don't know why, it doesn't pay enough to make a living. Not much lawlessness in LaFontaine besides mischief from rowdy boys, or the occasional chicken thief. I hope Jeb gets elected, he'd make a fine Town Marshal.*

When they arrived in LaFontaine they went first to the livery stable. Sarah tethered the team on the far side of the barn, then helped Henry get down from the wagon. When she turned to take Hathaway from Zeke, she found the baby standing alone in the bed of the wagon, arms stretched out, and a worried look on her tiny face.

"Come to mama, sweet girl. Did your rascal brother leave you behind?"

Zeke had jumped down and was headed toward Tom McVicker, the livery owner. "Hi, Mr. Micky Vickers. It's me Zeke." The boy turned in a full circle gesturing to the multiple teams of horses and single mounts. "Gee, Mr. Micky Vickers you sure are gonna have a lot of shit to shovel by the end of the day."

"Zeke Whitcome!" Sarah pulled the boy to her and buried his mouth in the folds of her long skirt. "Our apologies, Mr. McVicker. We'll be in town for about an hour. If it's all right, I'll settle up with you when we come back."

As it goes in small communities, one's personal business didn't usually stay personal. Sarah's circumstances were common knowledge among town folk and the old man seemed surprised to see the family in town. He tipped his hat, "Mornin' Ma'am. No apology needed. The boy's got my 'shitsheation' sized up just about right. You folks take all the time you need. Henry, it's good to see you out and about. I didn't know you'd come home."

There was no response from Henry. He stood staring off at the distance, arms hanging limp at this sides.

Tom McVicker looked at Sarah, placed his hat over his chest and said, "My condolences, Ma'am."

Sarah, Henry and the children walked a short distance from the livery to Branson Street, the street that ran through the heart of LaFontaine. Their attention was drawn to the long line of men waiting to enter the Town Hall.

"What's all them men in line for, Ma?" Zeke asked.

"Today's election-day. They're waiting in line to cast their votes for Town Marshal," Sarah explained.

"What's a vote? Do ya mean cast like you do with a rod when you're a fishin'? Can we get in line and get us some votes to cast too?"

Sarah was carrying Hathaway and holding tight to Zeke's hand. She was walking so fast that Zeke's feet near left the ground. The boy used his free hand to keep his hat from flying off.

"…hold up…hold up, Ma, we're a passin' the line and we're gonna miss our chance to throw us some votes," the boy gasped, trotting to keep up with his mother's pace.

"I'm sorry, son, only men are allowed to vote. You're too young and your father's too sick. Besides that, we're in a hurry. You be a good boy and when I'm through with my meeting, I'll stop by Wagoner's General Store and buy you a licorice stick before we go home."

Sarah looked over her shoulder and saw that Henry too was having a hard time keeping up with her pace. She quickly adjusted her stride to match his.

Sarah's heart ached for her husband who before the stroke, would have been the first in line to vote. He'd have taken the day off from farm work to hang out in town with the other men. They'd loiter and jaw about the recent harvest and county news.

*Thankfully it isn't a presidential election year. Teddy Roosevelt is finishing out McKinley's term and the next national election won't be until November '04. If Henry's not home and well enough to vote by then, he never will be.*

*All the years that we had a male school teacher, Election Day was a holiday for the children. Now that we have a female teacher, it's just another day of school. Well, at least for the girls. I see several boys that no doubt played hooky and came to town with their pas. The older I get, the more the unfairness of the process galls me. Maybe when the children are grown I'll have the time to join the suffragette movement.*

Sarah whispered in Hathaway's ear. "One day, girl, you and I will stand in that line together."

The baby smiled and gave her Mama a pat on the cheek.

When they reached the barbershop Sarah could see through the window that Nobel had someone in his barber chair, the seats for waiting were full and several men were standing. *I can't ask Noble to tend to Henry when he's this busy. All the hoopla might make Henry feel anxious. No, no… this isn't going to work.*

Sarah turned to look at Henry. He appeared diminished, as if he were trying to shrink down to be out of sight. *Oh, what have I done? I should've never brought him to town. Henry with his handsome face, tall stature and friendly disposition has been sought out and admired in this community. Now I've paraded him through town for everyone to see him with stooped shoulders, and a fearful, lost look on his face.*

Sarah took Henry's limp hand in hers and said, "Please forgive my foolishness."

She turned her little entourage toward the direction they had just come and began to steer them back to McVicker's livery.

Sarah heard fast approaching footsteps and someone calling her name. She looked over her shoulder and saw Doc Adams briskly walking toward them.

"Sarah, why is Henry with you?" Ben's call out brought the notice of onlookers.

Sarah waited until Doc caught up with them to respond, she didn't want others to hear. "Jonas brought him back to the farm yesterday. Henry's still sick. He's not happy about being at the farm and wants to return to the hospital. I came to town seeking legal protection that will prevent Jonas from bringing him home after I readmit him."

"So, you've been to see the lawyer and you're heading home?"

"No, I was going to leave Henry at the barbershop with Nobel while I went. Nobel's place is too busy for me to do that. Bringing Henry to town was a mistake. I've made him a spectacle...I need to take him home."

"Sarah, you have to get this taken care of today. Henry can come home with me. It will be quiet there and he can rest. You go on and make the necessary legal arrangements. A court action will likely take a few days. I'll keep Henry at my place until that's settled and we can get him back to the hospital."

"Ben, I'd be much obliged if you'd take him to your place while I have my meeting, but I'll stop by to get him on my way out of town. I won't subject him to staying in another place that's strange to him. He'll be better off at the farm until I can take him back to the asylum," Sarah explained.

"Sarah, I can't let you put yourself at risk. What if he acts out again, like he did in the barn that time?"

"Doc, I sincerely appreciate all that you've done and are doing for my family, but it isn't your call. Henry's my husband. I have to think of what's best for him. I can't just think of myself."

Ben's eyes followed Sarah as she took the children and walked in the direction of Parker's Dry Goods. *Dearest Sarah, when have you ever just thought of yourself?*

# Chapter 7

It had been two weeks since the trip to town on Election Day. After praying, Sarah had stopped dwelling on her misjudgment in taking Henry along and exposing him to public display.

The lawyer she'd met with assured her that he'd immediately file a petition to name Sarah as Henry's guardian. Once that status was awarded to her and on file in the county records, Northern Indiana State Hospital would be legally obligated to act only on Sarah's instructions when it came to Henry's care. A copy of the court's decision would be sent to Ma and Pa Whitcome, along with a letter admonishing them against any future interference with Henry's care. Sarah had ask that the letter also clarify that they were welcome to visit him at hospital.

Based on the lawyer's estimate, enough time had now passed since the filing of the petition for a court's decision to be rendered. Sarah was eager to re-admit Henry to the hospital. Several times daily he asked her to take him to the red brick house. The first week he accepted her response of *soon*. He napped some during the afternoons and maintained his daily ritual of pacing the distance between the house and the woodshed for long periods of time. This kept him occupied and exhausted by twilight, which aided him in sleeping through the nights.

Near the end of Henry's second week back at the farm his behavior changed. He became agitated when Sarah told him she couldn't take him to the red brick house that day, but would take him soon. The duration of his pacing sessions lengthened and he began mumbling more to himself. At times he punched at the air with fisted hands and shouted out, "Better take me back." It was almost as if he were giving a warning. Was the warning to her? Sarah didn't know, but the looks he gave her made her feel apprehensive and concerned.

Sarah was grateful that Henry had been content at the hospital. Knowing that he now considered it his home made it easier to think of him living there. How that could have happened after such a relatively brief stay there was hard to understand. Sarah believed that home is the place that a person felt the most accepted and peaceful. She was sad that the farm and family Henry had worked so hard for and nurtured so lovingly was no longer his safe haven.

Sarah speculated that at the asylum nothing was expected from him. Although she hadn't attempted to get him to do any chores at the farm, he could see that the rest of them had assigned work. He might have been aware of the looks of disappointment on the children's faces when he didn't join in the family's conversations. The people that he ate his meals with at the red brick house likely didn't care if he was responsive. Perhaps they were as frightened and confused as he was. She wondered that if on some level being in their company made him feel as if he belonged there.

Sarah kept up her vigil of sleeping on the floor next to the parlor door in case Henry tried to leave during the night. To make the pine floor more comfortable Abe had helped her drag the feather tick from her bed to the space. They placed it on top of several quilts making a soft pallet for her. It was comfortable enough, but she continued to awaken often, startled by night sounds.

Abe and Josh both offered to take a turn at sleeping guard, Sarah refused. She didn't want to chance them having to confront Henry if he did try to leave during the night.

Luke at seven years of age and Zeke at four, were completely oblivious to the strangeness of Sarah's sleeping arrangements. When they initially inquired about her bed on the floor she told them she was camping out. They thought that sounded like great fun and wanted to join in. She let them snuggle with her for bedtime stories, but insisted that they get in their own beds when it was time to go to sleep.

On the night of November 16th, Zeke slipped down the stairs and crawled under the covers with his mama. Sarah woke, but she was too tired to carry him back up the stairs to his own bed. Leaving him there was a mistake. Zeke wet the bed.

The next morning there was dampness in the air. Instead of hanging the feather tick outside on the clothes line, Sarah stretched it across two kitchen chairs in front of the cook stove. At 1:00 in the afternoon she checked its drying status. *Still damp. I hope this thing gets dry by bedtime.*

Sarah walked to the window. *What's keeping Elmo! He usually delivers the mail around noon. Today's the 17th, fourteen days since the lawyer filed the guardianship petition. According to his time estimation, I should get my response any day now.*

Sarah knew that when it did come, the entire rural community would find out about it. *No doubt Elmo Jones will delight in the telling. He's bragged to me that he learns a lot about people through the mail they receive. He said folks aught not use a postcard, with the message in plain view, if they didn't want it read by others. Of course, I've seen him holding envelopes up to the sunlight to make out their contents.*

*The notion that he'll gossip about my personal business makes me angry. Sometimes I wish I could stay mad at that rascal of a man.* Elmo had a jovial disposition and a lopsided grin attributed to his trademark chaw of Mail Pouch. The quirky man annoyed many, was tolerated by some, but was truly liked by most in the community.

Aggravated with her impatience she chided herself. *Sarah, you're wasting time. Get busy with your chores and get it off of your mind. The letter will come, when it comes!*

Sarah decided to increase the heat in the stove to promote faster drying of the feather tic. Stoking the fire would also take care of the chill that had settled on the house. The boys had been running late for school that morning and Luke hadn't had time to replenish the wood box. It now was empty.

"Zeke, I'm going out to fetch some wood for the fire. It won't take me but a minute or two. Please don't let Hathaway get near the stove while I'm gone."

Zeke and Hathaway were sharing a rare moment of congeniality, playing with blocks of wood in the corner of the kitchen. "Ok, Ma," was the boy's reply.

Henry was doing his afternoon pacing between the house and the woodshed when Sarah came out. As Sarah walked past him he had one of his outbursts, shook a fist at her and yelled, "Someone better take me."

Sarah quickened her pace. *I'll just grab a quick armload and hurry back. I think I'll fix Henry a cup of hot tea and add a spoon of Laudanum. When Elmo delivers the mail I'll send word back with him to have Doc Adams come out. This change in Henry's behavior is scaring me.*

Sarah had just loaded her arms with wood when she sensed a presence behind her. As she turned to see who it was, Henry pushed his hand into her shoulder with a force that knocked her off balance. Sarah fell with the arm-load of wood landing on top of her, a large piece striking her forehead, leaving her dazed.

Henry tossed the fire wood from atop Sarah as he yelled, "I want to go to the red brick house," over and over again. He straddled her and continued yelling his mantra with his face just inches from hers.

Sarah was struggling to gather her wits when Henry began hitting her about the face, arms and chest as he shouted his demand.

Sarah pleaded with him to stop. She tried to push him off of her. As she struggled beneath him, she saw the look in his eyes change. His whole countenance went from one of rage to a visage of pure lust.

Henry began to tear at Sarah's clothing until he had shredded her dress and petticoats, leaving her body naked and exposed. He pinned Sarah's arms to the ground above her head with his left hand. She watched with dread as he unfastened his trousers with his right hand and freed his now fully erect penis.

Sarah was physically useless against Henry's massive bulk. She screamed, then stifled it. There would be no one to hear except for Zeke and she didn't want him coming out. That would expose him to Henry's wrath and leave the baby alone in the house.

School would let out at 3:00 p.m. and the older boys would be home soon after that. She feared what might happen if they encountered Henry while he was in this fit of rage.

Sarah stopped struggling. She felt it was a useless waste of her strength. When she no longer resisted, Henry stopped hitting her. While he raped her Sarah forced herself to separate her mind from the act enough to pray. *Lord, make him stop. Don't let him hurt me anymore. Keep my children from harm. Please, please help me to think of a way to get him to leave the farm.*

Immediately after his sexual release Henry stood. Sarah had trouble focusing on the figure of the man that towered above her. Her eyes had already begun to swell shut from Henry's repeated hard blows to her face. Her head hurt and was bleeding. It was getting difficult for her to stay awake.

Gathering all the strength she had left Sarah raised her arm, pointed toward the pumpkin patch and told her husband a lie. "Walk across that field toward that line of pine trees. You'll find the red brick house in the clearing on the other side."

\*\*\*

It was about 11:30 a.m. on the 17th when Jonas walked in the kitchen carrying an envelope from the law firm of Hawkins and Pickering, Wabash, Indiana. "Emma, we got a letter from a law firm in Wabash. Wonder what this is about." Jonas tore it open.

The envelope contained a copy of the court's order naming Sarah as Henry's legal guardian. There was also a letter, but he didn't take time to read it. Jonas understood full well the implication of the guardianship. Sarah was planning on re-admitting Henry to the mental hospital.

"Get your hat, Emma, we're going over to Henry's farm. Sarah thinks she has had the last word on this, but I'm gonna let her know differently," he said as he angrily shook his fist that held the crumpled document.

\*\*\*

Before Jonas and Emma had climbed down from their rig they could hear the baby crying. They rushed to the house and jerked open the kitchen door without knocking. What they saw when they entered was Zeke down on his knees trying to feed his crying sister a hunk of dried bread.

"What's all the ruckus about, Zeke?" Jonas blurted out.

"I can't get Hathaway to stop her bawlin'. I tried givin' her this here piece of bread, but she don't want it. I think she done crapped in her britches cause she smells worser than a 'stinky stunk'!"

"Where's your mother?"

"She went out to fetch some firewood and she ain't come back."

"Where's your Pa?"

"I ain't got a Pa no more."

"Of course you do, we brought him back home to the farm about two weeks ago."

"That weren't my Pa. My Pa got stroked and that was the man that was left. But he ain't my Pa."

"Emma, you tend to the children while I go look for Sarah and Henry," Jonas said.

It didn't take long for Jonas to spot Henry off in the distance, sitting on a pumpkin in the now frozen patch. He started toward his son, but drew to a halt when he heard moaning. It was coming from near the woodshed. He ran that direction.

"Sarah! Sarah…oh, Sarah." Jonas took off his coat and used it to cover Sarah's nakedness. "Who did this to you?"

"The children, are they…"

"We found them alone in the house. They're fine, Emma's with them."

"What in tarnation happened out here, Sarah?"

"Henry…"

"Henry's all right, he's sittin' over …wait, are you sayin' Henry did this to you?"

Sarah lay limp and unresponsive. Jonas picked up his daughter-in-law's battered body and carried her toward the house. As he neared, he saw Elmo Jones coming up the lane.

Elmo started yelling while reining in his horse and buggy. "I got a letter from the County Circuit Court here for Mrs. Whitcome. I can't figure out what's in it. I made out the word guardianship, reckon it has…" Elmo caught sight of Jonas carrying a body covered in blood. In shock, he gasped and narrowly missed swallowing his chaw. "Holy Mackerel! Who's that you're carryin'?"

Jonas yelled, "Elmo, drive into town and fetch Doc Adams. Tell him there's been an accident and Sarah's hurt."

"What happened?"

"She looks bad Elmo. Get goin' and tell the doctor to hurry."

Elmo turned his rig around and gave his horse Nellie the whip. Nellie lurched in to a run so quickly the little man nearly lost control of the reins. Emo tightened his grip and eased Nellie in to the turn from the Whitcome's lane to the road. Once executed, he yelled, "Go girl go." The mare responded with a full out gallop. Elmo spewed his signature stream of tobacco juice over his shoulder and hunkered down for the bumpy ride.

The Postman considered it not only his job to deliver the mail, but also deliver the area's news. He'd tell Doc Adams to get out to Sarah's lickety-split, then he'd go notify the Riley's, Sarah's parents, that she was injured. After that, he'd continue delivering the mail while he spread the news of trouble out at the Whitcome farm. This was a banner day for Elmo Jones. He got to deliver *official* government mail and he was 'Johnny-on-the-spot' in Sarah Whitcome's time of need.

# Chapter 8

Emma was in the kitchen rocking her sleeping granddaughter. She heard Jonas call out to someone to go fetch the doctor and went to the window. Elmo Jones' rig was disappearing down the lane in a cloud of dust. Jonas was nearing the house, carrying Sarah's limp, battered body. A painful chill crept up her spine. "I can't let Zeke see."

Zeke was playing with blocks on the kitchen floor. "What can't ya let me see Granny?"

Emma fibbed. "I didn't say let you see, I said, let's play hide and seek."

The tyke jumped to his feet. "You ain't gotta ask me twiced."

On the way to put Hathaway in her crib she said, "You go hide somewhere upstairs. Now stay hid until I come and find you."

The boy took off calling over his shoulder, "I'm really good at this game. You gotta count to a hundret afore you come lookin' for me."

Emma flung the kitchen door open. "Jonas! Dear Lord in heaven, what happened?"

"I found her like this behind the woodshed." Jonas maneuvered Sarah's body through the doorway, taking care not to bang her head. "I asked who did this to her. She said Henry, then passed out. Where can I put her?"

Emma pulled the feather tic from its drying spot and started spreading it onto the floor. "Here, put her here. Jonas, she told you she was afraid of Henry…thought it was dangerous to keep him at home. You wouldn't listen!"

Jonas struggled to kneel and balance the weight he was holding. "Are you sayin' this is my fault? How do we know it really was Henry that did this?"

"Sarah wouldn't falsely accuse him," Emma said as she helped steady Sarah's body to the floor.

Jonas' mind went to the day a couple of weeks before when they'd brought their son home from the hospital. *When I left him standing in the yard his fists were clenched, he was angry…said he wanted to go back to the red brick house.*

Sarah moaned and moved her legs. Jonas's coat that'd been covering her naked body fell away. Blood was visible on her inner thighs. It was evident that she had been raped as well as beaten.

Emma jerked the crochet afghan from the rocking chair and covered her daughter-in-law. "My God, Jonas, how bad has she been hurt?"

Sarah murmured, "Zeke...Hathaway?"

"They're safe." Emma began plucking twigs and dried leaves that were embedded in Sarah's disheveled hair. "The baby's asleep in her crib and Zeke and I are playing hide and seek. He's waiting upstairs for me to come and find him."

Sarah grabbed ahold of Emma's arm and tried to pull herself up. "Got to get out of sight. School's letting out... can't let my boys see." Sarah was too weak to sit up, she lost her grip and fell back to the feather tic.

Sarah's eyes were swelling closed. "Jonas, Jonas, where are you?"

Jonas took ahold of Sarah's hand. "Here, Sarah, I'm right here."

Sarah pleaded. "Find Henry, don't let him harm the children. Check the woods... across the... pumpkin..." Sarah blacked out again.

Jonas picked up Sarah's limp body. Before he laid her on the bed, Emma stripped off Sarah's wedding ring quilt and spread out the soiled feather tick.

"I'll go see to Henry, the doctor should be here soon," Jonas said.

Zeke's sing-song voice rang out from his hiding place. "Granny, oh Grannnyyy, you done a countin' yet? I'm gettin' kinda tired of hidin'. 'Sides, you ain't never gonna find me." The small boy giggled as he sat huddled in the upper bedroom's wardrobe.

Emma called up the stairs, "Olly, Olly outs in free! I give up. Come on down and I'll set out some cookies and milk."

The boy entered the kitchen on a trot, grabbed a cookie and took a seat at the table. "I was hid real good wasn't I? Can't tell ya where, 'cause it's my secret place. I always hide there. My brothers generally find me right quick. I guess you ain't so good at playin' due to ya bein' so old. Was your skin always that wrinkled? How come your hair is ...?"

"Zeke, Zeke, please hush for a minute." Emma said as she poured water into a pan. "Hathaway and your mother are both taking naps, so be quiet as a mouse. Your brothers will be home any minute now. You can brag to them about how you skunked your granny at hide and seek." Emma grabbed a clean cloth and took the pan of water to tend to Sarah.

When a cool cloth was placed on her forehead, Sarah rallied enough to speak. "Did Jonas find Henry? Is he all right?"

"Shush, don't worry about that now." Emma crooned as she began to clean the dried blood from Sarah's facial wounds. "I never would have believed my boy could be capable of doing something like this."

"He wasn't. It was the stroke." Sarah replied weakly.

Emma heard a man's voice coming from the kitchen. When she peered out, Jeb Carter, the newly elected Town Marshal, was talking to Zeke who was still eating cookies. She called out to him, "Jeb, in here. Zeke, save some cookies for your brothers."

Spewing crumbs as he spoke, Zeke responded. "Ain't no need. We got us a plenty, I think. Iffin we don't, Ma always can bake us some more. I'm not the tallest, but my tumm…" The remainder of the boy's diatribe was cut off from hearing as Jeb entered Sarah's bedroom and Emma closed the door.

"Emma, Elmo Jones ran in to me on his way to fetch Doc Adams. He said there'd been an accident …." Jeb stopped cold when he saw Sarah's battered face. "What happened out here?" Jeb demanded.

"Sarah's been uh, uh, badly hurt," Emma responded.

"Badly hurt! She looks near beat to death. Who did this?"

"It seems that Henry might be at fault."

"Where is he?"

"Jonas left to go get him in the pumpkin patch." Emma explained.

"Zeke's in the kitchen. Where's the baby, she all right? What about the older boys, they still at school?" Jeb snapped rapid fire.

Wringing her hands Emma said. "Why isn't Doc Adams here? We need him to see after Sarah. She's hurt bad, real bad. I was trying to get her cleaned up when I heard you come in. She needs a doctor."

Jeb placed his hands on Emma's shoulders and gave her a gentle shake. "Get ahold of yourself, Mrs. Whitcome. Doc Adams is on his way. Now I'm asking you again, the other children, what about them?"

Emma shook her head as if to clear it. "The baby's sleeping, the older boys aren't home from school yet. They're due any minute now."

The sound of an approaching horse and buggy interrupted their conversation. "I'll go see who it is," the Marshal replied. From the kitchen window vantage point he called out, "Doc just pulled up." Jeb opened the back door. "Doc, glad you're here."

Ben stepped into the kitchen. "What's happened to Sarah? Elmo Jones told me she'd been hurt in an accident and that I needed to get here fast."

"Apparently Henry attac…"

Zeke interrupted. "My Ma ain't hurt. Granny said she and Hathaway are taken themselves a nap. I don't have to take a nap no more 'cause I'm gettin' big". The little man flexed his muscles.

"That's right, Zeke, your mother's napping." The Marshal said. "Doc, come with me and I'll show you where she's uh, uh…sleeping."

Jeb went with the doctor to Sarah's bedroom. "I'll take my leave so you can see to Sarah. I best go find Jonas and Henry."

"Jeb." Sarah tried to sit up, but couldn't.

Jeb stepped to the bedside and took Sarah's hand. "I'm here Sarah."

"The stroke…don't blame Henry. But Jeb, get him away from the children. He can't stay here on the farm."

"I understand, Sarah. I'll have him gone by nightfall. Now rest." Jeb left.

Jonas found his son sitting on a pumpkin on the far side of the patch. Henry was sweaty and his dirt-covered face had tear tracks. His clothes were in disarray. His left suspender strap lay limp at his side and the buttons to the front flap in his pants were undone.

The impact of acceptance hit Jonas hard. "Why, Henry, why?" Jonas felt the burden of guilt and remorse so heavily, he thought his legs would buckle under the weight. He lowered his bulk to a large pumpkin next to Henry. "What happened, son?"

Henry turned with a bewildered look on his face. "That woman wouldn't take me back to the red brick house." Pointing toward the stand of tall pines he said, "She told me it was over yonder, past those trees. I couldn't find it." Henry began to sob, his torso rocking back and forth. He reached over and grabbed Jonas's hand. "Mister, will you take me there? Please!"

Placing his arm around his son's shoulders Jonas said, "Yes son, I'll take you to the red brick house."

Jeb cleared his throat to alert Jonas that he was approaching. He laid his hand on the elder man's shoulder and gave it a reassuring squeeze.

Jonas looked up, and with a tone of resignation said, "I expect that my son's in trouble with the law."

"That would be up to Sarah, but I seriously doubt it. Her plea to me, just now when I left her bedside, was to not blame Henry. She knows his mind was severely damaged by the heatstroke."

Jonas shook his head. "Seems like I was the only one who couldn't accept the seriousness of Henry's condition. My boy wants to go back to the hospital. I said I'd take him."

"I heard you tell Henry that when I was walking up." Jeb took off his hat and ran his hand through his hair. "You know, Jeb, if you'd left him there, this would have never happened."

"That's a fact and one I'll have to live with. I hope Sarah can forgive me. Emma told me bringing Henry back to the farm was a mistake. I wouldn't listen. I think the Good Book says something to the effect that pride cometh before a fall. I guess I let my pride get in the way of my better judgment.

"Yep, Proverbs 16:18, not an exact quote, but close enough. Let's take Henry back to the house. We'll see how bad Sarah's hurt. I'll make the trip to Logansport with you." The Marshal put his hat back on and pulled it down snug. "We'll go tonight. No point in delayin'."

"I'd be much obliged for your company." Jonas reached out to Jeb for an assist up. "Can we catch a train this hour of the day?"

"The last run leaves at six o'clock this evening. If we hurry, we can make it."

"What if they won't take him back?"

"They'll take him Jonas. Obviously he was too sick to leave in the first place. We'll stop in town and use the telephone at my office to call them, let them know we're bringing him."

Jonas held a hand out to Henry. "Come on son, let's get you back where you belong."

\*\*\*

Sarah's parents had arrived just after Doc Adams. Emma gave up her beside spot to Mary, who continued applying cold compresses to Sarah's brow. Ben cleaned her wounds and inspected her injuries.

"These cuts on her face aren't deep. If they're kept clean, they should heal without leaving scars," Ben told Mary.

"What about her sight?" Mary asked. "Her right eye is swollen closed and there's only a slit left open in her left one. My girl can't even see!"

"We won't know if permanent damage has been done until the swelling goes down. I feel hopeful that her sight will be fine. I think it's just the tissue around the eyes that's been injured. These scrapes on her arms and legs will scab over. Keep them clean, and dry. These areas of red…" Ben lifted Sarah's right arm, then her left. "They cover much of her body mass. They're bruises, gonna look nasty…deep purple, then yellowish green… it'll take two, maybe three weeks before they're gone."

"Doc, what about her, uh…private area?" Mary whispered. "I know he violated her, but why was there blood? Has she been damaged down there?"

"I saw some minor tearing…because the act was forced. The tearing will heal. It's the blows she took to her head that concern me. She may have what's called a concussion. That might be why she's having trouble staying awake."

"I'm awake, I just can't open my eyes." Sarah whispered.

"Sarah, I'm here. Your Mama's here." Mary said as she applied a fresh compress to Sarah's forehead.

"My head hurts…hurts even more when I try to talk. Breathing hurts too."

Doc held a spoon full of medicine up to Sarah's lips. "Sarah, swallow this. I think a couple of your ribs are broken." Ben laid down the spoon and picked up a roll of cloth about six inches wide. "Mary, help me with this binding."

Mary laid the wet cloth she'd been holding down and helped Ben wrap the cloth snug around Sarah's rib cage.

Doc said, "This binding and the Laudanum you just swallowed should help. Laudanum will deaden your senses as well as take the edge off of your pain. Sarah, you've taken quite a battering. Healing is gonna take time and rest."

"I heard some of what you were telling Ma. Thanks for coming Doc," Sarah squeezed the doctor's hand. "It sounds like I'll mend. What about Henry? Is he all right?"

Mary was quick with a response. "Don't worry about Henry. Jonas and Emma will see to him. Me and your Pa will look after the children 'til you're able."

"Thanks, Ma, I just...want...to kno...," the Laudanum took effect, Sarah drifted off.

"I hear Jonas and Jeb talking in the kitchen." Ben said to Mary. "I think I recognize Henry's voice too. He sounds agitated. I'd better go check on him."

Jonas made his way across the room to ask Emma about Sarah's condition. Marshal Carter announced their plans to leave immediately for the mental hospital in Logansport. Henry nervously shifted back and forth on his feet with his head hung low. "Need to get back to the red brick house...tried to tell that woman."

Sarah's father Tom, was at the kitchen table helping Josh set up the checkerboard. When Henry spoke, Tom's hand, that held the checkers, froze in mid-air. It began to tremble. The checkers slipped from his grasp and fell to the board. The wooden disks already put in place scattered. Tom curled his trembling hand into a fisted ball and with deliberation, brought it down to his side. The look he gave Jonas was ominous. "I expect taking him back tonight would be best."

Doc Adams coaxed Henry to sit down. Emma brought her son a cup of hot chamomile tea. Doc added a few drops of Laudanum, just enough to take the edge off of Henry's agitation. "Henry, drink this. It'll bring you some comfort."

"I told that woman I wanted to go back to the red brick house. She wouldn't listen. I told her...she wouldn't listen."

"We understand. Drink your tea. Drink all of it. Your Pa and Jeb are going to take you there soon," the doctor told Henry.

The autumn days were growing shorter and it was nigh on to twilight when the trio began the long journey. Jeb carried a small bottle of Laudanum in his pocket. Doc had instructed him to give Henry a moderate dose if he got difficult to handle.

\*\*\*

Doc Adams prepared to leave. Mary came from Sarah's bedside to hear his parting instructions. "I'm leaving this bottle of Laudanum for Sarah. She can have a dose every six hours if needed."

Emma, Tom and Mary thanked Ben for coming. He assured them he would make a house call the next day to check on Sarah's condition and then he left.

Mary was watching out the kitchen window when Ben reached his rig. She saw his shoulders begin to shake and she saw him use his handkerchief to wipe his eyes. Mary stood silently, not wanting to draw attention to what she was witnessing. Since Henry's stroke, there'd been more than one occasion when Mary had observed the doctor looking at her daughter with admiration. Sarah always appeared oblivious to how much Ben Adams cared for her, but her mother was not.

Mary's heart ached for Ben as it ached for her daughter. Married until death do us part, was she feared, going to be a lifelong sentence for her Sarah. Henry was mentally ill, but physically he seemed healthy and as strong as a bull. Mary's eyes filled with tears. *Dear God, don't bind my child to a marriage in name only. If it isn't in your will to heal Henry, I beg you to help Sarah recognize that the man she loved is dead in soul and spirit. Lord, doesn't that free her to make a new life with someone else?*

\*\*\*

Tom Riley left for his farm to get his evening chores done, but said he'd be back to spend the night. Emma started cooking supper and Abe and Josh headed for the barn to do their usual chores.

Josh looked over at his older brother. "Abe, what's goin' on? Why was Marshal Carter at our house? Why'd he and Grandpa Whitcome take Pa away?"

"I don't exactly know." Abe responded.

"How come Grandma Riley's in Ma's bedroom with the door shut and why is Grandpa Riley coming back here, after he does his chores, to spend the night?"

"I think somethin' happened to Ma while we was at school. That's why they was all here when we got home."

"What do you mean, somethin' happened? Zeke said that Grandma Whitcome told him she was takin' a nap."

"I think she's been hurt or somethin'. When'd you ever know our Ma to take a nap in the middle of the afternoon? And, if she was, why ain't she got up to fix our supper?"

"Yeah, just now, when we left the house it looked like Granny Whitcome was fixin' to cook. Do you think Zeke told me a lie?"

"Na, I'm sure Granny told him Ma was nappin'. Zeke and Luke are young enough to believe what they're told without thinkin' otherwise. You and me ain't! I'll wait 'til supper is on the table. If Ma don't get up to eat with us, I'm goin' in her room."

"I'm goin' too."

"No, Josh. I'm the oldest, it'll be best if you leave it to me. I'll find out what's goin' on." *Pa hurt Ma, I just know it. He was tryin' to force himself on her that day in the barn, before he went to the hospital. Josh don't need to know about them things yet. Since Grandpa Whitcome brought Pa back to the farm, Pa's been scary actin'. Ma told me she was waitin' on some court decision about gettin' him admitted to the mental asylum again. If a decision come, I weren't told about it. Now Jeb Carter shows up to help Grandpa Whitcome take him back, all in a hurry like. Nappin', my foot. I ain't stupid!*

Tom returned from his farm. Emma called the family to the supper table. Mary came out of Sarah's bedroom to join them. Abe stood holding on to the back of his chair, but didn't sit down.

"Come on and join us, Abe. We need to say grace before the food gets cold." Emma said.

"Why didn't Ma get up to eat with us?" Abe asked.

"She's resting," was Mary's reply.

Abe started for his mother's bedroom. "I'm goin' in to see her."

"Abe, stop. I said your Ma is resting," Mary asserted.

"I don't mean no disrespect, Grandma, but I'm goin' in, now!"

"Let him go," Tom spoke up. "There's no way to keep this hidden and I expect the boy's old enough to handle the truth."

Abe fell to his knees beside the bed when he saw his mother's condition. "Did Pa do this to you?"

Sarah whispered, "Don't blame him, it was the stroke."

Abe laid his head down on the quilt that covered Sarah and sobbed. "I hate Pa. I'll never forgive him for doin' this."

Sarah reached out and smoothed the rumpled hair on her boy's head. "I'll be all right. We'll talk…in…the morn…" Sarah's hand slid to her side as she drifted off to sleep.

# Chapter 9

A dose of Laudanum at about six o'clock the night of the attack put Sarah in a deep state of oblivion to the rape and brutal beating.

Emma, Tom and Mary stayed the night, each taking a three hour shift of sitting vigil at Sarah's bedside.

When it was their turn to sleep, Tom and Mary used the double bed, in the upstairs bedroom that Luke, Josh and Zeke usually shared. The boys finally got their wish to camp out in the house and were set up with bedrolls on the floor in the parlor. Emma took what had been her son's makeshift bed to sleep on in the room with them.

Around nine o'clock that night rain began to fall. The music made by the rhythmic dancing of the liquid drops on the house's tin roof quickly lulled its occupants to sleep. About midnight when the mercury in the thermometer that hung outside the kitchen window dropped below thirty-two degrees, the rain began to freeze. As the icy crystals fell from the sky landing on the tin roof, the music was replaced by a sound akin to that of rocks being catapulted from a thousand slingshots, rapid fire. Except for the adults changing shifts, the family slept through the winter's onslaught.

Unknown to Sarah and the family who were warm and safe in the faithful old farmhouse, Jonas and Marshal Carter were facing an overnight stay at Northern Indiana Hospital for the Mentally Insane. Rain started to fall just as the men were preparing to leave after admitting Henry to the mental care facility. They knew the temperature would plummet with nightfall and the rain could quickly turn to sleet. It would be an hour's train ride back to LaFontaine. Hitching up the team and attempting to traverse an ice slick road in the dark, pulling a wagon, would amount to an accident just waiting to happen. The day had brought enough difficulties to deal with as it was, no point risking more. They'd stay put.

They were given a room furnished with two single beds. The pair slept poorly. The night was fraught with alien and disconcerting sounds coming from the hospital's residents who occupied the rooms adjacent to theirs. That, plus the sound of sleet and freezing rain hitting the room's windowpanes, made it nearly impossible to sleep.

Jonas had drawn some comfort from knowing that come morning, he would be able to find out how Henry had weathered his first night back at the hospital. There had been no positive aspect for Jeb who considered it a night spent in the bowels of hell.

The next morning Jonas and Jeb entered the staff-dining hall looking tired and disheveled. "You fellows have trouble sleepin'? One of the orderlies asked with a good-natured chuckle. A second orderly quipped, "This ain't your regular boardin' house and that's the gospel truth."

Over breakfast they got the report that Henry had slept peacefully during the night. He woke early and had already eaten his breakfast. He was now sitting out in the common relaxation room.

Jonas found Henry gazing out the room's huge windows at the frozen landscape before him. He took a seat next to his son.

The boughs of the huge pine trees that dominated the scenery hung low under their icy burden. Some appeared at risk of being severed from their connection to their life giving mother trunk. The rain had stopped and the sky was clear. It was totally void of any remnant of the havoc that it had spewed forth the night before. The rays of the sun, unobstructed by clouds, were making fast progress at melting the ice. As the majestic orb worked its magic its refractions bounced off of the frozen matter creating a glistening effect that looked like a million sparkling diamonds. Henry sat as if mesmerized by the beauty that was displayed before him.

Jonas realized his presence was of no consequence to his son. Seeing that Henry was finally at peace within himself, the father lovingly reached out, took his boy's hand and said goodbye.

*** 

Sarah woke to rays of sunshine lying on her pillow. Her mother was sitting at her bedside, breathing softly as she dozed.

Sarah watched her for a while drawing comfort from her presence. "Good morning, Ma," she gently called out.

Mary woke at the sound of her child's voice and in one fell swoop was on her feet. "What...what do you need? Are you hurting bad?"

"I'm sorry, Ma, I didn't intend to startle you," Sarah said as she took her mother's hand and pulled her down to sit on the side of the bed.

"No need to apologize, child. I shouldn't have fallen asleep," Mary said as she brushed back the ringlets of hair that had nested on Sarah's forehead during the night.

"Ma, have you been sitting here all night? You must be worn out."

"Your pa, Emma and I have taken turns sitting with you. I'm fine. Now tell me how you feel. Do you want a dose of Laudanum?"

"I'm sore and stiff, but I don't want anything for pain. It makes me sleep and I need to stay awake to talk to the children. Was Abe in my room last night? I seem to recall hearing him crying, but being too weak and sleepy to comfort him."

"Yes, he insisted on being let in to see you. Your pa thought he was too grown to keep the truth from him. Abe was near beside himself seeing you so badly hurt."

Tears rolled down Sarah's cheeks. "Oh, Ma, I'm so sorry we couldn't spare him from knowing."

Mary squeezed Sarah's hand. "He wanted to stay at your bedside, but we insisted he needed his rest. We told him he'd have plenty of opportunities to take care of you in the days ahead. He finally agreed, but would go no farther than the floor just outside your bedroom door. He's sleeping there now."

Sarah choked back a sob. "I fear this has cost him the small remnant of innocence he had left."

Mary sighed deeply. "I expect your right. Life has hard knocks, this was a big one. The boy's strong, he won't let it keep him down, nor will you, Sarah."

"Thank you ma. Would you please help me wash my face and comb my hair? I need to have a talk with Abe as soon as he wakes up. I want to look as fresh as I can."

While Mary helped Sarah with her morning toilette, they discussed the ice storm and the likelihood that it'd kept Jonas from coming back the night before.

"Rain's stopped. With this bright sunshine the ice will disappear in no time. I expect he'll be here to fetch Emma by early afternoon, if not sooner," Mary said.

There was a hesitant knock on the door just as they were finishing up. "Ma, its Abe. Can I please come in?"

Mary let her grandson in then left, closing the door behind her.

Abe leaned over and kissed his mother's brow. "How are you feeling ma?"

"I'm stiff and sore, but much better than yesterday." Sarah responded. "How about you? I want to know how you're feeling."

In a stone cold voice the boy said. "I hate him. Sick or not, ain't no excuse for hurtin' a woman. I wish that heatstroke had just killed him dead. We'd all be better off."

Sarah took a firm hold on her son's arm. "Now...you don't mean that. It's your hurting heart and fear that has you saying such a thing."

Tears slipped down the boy's cheeks as he reached out, but for fear of causing her pain withheld his touch. "Your face, your pretty face."

"Listen to me, son. Do you recall when you smashed your thumb with the hammer last summer? Remember how it was swollen and purple and hurt like the dickens? Look at it now. It's healed and you can't even tell it was ever hurt. It will be like that with my face and my body in a few weeks. Nothing has happened to me that won't heal."

Abe rubbed his once afflicted thumb with his other. "That was an accident. I didn't smash my thumb on purpose."

"What happened yesterday was like an accident too. The man that hurt me wasn't your pa. Through no fault of his own, your father's life was taken from him by the heatstroke. You lost your pa. I lost the man I loved. We were left with this hulk of a man who doesn't know up from down, right from wrong.

You and the other children must treasure the memories of the loving father you had just as I will treasure the memories of the dear sweet husband I had. We will respect him for who he was. The stroke can't steal away our memories unless we let it."

Abe swiped his sleeve across his dripping nose.

Sarah continued. "That man that hurt me yesterday didn't know what he was doing. He was frightened and confused and he wanted to leave the farm and go to a place where he felt safe. He got weary with waiting for us to take him there, so he struck out in anger. There's no point in blaming anyone."

Taking her son by the chin she raised his face to the level of hers and sternly said, "You will not fill your heart with hate. It will rob you of the happiness in life that God has in store for you. If I, the one who has been physically hurt, can forgive the man who hurt me, you will not harbor a grudge."

Abe took a deep breath and straightened his sagging shoulders. "I'll try to forgive him."

Sarah patted the boy's hand. "Thank you, son."

"Ma, how is it that you always have so much love in your heart? Even now, with what has happened, you say only loving things."

"Abe, the love in my heart comes from my faith in God. I let the love of His son, Jesus, that lives in me, carry me though times like this when the just plain Sarah in me wants to be angry and hurt. In the bible, Matthew 19:26, it says *...with man this is impossible, but with God all things are possible.* That includes allowing us to love even those who have wronged us."

"If you say so, Ma."

"It's not me that says so. It's God. Now go talk to your brothers. Tell them there was an accident and I got hurt. Don't tell them your Pa was involved. They're too young to understand the situation. Prepare them as best you can for the way I look so they won't be too frightened. Tell them I'll be alright soon. If they see that their big brother isn't worried about me, they won't be worried either. After you tell them, fetch Hathaway and you all come in to see me."

A few minutes later Abe returned with his siblings in tow. Josh and Luke approached the bed tentatively, each taking a turn at giving their mother a hug and kiss. They didn't have a chance to ask any questions before Zeke wedged his way in past them to be front and center at the bedside.

Briefly the four year old was taken aback and said, "Gosh ma, you look like you done fell out of the hayloft on your face."

Before Sarah could respond, the tike's mind moved past her battered look and he blurted out, "Grandma Riley made me eat oatmeal for breakfast. I tried to tell her it was pancake Wednesday, but she wouldn't make me none. If you're done with your nap, could ya please get up and make me some pancakes? It's Wednesday and I really need me some."

Zeke's selfish, but innocent request brought laughter to the room and the spirit of gloom that had shrouded Sarah's bed was pushed away.

Sarah reached for Abe to hand Hathaway over to her. If the baby noticed the difference in Sarah's appearance she gave no indication.

She immediately nuzzled her little face at the crook of Sarah's neck and breathed in the comforting essence that was her mama's.

Stealing herself to accept the pain the jostling would cause her broken ribs, Sarah invited her four boys to climb up on the bed. She tussled the hair on one head then another, but stopped at Abe. She'd shared adult things with her oldest child that morning. He'd handled it like a grownup. He was still her boy, but in that moment she wouldn't treat him as such. He had been irrevocably changed from the child who takes to get his own needs met while his mother gives, to that of a young man who knew how to give support to his mother's needs.

"How about you boys stay home from school today and keep me company. If you do, I'll ask Grandmother Riley to make us all pancakes for our noon meal." Sarah offered to her children.

"Boy howdy," the younger boys yelled while they bounced. Hathaway clapped her tiny hands to join in the excitement she didn't fully understand.

The children's rowdiness intensified Sarah's pain. No longer able to maintain a cheerful façade, she told them she needed to rest a bit and asked them to go play. Abe noticed the grimace of pain on his mother's face and responded quickly. He picked up the baby and ushered his brothers from the room.

As Abe was closing the door Sarah asked, "When your grandpa Whitcome gets here please ask him and your grandmother Emma to come in to see me."

"Sure thing, Ma. Now get some rest," the boy said smiling.

Sarah realized the air between her and Henry's parent needed to be cleared. She was standing at the precipice of deciding how to deal with Jonas in particular. Could she let go of her hurt and open the door to forgiveness as she had earlier told Abe he should do? Should she reckon with him in a way that would make it clear she was the head of her family... that there would be consequences if he ever again interfered with her decisions?

Sarah mulled it over in her mind. Unlike Henry who wasn't in his right mind, she felt Jonas was accountable for his actions. He had interfered with Henry's care. If he hadn't brought him back to the farm, the attack and rape wouldn't have happened. His bull headedness in refusing to accept Henry's impairments had caused her and the entire family great pain. She hoped he'd come to grips with his responsibility in the situation. Sarah had seen the grief on Emma's face when she realized what her son had done. Now Emma and Jonas' relationship with Sarah's parents was strained. There would be gossip among their friends and neighbors over what had occurred.

Sarah whispered aloud. "When will the hurting end? How can our family relationships be healed? What if Jonas doesn't think he's done anything wrong…has nothing to regret? How could I forgive him if that were the case?" As she spoke her troubling thoughts, the Lord's Prayer came to her mind, Mathew 6:12. "…and forgive us our sins, as we have forgiven those who sin against us." *Am I not justified in my resentful feelings toward Jonas? How could God ask me to see my way clear to let them go when my eyes are still so swollen I can't see the features on my own children's faces? Surely in light of the beating and rape God wouldn't be calling me to forgive… at least not this soon.*

Sarah wished she could get on her knees to pray, but knew the pain would be intolerable. Instead she leaned her head back on her pillow and lifted her eyes heavenward. "Heavenly Father, I know there's no point in confessing my angry feelings to you. You already know my heart is hard towards my father-in-law. When I see him and Emma later today, hold the bitterness that threatens on the tip of my tongue. Give me the words to say that will bring healing to my relationship with them and help bring a healing in the relationship they have with my parents. The children and I need to be surrounded with the love and caring that comes from family. No one in this situation will benefit from strife. I don't know what to say when I see them. You do. I trust you to give me the words. Father, I pray as it says in Psalm 19:14 …*may the words of my mouth and the meditations of my heart be pleasing to you oh Lord, my rock and my redeemer.*"

***

The train ride back to LaFontaine was uneventful. Jonas thanked Jeb for his help and said goodbye. Jeb headed for the Marshal's office and Jonas went to the livery to fetch his wagon and team of horses.

The sun had melted most of the ice from the road, but the intermittent patches of slush that remained made for slow going. It was nearly one o'clock in the afternoon when Jonas called "haw" to his team and they made the turn up Sarah's lane.

As Sarah had asked, her in-laws Jonas and Emma visited her room immediately upon Jonas's arrival.

At the sight of his daughter-in-law's face, swollen even more than when he had last seen her, Jonas lost his composure and wept. "I'm so sorry Sarah. I should have listened to you. I should have had faith that you were doing what was best for Henry when you admitted him to the hospital. Please forgive me."

A calmness spread throughout the room when three words were spoken in the spirit of remorse…*please forgive me.*

As if standing in a warm and gentle spring rain, Sarah felt her bitterness wash away. She reached out for the hand of the grieving man, took it in hers and said, "I forgive you Jonas. What's done is done. There's still peace to be made between you and my parents, but you and I don't need to speak of it again."

Jonas collapsed to the bedside chair where he drew in a deep breath and let it out slowly. "I'll tend to that directly."

Sarah motioned for Emma to come sit on the edge of the bed. When it looked as if Jonas had caught his breath Sarah took Emma's hand in hers and said, "Tell us about Henry. Did you get him settled at the hospital? Was he glad to be back there? Do you think he'll be alright?"

# Chapter 10

Sarah studied her face in the oval mirror atop her bedroom dresser. It had been three weeks since Henry's savage assault. The swelling around her eyes was gone. The scabs from her cuts and abrasions had flaked off and her bruises, no longer tender to the touch, had turned from purple to a light yellowish green.

As she looked in the mirror, Sarah caught a glimpse of her former self - the self whose life was filled with home and hope and a deep abiding happiness. As quickly as the reflection came, it left again. The image that held her gaze now was that of a worried mother alone with five children to raise and a farm to manage.

Sarah still had home and hope, but the happiness she had derived from being Henry's wife was no longer there. Her husband was gone. With him went that sense of well-being and wholeness that comes from the intimate sharing of one's life with another. The knowing that whatever occurred, there was a strong shoulder to lean on.

Sarah's facial features remained the same, but the beating and rape had changed her. The remnants of innocence that had transferred from being a young woman under her father's protection to being a wife with a protective husband had been ripped away. The reflection of her face held an altered, but not broken countenance. Sarah would accept this changed woman, it was her essence now.

Sarah's convalescence period was spent in near seclusion. With the exception of the trip to her parent's house for Thanksgiving dinner, she had kept to the farm. Her mother had stayed with her the first week to do the routine lifting involved with caring for the children and the house. Her father and brother brought in supplies and provided oversight for Abe and Josh in the care of the livestock. Ma and Pa Whitcome had been by a couple of times to offer their help. Both times had been when Sarah's father was there. The encounters were strained, so they hadn't been back.

Sarah wrote the mental hospital and requested a report on Henry's condition. They responded that he had adjusted quickly and seemed content. The news brought her comfort.

Doc Adams offered to make regular house calls. Sarah declined. She assured him that she'd send for him if needed. She thought that she just needed time to mend. The crestfallen look on Doc's face when she told him she didn't need him to come again had given Sarah pause. She wasn't naïve, nor had she been blind to the admiring looks she occasionally received from men. With Henry at her side, they had never given her a moment's concern. Now Henry was gone. Things were different.

She hoped Doc's reaction hadn't meant other than concern for her healing. She'd lost her husband, she didn't want to lose a dear friend as well.

While her body healed Sarah made use of the sedentary time to update the farm's ledgers. Sarah knew the basic operations of the farm, but she'd never had direct responsibility for managing the money. After making comparisons with previous years' income and expenses she realized that the bulk of their annual intake came from the sale of crops at fall harvest. The summer's heat that year, with spells of drought, had cost them the yield Henry had projected. The overall profit margin on the crops had been slim with corn and wheat producing more than beans. After paying off the crop loan from the bank, cash was alarmingly low.

Sarah sold several hogs for a quick infusion of money. She kept a couple of sows and a boar for repopulation. This brought temporary relief to her money concerns, but she knew she would have to skillfully manage the farm's expenses to keep things afloat.

At butchering time in October her father and brother had each given her meat. As a result, she was well stocked with enough ham, pork, sausage and bacon to see them through until spring.

Sarah had confidence that with advice from her father and brother she could make adequate plans for spring planting. Having the manpower to handle the work was another thing altogether. Her family and friends had their own farms to run. She wouldn't burden them with trying to help out with labor on her land too. The only alternative was to hire help. A hired hand would require money that, from the looks of the farm's ledger, she didn't have.

Sarah vowed to find a way to keep the farm from failing. Thankfully it didn't have a mortgage against it. Largely due to Henry's skillful management and planning they had been able to pay off all loans against the property the year before. That aside she still had property taxes to pay, upkeep expenses for the livestock and buildings as well as children to feed and clothe. The list seemed endless. If she sold the farm she would be left with no means to earn a living for her family. She couldn't bear the thought of moving in with her parents. They had raised their children and deserved freedom to enjoy their remaining years without the burden of her and the children underfoot. Her brother had a full house with four children of his own. Living with him wasn't even an option. The thought of being forced to move in with Jonas and Emma was beyond bearable.

She wouldn't allow any thoughts of failure to dampen her resolve. Sarah took to her knees with Jeremiah 29:11 on her lips. *"For I know the plans I have for you," says the Lord. "They are plans for good and not for disaster, to give you a future and a hope. In those days when you pray, I will listen…"*

After praying several days for guidance an idea came to her that she knew was God's response. It was unconventional and a long shot, but Sarah took a step in faith and ran an article in the LaFontaine and Wabash newspapers that read:

> **Experienced farm hand needed who will work for lodging, meals and a percentage of next fall's harvest income. Apply in person at the Henry Whitcome farm on America road LaFontaine or make contact by mail to Mrs. Henry Whitcome, Rural Route 1, LaFontaine. References required.**

\*\*\*

It was Sunday, December 6th, the second of the four Sundays in the Advent season. Sarah and the children had missed attending church the first Sunday and she didn't want to miss any more.

The Advent season, the celebration of Christ's birth, had always been a joyous time for her as a young girl and later for her and Henry with the children.

Sarah wondered if going to church and seeing her neighbors for the first time since the attack would be awkward. She had no doubt that tongues had been wagging about the incident. With Elmo Jones being the first on the scene and the one sent to fetch Doc Adams, there wouldn't be a soul in all of Liberty Township that didn't know that something terrible had happened at the Whitcome farm on November 17th. The details of just how Sarah had been hurt so badly weren't public knowledge. The news that Henry had been readmitted to the mental hospital was. That leak had likely occurred the day Jeb Carter and Jonas had taken Henry to the mental asylum. Jeb had used the telephone at his office to call ahead to let them know they were coming.

The local telephone operator, Myra Johansson, placed all calls. Making a connection to the Logansport mental hospital for the town's marshal would have been an unusual request. No doubt she'd listened in. Discretion wasn't one of Myra's virtues. The woman could spread gossip lickety-split. With additions or omissions made freely each time the news was repeated, the sharing at the end of the line often bore no resemblance to the truth.

The few telephones in the area were party lines. When a telephone's crank was turned to signal the operator for assistance in placing a call, the vibration through the lines caused a slight sounding on all telephones on that line. Once the call was transmitted they all got another jingle. The intended recipient knew it was for them when it emitted a specific sequence of rings that had been assigned to them, such as two longs and a short. Nothing however prevented a nosey neighbor on that party line from lifting their receiver and listening in on a call. The invasion of privacy occurred more often than not. One only had to claim they mistook the ring for their own if their intrusion on the call was discovered.

Elmo Jones stopped by the telephone office each morning before starting his mail route. He and Myra fueled one another's craving for gossip and freely swapped stories. One way or another, folks in and around town would have heard about the Whitcome's troubles.

Sarah believed that most of her neighbors were good people and meant well. She knew it was hard for folks to know what to say or keep from offering an opinion in a situation like hers.

The passing weeks had brought healing to Sarah's soul as well as to her body. For the most part, she again had her life in perspective. The process of living would go on despite what had occurred. She would not allow her family to be defined by that single, horrible incident. Nor would she allow herself to be seen as a victim or a helpless women estranged from her mentally ill husband. Sarah's soul was kindled with a will and determination to raise a healthy, happy family on a farm that prospered. She felt fueled up and ready to engage in society again with her head held high.

Sarah began her task of brushing her waist length mane one hundred strokes. Highlights of auburn and red glistened as if to punctuate her renewed fire for life.

While enjoying her coffee and reading her Bible that morning, Sarah came across Psalm 30:5 "...*weeping may last through the night, but joy comes with the morning.*" The phrase *joy comes with the morning,* was one Sarah's mother, Mary, used frequently. Countless times when growing up at home Sarah had heard her say that phrase. She used it when encouragement or strength was needed.

Reading the familiar passage had given her a feeling of joy, something she hadn't felt since the attack. She'd given thanks to God.

Sarah knew from experience that joy was revealed to the willing seeker in incremental and often indiscriminate amounts. It could come as a large, all consuming emotion that lingered, or it could flit across your consciousness as a mere thought that came and went in a snippet of time.

Joy wouldn't replace that deep abiding happiness she'd felt with Henry. They simply were two different things. Even still, Sarah would take joy whenever and however it came her way.

Drawn back to her grooming, Sarah twisted and pinned her hair atop her head. Several strands broke loose forming wispy ringlets that framed her face. She placed her wide brimmed, winter hat over the coiffure and secured it with her bejeweled hat pin. Henry had given her the pin as an anniversary gift. It had been an extravagant purchase for her usually practical husband. Although a tad ostentatious for Sarah's taste, she treasured it.

Sarah called, "Boys, it's time to load up and head to town. We don't want to be late for church." Leaving her bedroom she grabbed her handbag. The quick movement caused a sharp pain in her side. Her broken ribs were mending, but had not yet fully healed.

To her delight, all five of her children were in the kitchen ready to leave. They were lined up in stair-step fashion as if standing at attention. Nine-year-old Josh was holding baby Hathaway.

Sarah was awe struck that they were ready to go. She had dressed the baby and had helped the two youngest boys with their clothes before she got dressed. Abe and Josh were left to get themselves ready.

Abe was still the only one of her boys who knew how she had been hurt and the extent of her injuries. She suspected Abe was the one responsible for wrangling them together to be waiting by the door.

The other boys were left with the assumption that Sarah had been in an accident of some sort. They had been content with a vague explanation largely because they saw her health improving each day. Still, they had understood that going out for the first time after her extended convalescence was a big event for her. She felt immense pride and tears threatened to spill from her eyes as she looked at her brood.

"Ready for inspection, Ma," they shouted in unison as they threw their shoulders back and clicked the heels of their boots together.

Sarah assumed the role, affixing a stern look on her face as she walked the line, surveying her troops. She noticed that each boy had a severe part on the right side of his head. The hair on all their heads seemed to be plastered down with a substance that literally glistened. As she came to Zeke, the shortest step in the line of stairs, a lock of hair on the crown of his head where his cowlick was, sprung free and pointed skyward. The disturbance caused a tiny amount of a familiar odor to emanate from his scalp. It was at this point that it dawned on Sarah the likely source for their slicked down hair.

Trying not to be too obvious, Sarah cut her eyes to the cupboard shelf where she had left a plate with fat drippings from that morning's breakfast bacon. Sure enough, there were finger tracts through the congealed lard. A sense of mortification threatened but was pushed away as Sarah realized the boys were really quite proud of their hairdos. She uttered only words of praise as they walked to the waiting wagon and team. She would explain the possible ramifications later when they got back home. She hoped they didn't manifest before then.

The sanctuary of the church was nearly full when Sarah arrived with her family. She and Henry usually sat near the back in case one of their brood had to be taken out for one reason or another. Today her parents were expecting her and the children to sit with them. Tom and Mary Riley were in their customary pew, third row back, right side. The prized seats were smack dab in the middle of the Amen section.

Sitting in the Amen section at the Methodist Church carried with it certain responsibilities. Inhabitants were expected to stay alert and respond with an occasional 'Amen' at poignant utterances from the clergy or a 'praise the Lord' at the reading of particularly germane scriptures. Failure to do so was to reveal that due attention wasn't being given the sermon that morning.

Sarah took the lead carrying Hathaway. Her other chicks followed as she walked down the center isle to the seats her parents had saved for them. Several turned their heads as the entourage made their entrance while the organist enthusiastically pumped out the opening hymn, *There's A Song In The Air.*

Sermons in the Methodist church during Advent season as well as several other specifically chosen seasons throughout the year, were fraught with messages about tithing and giving money to the church. This particular Sunday the sermon had been titled, *From Every Side of Bacon Should Come a Few Slices for the Lord.* Shouts and murmurings of praise were plentiful as the Reverend Edward Sloan brought forth scripture upon scripture supporting his call to give and give abundantly.

It was approaching high noon and the preacher showed no sign of winding down the sermon. Sarah had long since abandoned attempts to keep her boys from fidgeting. She too was tired of sitting still. Her back hurt and she longed to free her ribs from the confines of the corset she wore.

The sun shown brightly through the stained glass windows. It refracted prismatic colors of red, orange, yellow, green and blue in the dust particles that danced about. Its rays mercilessly targeted Luke's head. The heat from the sun caused the grease on the seven-year-old's hair to release its hold. As his wiry unruly strands freed themselves the air was filled with the aroma of cooked bacon.

The airflow carried several whiffs toward the pulpit causing the preacher's stomach to growl loudly. Withdrawing his pocket watch from his vest he checked the time. Seeing that he had preached into what was normally his own dinnertime, he abruptly ended his sermon.

As the congregation stood to sing the closing hymn, Tom Riley leaned over and whispered to Sarah, "For the love of heaven, do the boys have bacon fat on their heads?" Sarah just looked up and smiled.

While the adults took a few minutes to visit, the children ran outside to play. Directly, Abe saw Josh walking toward him with tears streaming down his cheeks. Abe rushed to him and put an arm around his younger brother's shoulders. "What happened?"

"Ernie Brown made a crack about ma." Ernie was thirteen years old and had a reputation for bullying the younger children.

"What kind of crack, what'd he say?"

"He said, 'It looks like your ma survived the beatin' your pa gave her. Too bad she wasn't smart enough to keep him at the mental asylum after he went crazy.' I thought Ma had an accident, fell or somethin'. I thought that was how she got hurt. Did our pa really beat her up?"

The pent up rage Abe felt over what their father had done to their mother, now mixed with the anger he felt for his brother being subjected to embarrassment and public taunting, overwhelmed him. Through clenched teeth he growled, "It's hard to understand. I'll tell you what I know, but later. Right now I got me some business to take care of."

Abe shot across the church's yard. In short order, he closed the distance to where Ernie Brown stood with a group of older boys. "Ernie, I need a word with you," he said motioning for the kid to step aside for a private talk.

Ernie tossed back his head and standing with his hands on his hips said, "Hey squirt, whatever you got to say to me, you can say in front of my buddies here."

Abe hitched his shoulders back, "Alright, we'll do it your way. Don't be makin' cracks about my ma or my pa. Keep your nose out of my family's business. And another thing, my name is Abe use it. Don't ever call me squirt again."

"Or what? Squirt!"

Abe moved in close. So close that the warm breath from the two boys' mouths visibly mingled in the frigid air. Ernie, feeling intimidated, took a step backward. Abe made an aggressive move and stepped forward. He grabbed the older boy's shirt and pulled him so close their noses threatened to touch. Abe was two years younger but stood head to head with the thirteen year old. "Or I'll catch you out when you don't have all these body guards around and teach you some manners."

"Abe, time to go," Sarah called as she stood next to their horse and wagon that was already loaded with the other children.

Abe let go of Ernie's shirt, smoothed out the wrinkles he had created and said, "Gotta go now, it wouldn't be polite to keep my ma a waitin'."

When Abe hopped up in the wagon Sarah said, "It looked like you were having a serious conversation with that Brown boy just now. Anything you want to talk about?"

"Naw, nothin' to talk about. Him and me was just havin' us a discussion about the weather." Abe cut a look at Josh that conveyed, 'this is for us to handle, keep your trap shut'.

Sarah gave Abe a stern look. "The weather you say. Well I'm a good listener if you ever want to talk about the weather with me."

Abe turned away. He knew his story was thin on believability.

Sarah said to all in the wagon, "Your Grandmother Riley invited us over for Sunday dinner. She's fixing fried chicken, mashed potatoes with gravy, green beans, corn relish, hot rolls and apple pie."

"Boy howdy," they all yelled.

Sarah gave the reins a flick and called gettyup to the team. As if on queue, she and the boys broke out singing *Over the River and through the Woods to Grandma's House We Go.* Hathaway accompanied them by clapping her baby hands.

# Chapter 11

Sarah's ad for a hired hand appeared in the newspaper daily for two weeks. No one local had inquired. She wasn't surprised. Sarah knew most folks in the area and couldn't think of any likely prospects. She'd purchased several copies of the paper, clipped her ad and mailed it to grain elevators in counties adjacent to her own. Crops in neighboring territories had fared as bad as theirs in the recent harvest, some worse. That meant that farmers wouldn't be keeping hired help through the dormant winter months. As a result, she hoped some desirable inquires would come her direction.

Zeke was playing in his dirt pile and the baby was sleeping when, from the kitchen window, Sarah saw a horse and buggy turn up their lane. The time of day indicated that it might be Elmo Jones delivering the mail. The stream of tobacco juice spraying over the driver's shoulder confirmed it.

Instead of making a deposit in the mailbox Elmo jumped down, tethered his horse and scurried up to the house, mail in hand, and knocked.

Sarah stopped her task of sweeping the floor and opened the door to greet him.

"Got some mail here for ya, Mrs. Whitcome. Looks like responses to that there ad of yourn."

Reaching out to take her mail, Sarah replied, "Elmo, you didn't need to bring it to the door, but thank you."

The beady-eyed fellow didn't release his hold on the envelopes. "It's mighty cold out here deliverin' the mail today. I'd be much obliged if ya could spare me a cup of hot coffee to warm my internals a bit."

"Let go of my mail and I'll get you a cup." Sarah chuckled as she opened the door wider to let him enter.

Sarah laid the mail aside and fetched Elmo a cup of hot coffee. She placed a large dollop of her homemade strawberry jam alongside a couple of biscuits left over from breakfast and served those as well. After pouring a cup of coffee for herself, she joined Elmo at the table.

With his shoulders hunched over holding his biscuit like a hungry chipmunk as he nibbled, Elmo filled Sarah in on all manner of news about her neighbors. As their conversation waned, he kept glancing at the envelopes that lay unopened on her dry sink.

"Ma'am, I'd be happy to take a look at them inquiries for ya. I 'spect I might even know some of the fellers sending their application. Iffin I don't, I could still give ya my what-to and wherefores on which one ta pick."

Sarah guessed Elmo Jones' anxiety level was sky high, sensing that their visit was about to end and she hadn't shared the contents of her mail with him. She'd noticed that the seal on the envelopes had been picked at, hinting he'd already tried to sneak a peek before they were delivered.

Sarah rose from her chair, gathered both of their coffee cups and cleared the table. Smiling at the postman she said, "I don't want to keep you from your deliveries and I need to get back to my chores."

As he put on his coat and donned his hat the quirky little man said, "Ya know, if it weren't for my back that gives me trouble from time to time, I'd be happy to lend ya a hand with the farm during my spare time."

"How kind of you."

"Yes sir, I'd be Johnnie on the spot, iffin it weren't for this bad back of mine and that's a pure fact. I 'spect you get lonesome out here all by yourself with your man gone and all. I could come some evening and keep ya company. It's the least I could do since my bad back won't let me help with your chores." Seeing that Sarah's eyebrows had raised, Elmo quickly added, "We could play us a game of checkees, or whatever was your pleasure, Ma'am."

Sarah knew Elmo's bravado was about all the little guy had going for him in the area of romance. She didn't think his overtures were anything to worry about, but he'd crossed the line of being respectful and she wouldn't let that pass. "Elmo Jones, I'm still a married woman. Whether I'm lonely or not isn't your concern." Sarah took the postman's elbow. The little man was so short he only came to her shoulders. The difference in their heights caused Elmo's pants to hitch up and wedge. He stepped lively as Sarah ushered him to the door. "I've got five children to keep me company. My mother and father help out some and I've got my 6'4", 250 pound brother Jack who looks out for me. I'll be sure to tell him about your offer to come keep me company and uh… play checkers."

In a voice raised a couple of octaves, Elmo said, "No need. On second thought I likely won't have time to play the game anyway."

Nosey Elmo gone, Sarah sat down to read her mail. In the first letter the writer described himself as sixty-eight years old, strong and steady. He claimed considerable experience with crops and dairy cattle. The man's age concerned Sarah a bit, he was thirteen years older than her father. He provide two references, instead of the three she'd requested. Sarah laid the letter aside. The second of the two responses caught her attention. The writing was impeccable, with perfectly formed letters written in straight even lines, the grammar and spelling was good.

> Dear Mrs. Whitcome,
>
> My name is Sam Hartman and I'm writing in reply to your advertisement for a hired hand. I'm thirty-two years old and I have worked in farming since the age of thirteen. I have extensive experience with planting and harvesting crops native to Indiana; in particular corn, soybeans and wheat. I am knowledgeable about crop rotation to prevent soil nutrient depletion.
>
> My most recent livestock experience has been in hog farming where I developed a farrowing process that significantly reduces the risk of piglet loss due to injury from the sow.
>
> I have past experience in poultry farming and egg production and feel I can hold my own in that category. I have worked some in dairy farming and have a good working knowledge of the process, but less experience than in the other three areas I have mentioned.
>
> I have fair to middling carpentry skills and what I consider an above average understanding of the repair and maintenance of machinery. I have my own tools.
>
> Enclosed you will find letters of recommendation. Clem Hargrove owns the farm where I've worked for the past four years. Clem is retiring from farming and no longer needs my help which is why I'm looking for employment elsewhere. Leonard Sheline is proprietor of the local general store and has known me for twelve years.

Reverend Byron Alcorn is my pastor at the Free Will Baptist church where I regularly attend.

I understand that times are hard and I am willing to work for you under the terms you described in your advertisement. I may be contacted by writing to me, Sam Hartman, General Delivery Kokomo, Indiana. If you have access to a telephone you can make contact by calling Sheline's General Store and Mercantile in Kokomo. Leave instructions with Leonard and I will telephone you back.

Sincerely,
Sam Hartman

Sarah's hands, still holding the letter dropped to her lap. Sam Hartman was young enough to be strong and healthy. He claimed to have the skills and experience the farm needed. The way his letter was written indicated he had some education and was likely intelligent, both helpful characteristics. He attended church. She chuckled to herself and said out loud, "Aside from being a Free Will Baptist, Sam Hartman, you seem just about perfect. Tomorrow I'll go talk to Ma and Pa about this and get their opinions."

Hathaway woke from her nap and started fussing. Sarah hopped up to tend to her, checking first to see if Zeke was still digging.

\*\*\*

Tom Riley laid down the inquiry letter along with his reading glasses. He rubbed his eyes, folded his hands, resting them on the table before he spoke. "The man's qualifications seem good. If his references bear out his claims, he could be just what you need to help with the farm."

"Oh, Pa, I'm so happy you approve. I thought the same thing. I've read his letters of reference, all three of them support his work experience claims. I want to hire him."

"Hold on a minute, Sarah, I didn't say I approve. Your ma and I have some concerns about this plan of yours. Your ad says payment for work will be a percentage of next fall's harvest. What percentage did you have in mind? It's a creative idea, but have you worked your figures enough to know what you can offer and still pay off your crop loan with some left over for your own living expenses?"

"Yes, I have that all figured out."

Tom fired off with another question before Sarah had a chance to answer his first one. "You're offering lodging. Where will this man sleep? Your barn is too drafty to make suitable quarters during the winter months. If he eats all of his meals with you and the children, how will that affect your family time together?"

Sarah let several seconds pass before she spoke. "Pa, I've given all of that consideration and those concerns pale in comparison to my worry that I could lose the farm. What will happen to my children if I can't even provide a table for them to eat at, let alone one to share with a hired hand?"

"You can eat at our table," Sarah's mother said smiling.

Sarah smiled back and continued. "I think an eight percent profit share for the first year is reasonable. Working on the share system will be an incentive for the man to be productive with his time and crop management. The crop loan usually amounts to about twenty-five percent of the gross income. Since I'm paying the hired hand eight percent of the net, not gross income, I'm left with ninety two percent of the profit from the crops to help with family and farm needs. This doesn't count the income from livestock. I plan to buy more hens for increased egg production, add pullets to the flock to sell as fryers to area groceries and explore expansion of our hog operation. I'll work out some type of profit sharing with the hired hand on increased income related to livestock. It will depend on how much we need him to help in that area. The boys and I should be able to handle a fair amount of that workload."

"I'm impressed. That explains the financial side, but what about hired hand's living accommodations?" Tom Riley asked.

"As for where he sleeps, I thought I'd set up the parlor as his living quarters. It's a large room, big enough for a bed and a sitting area. The room is at the front of the house and has it's own outside entrance. Most folks come and go through the back door, so losing it for family use won't be a problem. I would keep the door from the parlor that accesses the rest of the house locked. This would provide privacy for the hired hand as well as the children and me. Except for meals and heating water for bathing, he won't need to be in our part of the house."

Tom Riley gestured to his wife, who sat nearby rocking baby Hathaway.

"I guess it's my turn," Mary said. Sarah, you're a beautiful woman and still young. What will people think about you being unchaperoned with a hired hand living in your house? Especially one as young as this Hartman fellow."

"Ma, the people I care about know me and won't think ill of me. As to other folks, I really can't worry about that now. What will people be saying about me if I lose the farm and can't care for my children? Uncle Jesse's wife died leaving him with three young children. No one thought it improper when he hired a housekeeper to move in to cook, clean and care for them. She slept in his spare bedroom and as I recall she was a young woman. Why is this any different?"

"It's different, Sarah, because you're a woman and your Uncle Jesse is a man. Him moving someone in to keep house for him was and still is a common practice for a widower. It just seems natural."

"Talk about what's natural… it doesn't feel natural for me to be alone without Henry. I physically feel his loss. It's as if half of me was severed and the other half is dangling in the wind. If I don't pull myself together and take charge, my dangling half will snap off and there won't be anything left of me to keep a hold on living."

Tom reached out and took his daughter's hand in his.

Sarah looked lovingly at her father. "Pa, I respect your concerns and you know I love both you and Ma with all my heart…but nothing and no one will stop me from doing everything I can to provide a happy and secure home for my children."

Tom replied, "You could always sell the farm and move back home to live with me and your mother."

"Pa, I know you worry about me but I'm not your little girl anymore. I want my own home. Not just for the children, for me too. I want to be the one to take care of them financially. I want Hathaway and the boys to enjoy you as grandparents, just like Jack and I enjoyed Ma's and your parents before they died."

The room grew quiet. Except for Zeke's playful banter with his toy farm animals, no one spoke.

Mary Riley was the first to break the silence. "Sarah, you've been through a lot, more than most women would experience in two lifetimes.

Your pa and I respect you too. Tom, we can't stand in her way of doing what she feels is right for her family. We had the freedom to make our own way in our lives without any interference from our parents. Sarah deserves that same chance."

Raising his hands as if in surrender, Tom Riley said, "I know when I'm outnumbered. Do what you think is best, Sarah. Your ma and I plan on being here for a long time yet. If you ever do need us, you're always welcome to come home."

"I'll always need you both," Sarah said as she hugged her parents, tears of blessing streaming down her cheeks.

\*\*\*

Before going back to her farm, Sarah drove the team through town to use the telephone at the Sheriff's office. She asked the telephone operator, Myra, to ring up Sheline's General Store for her.

Myra was reluctant, "Why are you calling the general store in Kokomo? Have you checked here at Parker's? They have just about anything a body could need."

"I'm quite sure Parker's Mercantile doesn't carry what I'm shopping for," Sarah replied. She knew she might come to regret her decision to use the telephone to leave a message for Sam Hartman. No doubt Myra would listen in. Before sundown, the whole town would know her business. "Please place my call."

# Chapter 12

Sarah washed strawberry jam from Hathaway's face. She told Abe, Josh and Luke, her three older boys, to clean up and comb their hair. Once finished with the baby she would tackle four-year-old Zeke's unruly mop. As Sarah fussed over the family's appearance she found herself questioning the effort. *I'm interviewing a hired hand, does it matter how the children look? Yes, the children's grooming is a reflection on me. I don't want this man to think I'm not competent or efficient. I don't want him thinking I would settle for shoddy performance from myself or someone I hire.*

The telephone message Sarah left for Sam Hartman at Sheiline's General Store gave instructions for him to come to the farm that weekend to talk about the job. She chose Saturday so, Abe, Josh, and Luke would be home. She wasn't going to bring on someone who would be overwhelmed by five young children who'd be underfoot. She hoped the planned exchange with her entire brood together would be sufficient for an assessment in that area.

Family meals had returned to a time of joy and telling about their day. Sarah was determined that she wouldn't bring in someone who might dampen their spirits. She expected whoever she hired to be pleasant and cordial to the children at all times. In turn, they would be taught to respect the hired hand's privacy.

With the family cleaned up Sarah retreated to her bedroom to tend to herself. She took off her apron and tucked a few errant strands of hair into her braided crown. As a matter of habit she brushed off her shoulders and smoothed out the folds in her pleated skirt. When her hand passed over her stomach, a nagging concern wiggled its way to the forefront of her mind. *My monthly's a week late. That's never happened except...can't think about that today.* Sarah leaned in to the mirror to pick off an eyelash that had fallen to her cheek.

"Ma, that man's ridin' up the lane," Abe called out.

Sarah headed for the kitchen. "I'm coming. We'll all go out and greet him together."

\*\*\*

The message to come to the Whitcome farm on Saturday to discuss their hired hand position was good news to Sam Hartman. The crops in Howard County had been hit hard by drought that year. Odd jobs were still available, but full time positions that offered room and board were scarce. Clem Hargrove, the farmer Sam worked for and lived with the past four years, was cutting back. He'd turned his acreage over to his sons to manage, and sold off all of his livestock except for a few chickens and a cow. Clem and his wife Clara were going to take it easy and not work so hard during their remaining years. Sam was happy to see them take a much deserved rest but he was sad to leave their employ. The couple had been good to him. *They gave me a job after my brush with the law. For that I'll be eternally grateful.*

It didn't take much for Sam to conjure up thoughts from that dark period in his past. Sounds sometimes brought remembrances of his time of incarceration. Certain smells triggered them instantly. He doubted he would ever be completely free from remembering the stench of the mattress in his cell, soaked with sweat and human desperation.

Sam was pleasantly surprised as he rode his horse up the Whitcome's lane. The barn, fencing and outbuildings looked as if they had been routinely cared for. The house was two-story with a yard clear of clutter. A small pile of dirt was mounded under a large oak tree that stood near a window. Although devoid of color due to their dormant state, there were flowerbeds on both sides of what he assumed was the back door. The house sat at an angle so that the rear had a direct view of the barn. He noticed that there was a minimally defined pathway around the left side of the home that he supposed led to a second entrance. It was evident the barn-facing egress was the most used. This was a common layout for rural Indiana farmsteads.

As he dismounted and tethered his horse to the hitching post his eye was drawn to a child's shovel and what looked like a small toy wagon protruding from the pile of dirt under the large tree. That's odd. Why would an old couple have toys? Grandchildren? Come to think of it I just assumed the Whitcomes are up in years. Families with children have a ready workforce.

Before Sam could speculate further the back door flew open and four boys of various heights ran out. It was a shock to him, but nothing compared to the jolt he felt when Sarah came out carrying Hathaway in her arms.

Sam thought she was the most strikingly beautiful woman he'd ever seen. She was tall and slender and the crown of braids atop her head glistened in the sunlight. Her chiseled features were flawless except for a yellow and purplish bruise under her left eye.

\*\*\*

Reaching her hand out Sarah said, "Hello. I'm guessing you're Sam Hartman."

"Yes, pleased to meet you, Ma'am," Sam said as his right hand clasped the one offered while he tipped his hat with his left.

"Welcome. I'm Sarah Whitcome and these are my children." Looking at the baby in her arms she said, "This is my daughter Hathaway. Hathaway can you say hello to Mr. Hartman?"

The baby, usually shy around strangers, surprised her mother when she responded with an ear to ear smile. Sarah put her down to walk about and gestured to the boys to introduce themselves.

Abe stood forward a couple of paces as if to make a statement that he was in charge. He offered his hand. "I'm Abe, the oldest. Pleased to make your acquaintance."

Sam reciprocated as Josh and Luke followed in kind.

When it was Zeke's turn, the boy blurted out. "My name's Zeke. I'm four years old. That's my dirt pile and my shovel over yonder. You might can use the shovel some time. Ya need to ask me first 'cause I'm generally busy usin' it ta dig holes."

Following this deluge, the tyke reached out his hand for a shake. It was then that Sarah noticed it was covered with strawberry jam. In her rush to get everyone ready she had missed that aspect of the child's spit and polish.

The man shook and with some difficulty due to the sticky goo, released the boy's hand. To his dismay, transference occurred. Sam didn't know what to do. He wanted rid of the uncomfortable residue, but didn't want to wipe it on his pants. Finding himself at a loss for a quick solution, he let his hand dangle uncomfortably at his side.

Zeke fired-off, "It's just strawberry jam. Ma makes it for us. It's real good.

It will lick right off." The tot demonstrated by vigorously wiping his tongue over the palm of his hand and then holding it up to show that it was now clean.

Zeke was the family's loose cannon, a fact Sarah could bank on. Even so, she found herself a bit chagrined at the boy's demonstration. Hoping to deflect the focus Sarah said, "Mr. Hartman, let's go in to the kitchen so we can talk." She motioned for Hathaway to come to her. The babe shook her head no, toddled over to Sam and wrapped her chubby arms around his leg.

Without a moment's hesitation, Sam reached down and gathered the small girl up in his arms. "That sounds like a good idea, Ma'am." His mind was racing with a multitude of thoughts and mixed feelings. Wow, five children. The mother's beautiful. Where's the husband? Need to wash this jam off my hand. This baby is as light as a feather. I smell apple pie. What! Oh no, something warm is running down my shirtfront. Don't let it be, oh no....

Sarah invited Sam to take a seat at the kitchen table. As she took Hathaway from him she saw that the entire front of his shirt was wet. "Oh, Mr. Hartman, I'm so sorry. Hathaway still wears a diaper."

Using only his index finger and thumb Sam gingerly pulled the soaked, clinging fabric from his skin. "It's alright, Ma'am. I expect it will dry... uh, eventually."

"Josh, please go get one of your Pa's shirts for Mr. Hartman to change into while his dries," Sarah instructed.

Sam hoped he hadn't acted appalled over the incident. He didn't want Mrs. Whitcome to think he was squeamish. That aside, he didn't relish the idea of discussing his future employment while his shirt was soaked in baby pee. "Thank you kindly, Ma'am, but I have a dry one in my saddle bag." Sam quickly went outside, discarded the wet shirt, donned the dry one and stepped to the pump to wash his sticky hand before going back inside.

Embarrassed by her indiscretion, but unable to tear her eyes away, Sarah watched out the window as the man stripped off his shirt and used it to wipe his chest dry. He was tall, nearly six foot two she guessed. His hair was curly dark brown. His shaven face showed a shadow of a sprouting beard. He was slim with broad shoulders supporting a chest covered with dark hair. Tears welled up in Sarah's eyes. *How many times I watched Henry strip down to bare chest and wash up at that pump at the end of the day. Dear Lord, I miss him so.* Sarah brushed her hand across the front of her skirt as if to remove something forbidden.

When the man came back in to the kitchen Sarah said, "I'm afraid we haven't made a very good impression, Mr. Hartman. I wish I could tell you things like the sticky hands and wet diapers are unusual happenings, but they aren't. My children are still quite young and those are typical occurrences."

Relieved that the woman's response was conciliatory Sam said, "No harm done, Ma'am. Let's talk about your hired hand position. Will your husband, the children's father, be joining us?"

Before Sarah could respond her three foot tall cannon discharged. "We don't got a pa no more. He got stroked and went away."

"Ma'am?" Sam said turning to Sarah with a quizzical look on his face.

"Sit down, Mr. Hartman. Abe and Josh, you join us too. I'll explain our situation to you and outline the duties for our hired hand position." Sarah walked over to Luke, handed the baby to him and whispered, "Would you mind putting a dry diaper on your sister and keeping her and Zeke entertained while we talk?"

The seven-year-old, pleased that his mother had given him a job of responsibility, replied, "Sure, Ma. Zeke, let's you, me and Hathaway have a block building contest. We'll see who can make the tallest stack without falling over."

"Boy howdy, I'm real good at stacking blocks," Zeke eagerly responded.

Sarah gave Sam a concise accounting of her husband's heatstroke, resulting impairments and subsequent admission to the mental hospital in Logansport. She was aware that he'd noticed the bruise around her eye. For a brief moment she struggled with her thoughts, then decided to keep the cause private for now.

Abe picked up on his mother's hesitation, reached over and patted her hand. A loving gesture that didn't go unnoticed by Sam.

Sarah efficiently outlined her plans for managing the farm and the help she was seeking from a hired hand. "In payment for the work, I'm offering room and board and eight percent of the profit from next year's crop. I'll pay a bonus for helping us get the egg and pullet business up and running. If we can't handle that new aspect of the farm's operations alone, consideration for a more suitable compensation will be discussed at the time. The position comes with Sundays off. Once we get caught up on the deferred maintenance around here and planting or harvesting doesn't require us to work, an occasional Saturday off could be taken too.

As Sarah gave her presentation Sam's head was awhirl. *It's clear this woman is in charge of her situation. Her ideas for the farm seem good. It would be exciting to be in on the beginning of her expansion plans like egg production and raising pullets to sell. I don't have any experience with children. They seem likeable, but would I have any privacy? Lord Almighty, she's a beautiful woman…with no husband at her side.*

Sam's attention refocused when he heard Sarah start to describe his accommodations. "I'm sorry, Ma'am, what was that you said about living quarters?"

"You would have the parlor with its own outside entrance all to yourself. We'd keep the door from the parlor into the hall locked to assure your privacy. I'll show it to you directly. Before that, I want to know if you or my sons have any questions."

Abe spoke first. "Mr. Hartman, I've been reading about the chicken business in the Poultry Tribune. Last month's issue gave a description and the measurements for building a chicken house. The article said the coop needs a lot of fresh air so the flock don't get sick with that fungus that can grow on their comb and cause them to die. It also said we should keep the cocks fenced away from the others 'cause they bully their way to the feed. If ya don't do that some of the chickens might be too scared to fight for food, go hungry and get puny. I think we need us a new chicken house first, before we buy more stock. The one we got now just ain't gonna work good enough."

Sarah looked at her oldest with pride. "Abe, I didn't know you'd been studying on the chicken business."

"Ma, you've had a lot to deal with recently what with Pa's stroke and the atta…uh, uh…I didn't want to burden you with the talk of it just now."

Sarah's eyes were misty as she gave the boy a nod of understanding.

Seeing the intimate exchange, Sam deflected the conversation by responding, "I haven't had a chance to inspect your existing chicken house. If it doesn't allow for ample ventilation and separating out the roosters, then I agree, a new structure might be needed. Building it before increasing stock would be the only way to go. Chickens are quite susceptible to colds and roup especially during the winter. Some say adding coal oil to their water helps prevent this and of course you could buy Conkey's Roup Cure to add to the water, but that would be an added expense."

"Well, gentlemen," Sarah said, "that sounds like some good information to add to the planning for the poultry expansion. Mr. Hartman, do you have any questions about the farming operation you want to ask?"

After determining there were none, the group left the table to take a look at the proposed hired hand living space.

"Ma'am, the accommodations you're offering are real fine. A body could be very comfortable sleeping and resting in this room with the fireplace and all. I'm just a bit concerned that if I took the job, folks might talk about me stayin' in the house with your husband being ill and gone. I wouldn't want you to be put in a difficult position over the arrangements. Can we take a look at the barn? Maybe I could set up quarters in there?"

"Mr. Hartman, I've given this a great deal of thought. Our barn is too drafty for human habitation. I wouldn't expect a dog to sleep there in the winter. I wish I had suitable separate accommodation for a hired hand, but I don't. I don't have the money to build anything now, or funds to weather proof a section of the barn for living purposes. My priority is keeping this farm running and bringing in enough money to care for my children. I won't let worrying about what others might think of our arrangement keep me from that. Converting this parlor is what I have to offer. If you want it and the job, it's yours."

Sam was taken aback by the woman's frankness about the issue. After a few moments of staring intently at Sarah he said, "Yes, Ma'am, I want the job."

"Good! We can start our working relationship the first Monday in January. Nineteen hundred and four will be a new beginning for all of us and hopefully a happy and prosperous year." Sarah reached out her hand to solidify the agreement.

"Now can we have us some of that apple pie you baked, Ma?" Luke said as he came in to the room trying to balance his baby sister on his right hip while he wiped beads of perspiration from his brow. "I can't hardly hold Zeke off it much longer."

Sarah looked at her seven year old and smiled. "Mr. Hartman has agreed to come and work for us so let's all have some pie to celebrate."

# Chapter 13

A light dusting of snow was falling the morning before Christmas. Sarah frequently looked out the window to check weather conditions while she cooked breakfast. Her father, Tom Riley planned to come around ten o'clock to pick her and the children up to take them to his farm. They would spend Christmas Eve and Christmas Day with her parents. If the snow turned to flurries, it could quickly accumulate, causing hazardous traveling conditions.

Sarah was grateful for her parent's invitation to spend the holiday with them. This was their first Christmas without Henry and not one Sarah relished handling on her own. The children's gifts from her, as well as those they would think came from Santa, were already at her parent's house. If the snow prevented them from going there she wouldn't have anything under the tree for them Christmas morning. Sarah chided herself, *I wish I had kept the gifts here. Weather this time of year can be unpredictable. I should have planned for the possibility of getting snowed in. Dear Lord, if it be in Thy will, please allow safe travels for us today.*

She reflected on the gifts waiting for her children, hoping they would be pleased and not left wanting. She recalled her own early childhood and how she expected a magical bearded man to slide down their chimney and bring her all that she'd conjured in her mind that she needed and wanted.

She wouldn't rob her little ones of their belief in a red-suited benefactor. All children reach an age of reasoning that reveals the truth about the bearer of gifts that magically appear under the Christmas tree. It often comes as an inward awareness before there is an outward acknowledgement of this truth. She would let that happen in due course even though she knew that the knowing made the giving and receiving of gifts a much sweeter experience.

Sarah's gifts for the children were homespun. She reworked some of Henry's long-sleeved shirts to make clothing for them. Henry had such broad shoulders and large muscled long arms that a single garment made a dress for Hathaway as well as a shirt for Zeke. The shirt she chose to alter for them was made from a printed fabric with tiny dots and squares on a field of light blue.

Making the alterations brought bittersweet memories. She'd purchased the fabric at Parker's Dry Goods and made the shirt the year before as Henry's birthday gift. He'd dubbed it his Sunday best, wearing it only to church and on special occasions. Sarah buried her face in the garment and breathed in the lingering scent of the man she loved. *Oh how the blue in the fabric made your blue eyes sparkle.* Tears welled up in Sarah's eyes. *The tender embrace you gave me in thanks led to a time of lovin' that I'll never forget.*

The fabric's color and pattern was such that it suited boy or girl. She wondered if Zeke would take offense to his sister having a garment like his or if he would think the matching clothing looked quite fine. With Zeke it was hard to predict.

Although considerable downsizing was needed to alter shirts for Luke and Josh there wasn't enough fabric left to make anything else. The remnants were placed in her scrap sack for use in a rag rug at some future point.

Abe's shirt required the least downsizing. The boy was growing like a weed. His shoulders were beginning to broaden and his arms were getting long, still he lacked the bulk of a man. That would come soon enough. Likely it would come too soon for the comfort of Sarah's tightly held apron strings.

Each of Sarah's children, as well as her nieces and nephews, would receive a knitted hat and matching mittens from Sarah. Knitting brought Sarah comfort and provided an outlet to relieve her tension. The hardships of the past several months led to many nights of knitting until late hours while she rocked by the fire.

With the exception of the hand-made rag doll for Hathaway, the gifts from Santa were mail ordered from the Sears and Roebuck Catalogue. Zeke would receive a wagon for hauling dirt. The tike had expressed repeated concern that Santa might not understand how much dirt he had to haul and forget to bring him a larger wagon.

Luke's gift was a harmonica. His sights had been set on obtaining the musical instrument after hearing Slim Kilty play his when the band performed at the town's Halloween party earlier in the fall. The catalogue advertisement had promised the mouth organ would come complete with playing instructions. *For the sake of the family I hope Luke catches on quickly.*

*Played well the harmonica is pleasing to the ear. Played poorly it reminds me of a cat with its tail stuck in a wringer.*

Josh would receive his first jackknife. Sarah believed he had matured enough to handle the responsibility of carrying one.

Abe no longer believed in Santa and had asked Sarah not to get him anything. He mentioned that money was scarce and he thought the family should save where they could and put it toward building a new chicken house. Sarah was proud of him for his selfless overture but didn't want Christmas morning to come without something special under the tree for him. Abe's gift was a new pair of boots. He'd outgrown his current pair. He'd told Sarah that he would make do by wearing his father's work boots that sat unused by the back door. Sarah felt Abe's feet literally weren't big enough to fill his father's boots and she didn't want him striving for that on a figurative level either. *My sweet, sweet boy, I want you to find your own path to tread. I hope getting a practical gift will relieve your concern over the money I spent.*

While Sarah worked in the kitchen, Abe was alone in the barn finishing morning chores. When Sarah had inquired why he hadn't awakened Luke to help him, he'd told her that letting his brother sleep longer was his Christmas gift to him. Sarah stretched to relieve a kink in her back. *To sleep in…what a special gift.*

Sarah called up the stairs. "Wake up, breakfast is on the table. We need to eat and get ready to go to your grandparent's house. Grandpa will be coming to pick us up directly."

Abe came from the barn and they sat down to eat. "Ma, the snow has changed to large wet flakes. The tree branches are covered in it."

Sarah was cutting up pancakes for Hathaway. "It appears we might be headed for a full-fledged winter storm."

*\*\*\**

It was half past nine when Tom Riley drove his team and wagon up the Whitcome's lane. Zeke jerked the door open while Tom was tethering the horses. The four-year-old stood on the stoop, jacket, hat and mittens on. "I'm the first to be ready, Grandpa, so can I set on the wagon seat with ya?"

"Well if you're ready, where's your pants," Tom said as he looked at the boy's legs covered only in his red long johns.

"I got my pants right here under my arm. I can put them on later."

"We do need to hurry since the snow is falling heavy, but I think we have time for you to put your pants on."

Sarah gave her father a hug. "I'm so glad to see you. How are the roads? Can we make it back to your farm safely?"

"I think we'll be ok if we get moving. Abe you sit in the back and keep the little ones bundled up. Under the tarp you'll find dry hay and blankets."

Once loaded and tucked in, all that could be seen from the bed of the wagon was a row of various sized heads poking up from their warm nest. Sarah sat up on the wagon seat with her father while Zeke got his wish and sat wedged between them wrapped head to toe in a quilt. When they got down the Whitcome's lane to the main road they started to sing Jingle Bells at the top of their lungs. Baby Hathaway, too young to sing, entertained herself by catching snowflakes on her tongue.

"Hathaway, put your tongue back in your mouth. You're going to get chapped lips." Abe said as he ran his mitten-covered hand over her mouth to wipe it dry. His efforts were futile. The baby continued to capture the lacy crystals, her eyes crossing in their struggle to watch each one melt.

Traveling in the snow that had started to drift was treacherous. The horses soon were covered in sweat and breathing hard. The depth in some spots was almost more than the team could plow through. When it reached to midway up the horses' legs, they baulked and refused to move forward.

Tom handed the reins to Sarah. "Take the reins. I'll jump down and walk them through."

With coaxing the team trudged through the drift. The snow leveled to a more manageable depth and Tom climb back up on the wagon and took the reins. Sarah gripped the edge of the wagon seat. Tom patted her hand. "We've gone more than half way, too far to turn back. Might as well keep goin'."

The children clapped and cheered when they caught first sight of their grandparent's home. Smoke from the chimney atop the house's snow covered roof curled skyward signaling a promise of warmth for all who entered.

Sarah put her arm around her father's back. "Praise be to God. We made it here safely."

The ground was blanketed with what looked to be at least four inches of snow by the time they arrived and the flakes were multiplying at a fast pace. The quilt wrapped around Zeke was obliterated in a white mass. He looked like a snowman riding between the two adults.

Mary Riley came out to greet the entourage. Abe flipped the tarp back sending snow flying, handed Hathaway over the side of the wagon to his grandmother, and then jumped down. Zeke had been lifted down and stood like a frozen statue. Sarah was busy getting the pies she'd brought out of the wagon.

Josh and Luke were already in the yard throwing snowballs at one another. Abe barked at them. "You two need to help out. Clean that snow off of Zeke and take him in where it's warm. I'll help Grandpa rub down and feed the horses."

\*\*\*

After a supper of hot cream of potato soup and biscuits the family spent Christmas Eve telling stories, playing checkers and enjoying being together.

While everyone was occupied Abe knelt down by the Christmas tree and slipped a small package from his pants pocket and placed it amongst the other presents. His thoughts took him back three days previously to when he'd found the gift.

\*\*\*

He was getting corn out of the bin to feed the livestock when his scoop hit on something metal. It was an old coffee tin and the small package was inside it. Abe recognized it. He'd been with his father when he'd purchased the locket that it contained. A Christmas gift for his ma.

They were in Parker's Dry Goods, it was early spring, just a few months before his father's heat stroke. *I was surprised when Pa stopped at that counter to look at them trinkets on display. When he asked Mrs. Parker to take out the oval shaped gold locket for him I asked him why he was looking at women's stuff and he said,* "Because I want to buy something special for your ma for

Christmas." *I told him Christmas was months away and besides the durned thing cost three dollars.*

Abe had to take a swipe at his eyes when he recalled his pa's response. "Yes, son, three dollars is a lot of money but your Ma is worth every penny of it. Some day I hope you find a girl to love as much as I love your ma. When you do you likely will find yourself willing to spend the last penny you have in your pocket to buy her a fancy bobble just like I'm gonna do now."

Finding the package was a turning point in Abe's battle with the grief over losing his pa and the all-consuming anger he was harboring against him for attacking his mother and hurting her so badly. *Pa was a good man who loved Ma somethin' fierce. I can't remember a time he ever raised a mean hand to any of us when he was in his right mind.* Abe had dropped to the barn floor and bawled like a baby.

\*\*\*

The snow continued to fall the rest of the day and night. Nearly twelve inches accumulated before it stopped on Christmas morning. Sarah and her parents were up early enjoying a quiet cup of coffee.

They stood at the kitchen window looking out at the winter wonderland that lay before them. The trees were heavily laden with wet snow. The branches of the pine tree just outside the back door bowed low as if paying homage to the force of nature. The blanket of snow covering the ground was pristine, except for Tom's footprints between the house and the barn from doing the morning chores.

Sarah blew on the hot, rich brew in the mug she was holding. "Those drifts along the fencerows and the smoke house look to be nearly ten feet high."

"Thankfully there wasn't any drifting at the entrance to the house or the barn door," Mary said.

"Do you remember the blizzard about five years ago when the snow drifted higher than the kitchen door and we had to dig our way out of the house?" Tom asked.

"I'll never forget that. We filled the dry sink, all my pots and pans and the washtub with snow before we tunneled through." Mary shook her head. "What a mess that was to clean up."

Sarah pointed to the thermometer on the opposite side of the window glass. "Thirty-two degrees. Hopefully it will get even warmer by midday. A lot of this needs to melt so Jack and his family can come to dinner."

The eventuality of melting snow aside, Sarah knew that she and the children wouldn't be going home Christmas night as they'd originally planned.

Sarah's neighbors, the Carters, were feeding her livestock while she and the children were gone. They'd realize the road condition wouldn't allow travel. The helping hand would be extended until they got back. The Carters would know that the favor would be returned, should circumstances require.

Giggles and the shuffling of feet were heard overhead. Tom set down his coffee cup. "Peace and quiet is over. Sounds like the festivities are about to begin."

It was Zeke who'd woken first. Luke was sleeping with him and Zeke shook him awake. "It's Christmas. Get up, time's a wastin'."

The ruckus roused Josh and Abe who were sleeping in the bed next to them. The three youngest boys, still in their night shirts, ran down the stairs. Abe took time to dress before going to fetch Hathaway who had slept across the hall in the bedroom she'd shared with her mama.

Her brother's loudness woke the baby who had toddled to the closed door and was patting on it as she called, "Me out. Me out."

Abe opened the door and scooped her up, holding her at arms-length. "Let's change your britches before we go down stairs."

Hathaway wiggled and kicked. "Me down. Me down."

Abe pulled her close enough to kiss her on the cheek. "Hold still so we can get this done. I won't let you miss anything."

Sarah who'd come up to tend to Hathaway, found her smiling in her big brother's arms. "Well...look at this. You've got on dry britches. Can you tell your brother thank you?"

The baby's response was, "Me hungie".

Zeke, Luke and Josh were jumping, whooping and hollering in front of the Christmas tree. The loud hullabaloo frightened Hathaway who eagerly went to her mama's outstretched arms.

"It's ok. Your brothers are just happy," Sarah crooned and patted the child's back as the three went down the stairs.

"Let's get ta openin' these here presents!" Zeke shouted.

"Whoa Nellie! No gifts will be opened before we have us some breakfast and I read the scriptures about the birth of baby Jesus," Tom called out above the mayhem.

Zeke slowly turned to face his grandfather, a look of incredulousness on his face. "You's just pullin' our tails ain't ya, Grandpa?"

"No, I'm serious. Christmas comes just once a year and we can take time to have breakfast together and read the story from the bible that tells us about the true reason we celebrate this season. Then we'll open the presents one at a time so we can enjoy seeing what one another receives."

The rowdy trio pleaded in unison for their mother to intervene. "Ma!"

Sarah didn't respond. She didn't need to, the expression on her face gave no doubt. Together with heads bowed in defeat, the three trod to the breakfast table to eat and await the reading of the scriptures.

Pancakes, eggs, sausage, biscuits, gravy and fried potatoes were placed on the table. After grace was said the children eagerly dug in, eating with a speed that would put a hungry dog to shame.

Zeke was the first to clean his plate. He threw his arms in the air and yelled "Yes" after each person at the table laid down their fork.

Tom, in a deliberate effort to prolong Zeke's agony, had taken a second helping of biscuits and gravy which he'd been slowly consuming. He paused, with his fork mid-air, and stared out the window as if in a daydream.

Zeke reached his full level of tolerance. The boy jumped up fork in hand, ran to his grandfather's side, scooped up the man's remaining food and shoved it in his own mouth. With his cheeks bulging he declared, "Your plate's clean. Now get ta readin' them scriptures!"

"Zeke Whitcome!" Sarah exclaimed. "Don't talk to your grandfather like that and apologize for eating his biscuits and gravy."

Zeke, more in defense than contrition said, "Sorry Grandpa. A boy has his limits. I couldn't hold myself off no longer."

With a grin Tom said, "I expect you're not the only one at this table that's neigh stretched to their hold-off limit. We can open the presents now. I'll read the bible story later after Jack and the family get here."

"Boy Howdy", the three youngest boys yelled, jumping up and running to the parlor and the waiting gifts.

Eager as they were, Tom stuck to his plan of having everyone take turns at opening a present. Sarah was appreciative. She wanted to savor the look of excitement on each child's face as they unwrapped their gifts.

Josh's eyes sparkled with pride when he opened his package. A jackknife was a right-of-passage for a nine year old boy. "I sure hoped Santa thought I was old enough to have one of these. This is just what I wanted."

Luke nearly burst into tears of joy when he unwrapped his harmonica. "How did Santa know I wanted one? I'm gonna be playin' with Slim Kilty and his band come next Halloween, you just wait and see."

Zeke was elated with his gift. He was so excited he was speechless, a first for the boy who kept rubbing his hand across the wagon's shiny red painted sides.

Hathaway instantly hugged and then cradled her rag doll. Sarah and her mother traded knowing smiles over the baby's instinctive act.

Abe was overcome with emotion when he opened his boots. He was old enough to realize the sacrifice his mother made to purchase them. He couldn't risk looking at his ma just then so instead he said, "Thank you, Santa."

When everyone had taken a turn there remained one lone gift under the tree. It was a small gray box with a length of pink ribbon tied around it. Tom reached under the tree and fetched it. "The tag says 'To Sarah'."

Sarah took the box from her father's outstretched hand. "Now, Pa, Ma, what have you done? I thought we were keeping our gifts for one another to homespun items."

"It isn't from us, Sarah," Mary replied.

Sarah untied the bow and lifted the lid. Nestled in the box was a gold oval shaped locket with intricately carved filigree on the face side. When she turned it over she found "I love you" inscribed. With trembling hands Sarah opened the locket. On one side there was a picture of Henry and on the other side the word "forever" had been engraved. Sarah's eyes filled with tears. "How, when?"

"Pa bought it for you last spring and hid it out in the barn in the corn bin." Abe told her. "I was with him when he bought it at Parker's Dry Goods. It cost a whole three dollars. I thought he was crazy to spend that kind of money on it. He said you was worth every penny. I'd forgotten about it. I just happened to find it this week when I was scoopin' out feed."

Abe went to his mother and wrapped his arms around her. "I remember him, Ma. I remember him like he was before he got sick. Oh, Ma, he was so full of love and goodness." The boy laid his head on his mother's shoulder and wept.

Josh, Luke and Zeke, followed by Tom and Mary joined them. The family stood intertwined, remembering the dear one they missed. Hathaway's tiny bare feet padded to the huddle and she started to wedge her head between Luke's legs then paused. She went back, grabbed her new doll by the leg and drug it behind her as she ran to her family to join in the love.

# Chapter 14

As she thought about the day ahead Sarah was in her bedroom finishing her morning grooming. Sam Hartman, the man she'd hired to help with the farm would arrive that afternoon.

*I hope the living quarters are adequate and to his liking. We gave it our best...*

"Ma, Hathaway done ett all of her breakfast and now she's tryin' ta steal my bacon," Zeke yelled from the kitchen.

"Move your plate out of her reach. I'll come and get her directly." Sarah sat down on the edge of her bed. *I can't believe it's the first Monday of the New Year. This day seemed a long way off when we set the date.*

***

The week following Christmas Sarah and the children had worked hard to transform their parlor into living quarters. Each child was given a specific task. Sarah wanted them to understand the importance of what they were doing.

They weren't just transforming a room, they were setting up a private living space for Sam Hartman, a space the children were forbidden to enter without her consent, even if invited.

Moving the horsehair sofa to create a new gathering place for her family and guests in the kitchen had been the hardest task. The door from the parlor directly in to the room was too narrow for passage. Abe and Luke helped her take it out the front door, around the house and in through the back entrance. Although there was a cleared path through the snow, the surface was icy and treacherous as they carried the heavy piece of furniture.

A full sized rope bed with a feather tic mattress covered in white linens now occupied the vacated space in the parlor. A thick comforter was added to provide warmth. Sarah chose one whose pattern dubbed it a Crazy Quilt. She felt its mismatched and eclectic shaped swatches of fabric sewn together, were representative of the life they now lived on the farm, the life the man would be joining. The pieces, while colorful, all appeared to have come from something once beautiful that had been broken and shattered. Now collected and pulled together they formed into something with a purpose.

A plank of wood with eight pegs for hanging clothes was secured to the wall opposite the foot of the bed. A relaxing seating area was created next to the fireplace by bringing in a wooden rocker with arms and a small side table with an oil lamp.

Sarah knew the room needed a rug to add a sense of coziness to the space. She'd gone to her cedar chest and pulled out one that was just the right size and mix of color. When she'd smoothed her hand across it, memories began to flood her mind.

The hand making of the rug had been her evening project the winter before. After the children were in bed she'd sat braiding the fabric pieces while Henry worked nearby on his own projects. Often times he'd lay his work aside and come join her by the fire where he'd rock and read his bible. The togetherness they had shared in the glow of the kerosene lamp had formed tender memories for her.

The floor adornment was made from remnants of cloth that represented milestones in Sarah's married life. There were treasured pieces from her wedding dress and the shirt Henry wore when they exchanged their vows. Swatches of red and white gingham were included in remembrance of the first pair of curtains she'd made for their kitchen windows. Intertwined with more sturdy fabric were snippets from scraps left after she'd made Abe's christening gown. The gown was worn by each baby that followed him.

Making it had been a labor of love that had resulted in a beautiful work of art. Sarah kept the rug stored in her cedar chest. Her plan had been to safeguard it until the children were grown and gone. It was to have been a focal point in front of their fireplace in later years. She and Henry would rock and remember days gone by while they enjoyed the comfort of the rug beneath their feet.

Although it was a perfect match for Sam Hartman's living space, when it came down to it, she couldn't part with the rug. She'd placed it back in her cedar chest and selected an older rug made of sturdy fabric. The replacement was a bit faded but still brought an additional splash of color to the room and added warmth.

The attention to detail for the hired hands living quarters was symbolic for Sarah. It represented her unspoken commitment to their working partnership. She was giving her best effort to provide comfortable accommodations and expected in return that he would give them his best effort to work hard and help make the farm profitable.

Their final task in readying the room was to bring in firewood. Each child carried a piece and stacked it neatly on the hearth. The piece they gave Hathaway was tiny in comparison, yet she carried it with pride. After placing her offering on top of those of her siblings she brushed bits of bark from her tiny hands. "Hebby."

***

Sarah's attention was drawn back to the present when she heard Zeke yell, "Ma, Hathaway done climbed out of her highchair to the top of the table. It's ok.... I got my bacon protected. I took my plate and crawled under the table. Hathaway is eatin' scraps off a Josh's plate....no need ta hurry."

"Lord, give me strength," Sarah said out loud. Getting her morning toilet routine and chores done had recently become a struggle for Sarah. She was inexplicably tired and sometimes felt irritable. She couldn't remember when, if ever, she'd cooked breakfast before properly dressing for the day.

Sarah winced at the discomfort in her breasts when she attempted to fasten her bodice. They were swollen and tender to the touch.

With five children, Sarah was familiar with the signs and symptoms of pregnancy. For the past few weeks she had chosen to ignore the message her body was communicating to her. She was intent on getting through the holidays and attributed some of her body's signals to stress and worry. Likely on a subconscious level Sarah had known for some time that she was again with child. Finding it difficult to fit in to her clothing was the defining moment; she was no longer able to push the reality aside.

Sheer panic filled Sarah's mind. *Not today. I can't deal with this today. Sam Hartman is coming in a few hours. I'm not dressed yet. The breakfast dishes are still on the table. I have bread to bake. No, not today. I can't deal with this today.*

Overwhelmed by emotion and suddenly sapped of all of her strength, Sarah dropped to her knees then lay down on her bedroom floor. Forlorn and weary she gave in to her pent up emotions and began to cry and pray aloud, her words wracked with sobs. "Why, wh…why, Lord? I…I didn't lay blame when Henry had the sun stroke. I…I didn't deserve his brutal attack and rape, but I bore it. How can I carry a child conceived in violence? I'm not that strong. I'm not. How can I add a sixth child to rear alone?"

As Sarah cried she ran her hand back and forth across the bedroom floor. The planks once rough-hewn, were now worn down from much treading and shuffling of feet. They were as smooth as glass in many places. Sarah drew solace from feeling the polished wood beneath her fingertips and after a time her crying stopped. Forcing herself to accept that she was pregnant brought a sense of relief and Sarah felt the tenseness draining from her body.

\*\*\*

Sarah's thoughts drifted to memories of when she discovered she was pregnant with Abe, her first born. At the ages of twenty-three for Henry and twenty-one for Sarah when they married in October 1890, they were older than most newlyweds. They made a decision to start a family as soon as possible. Sarah was healthy and strong and exceedingly happy in her life with Henry, yet after six months of marriage there was no sign that she was pregnant. Sarah began to worry that she might not be able to conceive.

June that summer was a farmer's dream of good weather with frequent gentle rain showers in the mornings, followed by bright sunny skies in the afternoons. With average to above temperatures the humid climate brought ideal growing conditions.

Their strawberry crop flourished, producing more berries than Sarah had ever seen for the size of the patch. Even after sharing with their neighbors and family there were enough berries to put up forty pints of strawberry jam. Daily she treated Henry with strawberry shortcake or some other variation of dessert she'd made from the fruit.

With berries at risk of spoiling, Sarah decided to try her hand at making strawberry cordial. Her grandmother Riley extolled the dangers of the inviting elixir. Being a staunch teetotaler Methodist, she'd contended it was skirting too close to partaking of the devil's brew. Sarah lived by the *waste not, want not rule* which in her mind, overruled her grandmother's warning. Sarah wasn't about to let the fruit wither and die in the patch.

Standing at the stove, cooking up a batch of the forbidden recipe, Sarah was hit with a wave of nausea. The queasiness added to other common symptoms, confirmed for her what she had been hoping and praying for, she was pregnant.

When Henry came in for lunch that day he found Sarah pouring the cordial mixture in to quart jars and weeping. When she explained to him that they were tears of joy, he too cried as he smothered her face with kisses. The kisses had led to caressing and then to the most intimate of encounters. They'd spent most of the afternoon cuddled in bed discussing names for the baby and making plans for their future.

The neglected cordial turned foul when the canning process was interrupted. Henry had thereafter teased her that it was God's intervention to keep her from imbibing the brew.

***

Sarah's thoughts returned to the present. *Henry's gone. There'll be no intimate moment to share the news of this pregnancy. There's no one to smother me with kisses and hold me close.*

The comparison of then, to what was facing her now, made her more melancholy. Vowing to shed no more tears over the situation she forced her thoughts to be positive.

*I'm not the first woman to find herself pregnant without a husband's support. I've got a hired hand coming today to lessen the burden of the farm's management. I'm doing alright caring for five children alone. Six is just one more than five. Hathaway likely will be potty trained before this baby arrives. Having only one in diapers will lighten the workload.*

As she lay on the floor, a scripture came to her. Philippians 4:13, "For I can do everything through Christ, who gives me strength." Sarah felt God was speaking to her. He was telling her that she would not be alone to raise this child she carried. He was with her now and He would continue to be her source of courage and strength in the months and years ahead.

In that moment Sarah knew she could raise this child that grew in her. Although conceived through rape, the child bore no guilt for the violent act. This baby deserved the same measure of love that she willingly gave her first five.

The wooden planks beneath her hand were warm from the penetrating rays of sun coming through the window. Sarah felt relaxed and at peace. *If I let myself. . .dare I let myself. . .fall. . .asleep. . .*

Zeke's voice jolted her awake. "Ma, Hathaway done crapped in her britches and she stinks something awful."

Startled and alarmed that she had lost all track of time and left Zeke and the baby unattended for too long, Sarah jumped up and yelled, "I'm coming."

Sarah ran to the kitchen as she struggled to button her bodice.

Zeke greeted her with, "Oh and Ma, someone knocked at the door."

*Who?* Sarah went to the window and peeked out. There on her stoop stood Sam Hartman, his knuckles poised to knock again. He had arrived four hours early and looked fresh as a daisy to boot. He was clean shaven, his hair was slicked back, his shirt creased as if it'd been starched and ironed that morning.

Sarah was embarrassed by her disheveled appearance and the disarray of her kitchen but thought as she softly brushed her hand across her abdomen, *what's a little wounded pride compared to other more important things?*

She opened the door. "Good morning, Mr. Hartman. Please come in."

Deciding there was no need to make apologies for life on the Whitcome farm, Sarah pointed toward the cupboard. "Grab a cup and help yourself to some hot coffee while I get the baby cleaned up. I think we'll have time to get you settled in to your living quarters before the noon meal. After we eat we'll go over my thoughts for managing the farm and you can tell me what you've been figuring we should do. With luck we can set some ideas to paper to share with Abe and Josh while we eat supper tonight."

As Sarah left the kitchen carrying the baby she called over her shoulder, "The older boys get home from school around three o'clock each afternoon and start tending to the livestock and other chores. Evening meal is generally on the table by five o'clock. You'll find time goes fast around here."

Sam was standing just inside the door with his hat in hand. He looked to his right and saw a wall rack with pegs. After hanging his coat and hat on the rack, he squatted down and peeked under the table. "Good morning, young man. Guess I'll have me some coffee. You want to come up and join me?" He fetched a cup from the cupboard and filled it with hot brew. After clearing a spot at the table he sat down and tried to relax.

Zeke crawled out from under the table. "I'm Zeke. Ma says I ain't big enough to drink coffee yet." The child thrust his hand toward Sam's nose. "Ya can have my piece of bacon if you're hungry."

Sam looked down at the gnarled length of pork laying limp atop the boy's jam soiled palm. "No thanks, this coffee will hold me 'til noon meal."

# Chapter 15

Sam settled into bed savoring the smells around him. Aroma of apple pie served at supper lingered. The air was permeated with the pungent odor from hickory that burned in the fireplace and set the room aglow. Holding the sheets under his nose he took a deep breath and drew in the fragrance of lye soap mixed with pine. The smells complemented one another giving the space a scent of comfort.

The living quarters Sarah and the children had prepared for him were beyond his expectations. The space was more than adequate to meet a single man's needs. The room was warm and cozy. The rag rug in front of the fireplace had a predominant hue of blue, his favorite color. There were interwoven highlights of red, orange and green. The rug's kaleidoscope of colors, added to the mixture of eclectic patches in the Crazy Quilt on the bed, provided a touch of cheer. The armed rocking chair with side table and lamp would be perfect for evening relaxation and reading adventure novels.

Sam's much anticipated first day at the Whitcome farm hadn't been awkward like he had expected it would be. Three weeks had passed since he'd first met Sarah and her brood. He was pleased that he had the children's names and faces sorted out.

Despite their rambunctious nature, he found them all delightful. Their show of hospitality was touching. Luke had suggested he be served first and Josh had anticipated his desire for more gravy, offering it without him asking. When the biscuits were passed the three older boys each declined taking the largest. Zeke had sat next to Sam and although he reached for it, he'd chosen a smaller one instead when Abe gave him a soft elbow to his ribs.

Sam liked Sarah's plans for running the farm and the order in which she had prioritized them. She presented the building of a larger chicken house as a priority project. He admired that she had listened to her oldest son's idea to expand in that area. The boy had literally beamed with pride when they discussed the project.

Sam was excited to be involved at the beginning of this new venture. The Farmer's Almanac predicted an early winter's thaw. With luck they could lay the foundation for the structure the first week in March and have the building completed by that month's end.

Once it was done they would increase the stock of laying hens. Sarah had a plan for distribution of the expanded egg production. It included selling eggs to the general store in their local town of LaFontaine as well as marketing to mercantiles in the tiny adjacent bergs of Lincolnville, Treaty and Banquo. She also hoped to garner business from some of the larger groceries on the south side of Wabash, the county's seat and namesake. Sam was impressed.

Developing an efficient egg production large enough to meet the plan's demands would be quite an accomplishment. The venture had potential for a lucrative business.

They'd also discussed spring planting. Sarah wanted to increase the size of her vegetable garden by adding more lettuce, tomatoes, green beans, onions and carrots. She said they were all marketable items that could be easily transported to Wabash for the Saturday farmer's market held during the summer on the courthouse square. Additionally, she wanted to plant a fair amount of watermelons and cantaloupe for late summer harvest and pumpkins for fall. Most of the farm's acreage would be cultivated for corn and soybeans. These were both hardy crops that could be sold locally.

In the intervening months before building the chicken house, Sam decided he would work on deferred maintenance around the house and barn. Cleaning and oiling the team's harness, inspecting and tending to their shoeing and general health were at the top of the list.

Of high priority would also be sharpening the plow blades and other cultivation tools. Intermixed with those chores would be gathering and chopping firewood. The farm's three acres of woods was adequate to meet their immediate and long-term needs for firewood if appropriately maintained. That required clearing out dead brush and felled trees so that sunlight and rain needed for growth could penetrate the canopy of foliage. Sam was anxious to survey the woods. Judging from the smell of hickory coming from his fireplace, he thought there might be some valuable trees that could be sold when thinning was required. Purging to that extent occurred about every ten years and he would have to ask Sarah when that had last been done.

*The roof on the barn needs some patching. I noticed a loose hinge on the cellar door. The windmill needs some attention. It makes enough racket to wake the dead. Hope a good greasing of the gears is all it will take to fix it. The list of things to do around here is endless.*

The smile that graced Sam's face was big as he ruminated about his responsibilities to get the Whitcome farm in shape. He was confident he could handle the workload, but thinking about all of it at once made him tired. Savoring the feel of the soft feather tic mattress beneath him, he turned on his side, pulled the quilt up around his shoulders and quickly fell asleep.

*** 

Sarah lay in her bed thinking about the events of the day. With all of the children tucked safely in their beds and the new hired hand off to his private quarters, she was finally free to be alone with her thoughts.

The pregnancy was foremost on her mind. She was about two months along. That meant a mid-August or there about due date. Smack-dab in the middle of summer, the timing couldn't get much worse. She'd have a newborn to care for when the chores of gardening would be at their peak and the other demands of running the farm would be in full swing.

Sarah decided to confide in her mother, woman to woman, about being pregnant. When it became obvious that she was expecting, she'd tell the children and Sam. Their hired hand was now a part of the farm's family. With them working so closely together on a daily basis, keeping her condition private wouldn't be possible.

Being out and about while she carried this child was going to be different for Sarah than with her previous pregnancies. There would be no husband at her side. Some women padded themselves so as to feign weight gain in an attempt to disguise the protruding bulge of the baby. Sarah chuckled when she recalled a schoolmate's story. She and her friend Margaret Simmons were sixteen years old and in their last year of schooling. Margaret said she woke up to the sound of what she thought was a newborn kitten mewing. She told Sarah she ran downstairs excited to see how many were in the litter, to discover that she had a baby brother instead of kittens. The mewing she heard was actually the baby's first cry. Neither Margaret, nor any of her siblings had the faintest idea that their mother was expecting a baby. Margaret's mother had padded herself to disguise her protruding abdomen.

*Padding, pashaw! I won't hide my condition once it's obvious. I've nothing to be ashamed about and I don't want this newest Whitcome born in a shroud of secrecy. Newest Whitcome! Oh my! I have to tell Jonas and Emma that they will be getting a new grandchild. I'll make a trip to the farm soon. I wouldn't want them to hear the news from anyone but me.* Despite her emotional scars from the child's conception in violence, Sarah felt the familiar soft kiss of joy from knowing life grew within her.

Sarah's thoughts shifted to her discussion with Sam regarding her plan for managing the farm. She was pleased that for the most part he seemed in agreement and was relieved that he acknowledged respect for her authority to make final decisions.

Sarah intended to hold tight reins on the farm's management for the time being. Once she felt comfortable that Sam was equal to the skills and working abilities he claimed, she would take his advice into consideration.

She wanted Abe, who would soon be turning twelve, to be involved in decision- making appropriate for his age. She knew he was excited about expanding the egg business. She hoped it would provide an opportunity for him to experience personal successes and build his confidence in decision-making. There wasn't anything much worse to stall a person than being afraid to make a decision or take a chance on an idea.

As each of her children showed an interest in the farm beyond their assigned chores, she would draw them into planning discussions, Hathaway included. The wisdom she had gained through her own circumstances gave her insight into the importance of educating her daughter as well as her sons in the workings of the farm.

Sarah knew there was no way to have predicted she would be in her current circumstances. Life had a way of taking unexpected twists and turns. If a person wasn't flexible enough to move with the ebb and flow of living, they'd drown in regret, right where they let themselves get stuck. The key to accepting change without fear was self-reliance. No amount of schooling could best life on a farm for teaching one how to thrive amidst change. Planning for planting and crop yield was important, but in reality it was left to the whim of nature to produce a harvest substantial enough to support a family. Sarah reckoned it was a farmer who coined the phrase,

"Don't put all of your eggs in one basket." A family farm like hers, with cows, chickens, hogs, fruit trees and vegetable gardens was diversified enough to sustain life even under adverse circumstances. City folks were dependent on the local mercantile for their needs.

Sarah smiled at that thought, realizing she was being hypocritical about city folk's dependency on store shopping. Wasn't she counting heavily on that need to grow her own egg business?

It was late. Sarah knew she needed to let her mind shut down so she could sleep. As was her routine, she ended her day by talking with God.

*Thank you, Lord, for seeing me through this day. I appreciate that you listened when I cried out to you in my anguish over being pregnant again. I'm grateful for your tolerance to allow me to complain and feel sorry for myself. I praise you for giving me a good plan to manage the farm and a hired hand to help with the work. I especially praise you for the love I feel for this unborn child. My day began with fear and resentment and because you lifted me up and reminded me that you daily walk by my side, my day ends with a sense of confidence, acceptance and hope for the life ahead. Amen.*

Sarah snuggled deeper down under her warm bedding and succumbed to much needed sleep.

# Chapter 16

"Hold it steady. A couple a more nails, then you can let go," Sam instructed. Abe was helping Sam by holding a two by four that served as a temporary support to the west end of the new chicken house.

Sarah had provided money for the purchase of building materials at the end of January. Having them on hand made it possible for Sam to seize the opportunity of an unexpected February thaw to start work on the new chicken house.

Digging away in some spots and adding fill dirt in others had resulted in a level earthen surface on which the base of the building had been laid. When the structure was finished sand would be placed on top of the ground to form the floor.

That morning they'd started the framing phase. Two workers were required to lift and steady the longer beams until they were secured in place. Abe was happy to be excused from school for the day to help. He was also grateful that his Grandfather Tom and Uncle Jack would be arriving later that morning to pitch in.

Construction was hard, physically taxing work. Abe's muscles at age eleven were being challenged to their maximum capacity, but holding up. It was the buttons on his coat that threatened to pop. His chest was puffed out with pride over his suggestion of a new chicken house becoming a reality.

Sarah opened the kitchen door and stepped out on the stoop. "You men need to take a break. Come in and have a cup of hot coffee and warm yourselves. Save some strength to work with Pa and Jack when they get here."

"Yes, Ma'am," was their joint reply.

Sam was up on a ladder. He took his hat off and used his handkerchief to wipe the sweat from his brow. He was immersed in a beam of morning sunlight and he held his hat at an angle to shade his eyes so he could get a clear view of Sarah. *There she goes again, rubbing her back with her right hand while holding her left one over her stomach. I've seen her do that a lot this week.*

Sarah turned from a full front view to a profile stance, bent over and picked up one of Zeke's toy wagons laying in the yard. As she straightened back up, Sam noticed that her apron appeared to pooch out just below her waistline. *Is she gaining weight? Her arms still look slender. Her face is the same. But…something is different.*

Sam kept looking at Sarah while he mulled about nettling thoughts of what was different about her. When his errant notions lined up, the implication hit him with a jolt. He lost his grip and the hammer he was holding fell to the ground.

The thud startled Sarah. "Everything alright?"

"Everything's fine," Sam lied. "I'll be in directly."

Sam wasn't fine, he was stunned. He thought back to that day in December when he'd come to apply for the job. Sarah had told him that her husband's heatstroke occurred in July that year and that he was never well again. She'd said that afterward the man didn't even know who she or the children were. His instincts were telling him that Sarah might be with child. *How can she be pregnant and barely showing if he was struck sick nearly nine months ago?*

A comment Abe had made that same day came to him. *What was it Abe said…something about Sarah having been through a lot, or having had a lot to deal with.* At the time Sam had assumed the boy's comments were in reference to the husband's illness. He remembered seeing several large bruises with yellowish hues on her face. There'd also been deep looking scrapes, not fully healed, on her arms. She looked as if she'd been in a knock-down, drag-out bar fight. *Was the boy referring to something besides the heatstroke? Might Sarah have been physically attacked? Could she have been, nah,…surely she wasn't,…violated by someone?*

One thing was certain, if his suspicion about her being pregnant was true, time would confirm it. Meddling in Sarah's personal affairs wasn't what he'd been hired to do. Still, Sam couldn't help but feel concern for his employer. She already carried a heavy load with five children to rear and a farm to manage. He couldn't imagine how she could handle having another child.

"Sam, aren't you coming down?" Abe yelled.

The boy's call-out interrupted Sam's thoughts. "Yeah, be right there."

\*\*\*

Sam and Abe finished their morning break, left the kitchen and were headed back to the worksite when Sarah's father, Tom, and her brother, Jack, arrived. Before the four got tasks sorted out and commenced work again, Jeb Carter, the Town Marshal, and his nineteen-year-old son, Julib, rode in on horseback.

"Jeb, Julib, good morning," Tom said, tipping his hat.

Jack teased, "Is this an official call, Marshal, or are you two just out for a fair-thee-well pleasure ride through the country side?"

Jeb swung his leg over his saddle and stepped to the ground. "We heard you was havin' a barn raisin' of sorts. We come to see if you could use a couple more hammers."

The Riley men accompanied by Abe dropped their tools and walked toward the Carters with outstretched hands. "A man with a hammer and a sidearm to boot, now that surely does add new meanin' to comin' prepared," Tom quipped.

"Haven't you fellers heard about Carter's fast style for buildin'? I shoot holes in the lumber and Julib comes along behind me and slips in the nails." Jeb patted his gun. "Job goes twice as fast that way."

Having at first hung back, Sam now sauntered forward and stood next to Tom.

Tom put his hand on Sam's shoulder. "My apologies. We're forgetting our manners. Jeb, Julib, this is Sam Hartman, Sarah's hired hand. Sam meet our Town Marshal, Jeb Carter, and his son, Julib."

"Pleased to meet you both," Sam said extending his hand.

"I don't think I've seen you in our neck of the woods before. You're not from around here are you?" Jeb said shaking Sam's hand.

"No," was Sam's blunt response.

The awkward moment was interrupted when Julib reached over and snatched the knit cap off of Abe's head. "I do believe you've grown an inch taller than the last time I saw you."

"Yep! A couple a more inches and you'll have to jump up to get to my hat," Abe said with a playful fist jab at the older boy's arm.

Julib grabbed Abe around the neck and gave his head a knuckle rub. "You best learn to respect your elders, boy!"

Sarah saw the Carter men arrive. Instead of taking time to go outside and greet them, she set to mixing more dough for additional dumplings. She'd put a large hen on to stew that morning. A rich broth for cooking the bite sized savory morsels was brewing.

Sarah lifted the chicken from the broth and placed it on a platter to cool. The meat would be picked from the bones and shredded. *Chicken and dumplings is a stick-to-the-ribs meal. A hardy helping along with a few slices of bread slathered in butter and topped off with strawberry jam, should hold the men until suppertime.*

Zeke and Hathaway sat contented at the table playing with scraps of dough. "What ya makin', Hathaway?" asked Zeke.

"Pie."

"What kind of pie?"

"Straw pie."

"Straw pie! That's just silly. No one would eat straw pie."

"Me eat."

"Ma, tell her she can't eat straw pie. Tell her that's just stupid."

Sarah interpreted. "Zeke, your sister is saying she's making strawberry pie."

"Well she better learn to add some berries to her straw or ain't nobody never gonna eat her cookin'," Zeke blurted.

\*\*\*

By mid-day the work crew had the gable ends of the building framed and had started on the sides. The kitchen clock began its series of twelve chimes at the exact moment Zeke climbed on a wooden crate and rang the dinner bell. The small boy had been eagerly waiting to sound the signal that their noon meal was ready. He couldn't tell time, but Sarah had told him that when both hands on the clock pointed straight up, he could commence pulling the rope.

Sarah stood at the kitchen window and watched as the men took turns washing their hands and face at the pump. Early that morning she'd placed a fresh towel there for their use. Sarah winced when Abe, was the first to grab it. Moisture in the air had collected on the cloth causing it to freeze stiff as a board. She knew it would feel scratchy on his tender skin.

The scene before her brought back bitter-sweet memories of Henry cleaning up in that same spot. The sight had always given her a tingle of excitement. It was his habit to pull her into an embrace and give her a kiss when he entered the house. Although they'd been married a long time, the nearness of him had never ceased to give her a thrill and cause her breath to catch.

Sarah stepped out on the porch to greet the men as they one-by-one filed in to her kitchen. Abe was the first in and saw the food on the table. "Boy howdy. Chicken and dumplins', my favorite meal."

Sarah lovingly patted her father and brother on their backs as they passed by. She gave Jeb a welcome hug and whispered "thank you" in his ear.

When Julib stepped up on the porch Sarah turned him so he was facing her. "Let me get a good look at you. Whiskers! When did you start growing whiskers? Seems like yesterday you were sitting in my kitchen eating oatmeal cookies and bragging about catching crawdads down at our creek."

"Yes, ma'am. They sure was big enough to brag about," Julib said blushing.

The last to approach was Sam. He took off his hat and motioned for Sarah to enter while he held the door. "Ma'am."

Sam ate in silence as the family and their neighbors exchanged stories and brought one another up on the news of the community. Sarah asked the Marshal about his wife, "How's Judith these days, Jeb?"

"She's stove up with rheumatism again this week. Seems like it hits her hard every time the temperatures drop to freezin'. That warm spell a couple of weeks back was a Godsend. It allowed her to get caught up on her house work. Now that it turned cold again, she's gettin' behind."

"Please give her my regards and tell her I'll try to come over tomorrow and help a bit."

"My goodness, Sarah. You've got your hands full with five youngin's to tend to and a hired hand to feed. I wouldn't want the word to get spread around, but I do reckon I could cook up a pot of stew and wash a plate or two if push comes to shove."

"Well, at least let me send some fresh baked bread and an apple pie home with you. Unless you've taken to baking in your spare time."

"No, Ma'am! At our house that rollin' pin is hands off to anyone except my Judith."

Sarah, her father, brother and Julib all broke in to full guffaws at Jeb's comment. The story of Judith Carter chasing Jeb out of her kitchen with a rolling pin was legendary. She'd caught him eating the blueberry pie she'd made for the County Fair pie-baking contest. The laughter was so contagious that Sam found himself smiling even though he didn't have a clue as to what was funny.

Tom was the first to catch his breath. "Sam, there's a story behind this foolishness but not enough time to tell it and give it justice. Come on, let's get back to work."

***

By 4:30 p.m. the sun had started its descent. The work crew gathered up their tools and called a halt to the day's work. Four tired men and one strapping boy stood shoulder-to-shoulder surveying their accomplishment. The day had started with a partial skeleton of a structure and ended with a building enclosed on all four sides with a roof ready for shingles.

Tom wrapped his arm around his grandson's shoulders. "Abe, that's the fanciest chicken house I've ever seen. Nothing but high stepping hens for this fine abode. Hope they won't get too uppity to lay eggs."

Red-faced, the boy laughed. "Oh, Grandpa!"

Sarah, Zeke and Hathaway, accompanied by Josh and Luke, who were now home from school, came out of the house to join in admiration of the near finished structure.

Sarah stood hands clasped as if in prayer. "Words can't express how grateful I am to all of you for helping to bring the building along this far. Shingles, windows and door and we'll be ready to buy our poultry stock. This new venture started out as Abe's dream. Now that we're close to making it a reality, I have to admit that I'm floating mighty high with anticipation myself."

Sarah gave the Carter men hugs, handing an apple pie to Julib and a loaf of fresh baked bread to Jeb. "Thanks until you're better paid."

"Glad to be of help, Sarah, and much obliged for the pie and bread.

I'll give Judith your regards," Jeb said. The Marshal locked eyes with the hired hand, tipped his hat and said, "Sam."

Sam responded in kind. "Marshal."

Tom and Jack left too. Both were anxious to get to their own farms where evening chores had to be done before their day of work would be over.

Sarah picked up Hathaway and started toward the house. "Luke, you pitch in and help the others with the evening chores. I'll get busy in the kitchen. Supper will be waiting for you when you're done.

\*\*\*

By 5:30 p.m. the livestock had been fed, the wood box replenished and the reservoir on the cook stove filled with water from the pump. A table of hungry faces watched as Sarah dished up ham hock and beans and set it on the table next to a platter of hot cornbread.

Sarah gave grace, thanking God for keeping the workers safe and for all that had been accomplished that day. As she said amen, Zeke blurted out, "Look at Abe, he done fell asleep in his chair."

Abe's head was resting on the back of his chair. His mouth was open and he was softly snoring. The laughter of his siblings jolted him awake.

"What,…uh sorry, guess I fell asleep." The boy yawned. "Ma, could I be excused?"

"Yes, get yourself to bed." Sarah gave her son a hug and a kiss before he left the room.

"Wow, Abe must have worked awful hard today to be too tired to eat ham hoc and beans," said Josh.

Luke sang out, "Beans, the more you eat the more you tweet."

Sarah reached over and ruffled her boy's hair. "Luke, mind your manners."

"More pweze, more pweze." The baby pleaded, holding up her empty bowl.

"My goodness girl, did you eat your helping already?" To stifle the child's whining for food Sarah had put Hathaway in her highchair with a serving of beans before the others were called to the table.

Sarah reluctantly dished up a second portion of ham and beans for the child. "Honey, don't eat so fast."

"Ma, can I have Abe's piece of pie?" Zeke inquired.

Sarah shook her head. "I don't think your tummy can hold your piece of pie and Abe's too. Besides, your brother might wake up in the night and be hungry. We'll just leave it in the cupboard for him."

Sam reached for a piece of cornbread. "If I were a bettin' man, I'd wager you won't see hide nor hair of Abe until you call him to get up for chores tomorrow mornin'. I didn't know a boy his age could work as hard as he did today. I think he's plum tuckered out."

"Do you think the work was too hard for him?" Sarah asked.

"I don't think so, Ma'am. Besides I won't need his help tomorrow. He can go to school and give his muscles a rest."

"Ma, if a feller was to stay awake until midnight and if at midnight Abe still ain't ett his piece of pie, then could that feller have it?" Zeke asked.

From the other end of the table a distinct and discernable sound emitted from Hathaway, reverberating loudly off the wooden seat of her highchair. Un-affected, the child just kept shoveling in beans while her brothers giggled. Sarah breathed out a deep sigh and Sam hunkered down over his bowl of beans, a smile on his face.

# Chapter 17

At the first clang of the teacher's bell, Abe left school and ran home. About two-thirds up the farm's lane he saw the hired hand working on the barnyard gate. He veered in that direction and yelled, "Mr. Hartman, hey...Mr. Hartman, how'd the work go today?"

The hired hand raised his arm, hammer in hand. "I got the windows installed."

Abe closed the distance that separated the two. He bent at the waist and rested his hands on his knees while he gulped air. "Sorry...but...I... couldn't make out what you was sayin'."

Sam spat nails from his mouth to the palm of his hand. "I was sayin', I got the windows installed."

"Boy howdy! That just about finishes 'er up. Can we start layin' the sand floor tomorrow?"

"Well, that depends."

"Tomorrow's Saturday...no school. I'll be here to help and there ain't nothin' more important than finishin' that chicken house is there?"

Sam put the nails back in his mouth, then steadied the gate's hinge with the freed hand. His words were garbled but, at close proximity to Abe, understandable. "The buildin' is ready. Movin' ahead to the floor depends on a couple of things. First, we need to see if your ma has money to buy the sand. Second the weather needs to cooperate. Sand's gotta be dry when we put it in. Can't chance hauling it if it's rainy or damp. Let's discuss it with your ma at supper tonight."

"Thanks, Mr. Hartman, much obliged." The boy started walking backwards toward the chicken house. "I'm gonna take a look at them new windows then I'll change to my work clothes and start the evening chores."

Sam again deposited the nails, mouth to palm and called out. "Abe, you can call me Sam."

The boy stopped, drew his shoulders back and stood tall. "It'd be an honor." He turned and hollered over his shoulder as he sprinted toward the chicken house. "Thanks, Mr. Hartman."

Sarah stood at her kitchen window watching Abe as he inspected Sam's work. It had been around three o'clock when she'd seen Sam close the door on the chicken house and head toward the barn. She figured he'd finished up, but resisted the urge to go take a look. She wanted Abe to be the first to see the finished structure.

Sarah scooped Hathaway into her arms as she left the house. She walked past Zeke on her way to join Abe. "Zeke, want to go with us to see the finished chicken house?"

"Nope. I ain't done haulin' dirt." The tyke dumped his wagon and commenced shoveling another load.

The responsibility for moving ahead with the egg business was squarely on Sarah's shoulders. The money she'd borrowed from her parents had covered the purchase of building materials. Going any further would take a bank loan. The mortgage on the farm had been paid off five years previously. Henry, like most farmers in the area, had taken out annual loans to finance spring planting. The Whitcome's debt was honored in full after each fall's harvest.

Sarah had followed suit the previous fall. The slim margin of profit had been just enough to pay off the crop loan. They'd been solely dependent on the sale of hogs for income and their finances were in a bind. That aside, she was grateful the farm remained mortgage free.

Knowing that dealing with the bank was considered a man's territory, Sarah challenged the boundary by going alone, a few days before, to meet with the bank's president. Sarah shuddered in disgust as she recalled the unpleasant encounter.

\*\*\*

Cleavold Anubis was the President of the LaFontaine Bank. Although new to the position he'd quickly established a reputation of being ruthless, hard-hearted and heavy-handed when it came to making loans to farmers. Sarah knew this when she made her visit to the bank. Mr. Anubis had replaced the bank's long-standing president, Hickory Ramsey, who had retired six months earlier.

Mr. Ramsey, known as just plain Hick to most folks in the area, was bank president when Henry and Sarah applied for the loan in 1891 to buy their farm. Hick was a highly respected leader in their community and a good family friend. He'd been the one to strike the match at their mortgage burning celebration in 1898. He'd approved many crop loans for them, the previous year's included.

Although armed with a well thought out plan for adding an egg business to the farm, Sarah was nervous when she walked into the bank. She'd wished old Hick was still there to greet her.

Chairs for customers were situated near the potbellied stove in the bank's lobby. After being kept waiting for what seemed a very long time, Sarah grew warm in her winter coat and took it off. Eventually she was ushered into the office of the president.

A short, stocky man with a receding hairline introduced himself as Cleavold Anubis. Sarah introduced herself and took a seat in one of the chairs facing the man's desk.

Sitting in the oversized desk chair designed to fit Hickory Ramsey's six foot, six inch frame, Cleavold looked like a child play-acting as a bank's officer. His legs were too short to reach the floor. Cleavold wore two inch lifts in his boots; which gave him a height enhancement when he was standing or walking. Seated, the lifts did nothing to elevate his five foot, two inch stature. To compensate he had equipped the desk's blind kneehole with a wooden apple crate turned bottom side up. He used it as a footrest.

For the umpteenth time the banker mentally cursed Sears and Roebuck for the delay in shipping the newfangled chair he'd ordered. It was advertised to have a mechanism whereby the seat could be spun around causing the shaft to the base of the chair to extend, thus elevating the seat. It reportedly would heighten up to six inches. Currently the little man was using a thick cushion under his buttocks to add some height.

There were times when, in the presence of someone Cleavold deemed important, he felt especially self conscious of his short stature. For some inexplicable reason he had that feeling with Mrs. Henry Whitcome sitting before him. Why, he didn't know. She was a farmer's wife. She wasn't anyone of particular prominence in the community as far as he knew. Yet there was something about the woman that intimidated him.

Cleavold wanted to impress this woman who he'd been told had no husband at home. In an effort to appear taller the little man used his bicep muscles to push off the arms of the chair to put himself in a more elevated position. He used his toes on the apple crate to balance and maintain the advantage.

Sarah, who up to this point had been busy smoothing her skirt and removing her written proposal from her handbag, looked up. The banker's strained look startled her such that she flinched. His exerted and flushed countenance reminded her of a person straining to have a bowel movement.

"Mr. Anubis, are you alright?"

The man's arms began to tremble under the strain; he lost purchase and plopped down on his cushion. Embarrassed by his foiled attempt to appear taller, Cleavold Anubis barked, "Mrs. Whitcome, what's the nature of your business with me today?"

Sarah handed the banker her hand written proposal. Referring to notes she'd made for herself, she stated the amounts needed for a start-up loan to buy a flock of laying chickens and a six month supply of poultry feed. Her proposal called for purchasing young, one-month old birds, seventy-five percent Rhode Island Reds diversifying the flock with twenty-five percent Barred Plymouth Rocks. The expectation was that the pullets would begin producing eggs four to five months into the operation.

The loan would also cover a six month supply of poultry feed which had a built in contingency of six to eight weeks. She wanted to assure their feed was planned for up to the time they were mature enough to produce eggs. Once that occurred she would use the revenue from the sale of the eggs to buy feed. From that point forward the plan called for the egg operation to be self-sustaining and profitable. Sarah asked for a three-year loan with the first payment due in twelve months and at six-month intervals thereafter until satisfied.

\*\*\*

Cleavold Anubis hadn't agreed to the meeting blind to Sarah's circumstances. He'd made inquiries and knew the story behind her husband's absence. He wouldn't be approving any loans for the woman. To do so without a husband available to work and manage the farming operation would be ludicrous. He'd agreed to meet with her for appearance sake because the family had a loan history with the bank. Cleavold had personal reasons too. He'd seen Sarah Whitcome in town several times and had admired her from his office window. He thought she was beautiful, albeit taller than he preferred. The story as he had heard it from the postman, Elmo Jones, was that her husband had been gone a few months and the woman was getting lonely.

Romance and its inherent proprieties had eluded Cleavold in his younger years. He now considered the niceties associated with courting a waste of time. He was a man of importance. He was the president of a bank. He had needs and desires that couldn't randomly be met in this two-bit town. Wabash had resources, but was twelve miles up the road. He'd made a few trips into the city but he was tired of the inconvenience. He was on the hunt for a local source to provide the occasional 'companionship'.

A bank president was in a position to use certain tactics with women when cooperation wasn't voluntary. He'd successfully employed those tactics in other towns without repercussions. In the absence of a man to provide for them, a woman was pretty much up the proverbial creek without a paddle when it came to money matters. Cleavold planned on using his tactics on the lovely Mrs. Whitcome.

The man had worked himself into such a state of anticipation that beads of perspiration popped out on his brow. The act of taking out his handkerchief to wipe it dry brought him out of his lascivious thoughts. He realized that the woman was waiting for him to speak.

"Mrs. Whitcome, it would be impossible for the bank to loan you money when you don't have a man standing by your side. An egg business, on the scale you're proposing, would be a risky venture even for a man. You'd best stick to tending to your housework and such."

"Mr. Anubis, I can assure you that I know the risks involved in poultry farming and I have studied the operation enough to feel competent to handle the challenge."

"Again, I'm sorry Mrs. Whitcome, but without a man securing the loan for you, you won't be getting one from the LaFontaine Bank."

"No loan at all? What about my crop loan for spring planting?"

"No, we won't be giving you a loan for that either. Not this year. Not without a man at your side."

"Is there a law against loaning money to a woman?"

"While I have the authority to approve a loan from the bank for you, I don't consider it to be a prudent action. It goes against good banking practices, not to mention the natural order of society. Women are known for their frivolous spending. It's my responsibility to guard against having this bank's money squandered."

"Mr. Anubis, I own my farm free and clear. I'm willing to take out a mortgage for a collateral secured loan if you aren't comfortable approving a promissory note."

Cleavold Anubis rose from his seat and came from behind his desk. He picked up Sarah's coat and held it open for her. Sarah obliged the offer and put her arms in the sleeves. Cleavold stepped in close behind her and squeezed her shoulders. The little weasel of a man was a full head shorter than Sarah. When he spoke his hot, foul breath assaulted the back of her neck.

"Mrs. Whitcome, you're a beautiful woman. Although I won't make you an official bank loan, I think we could make some type of mutually beneficial arrangement on the side."

Sarah went from being befuddled to belligerent. In one fell swoop she turned around and without taking even a single step away faced the man down. "Mr. Anubis, keep your stubby-fingered little hands off of me. I will be borrowing money from this bank to start an egg business and I will be borrowing money to buy seed for spring planting! That can be done with or without your cooperation."

Holding his ground Cleavold said, "Mrs. Whitcome, you underestimate the power I wield as the bank's president. I believe I've made myself clear. There's only one way you'll get money from me. After you think it over perhaps you'll come to appreciate the generosity of my offer."

Smoothing down the collar on her coat Sarah stepped toward the door, stopped and looked back at the man. In a measured tone she said, "Mr. Anubis, my husband and I have honored every agreement made with this bank, paying our loans off either on time or before they were due, for over fifteen years. *You sir,* underestimate the power of a mother determined to care for her children. I'm sure that after you've had an opportunity to think over what has transpired here in your office today, you'll come to appreciate the prudence of approving my loan requests.

I'll see Hickory Ramsey at church this Sunday. Hick is a close family friend and as you know Chairman of the Board of Directors for this bank. If necessary I'll share what you referred to as a 'mutually beneficial proposal' with him. I'll be asking if the bank approves of that practice when dealing with women who have no man at their side. You may also know Tom Riley who serves on the bank's board. He's my father.

I'll require the same amount as last year for my crop loan. You have my egg business proposal to refer to for the loan amount needed in that area. I'll be in Monday morning to sign the papers. Please have them ready." Sarah adjusted the hat on her head and exited the man's office, leaving the door ajar.

Cleavold Anubis stood frozen in place. He couldn't have been more stunned by Sarah's revealed association with Hickory Ramsey and Tom Riley than if she'd hit him over the head with a two-by-four. If the woman talked he'd be lucky to get out of town without being tarred and feathered, let alone keep his job. His future looked bleak, very bleak.

Sarah left the bank feeling violated and angry. Thankfully the latter was the stronger of her emotions. She'd left the children with her neighbor so she could stop by to see Doc Adams while she was in town. She'd planned to have him confirm her pregnancy. Ben was her family's physician, but also a close friend. She was so shaken by the encounter at the bank that she feared she might break down and tell him what had happened. She needed to gather her wits before seeing him. She didn't want to risk him feeling the need to heroically defend her honor. Sarah decided just to pick up the children and go home.

The afternoon following the encounter Sarah made bread. Kneading and pounding the dough brought some release, but not enough to assuage her bitterness. Cleavold Anubis's actions had been so dastardly, Sarah felt justified in harboring her anger. As a result, she'd ended the day without her usual talk with the Lord. She'd slept poorly.

\*\*\*

As she approached the chicken house Sarah's attention snapped to the present when Abe called, "Hi, Ma. Sam got the windows in. We're ready to get 'er set up for the new flock. Can we talk about that over supper tonight?"

Sarah pulled Abe in to a one-armed hug. The boy had grown such that she could access his forehead without bending over. She gave it a kiss before she released him. "That sounds like a good idea. Now give me the grand tour, I want to see those windows."

After oohing and awing over each construction detail pointed out by Abe, she asked him a favor. "Would you please watch Hathaway and Zeke for just a few minutes? I need to do something in my room. You can ask Luke to take over once he gets in from school." Sarah didn't want the sun to go down again with her heart filled with anger. She needed a talk with the Lord.

"Sure, Ma," Abe said. "Luke and Josh weren't far behind me. They'll be home directly."

Sarah's knees made a popping sound as she knelt at the side of her bed. "Here I am, Lord. I'm sorry I skipped our talk last night. I wasn't ready to let go of my anger. I'm not apologizing for losing my temper with Cleavold Anubis. I'm telling you straight out, I'll make good on my threat to tell Hick and Pa if he doesn't have those loan papers ready for me come Monday. I hope it doesn't come to that. If I'm forced to tell, he'll likely get fired.

Heavenly Father, fill me with your spirit of love so that I can release this anger that I'm holding. Staying mad isn't going to change what happened and it's sapping my energy. Lord, thank you…"

A loud crash coming from the kitchen diverted Sarah from her prayer. "Ma, Ma," Luke called out. "Hathaway pulled a pan of bread off the cupboard. She's sitting on the floor eatin' it. When I went to take it from her she tried to bite my hand. What should I do?"

Zeke chimed in, "Ma, Hathaway won't share her bread. I tried ta sneak up on her and swipe a piece but she saw me comin'. I'm hungry but I'm scared of them teeth of hers. Can I eat one of them other loaves of bread that's up there on the cupboard?"

"Sorry for the interruption, Lord. I'll talk to you later." Sarah jumped up and ran to the kitchen in hopes of salvaging enough bread to get them through the evening meal and the next morning's breakfast.

# Chapter 18

"The new chicken house gots some fine lookin' windows," Zeke said, his mouth full of food. The four-year-old child's legs swung back and forth as they dangled from his chair. His elbow was on the table, fork in hand suspended mid air, eyes staring off as if deep in thought. "Do ya reckon they'd break if a feller was ta throw a rock at 'em real hard?"

"Yes, they'd break! Don't you be throwin' rocks at the chicken house windows," Abe warned.

Sarah scolded. "Zeke, I've told you it's dangerous to throw rocks. Unless you're skipping stones at the creek, I don't want to hear tell of you throwing rocks at anything. You might hit someone in the eye and make them go blind. How would you feel if that happened? Would you want someone to thro...?"

"Sorry, Ma," interrupted the tyke. "I didn't mean to say that out loud. I was havin' me some private thoughts. Reckon they just popped out of my mouth when I wasn't payin' attention."

Abe reached over and patted his little brother's hand. "The egg business is a chance for this family to make some good money. The chicken house is just the start. We'll be bringing in young chickens that will need to be fed three times a day at first. There'll be plenty of work. I'm sure your help will be needed somewhere."

"Well I already got me chores to do like diggin' holes in my dirt pile and pickin' up blocks that Hathaway throws all over tarnation," Zeke responded.

Nine-year-old Josh said, "Ma, Zeke said, 'all over tarnation'. It's supposed ta be all over creation, ain't it?"

Sarah smiled. "Yes, Josh, the expression is 'scattered all over creation'. Some folks use a phrase 'what in the tarnation are you doing'. I'd prefer you boys wouldn't. The word tarnation is another way of using the word hell as a cuss word. I don't want my boys cussing.

"Zeke is right about Hathaway throwing the toy blocks all over the place. He helps me out by picking them up because she's still too little to do it herself. Zeke's a hard worker, but a bucket of chicken feed might be too heavy for him to carry at his age."

Sam spoke up. "Ma'am, do you suppose now that Zeke understands the importance of protecting the windows in the chicken house he could have the job of guarding them. You know, watching out for rock throwing hoodlums that might come by."

Zeke's eyes grew big as saucers. "I could do that, Ma. I could carry my wooden rifle. It don't shoot real bullets so I can't kill me any hoodlums, but I sure can scare 'em away. Uh, Ma, what's a hoodlum look like?"

Sarah struggled to keep a straight face. "A hoodlum looks like a fellow fixing to get himself in trouble by doing something bad. Zeke, I think you'd be a perfect chicken house window guard."

Sarah whispered to Sam, "Thank you."

"Ma'am, are you in position for Abe and me to make a trip to town tomorrow to buy sand for the chicken house floor?" Inquired Sam. "We need to lay it an inch thick. One full wagonload ought to do it. Three dollars should be enough to cover the cost."

Sarah was slow to answer. She wasn't sure how she wanted to broach the subject of money with her hired hand. He'd helped figure the amount needed for a loan to start the egg business. However, circumstances surrounding the loan's delayed approval were private.

Deciding to deflect the answer another way she said, "Jonas Whitcome, my husband's father, has a gravel pit on his farm. He has plenty of sand. It's about four miles east of here. I saw him a few days ago and filled him in on the chicken house construction progress. He offered to help out any way he could. Going to his farm is a bit further than the quarry at the edge of LaFontaine, but I think it might be worth the extra distance to take him up on his offer. Abe can tell him I'll settle up with him later."

"Grandpa Whitcome won't charge us for a load of sand, Ma. We're his family," Abe said.

"You're probably right," Sarah replied. "Just the same, I want you to make the offer."

"Sounds like a good plan. Abe can show me the way there," Sam said.

Seven-year-old Luke asked, "Ma, will Butter Cup and Butter Ball get to live in the new chicken house."

Abe popped off, "You mean Crow Bait and Reprobate don't you?"

"Don't be calling my chickens bad names."

"We're lucky to get six eggs a week between the two of them," Abe said. "They're long overdue for the stew pot if you ask me."

With a raised fisted hand Luke countered, "Yea! Well you're long overdue for a fat lip."

Sarah intervened. "Stop it, both of you. Abe, Butter Cup and Butter Ball are pets to Luke. He's looked after them since they were new-born chicks."

Sarah lovingly brushed her son's hair from his eyes. "Luke, we can't put Butter Cup and Butter Ball in with the new flock. They and the few other chickens we have are being raised free-range. We don't keep them cooped up. In this cold weather some of them have caught a disease to their combs called Roup. Butter Ball and Butter Cup don't have any signs of the disease now, but they have been exposed to chickens that do have it. We can't take a chance on infecting the new flock."

Luke, the most sensitive of the Whitcome children began to softly whimper. "It…it don't hardly seem fair, Ma."

Patting her son's arm Sarah said, "Well I guess I have to agree with you on that son. A lot of things happen that don't seem quite fair."

Abe wiped Hathaway's face and hands and lifted his sister out of her highchair on to the floor. The baby toddled as fast as her chubby little legs would carry her, to the corner of the kitchen and the crate that contained the toy wooden blocks. She gleefully began pitching them around the kitchen.

Zeke yelled, "Hathaway, what in the tarnation are you doin'?"

"Zeke, I told you I don't want you using that word!" Sarah chided.

"Sorry, Ma, that's another one of them thoughts that popped out of my mouth when I wasn't watchin'."

\*\*\*

Monday dawned with no promise of sunshine. The overcast sky matched Sarah's dreary mood as she drove her horse-drawn wagon in to town.

She'd left Zeke and Hathaway with her neighbors, Josephine and William Johnson. The Johnsons were brother and sister, born and raised on the farm next to Sarah's. Neither of them ever married and continued to live together and run the family's farm after their parents died. The children loved the focused attention they got from the pair and they in turn seemed to enjoy having the children visit them.

Sarah was going to the bank about her loan requests and to see Doc Adams about her condition. She didn't look forward to either appointment and not having the children in tow would be helpful.

She sought to lift her spirits by focusing on positive happenings. Sam and Abe had fetched a load of sand from Jonas' gravel pit the Saturday before. Jonas had refused to take any money. Jack had delivered a load of straw from his farm. He also refused payment. The new chicken house now had a one inch sand floor covered with a thick layer of fresh straw. It was ready and waiting for a new flock of chickens. Her family's generosity gave her a warm feeling.

Her thoughts wandered to the elder Whitcomes. She'd visited them about ten days prior, to tell them about her pregnancy. *Jonas and Emma appeared stunned when I told them I was expecting another baby. Although we didn't speak of the circumstances shrouding the child's conception, Jonas's head hung low and an air of gloom, rather than joy, permeated the room.*

Sarah and Henry's parents were in agreement that they wouldn't tell Henry about the coming baby. When they'd visited him a few weeks after Christmas he hadn't recognized them. *If he doesn't know his own ma and pa, or remember that he has a wife and five children, why burden him with news he won't understand.*

***

Sarah's mood again turned dark as she drove the team of horses toward town and her impending visit to the bank. Initially she'd felt just fine about the way she'd handled the sleazy Cleavold Anubis. Threatening to use her connections with the bank's board of directors, to expose that he had propositioned her, seemed justified. What had started to tickle at her conscience was her talk with God about the incident.

*I didn't ask God for guidance. I told Him what I was going to do... that I'd make good on my threat to expose Anubis for his dastardly deed. I even boldly asked God to make my threat work. Cleavold Anubis thought he could force me to do his bidding because he held the power over granting my loan.*

*His actions were unconscionable, but mine weren't honorable. I used coercion when I threatened to tell on him if he didn't grant my loans.*

Sarah felt embarrassed before God for her resolve to get her loans by hook or by crook. Contrite, pregnant, and penniless she felt as if she were sinking in a quagmire of problems.

A drop of moisture trickled down her cheek. Then the dam burst flooding her face in torrents of tears that turned to sobs. Her sobs were so loud they spooked the horses causing them to break in to a run. The wind tore at Sarah's hat threatening to dislodge the only good bonnet she owned and send it blowing to the side of the road. Her breach with God grieved her so much that she physically felt pain in her chest.

In her anguish, words wouldn't come to her. In desperation Sarah recited the Lord's Prayer. "Our Father, which are in heaven, hallowed be Thy name. Thy kingdom come, Thy will be done in earth, as it is in heaven. Give us this day our daily bread. And forgive us our debts, as we forgive our debtors. And lead us not into temptation, but deliver us from evil; for thine is the kingdom, and the power, and the glory, for ever. Amen."

The two verses, Mathew 6:14-15, that immediately follow the Lord's Prayer came to Sarah's mind. *"For if you forgive men their trespasses, your heavenly Father will also forgive you. But if you do not forgive men their trespasses, neither will your Father forgive your trespasses."* Sarah prayed. "Father, forgive me for telling you how I would handle my bank situation instead of asking for your guidance. I want to be in your will with all that I do and say. I trust you, Lord, and I surrender this problem to you."

Sarah knew what she had to do and it wasn't going to be easy. She pulled back on the reins. "Hup, hup, whoa." Responding to her command the horses slowed from a run to a walk. Sarah maneuvered the team and wagon through the turn off of the county road on to Main Street, LaFontaine. While she held the reins in one hand, she used the other to right her hat and tuck in wayward strands of hair.

After traveling a couple of blocks, Doc Adam's office came in to view. Sarah made a change in her plans and passed on by. *The bank first, then Doc. I might need a good friend to talk to after seeing Cleavold Anubis.*

Sarah pulled up in front of the bank and climbed down from the wagon. The horse's backs were lathered with sweat. They stretched forward in an attempt to reach the water trough directly under the hitching post.

Sarah tethered them, leaving enough slack in the reins to allow them to drink freely.

Standing with her back to the bank, Sarah used her handkerchief to dry her eyes. After smoothing out the wrinkles in her skirt she turned, held her head high and walked in to the bank where its president and their unfinished business waited.

# Chapter 19

Monday morning, Cleavold Anubis paced the floor in his office with angst and anticipation. He expected Hickory Ramsey, chairman of the bank's board of trustees to come charging in at any moment. Mr. Ramsey would demand an explanation of Cleavold's actions with the Whitcome woman the week before.

Of course Cleavold would out-right deny the allegations. That was a foregone conclusion, denial being his standard first line of defense. After labeling the accusations preposterous, he would pull out the loan documents he'd prepared after the fact. They would support his rebuttal, proving that he was planning all along to give the family conventional bank loans.

What he needed to wrap up his defense package was a scenario of events he could relay that would support his claim that Mrs. Whitcome somehow mistook his comments and got the wrong impression. Cleavold took pride in his ability to contrive and connive especially when it came to women. Yet after mulling it over and over in his mind, he had nothing that sounded particularly convincing. Certainly nothing that would stand up to the woman's self-confidence and credibility.

Earlier that morning Cleavold had offered a cup of coffee to Elmo Jones, the postman. It was a ruse to pump his short friend for anything and everything he could find out about Sarah Whitcome.

To his dismay Elmo confirmed that the Whitcomes as well as Mrs. Whitcome's family, the Rileys, were well respected in the community. They were close personal friends of the town's law enforcer, Marshal Jeb Carter. They were active at the local Methodist Church, admired by their neighbors and considered by all fine upstanding folks.

Elmo told Cleavold about the grand size of the Whitcome's newly constructed chicken house and that the farm now had a hired hand. According to Elmo the man was good-looking. Cleavold had gotten nothing to help him with his current dilemma. What he'd learned only made him feel more anxious about his future.

His unscrupulous ways of quenching his thirst for passion had cost him before. He'd been fired from his position as president of the bank, in Nappanee, Indiana for similar actions.

His dismissal was a public embarrassment and a blow to his ability to find employment elsewhere in that area. After being unemployed for nearly four months he'd found anonymity in this small, hick town and was hired as LaFontaine's bank president. He'd settled in without anyone finding out about his past transgressions.

If he lost this job after holding the position for only six months, he knew he'd be lucky to find a job elsewhere as a bank janitor, let alone a bank president.

Cleavold just couldn't believe his bad luck. In the past he'd been able to pick women to proposition that were not only vulnerable, but also weak in spirit. He'd certainly misjudged Sarah Whitcome. She was by far the most beautiful of all the women with which he'd tried his dalliances. Maybe her beauty had clouded his judgment.

Cleavold reflected on the news that Mrs. Whitcome had a handsome hired hand working at her farm. Elmo was fairly sure that the man lived in the house with Mrs. Whitcome and her children. The postman didn't know that conclusively but being the good hound dog he vowed to sniff out the truth. If the hired hand was living in the house, that most certainly would be considered a stretch of decorum. Perhaps this explained why the lovely Sarah had rejected his proposal. She might not be as lonely now as she had been before the hired hand came on the scene.

He disgusted himself with his sleazy thoughts. What difference did any of his speculations make? The woman had undoubtedly told on him to her father and Hickory Ramsey. One or both of them would come charging through his office door any minute to fire him. He had nothing but a flimsy lie to defend himself.

The bank's clerk knocked on Cleavold's office door and poked his head in. "Mrs. Whitcome is here to see you."

"Is anyone with her?"

"No, she's alone."

"Alone. Are you sure she's alone, no man with her?"

"Yes, I saw her pull up and tie her team out front. She came alone."

"Have you seen Hickory Ramsey or Tom Riley in town this morning?"

"No. I haven't seen either one of them."

"Send Mrs. Whitcome in."

Cleavold hadn't really expected Sarah Whitcome to come to the bank at all that day. If she did show, he never dreamed she'd be alone. Nothing about this woman was predictable.

Desperate for a bulwark of any kind, the little man retreated to his oversized chair behind his massive desk and braced himself.

The clerk ushered the tall woman in and closed the door. Cleavold was taken aback by her presence. It wasn't just her height and beauty; Sarah Whitcome had a spirit about her that seemed to literally bring more light in to the room.

He motioned for her to take a seat.

She took the chair directly in front of his desk sitting with her back straight and head held high. She looked into his eyes with such intensity that despite his trying, he was unable to break their hold. "Mr. Anubis, I've come to give you an apology. I was insulted and angry about the way you treated me last week when I made my loan requests. Those emotions led me to threaten to tell Hick Ramsey and my father Tom Riley what you proposed. I knew when I made the threat that if I carried through with it, you would be fired. At the time I felt my threat was justified. My intent was to come here today to see if you were going to give me the loan. If you didn't, I planned to go to the bank's Board of Directors.

"This morning I was reminded that retaliating against you is not an option for me as a Christian. God alone has the authority to stand as your judge. I will be praying that you might come to know God personally and that you will never again use your authority as bank president to harm others.

I need you to know that I forgive you for propositioning me. I'm sorry I threatened you. I still need money to support the farm, but no matter what your decision is, I'll trust God to provide the way I get it."

Cleavold Anubis was dumfounded. After an awkward few moments he silently slid the loan papers, fountain pen atop, across his desk. He had to stand, his arms were too short to traverse the large expanse while seated.

Sarah signed the papers, leaned forward and pushed them and the fountain pen back across the desk to Cleavold. "Do you need anything further relevant to these loans?"

Remaining mute, the banker shook his head.

"May I expect the funds to be available in my account by the end of the day?"

Cleavold nodded.

"Mr. Anubis, thank you for the loan and I'll be praying for you."

No longer able to bear the look of sincerity and kindness in Sarah Whitcome's eyes, the little man hung his head. Still he felt her eyes upon him. Cleavold placed his arms over his bowed baldhead to shield against her radiating grace.

"Good bye, Mr. Anubis. May the rest of your day be blessed."

Cleavold didn't understand what had just transpired. The woman had apologized to *him* and had asked *him* to forgive *her* for threatening *him*. She said she would pray for him. No one in all of his life had given even two cents worth of care about him, let alone say they were going to pray for him.

He'd dodged a bullet that was aimed right at his livelihood. He wasn't going to be fired. He should feel happy. He didn't. He felt shame.

# Chapter 20

Coffee cup in hand, Ben Adams stood gazing out his parlor window. *More hustle and bustle than usual for a Monday morning. I'd appreciate some folks with minor ailments and folding money in their pockets stopping by.* As soon as the doctor had the thought, Sarah pulled her team up in front of his house. He watched in admiration as she tethered the horses.

When Sarah stepped up on the porch, Ben opened his door. "Sarah, so good to see you. Come in, come in."

"Good morning, Ben."

"Let me take your coat. I'm having a late morning cup of coffee, would you join me?"

"Yes, thank you. A cup of coffee would be nice."

The doctor hung Sarah's coat on the hall tree and went to the kitchen to get her coffee. Sarah stood, taking in the sight of Ben's parlor. It was pristine, unchanged from when his wife, Beth, her dear friend, kept house. Sarah gently touched the doily that lay under the oil lamp atop a round pedestal table. Sarah leaned in to study its intricate design. She'd always envied Beth's crocheting skills, each stitch beautifully executed.

"Here you go. You take your coffee black as I recall," Ben said handing the cup to Sarah, then retrieving his own from the window ledge by his front door.

"Please, sit." Ben said gesturing to his rocking chair. "How are you?"

"Oh, fair to middling I guess." Sarah took a sip of coffee and nodded toward the doily. "I was just studying Beth's crochet stitching. So delicate and beautiful, just like she was."

Ben held his mug with both hands and studied its brew. "Yes. That she was. Hard to believe she's been gone three years." The doctor looked up and forced a smile. "Jonas and Emma stopped by a few weeks ago and told me they'd been to visit Henry in January and that he was doing well."

"Yes. He seems to be settled and content. It's such a comfort to know."

"So, Sarah, what brings you to town on a cold winter's day? I'm glad to see you, but I'm sure you didn't make the trip just to visit with me."

"I had some business at the bank to tend to as well as stop here. I came to see you because I think I'm about three months pregnant."

Sarah's announcement caused Ben to jolt and his coffee sloshed out on to his trousers. "From Henry violating you!" Ben said jumping up, dabbing at the hot spill with his handkerchief.

"Yes…that was November 15th. I figure I'm three months gone."

He went to Sarah, startling her when he pulled her up and into a hug. "My dear, Sarah, I'm so sorry."

Pushing from the embrace, Sarah patted Ben's arm. "Don't be, Doc. I've made my peace with it."

"Well…I need some time before I can."

"Doc. Don't think about the attack. Remember Henry as your friend and the good times you had together."

Ben shook his head as if to clear his mind. "How are you feeling?"

"I'm feeling fine, just tired."

"As you well know, that's common during the first three months of pregnancy."

"In a couple of weeks I'll be well in to my fourth month. As memory serves, my energy should return by then. I'm going to need it. We should have our new flock of pullets by then."

"I was talking to Elmo Jones last week. He didn't say anything about you getting a new flock."

"Well, well. It's comforting to hear that Elmo doesn't know and tell all of my business."

"He did say you were building a large chicken house. I guess it follows that you'd be getting more chickens. Elmo also told me that you've taken on a hired hand…a stranger. How's that working out for you?"

"It's working out just fine. His name is Sam Hartman and he comes from Howard County. He's a hard worker. Having him at the farm has been a big help. We're planning to start an egg business and just finished building the new chicken house. You should come out and see it."

"I'll do just that."

"Abe will be proud to show it to you. This new venture was partly his idea and he's really exited to get started."

"Sarah, the egg business can be risky, but I'm sure you already know that. I wish you all the best."

"Thanks, Doc. How about coming out for dinner next Sunday after church? We could show you the chicken house. I'll introduce you to the hired hand, I'd guess you two are about the same age."

"I'd like that. Now let's take a look at you."

Doc Adams found Sarah to be fit as far as he could tell and suggested she get some extra rest. They both chuckled, realizing the futility of the advice.

Sadness enveloped Ben Adams as he watched Sarah climb up on her wagon and drive her team out down Main Street, toward the county road that would take her back to her farm. He was helplessly in love with Sarah. Before Henry's heat stroke, he'd denied the reality. Once Henry's mind was stricken, never to return again, he privately owned his feelings.

He'd been holding the hope that after a year of Henry being institutionalized, Sarah might accept that her marriage was over and seek a divorce. Divorce was uncommon, but not unprecedented in such situations.

Folks didn't expect a woman to raise a family without a man's help. Those who knew and loved Sarah might even consider it a necessity for her to divorce and take another husband.

Ben cared deeply for Sarah's children as well for as her. Nothing would please him more than a chance to win her heart and be her helpmate. His hopes for a future with Sarah were now threatened. By the time Henry had been away a year, Sarah would have a newborn, a sixth child. Neither Sarah's condition, nor the prospect of her having another child to care for did anything to dampen Ben's ardor for her. The question was, would she ever have time to think of her own needs and reach out for love?

Ben was lonely and wanted a wife and children. If he could have Sarah by his side, he felt he could be content with raising her children as his own. *Sarah's strong and self-reliant. What if the egg business turns profitable? What if she successfully makes it through her first year alone? What if she gets so independent she doesn't want a husband? What if she's already taken a liking to the Hartman fellow?*

At age thirty-six, Ben Adams was unfulfilled and he felt as if life was passing him by. *Is it healthy for me to wait for the mere chance to win Sarah's heart? What if she never considers divorcing Henry? Is it time for me to move on and try to find someone else to love…someone free to love me back?*

Ben picked up his wife's bible from the table beside the settee. The bible hadn't been opened even once during the time she'd been gone. Doc stroked the leather cover. *I wish I could believe... I almost did once. How can I now? I prayed for Beth and our child to be spared. God didn't listen, childbirth took them both. Even if I wanted to...how after all this time would I pray?*

Ben plopped the bible down on its spine. It fell open to an underlined passage. Doc picked it up. The scriptures singled out by Beth were Romans 8:26-28. *"And the Holy Spirit helps us in our weakness...we don't know what God wants us to pray for. ...And the Father who knows all hearts knows what the Spirit is saying,...*

Tears streamed down Ben's cheeks. The bible's parchment pages puckered as the wet droplets fell upon them. He closed it and held it close. Breathing in a faint lingering of his wife's essence he said. "God, help me."

# Chapter 21

Breakfast at the Whitcome's table on Saturday morning was charged with anticipation. Reinhold's Chicken Hatchery would arrive before noon with a wagonload of one-month-old laying hens. They'd be the first to inhabit the new chicken house. Abe worked until dark the evening before filling water containers and fussing over aesthetic details in readiness for their arrival.

"Abe you pert near rubbed holes in the chicken house windows yesterday, you was a shinin' on 'em so hard, I thought the new hens was supposed to lay eggs, not gawk out the windows." Josh teased.

Abe face flushed, he kept it bent low over his biscuits and gravy. "I was just makin' sure the place is clean. The birds that's comin' are young and we need 'em to settle in real quick. We can't afford for any of 'em to get sick on us."

Zeke piped up. "Should I set up with my shotgun to guard 'em windows when the chickens arrive? They might be some of 'em hoodlums hidin' in the delivery wagon with rocks in their pockets."

Sam reached for another biscuit. "I don't think we'll have to worry about hoodlums today, Zeke, but it might be a good idea to be prepared. Instead of walking guard next to the chicken house, why don't you set up along the fencerow? That will put you close enough for Abe or me to holler if we need your help."

Zeke saluted, "Yes, Sir."

Sarah was proud of Abe's commitment to their new egg business venture, but worried he'd burdened himself with a load of concern that she felt was hers to carry. "When you're finished with your breakfast, how about you boys fill the wood box instead of leaving it for evening chores. When you're done get your baseball and gloves and play some catch. You all need to take some time to relax this morning."

Abe wiped his mouth with his napkin and laid it on his breakfast plate. "Ma, I might should check on the straw on the chicken house floor again and the hinge on the door has a squeak. I thought I would oil it."

"Son, you've done a wonderful job of getting the chicken house ready.

Go play some catch with your brothers. It will help the time pass while we wait for the flock to arrive."

\*\*\*

Sarah took three steaming hot apple pies out of the oven and sat them on the cupboard counter to cool with the other, already baked, three. Ben Adams had accepted her invitation to come and see the new chicken house. Doc and Sarah's parents were coming the next day after Sunday morning service. The dinner would be a celebration of their new egg production venture. Sarah planned a special meal of, smoked ham, mashed potatoes with red-eye gravy and home canned green beans, slow cooked with a big slab of bacon for seasoning. Apple pie with thick cream on top would be their dessert.

Sarah rubbed at a niggling ache in her lower back as she poured herself a late morning cup of coffee. She sat at the table to rest a bit, positioning herself so she could watch the road for the arrival of chicken flock. Sarah looked down at the bump below her thickening waistline. A week short of four months in to her pregnancy and she was showing more at this point in the term that ever before. *I need to cut back on my eating portions. I don't want to gain other than baby pounds. Extra weight will make it harder to carry the baby and I sure don't want it after the child is born.*

Both sets of grandparents were now aware they'd be getting another grandchild. *My tummy's protruding to the point of being noticeable, guess it's time the children found out they'll be getting a new baby sister or brother. The whole community's going to know soon enough.*

\*\*\*

Sarah reflected on the day about three weeks before when she had broken the news to her parents. They were loving and supportive as she expected they would be and knowing that gave her comfort. Sarah and her mother spent time together, talking and crying. Their conversation that day started with discussing regrets and concerns and ended in joyful planning for the birth.

Mary took on the responsibility of inventorying available newborn layette items. She would look at what Sarah had on hand and check with her daughter-in-law Rebecca to see if she had anything to loan. Mary would sew whatever additional garments were needed to assure a sufficient supply was ready for the new arrival in mid August.

Sarah appreciated her mother's help. Although she enjoyed the "nesting" phase of pregnancy, stitching tiny baby gowns and knitting booties, she didn't have the time to do that now. Keeping house, cooking and caring for her five children along with the added work of managing the farm's operations and finances didn't leave her with a minute to spare. Sarah couldn't fathom how she would handle it all while breast feeding and caring for a newborn. The enormity of her workload bore down heavy and threatened to dampen her spirits.

***

Her attention was diverted from her thoughts when she saw Reinhold Chicken Hatchery's wagon turn from the county road to the farm's lane. The sight of her boys breaking from their game of catch to greet the arriving delivery filled her with joy. She watched from her position at the window as the wagon stopped near the chicken house and Abe reached up and shook the driver's hand. Sarah threw a shawl around her shoulders. She quickly put a sweater and knit cap on Hathaway, picked her up and left the house so they could join in the excitement.

As Sarah approached the greeting party that now included Sam she noticed that Zeke had already set up sentinel duty. He had his shotgun over his shoulder and was walking the fencerow adjacent to the chicken house.

"Good morning, Ma'am," the deliveryman said tipping his hat to Sarah.

Directing his comments to Sam as he gestured toward the chicken house the man said, "Looks like these birds are comin' to a mighty fine home."

Sarah stepped forward, reached out and shook the man's hand. "Let's just hope they enjoy our hospitality enough to repay us with a lot of eggs in a few months. Hello, I'm Sarah Whitcome, owner of the farm." She gestured to the others. "This is our hired hand, Sam Hartman, and my son's, Josh and Luke. You've already met Abe my oldest. The one I'm holding is my youngest, Hathaway."

"Pleased to meet you, Ma'am. Sorry for the confusion. I assumed that Sam here was your mister."

"No harm done. We're happy you've arrived."

"So, who's that feller over yonder toting the shotgun? He looks mighty fierce."

"That's our security guard, Zeke. There's a story behind his sentinel duty, but you all have chickens to unload."

"Yes, Ma'am, that we do. I've brought you one hundred and ten Rhode Island Reds and forty Barred Plymouth Rocks. That makes a flock of one hundred and fifty all together."

"That's what we ordered. I'll leave it to you men to do the unloading."

\*\*\*

The chickens remained in a state of agitation a couple of hours after they were unloaded and closed up in the chicken house. Sarah had a hunch that the flock needed some quiet to settle themselves. She told the boys to get clear of the structure and keep the noise down. It worked, the squawking subsided.

Since the birds were only one month old they required feeding three times a day. To minimize their agitation, a feeding schedule was established during supper that evening. Sam would handle the three feedings per day for the first week so they could get comfortable with him entering the chicken house. At the second week point, Sam would feed them in the mornings and at noon. Abe would cover the evening feeding. If they tolerated both Abe and Sam tending to them, Josh would be introduced to their feeding crew after another week's time.

"Well, gentlemen, I'd say we've got a good schedule for feeding figured out. Let's celebrate with a piece of apple pie." Sarah said.

"Yeah!" the boys yelled in unison and clapped their hands.

They were finishing up dessert when Zeke plopped first one bare foot, then the other up on to the table.

"Ezekiel Whitcome, it isn't polite to put your feet on the table, especially when we're eating," Sarah chided.

"Well, Ma, I need you to look at my toes, they hurt. 'Sides, everyone done ate their pie," the boy said matter of fact.

143

Sarah pulled Zeke's feet off the table and laid them in her lap. "They hurt Zeke because you've got blisters on each of your big toes. You best retire from marching guard for a day or two so your 'piggies' can heal."

Zeke put his feet back on the floor. "What about them hoodlums?"

Sarah reach over and affectionately pinched Zeke's cheek. "You can sit by the window and keep watch."

\*\*\*

After supper that evening, Sarah, the children, and Sam stood out under the stars in a glow of white lunar light, listening to the chicken's soft contented clucking and flapping of wings. With day one under their collective belt, it was official. The Whitcomes were now in the egg production business.

"Grow, birds grow." Abe, softly encouraged as he stood hands in his pockets chewing on an errant piece of straw. "We need you to start producing eggs so we can make us some money."

Josh, bent down, plucked a long stemmed piece of crab grass, stuck it between his teeth and pocketed his hands. "How much do they have to grow before they start layin' eggs?"

Sam, stooped low and fetched his own blade of grass to chew on. In a quiet voice he said, "Pullets don't start layin' until they're at least four months old, sometimes five."

Luke, who'd recently learned how to do his sums and minuses, pulled a pencil out of the narrow pocket on the bib of his overalls. He calculated midair. "If the new chickens are one-month old today and they have to be four months old before they start layin' eggs, one from four equals three. We have three whole months to wait before we can gather eggs from them." Feeling quite proud of himself he stuck his, already well chewed, pencil in his mouth and nested his hands in his Oshkosh's bib.

Zeke inquired. "How many eggs a day can one of them new chickens lay when they set their mind to it?" He reached down, pinched off a couple of long-stemmed Sheep Shire blooms, stuck them leaf first, in his mouth and shoved his hands deep in his overall pockets.

"One egg a day. That's all any chicken can lay." Was Sam's relaxed response.

Hathaway was quietly sitting at her mother's feet playing in the dirt. She looked up and noticed that Sam and each of her brothers had something protruding from their mouths. The baby snatched up a small twig and followed suit, letting it dangle from her tiny lips.

Sarah who'd been standing with her arms folded while she soaked in the myriad peaceful sounds that come in the night, glanced down at her daughter. "Hathaway, what on earth are you eating?"

Sam and the four boys were standing stair-step height in line. Their act of turning in synchrony, to look at Hathaway, caught Sarah's attention. The sight of them all with their hands in their pants, various and sundry objects protruding from their mouths made her burst out laughing.

Simultaneously the five said, "What?" When they looked at one another, it was evident.

The group burst into unbridled laughter. At the sound of their collective guffawing, the chickens began to squawk and flap. This made the bunch laugh louder which in turn caused the chickens to ratchet up a few notches.

After hee-hawing until they couldn't laugh anymore, Sarah, her brood of chicks and Sam, said goodnight to one another and went to their respective living quarters. In short order the flock got quiet.

Luke, lay awake long after his brothers had commenced sawing logs. He'd shared in the pride of the new flock and the anticipation of a profitable egg business, although he didn't see the need. *Don't see why we need money. We got us pert near anything a fellow could want. Ma cooks us good food to eat. Got me a jackknife, don't no other boy I know that's my age have one. I even got me an extra pencil in case the one I keep in my bib pocket should happen to break.*

*I don't see why all the fuss over puttin' them new chickens in a fine house to eat and sleep. Butter Cup and Butter Ball has lived on this farm all their lives. Looks like them two should get first crack at livin' in that new house, if it's so all fired special. I asked Ma, she said they can't sleep in there 'cause they might spread sickness to the new pullets.*

After contemplating the inequity of the situation, Luke came to what he thought was a good compromise. *I'll let Butter Ball and Butter Cup sleep in the new chicken house just for tonight. They ain't sick. I'll get up early and take 'em out before anyone gets out of bed. Won't no one but me and my two "B's" know.*

Luke, climbed out from under the covers, careful not to wake Zeke, who shared a bed with him. He gathered up his boots and tip toed down the stairs and out to the barnyard.

The moon was bright, lighting up the barnyard such that Luke quickly found Butter Cup and Butter Ball nested together in an old tree stump on the far side of the barn. He quietly gathered the hens, one under each arm and like a man on a mission stealthily made his way through the dark. Using his elbow he pressed down the lever and unlatched the door to the chicken house. He tossed in Butter Ball first followed by Butter Cup and quickly shut and fastened the door.

Startled by their intruders the pullets commenced to squawking and flapping their wings. Luke, ran for cover behind the maple tree. He was breathing heavy while hoping hard, with his fingers and legs crossed, that the chickens would get quiet before Sam, Abe, or his Ma came out to check on the ruckus.

The flock settled down quickly. Luke was able to slip back to his bed without being noticed. The boy fell fast asleep and didn't wake until he heard his Ma call him down to breakfast the next morning.

\*\*\*

Sam woke on Sunday morning prompted the Leghorn's faithful crow. He dressed and went straight to the chicken house to see how the flock had faired their first night on the farm.

The hired hand could hardly believe his eyes when he opened the door and found two full grown, white hens in with the pullet mix of auburn feathered Rhode Island Reds and gray speckled Barred Plymouth Rocks. He hadn't grown personally acquainted with Butter Ball and Butter Cup, but had a strong suspicion they were the two strangers in the house. The structure was secured from unwanted intrusion. There was only one way they could have gotten in, someone had to put them there. A culprit came to mind and his name was Luke.

Sam had no choice. He would have to tell Sarah what he found. He fed and watered the flock, then went on to the barn and started the morning milking. *Guess I best leave it to Sarah to decide if Abe needs to be told. Only time will tell if harm's been done. They're young birds...been livin' in a highly controlled and protected environment. Their immune systems are fragile. The risk of some of them catchin' Roup is high and the threat of dying for them that do, even higher.*

*We went to sleep last night with dreams of a lucrative egg business and now this.* "Dad-blame!" Sam kicked the milk bucket sending it sailing across the barn's floor.

Abe walked in to help with morning's chores. "What's wrong, Sam?"

# Chapter 22

"Luke, rise and shine. Breakfast is ready," Sarah called up the stairs.

The boy, came awake with a start and jumped out of bed. He was so flustered that he put on his bib overalls and pulled up the straps before he put on his shirt. He didn't take time to button up and his shirttail billowed out behind him as he ran down the stairs to the kitchen in his bare feet.

Luke, had his hand on the door knob when Sarah called out, "Whoa, whoa, where're you going? I've just put breakfast on the table, sit down and eat."

Luke, turned toward the table and saw his mother, brothers, sister and Sam staring at him. "Why's everyone up so early?" he said.

"It isn't early, son," Sarah said. "It's almost seven-thirty. We need to eat breakfast and get on the road for church by eight-thirty."

"I...I got me somethin' I need to tend to outside. It'll only take a minute."

"No need, Luke. I took care of it first thing this mornin'," Sam said in a steel-cold tone.

Sarah, didn't like Sam's tone, nor the troubled look on Luke's face. "Took care of what?" She said.

Sam, started to take a sip of coffee, stopped and said, "Ma'am, I'd best discuss it with you in private. Luke, come on and eat your breakfast."

Luke's head hung low as he took his seat. The boy placed his elbow on the table and leaned in resting his palm against his temple to block his view from Sam.

Sarah, was shocked at Sam's breach of the boundaries she'd set for their working relationship. He had no authority to scold her children. What could a seven-year-old boy have done that would anger Sam enough to cause him to forget his place? A chill of alarm shivered down Sarah's spine as she turned and made eye contact with Sam.

Josh's face broke out in a big smile. "Luke's in trouble, Luke's in trouble."

"Ma, if Luke's in trouble and you're gonna send him to bed without his breakfast, can I have his bacon?" Zeke asked, as he reached for his brother's plate.

Sarah, swatted at Zeke's hand. "Leave Luke's bacon alone! Josh, don't let me ever again hear you taking pleasure over someone else's grief. Now eat!"

It was rare for Sarah to use a stern tone. Without a mumbling word they all, including Sam, ate their breakfast. When they were finished Sarah said, "Boys, go upstairs and finishing getting dressed for church."

"Ma, you want me to take Hathaway with me?" Abe asked.

"No, I'll tend to her." Sarah handed the baby another biscuit to chew on.

Luke, was sitting to the right of his mother. When his siblings left the room the boy began to cry. Sarah pulled him from his chair to her lap and snuggled him close. "Son, I need you to tell me what's happened. Before you do, I want you to know that whatever it is, it won't stop me from loving you. If it can be fixed, we'll work on it together. If it can't be fixed, we'll figure out how to replace it or live without it. Now, tell me what happened."

Luke, struggled to tell his story between sobs that wracked his small frame. The front of Sarah's bodice became wet with his tears. "They... they...aren't sick. "I...I...I just wanted 'em to enjoy one night in a nice house. I...I...planned on gettin' up before everyone and takin' them out so it would be my secret. I overslept. Sam must have found 'em in there."

Sarah, had it figured out before she asked, "Sam, tell me what you found."

"Ma'am, what I found was two full grown hens in the chicken house with the flock of new pullets. I wasn't certain, but I guessed they might be Luke's pets. Since the building was secured, I knew someone, likely the boy here, had put them there."

Sarah said, "I'm guessing you didn't tell Abe what you found. He didn't say anything about it when he came in from doing chores."

"No, Ma'am. I thought I should discuss it with you and you would decide about tellin' him," Sam replied.

Sarah, looked at Luke. "Is Sam right, did you put Butterball and Buttercup in the chicken house?"

The boy wiped his nose on his shirtsleeve. "Ye..yes, I did."

"Sam, I appreciate that you didn't tell Abe. This is an unfortunate turn of events, but we'll get it sorted out," Sarah said.

"Ma'am if those pullets catch the Roup, they..."

Sarah, cut in. "Yes, I'm fully aware of the implications and what we might be facing. I'll discuss it with you this evening. If you would excuse us, Sam, I need a private word with my boy."

"Yes, Ma'am," Sam, said in a crisp tone. Avoiding eye contact with Sarah he left the table, retrieved his hat and left the house.

Sarah, used her apron to wipe tears from Luke's cheeks. She cupped his face in her hands and studied his eyes. "Son, your accounting of what happened tells me you knew you were doing something wrong. If not, you wouldn't have felt the need to sneak out in the dark after everyone was asleep to put Butterball and Buttercup in the chicken house. Only you know the reason you're crying now. Is it because your wrongful deed was found out? Or, is it because you're truly sorry about doing something you had been told you shouldn't do?"

"Well, it's both of them things, Ma. I was real scared after I tossed the two B's in the chicken house. The flock started to make a ruckus and I hid behind a tree for fear you, Sam or Abe might come out to see what was goin' on. I felt bad about doin' somethin' you told me not to do. But, Ma, I also felt really good about doin' something special for my pets. How can doin' somethin' good, also be somethin' bad?"

"Luke, it's fine to do something nice for those we care about. However when the thing we want to do might bring harm to someone or something else, then it mustn't be done. You could have fixed a special place for Butterball and Buttercup to sleep, a place just for the two of them. That would have shown them kindness and wouldn't have put the new flock at risk for catching Roup.

"While you're still a growing boy and living here with me, you have to trust that when I tell you not to do something, it's for a good reason. If you don't agree or don't understand the reason, tell me. I'll discuss it with you if I'm able."

"What's goin' to happen now? Will the new flock get the disease even though Butterball and Buttercup aren't sick?"

"Your pets might be carriers of the disease. That means they have the germ although it hasn't made them sick. They can spread that germ to other chickens that might not be as strong. That's a likely chance with the new flock since they're young birds and have lived in a protected environment."

"When will we know if they're goin' to get sick?"

"If two weeks from now the new flock doesn't show any signs of the illness, they likely weren't contaminated. We'll just have to wait and see."

"What happens if they do get sick?"

"We'll treat with them medicine and hope for the best."

"If they get sick, will they die?"

"Yes, I expect some of them will die."

"I...I...I didn't mean for nobody to die," sobbed the child.

"I know you didn't." Sarah hugged him close.

"Do...do we have to tell Abe what happened?"

"Abe has worked really hard to build the chicken house and bring in a new flock. Don't you think he has a right to be told?"

"I guess he does, but he'll be real sore at me if he finds out. I don't want to tell him. Wha...what if Sam tells? Wha...what if the chickens start dyin' and Abe figures it out?" Wha...wha...what if Abe gets mad and beats me up?" The boy started to sob again.

"Yes, what if can be a mighty big weight to carry. Do you want go around in fear of being found out? Doing wrong has consequences. I can't stop Abe from being angry. However, I can and will make sure he doesn't beat you up. It's for me as your parent to decide what your punishment will be."

"Punishment? You're gonna punish me?"

"Luke, you disobeyed me. Yes, there will be a punishment. Abe needs to be told and I think you'll feel better if you tell him yourself. I hope you're sorry for what you did. I hope you'll let your brother know that. Asking for forgiveness is important."

"Ma, I'm sorry I did it. Can you forgive me?"

Sarah, kissed her son's right cheek and then his left one. "Yes, I forgive you."

"Should I go now and tell Abe what I did?"

"No. Today's a day of celebration and we're having company. You can tell him this evening after our guests leave.

"Ok...Ma, what's gonna be my punishment?"

"Luke, I need to think on that some. This is a very serious thing you did. I'll let you know tomorrow. Right now you need to skedaddle and get dressed for church.

# Chapter 23

Ben Adams wiped his mouth with his napkin. "Sarah, I haven't had a meal this fine in a really long time. Thanks for inviting me."

"You're welcome, Ben. We wanted you to see the new chicken house and help us celebrate the start of our egg business."

Doc buttered a yeast roll. "Abe, I heard the new building was your idea."

"Well I did do me some studin' on different buildings I saw in the Poultry Monthly, but I can't take all the credit. Sam's real good with tools and everyone pitched in to help."

Doc held his roll mid-air and turned to the hired hand. "Sam, do you have a lot of experience in raising chickens for egg production?"

With a growl like a dog protecting its territory Sam said, "I reckon I've got fair to middlin' experience. I'm up to the challenge."

Ben raised his eyebrows then turned away. "Sarah, I think you're getting in to the market at just the right time. Wabash's population has increased considerably the last few years. A growing number of city folks prefer to buy their eggs rather than keep chickens. Myself, included."

"Let's quit a talkin' about them chickens and go look at 'em." The call to action came from Zeke who was standing at the door, shotgun over his shoulder ready for guard duty. "Doc, you ain't one of them hoodlums are ya? 'Cause we don't allow no rock throwin' hoodlums ta gets near the new chicken house winders."

"Zeke, I don't think I've ever been accused of being a hoodlum."

"Well they's a first time for everythin'. I best check your pockets to see if you're a carrin' any rocks afore I let ya get past me."

"Zeke, don't be disrespectful to Doc Adams," Sarah scolded her four-year-old.

"No disrespect taken," Doc said as he stood and started to empty his pockets. "I can't fault a man for taking his job seriously."

"Ben, no!" Sarah said, rising from her chair. "Zeke, Doc Adams is a close family friend. I'll vouch that he isn't carrying any contraband. Abe, you lead the grand tour."

Zeke, a bit crestfallen due to his mother's chastisement, whispered to Josh, "I don't care 'bout no contraband. Its rocks that's got me worried."

As the entourage left the kitchen for the tour, Tom pulled his daughter to his side. "Sarah, you best rein that tyke in a bit or he'll be tellin' you what's what, instead of the other way around."

"I appreciate your concern, Pa. But I was the one who assigned Zeke guard duty. He's showing me he's up to the task."

"Is that your way of tellin' me to mind my own business?"

Sarah kissed her father's cheek. "I love you, Pa."

Sarah made a mental note to ponder her father's advice about Zeke. Truth be told she was really proud of the little guy. She would rather have the burden of needing to tame a child a bit, over the worry of how to instill gumption in one.

With the tour finished and the talk about poultry farming and egg production exhausted, Ben bid his farewell. "Sam, glad to meet you. My shingle is hanging on Main Street if you ever need any doctoring."

Sam tipped his hat at Doc and said, "Much obliged, but I'm doing real fine these days."

Ben eyed Sam a few seconds longer than was polite, then diverted his attention to Sarah. "Thanks again for the delicious meal. Abe, you take good care of your ma. Don't let her work too hard."

"I'll watch out for her, Doc," Abe said.

Sarah's parents were standing together. Tom leaned down and whispered, "Mary, it looks to me like those two men just drew a line in Sarah's sand. Hope neither of them try to cross it."

"I expect Sarah can handle it if they do," Mary replied. "Our girl looks tired. I'm going in to tackle those dishes."

***

As Sarah's parents prepared to leave her father said. "Luke, you've been mighty quiet today. You a feelin' ok?"

Sarah put her arm around her son's small shoulders and pulled him close. "He's got a lot on his mind. He'll be fine after he unburdens himself."

Luke nodded his head, but the weight he carried was too heavy to pull his cheeks into even a fake smile.

\*\*\*

Sarah stood at her kitchen window surveying the farm. The sun still shone, but rode low on the horizon. It was evening and time to put together another meal. Cooking was a routine Sarah didn't generally give a second thought. Now in light of the distasteful task that lay ahead it seemed daunting. She didn't know whether to have Luke talk to Abe before or after supper. Knowing that breaking bread together could be a bonding experience, she decided to get the two together before they ate.

"Luke, Abe, would the two of you come in my room please. Josh, I need you to look after Hathaway and Zeke."

Josh looked from Abe to Luke, then to his ma. "Uh, ok," he said.

Abe followed his mother and brother into the bedroom. "What's this about Ma?"

"Abe, Luke has something he needs to tell you."

"What?"

Luke couldn't stop tears from flowing down his cheeks as he told his brother about putting Butterball and Buttercup in the chicken house the night before. "So...so that's the whole story. I...I was just tryin' to do somethin' nice for my pets."

Abe exploded, "Why? Why would you do such a stupid, stupid thing? We told you the new flock couldn't be exposed to the free-range chickens. What if they come down with Roup? Don't you know that some of them could die?"

"I...I...do now. At the time I didn't think that could happen. I'm sorry. Will you please, please forgive me?" Luke pleaded.

"Forgive you!" Abe threw his hands in the air. "How can I forgive you? Your stupid move likely will cost us a lot of money. No, I ain't gonna forgive you."

Sarah tenderly brushed the hair from Luke's forehead. "Go on out with the others Luke, I want to have a private talk with Abe."

"I'm sorry, Abe, I wish you could forgive me." With his head hung low, Luke left the room.

"Abe, please sit. I want to tell you a story."

"I'm too mad to sit." The boy paced while holding a bed pillow, using it as a punching bag. "I ain't in no mood for a story."

"I didn't ask you if you were. Now sit!" Sarah said pointing to the bed. Knowing better than to push his obstinacy further, Abe complied.

Sarah began. "There was a farmer who saved his money for a very long time to buy himself a coon-hunting dog. He didn't want just any old hound dog. When he heard that the Indiana State Coon Hunting Champion had a litter, he paid the high asking price and bought one of her whelps.

"He brought the pup home where he lived with his wife and three little boys, ages seven, five, and three. The boys loved the puppy and enjoyed playing with him. It was summer and the farmer built a pen so the little dog would stay confined to the yard. He told his boys to never let the pup outside of the pen unless it was on a rope.

"The boy, who was seven at the time, the same age Luke is now, didn't think it was fair for the puppy to be kept in a pen all the time. He wanted it to run up and down the lane with him. So one day when the farmer was out working in the field, he let it out and didn't put it on a rope.

"The pup loved running free. He followed the boy up and down the lane a couple of times and then decided to go exploring on his own. Before the boy could catch him the puppy ran under the fence and in to the corral where the farmer kept a breeder bull.

"The puppy started to bark and chase after the bull. The bull turned and chased the puppy. The bull caught up with the puppy and gave it a head butt. The puppy flew through the air, bounced off of a large rock, and fell dead to the ground."

Tears were flowing freely down Abe's cheeks as his mother continued the story. "The boy was heart-broken that the puppy died. He'd just wanted to let it run free. If he'd obeyed his father, the puppy wouldn't have been killed.

"That night when the farmer came in from the field the boy had to tell him what happened. The father was angry that his son had disobeyed him and let the puppy run free. The boy told his father he was sorry and asked to be forgiven.

"When the father saw how sad and how sorry his little boy was about what had happened, he gathered him in his arms and told him it was ok. He told the boy he was forgiven."

Abe had tears streaming down his cheeks when his mother finished the story. "I get your point Ma. I don't recon I could have survived if Pa hadn't forgiven me. He was hurt real bad over losing that pup. After that one got killed we never had another one."

The boy let out a deep sigh. "May I be excused?"

"Yes, son, I'm finished with our talk."

Abe left the room, found Luke and pulled him in to a hug. "I forgive you, Brother."

# Chapter 24

Ben's mind was filled with bittersweet thoughts as he made the trip from the Whitcome farm back to town and his empty house. He savored the time spent in the company of Sarah and her children and he enjoyed the chance to catch up with Tom and Mary Riley.

The opportunity to meet the elusive Sam Hartman was appreciated. What little he knew of the hired hand before that day he'd learned from Elmo Jones. Anyone with a lick of sense sifted through the mailman's gossip and then took what was conceivably believable with a grain of salt. Ben hadn't gained any first-hand information while out at Sarah's farm.

*Does that mean the man has something to hide? Could be. Might not be. The guy could just be the private sort. The fellow seemed agreeable enough, a bit testy but tolerable.*

*I can't shake the feeling that Sam's attracted to Sarah. There was nothing in particular I could name, but there was something about the way he looked at her. It just doesn't sit well with me.*

*Truth be told, what has me feeling agitated toward the guy is that he'll be sleeping in Sarah's parlor tonight and I'm going home by my lonesome.*

*Soon it'll be evident that Sarah is pregnant. Will that dampen Sam's ardor for her? Likely not. I've seen Sarah with child several times over the years. The glow that comes with pregnancy suits her well. If anything her condition will be an enhancement to her beauty.*

*Due to the circumstances she'll need more support, both physically and emotionally. Problem is, Sam's already got his big foot stuck in her door... willing and able to provide support. I should visit Sarah and the children more often, or Sam's foot might get wedged in too tight to remove.*

*I wonder what Jeb Carter's take on the guy is? Abe said Jeb and his son Julib helped some with the building of the new chicken house. Jeb would've had an opportunity to observe Sam and form an opinion. Tomorrow I'll drop by the Marshal's office and see if he's willing to share anything.*

A doe and her fawn jumped in the path of the Doc's rig. The horse broke stride and jolted Ben from his thoughts to the here and now. *I'd better tend to the business of handling this rig. Many a horse and driver have met their demise or some lesser calamity on these poorly paved country roads.*

*There'll be plenty of uninterrupted time to ponder on Sarah tonight before sleep comes to my rescue.*

\*\*\*

Sam stoked the fire in the fireplace. After adding another log he settled in his rocking chair and popped the cork on a bottle of beer from the supply he kept stashed in his room. The hired hand propped his sock-covered feet up on his footstool and breathed in the essence that was his home.

*Life's good. I've got a good job, comfortable living quarters and three squares a day. I've got the promise of more than just pocket change come harvest time. When I left the Hargrove's employ I was afraid I wouldn't find comfort elsewhere.*

Running his calloused hand across the smooth wooden arm of the rocker Sam thought about the contrast of his homey quarters to the six by eight foot cell he had occupied a few years back. He didn't like remembering those difficult months of incarceration and tried to avoid their memory altogether.

Tonight foreboding pressed heavy on his chest and whispered in his ear…*don't get too comfortable, don't let your guard down, don't open yourself up to hurt.*

Clem and Clara Hargrove had been good to Sam from the start, but he'd been slow to accept their kindness. Eventually the broken pieces of his life pulled together and he felt as if he fit in while he lived on their farm.

The job change and the uncertainty of acceptance in his new location had put a crack in the barrier to the past that he'd erected in his mind. Memories of long ago events were seeping through. Along with them came the fear that he would be unable to hold on to his good fortune if his past became known.

Sam drained the bottle he was holding and reached for another. The cumulative draught from the two would work just enough magic to push his demons back into their hiding place.

Sam's living space provided him with considerable privacy. It had its own door to the outside. An approximate inch and a half high band of light that showed under the crack of the parlor's interior door was the only visible breach. *It'll take a determined soul with the flexibility of a contortionist or a midget to peek under and invade my privacy.* He thought as he drew hard and long on the neck of the friend he held in his hand.

Sound separation between his quarters and the rest of the house left room for improvement. Sam intentionally tried to filter out the conversations between Sarah and her children. They needed their family time and Sam needed the peace and rest from the children's chatter. It wasn't that they annoyed him. It was quite the contrary. He really enjoyed their banter and even their bickering. He didn't mind when they asked him questions. What he needed a respite from was the constant being on guard. On guard so he didn't respond when they asked their mother something, or interject his opinion when it came to their care and discipline. Sarah Whitcome had made it crystal clear that he needed to keep his place when it came to her children. She had reminded him of the unequivocal fact just that morning when the incident of Luke and his pet chickens was discussed.

Sam emptied his comforting companion. *No worries ma'am. I got the message.* Sam guessed the demons had been able to break through his mind's barrier because of the visit they'd had from Ben Adams. *What gave Doctor almighty Adams the right to question me about my skills to help Sarah start up an egg production business? I figure I've handled a few more chickens than the good doctor. Likely a man of his education and means hasn't ever cracked an egg. Besides I don't like the way he looked at Sarah. Why doesn't he have a wife and family of his own? You'd think it would be easy for the only doctor in town, good looking to boot, to find his own woman.*

*His own woman…whoa boy…watch yourself. If the wrong person knew you were thinking that, you'd be in a heap of trouble with no way out but gone. Sarah's a married woman. She's never acted or behaved any way to the contrary. Neither you nor Ben Adams has any right to lay claim to her.*

Sam started toward his bed when movement broke the band of light under the parlor door, catching his attention. He stood still and watched as two chubby, child sized, fingers reached under the threshold and wiggled. The mouth connected to them whispered, "Sam, we's havin' us some popcorn. Want some?"

Simultaneously dimpled baby fingers pushed three pieces of popcorn to his side of the door. "You, pacorn?"

"Sam, they's more where that came from. We got us a plenty. Go ahead, Hathaway, and give Sam some more of your popcorn," the voice instructed.

"No, my pacorn."

"Now, Hathaway, what have I been a tellin' you about sharin'. Here, let me get a handful of your popcorn and I'll push it under the door."

Sounds indicated that a scuffle had ensued. "No, my pacorn, my pacorn."

Sarah's easy to discern footsteps closed the gap between the kitchen and the hall. "Zeke, Hathaway, get away from Sam's door and give him some peace. If Sam wanted popcorn he would have come and got a bowl for himself when I offered it to him earlier."

Sam chuckled as he bent down and scooped up the offering. He could forget worrying about contortionists or midgets invading his privacy. It was a precocious four-year-old and a not so gullible toddler he had to watch out for. He tossed the kernels of corn in the fire, adjusted the screen to make sure no embers could escape to the wooden floor and crawled into his welcoming bed.

The whispering in his ear came again...*watch yourself, you're getting too fond of this family, keep your distance.* Was it one of the demons taunting him, or was it simply common sense dispensing sound advice?

# Chapter 25

Home from school, Abe came rushing into the kitchen with a smile on his face. "Ma, it's been nearly two weeks since Luke put his two hens in with the pullets. I just checked on the new flock. None of them look sick. They're cluckin' and peckin' like they don't have a care in the world."

"Son, don't get your hopes up too high. We need to give the flock a couple of more days to know for sure that they're out of danger. Remember the incubation period for Roup is fourteen days, today's the thirteenth day," Sarah said.

"I got me a good feelin', Ma. I think things are gonna be just fine. One more day, maybe two and then I say we celebrate. You could make us one of your special occasion carrot cakes."

Sarah reached her hand out for a shake, "You've got a deal."

"Ohhh...Ma, sometimes *you* take the cake," the boy teased clasping his mother's hand.

"Where's Josh and Luke? Didn't they leave school the same time as you?" Sarah asked.

"They'll be home directly. It takes about three times as long as it should when you're walkin' with Luke. He can't pass a rock...has to stop and pick it up. Stoppin' and startin', stoppin' and startin'. It's enough to drive a busy man crazy. I ran on home ahead of them."

"Be patient with Luke, he's still young. I seem to recall that you once thought gathering interesting rocks was important," Sarah said. "Get changed and start evening chores. It'd be nice if you'd finish early this evening."

With Zeke and Hathaway out playing in the dirt pile, Sarah took a deep breath and savored the quiet that came when she was alone in the house. She hummed while she started preparing their supper. *How blessed I am to have five healthy children.* Sarah ran her hand over the bump under her expanding waistline. *Anyone who looks at me twice would know I'm with child. I didn't expected Josh, Luke, or Zeke to notice, but I'm surprised that Abe hasn't asked questions. The excitement of building the new chicken house and now concern over the health of the new flock have likely kept him from seeing what's obvious.*

*Before I put supper on the table I'll gather the children and tell them that they're getting a new baby brother or sister.* Sarah walked to the window to check on Zeke and Hathaway. *Those two never seem to tire of digging in the dirt.* The sky was filled with interwoven ribbons of pink and purple, accentuated by golden highlights, as the sun lost its hold on the day and started its descent into the night.

Sarah silently prayed, *thank you Lord for the gift of this glorious sight. Thank you for the assurance that the sun will rise tomorrow. Be with me as I tell the children about the coming baby. Give me the words to share the news in a way they can understand and be joyful. For Abe, the news will bring back painful memories of the day his Pa attacked me. He will know that was the day I conceived. Please help him accept the news without fear, regret, or feelings of recrimination against this unborn child.*

\*\*\*

Supper was ready and simmering on the cook stove's back burners. Sarah was anxious to have her talk with the children. She went outside to see if Abe and Josh were coming up from the barn so she could gather everyone.

Luke was in the rope swing that hung from the large maple tree. He'd pumped himself so high the ropes went slack on the upward swing and jerked taut on the return downward. Sarah called out, "Luke, you're too high. I've told you before that's dangerous."

"Sorry, Ma, I forgot," the boy called back.

"When your brothers are finished with their chores, I want all of you to come in the house so I can talk to you," Sarah instructed.

"I see 'em," Luke called out from his vantage point. "They just come out of the barn and are headin' this way." The boy eased off of his pumping. As the swing slowed, Luke's legs lowered, his tiptoes touching the ground. He started dragging his feet creating billows of dust with each pass.

The digging pile was in close proximity. Zeke and Hathaway covered their faces as protection against the airborne soil. Switching to a one-handed shield, Zeke shook his fist at Luke. "Hey, can't ya see they's people workin' over here. You're a throwin' dirt all over us."

Sarah walked to the dirt pile. "Hathaway, take mama's hand. Zeke, it's

162

time to stop digging. I want all of you children to come in the house for a talk." She called over to Luke. "Wait for your brothers. When they get to the pump, tell them to go ahead and wash up, then you all come on in too."

\*\*\*

"What's wrong, Ma? Why are we all huddled here in your bedroom?" Abe asked, taking his hat off and running his fingers through his hair. "Did someone...uh, do somethin' again."

Zeke's face turned beet red. He reached in his pocket and pulled out Josh's jack knife. "Ma, I didn't steal it. I was just keepin' it in my pocket so I could...so I could uh, appreciate it," Zeke lamely explained.

"My knife! I wondered what happened to it," Josh squawked as he grabbed it from Zeke's hand. "I thought it was lost. Appreciatin' it my foot! You done stole it," Josh huffed.

"Zeke, apologize to Josh for uh, uh, appreciating his knife. Later you and I will have a talk about the difference between appreciating and stealing. You walked a mighty thin line on this knife business. I'm not convinced that you didn't know it when you put it in your pocket," Sarah scolded. "Now listen, I have some exciting family news to share..."

"Let me guess!" Josh shouted, "We're gettin' us a dog. That's the most excitin' news a feller could get."

"No, we aren't getting a dog," Sarah said as she sat down on the bed and pulled Hathaway up on her lap. "My special news is that near the end of this coming summer, in August, we're going to have a new baby join our family. You'll be getting another brother or sister."

Sarah saw anger wash over Abe's face and sadness take its place. Tears welled in the boy's eyes as he struggled to maintain his composure.

The emotional tone shifted when Zeke blurted out. "I don't call that special news. What's so special about gettin' another baby! We got us one of them. I agree with Josh. What we need is a dog. 'Sides, Hathaway still craps in her britches. Now you're tellin' us we're gonna have two babies smellin' up the house." The tyke had taken a stand directly in front of Sarah with his legs spread and his arms folded across his chest. "I vote no."

For once having a loose cannon in the house paid off. The sight of Zeke making his objection, as if he had a voice in the matter, caused Sarah and Abe to burst out laughing. Josh and Luke, didn't get the full gist, but joined in. Hathaway, oblivious to the derogatory comments directed at her, clapped her tiny hands.

"Laugh if you want, but when the house smells like a stinky stunk done crawled in, I ain't feelin' sorry for no one 'cept me," Zeke forewarned.

"Whew…! Zeke, enough with your pontification," Sarah said.

Zeke was quick to respond, "It weren't me, Ma. I generally don't do no *puffacation* unless I've had me some beans to eat. I think that smell's a comin' from Hathaway. I saw her face pinch up and get red, I think she done cra…"

Sarah tuned the boy out, her thoughts had moved on. "Josh, take your sister and change her britches please. Supper will be on the table directly."

The children started filing out of the bedroom. "Abe, stay. I want to talk to you," Sarah said.

Sarah took Abe's hand in hers. "Son, everything will be fine. I've made my peace with the pregnancy. I need to know that you don't blame this new baby for what happened to me. He or she will need your love and big-brother protection as much as the other four."

"Ma, I'll treat the new baby the same as the others." Abe squeezed his mother's hand. "I didn't get angry over the news we'd be gettin' another brother or sister. I got upset because the news caused me to think about what Pa did to you. I like to pretend I don't know."

"I understand. Son, this baby is growing fast. It won't be long before it's obvious that I'm expecting. Folks will talk. Some might even gossip. They'll count on their fingers and speculate about how long your pa's been gone."

"Ma, if I hear tell of anyone talkin' ugly about you, they'll wish they hadn't," Abe vowed.

"It's sweet of you to say that, but I don't want you to worry about having to defend me." Sarah released the boy's hand. "Now please go ring the dinner bell so Sam will know that I'm putting supper on the table."

Sarah, the children and Sam sat down to a supper of roast beef, mashed potatoes with gravy, and butter beans. Sarah asked everyone to join hands and she started giving the blessing. Before the Amen, the loose cannon discharged again. "Sam, Ma done said another baby is a comin' to live with us. Everyone but me acts like it'll be just fine. I voted no. What've you got to say about it?"

Sam had suspected for a few weeks that Sarah might be with child. Even though, Zeke's blunt announcement left him momentarily speechless. Sam's hesitation in responding caused Zeke to interject. "Ma, you ain't gonna add changin' diapers to Sam's list of chores are ya?"

"No, Sam won't have any responsibilities to care for the new baby." Sarah quickly responded. "Zeke, I'm not angry with you, but the special news was mine to share, not yours."

Sam found his voice and raised his coffee cup. "I can't think of anything more exciting than adding someone new to your family. Congratulations!"

# Chapter 26

On day fifteen, Sarah was putting the icing on a three-layer carrot cake when Sam knocked on the kitchen door. "Ma'am do you have a minute?"

"Sure, come on in Sam. I was just finishing up on this cake. Grab a cup of coffee and tell me what's on your mind."

"You might want to take a seat before I do that." Sam said as he fetched himself a cup of coffee.

Sarah dropped the knife she was holding and clutched the edge of the table. "No, no, oh, no...is it bad news about the pullets?"

Sam took Sarah by the elbow and ushered her to a chair. "I'm afraid so, Ma'am. I just came from the chicken house. Several of the pullets are lookin' poorly...breathin' seems labored. I inspected about a half-dozen and found warts on their combs."

Sarah rested her elbows on the table and laid her face in her hands. "Dear God, why? They made it through yesterday, two weeks without symptoms. I thought they were going to escape contamination."

"Me too," Sam shook his head. "I'm so sorry, Ma'am. I know this is hard news to take. When you had us hold hands and pray over the flock, I wanted to believe all would be fine."

Sarah reached over and patted Sam's hand, "all will be fine. It just doesn't seem like it right now. Thankfully God's in control."

"How can you keep the faith when God didn't answer your prayer that the pullets would stay healthy?"

"Sam, a flock of sick chickens can't shake my faith. God has sustained me through much rougher circumstances. I don't know why this happened. Maybe someday I will, or I may never know."

"You're a strong woman, Sarah Whitcome. I mean that with the utmost respect," Sam ran his hands across his face. "I'll separate out those noticeably affected, put them in the make-shift hen house, and start doctorin' them."

"Thanks, Sam. Abe will be home from school soon and can help. He'll take the news hard too, but don't try to shield him. There's no denying this is a setback, but that's all it is. We'll do what we can and push forward. I don't want the boy wasting energy on what if or if only."

"Cull and dose them, that's all we can do. I best get to it." Sam swallowed the last dregs in his cup and stood.

"Sam, that's not all we can do. We can continue to pray," Sarah said as she pushed herself up from her chair.

Home from school, Abe had entered the kitchen and caught the tail end of his mother's conversation with Sam. "Pray! For what? Did somethin' happen? Is it the new flock?"

"Yep, it's the pullets," Sam said. "Sorry, boy. Your Ma will explain the situation. I'll head on out and see to them. Thanks for the coffee, Ma'am."

Abe's eyes were ready to spill over. "Why? Why? This is day fifteen. I thought we were in the clear."

Sarah picked up the wooden spatula to finish icing the cake. Abe grabbed her hand. "You can stop icin' it! There ain't no cause for celebration now!"

Sarah jerked her hand free. "Listen to me, boy, Christ died for our sins and rose again. Because He lives, is reason alone to celebrate every day of our lives. Now get your clothes changed and go tend to the pullets."

"Yes, Ma'am." Abe turned to leave, then stopped. "Ma, do you really believe what you just told me about a reason for celebration?"

"With all of my heart, son. With all of my heart."

"Well...I ain't so sure," Abe left. If his Ma had a response, he wasn't ready to hear it.

✳✳✳

Ten days had passed since the infected pullets were culled, doctored and summarily prayed over...again. The first infected chickens grew sicker while more succumbed to the illness. In all about one-third of the new pullets were sick with Roup. Hopes for a cure were dwindling. Death for many of the ailing fowls was imminent.

Sarah sat at her table, her head in her hands, reviewing the farm's account ledger. She faced a potentially catastrophic loss to her new egg operation. Usually she could see a bright side to a dilemma, but not this time. Emotionally she felt utterly and completely drained; beaten down with no foreseeable way up.

Without the projected income from the selling of eggs, Sarah didn't know how she was going to pay off their bank loan. She held hope for a good crop yield in the fall that would cover a portion of the debt. The remainder was to have come from the egg production. With a much-dwindled flock, breaking even was questionable, let alone have money to provide for their living.

Sarah reasoned it was an accumulation of loss that had her feeling devastated. *I've lost Henry, my helpmate and the love of my life. I've lost family privacy with Sam living in close quarters and taking meals with us. I've lost control of my plan to make the farm profitable and provide for my children.* Sarah looked down at her protruding tummy and groaned. *I've even lost my figure!*

Sarah knew she had taken a bold step when she started her egg production business. It was a new concept for the family farmer and considered a foolhardy venture by many. *I'm the first in this area to take on such a large egg production. I just can't fail, I can't.*

Weary of her self-pity, Sarah got up and poured herself a late morning cup of coffee. Before going back to the table she opened a drawer in the sideboard and got a pencil and a scrap piece of paper.

*What would Henry do if he were in this situation?* Sarah pictured him storming through the kitchen door to break the news about a Roup-infected flock. *"Put your thinking cap on, Sarah, we've got a problem to fix."* Between the two of them, Sarah was the more creative thinker. Henry had been methodical, steady and sure, but never creative when plans went awry.

*Well…until I figure something out, we'll just have to tighten the belt! No matter how lean the income, Henry and I never put provisions on account at the general store and I'm not starting that practice now.*

Sarah held her cup under her nose and took a deep breath, savoring the aroma. She put the cup down, picked up the pencil and started to write down ideas as they came to her. *Coffee will be the first cutback. One pot of fresh grounds per day, no more. I'll add eggshells to the morning's used grounds to extend them enough for an evening pot. Sam won't like it any more than me, but it has to be done. No more buying yeast for baking. I'll get a start of sourdough off Ma, keep feeding it and switch to it for bread and other baking needs. Bacon…need to conserve our supply of that. I'll cut from cooking it every morning to three or four times a week.* Sarah tapped her pencil on the table as she struggled to expand her thinking.

Another flood of ideas came to her. She licked the lead in her pencil and continued to write. *No more buying soap. I haven't had to make my own in years, but I still remember how to make lye soap. The curing time is about four weeks, so I need to start saving extra lard. We've got lye on hand and the recipe doesn't call for much. We'll cut back a tad on the amount we put in the privy...save it for making soap. Make soap! Where will I find the time to make soap?*

Sarah sipped from her coffee cup and switched thinking from purchase cut backs, to ways for creating income. *Spring is coming soon. What could I plant for easy sell...?*

*Vegetables! I'll devote another half to full acre of ground to growing vegetables. We can haul them to Wabash...set up on Saturdays on the court house square, market with other area farmers. Which vegetables...?*

*Cabbage and squash! They're easy to harvest. Potatoes!...they sell well but take time and labor to dig up. What else...?*

*Green beans are easy to grow. ...backbreaking to pick. Josh! Josh is still low to the ground and can pick. Luke can help him, maybe Zeke too. No... forget Zeke...too much potential for waste. He'd be apt to snap the beans on the vine. They need to be pulled off at the stem.*

Routinely after opening her mail, Sarah stuck empty envelopes in the sideboard drawer to use as scrap writing paper. She was recording her list of ideas on one of them. She felt a twinge when she realized the one she was using had a Wabash County Court House imprint on the face of it. *How ironic that the envelope I grabbed to write on is the one that delivered the declaration of my guardianship over Henry. It arrived the same day he attac...can't think about that now.*

*Livestock, I'll need to sell off several hogs and what few head of cattle we have. That'll cut down on feed cost, bring in some income. I'll keep the two milk cows.* The sound of loud squeals snapped Sarah's mind from planning to the present. She glanced at the clock. *Oh...no, it's been an hour since I last checked on Zeke and Hathaway.* With a sense of foreboding she went to the window and looked out. The two blobs she saw, standing in the dirt pile, bore no resemblance to the children she had scooted out the door earlier that afternoon. Zeke and Hathaway were caked head to toe in mud.

Going outside for a closer look Sarah found the water source the pair had used to create the sludge. It was her precious rain water. Sarah kept a barrel under the downspout coming off of the back porch roof. Rainwater was soft, not hard like their well water. It didn't cause rust stains. Sarah collected the runoff to use for washing her finer linens and her hair.

The precious elixir had been contaminated beyond salvaging. A tree stump had been pulled to the side of the barrel and used for the height advantage needed to dip the contents. Small sized, muddy hand prints dotted the barrel's sides, leaving no doubt as to who the culprits were. Twigs, leaves and other debris floated on the surface of the remaining water.

"What are you two supposed to be?" Sarah said to the blobs.

"We's brown babies, like those ones we saw in town last week," Zeke answered. "We look pretty good don't we, Ma? Ya can't see nothin' but the whites of our eyes."

Sarah stripped off Hathaway's clothing first and took her naked to the pump. It took several buckets poured over the baby's head to remove the layers of mucky goo. She wrapped the child snugly in a sheet she'd fetched and sat her off to the side.

While she tackled the mess named Zeke, she explained, "The children you saw are referred to as colored folk, not brown."

"Well they ain't a lot of different colors, they's just brown. So why ain't they called brown?"

"Zeke, your skin is white. Do folks call you white?"

"No, I got a name. Folks call me Zeke, 'cause that's my name."

"The children you saw in town have names too."

"Well then why does folks call them colored? Why not just call them by their names?" Zeke asked through chattering teeth.

"Zeke, that's an excellent suggestion. Just call them by their names."

"Ma, what if I'm too scared to ask them their names?"

"Zeke Whitcome, I've never known you to be too shy or too scared to strike up a conversation with anyone."

A figure coming up the lane caught Sarah's attention. The person was too far off to see just who it was, but it looked like Abe. She told herself it couldn't be him as it was only 2:00 in the afternoon and school wouldn't be out for another hour.

As the figure drew closer Sarah could see that it was Abe, but he was hurt. His nose was crusted with blood, his left eye was swollen near closed, and he was walking with a limp. Sarah grabbed another sheet off of the clothes line, wrapped Zeke up and left him standing while she took off running.

"What on earth has happened to you?" Sarah said when she reached her boy, grasping his arms to hold him still so she could inspect his face.

"It ain't nothing to worry about, Ma. I got in a scrap with Ernie Brown and teacher sent me and him home early.

"What do you mean it isn't anything to worry about? You look like you've been run over by a hay wagon. What were the two of you fighting about?"

"I'd rather not say, Ma. It's a kinda private thing."

"So private you can't tell your mother?"

"Well I'd rather not have to tell you, Ma."

"Did you get your differences settled?"

"I hope so. Ernie looks worse than me. I'm sorry I had to fight him, but there weren't no choice."

"I seem to recall that you and Ernie had a scuffle in the church yard a few months back. Was it related to that incident?"

"Yeah, I guess you could say it was. Like I said, I don't look for him to be causing no more trouble."

"I won't force you to tell me what the two of you fought over if you promise me you won't fight again. Ms. Kirsh has enough to handle teaching, she shouldn't have to deal with two rowdy boys."

"Ma, I ain't gonna lie to you and say I'll never fight Ernie again. I will promise you I won't do it at school. That's the best I can do right now."

"Get over to the pump and clean yourself up. You've got a couple of hours before chore time. I'll fix you some milk and cookies and you can lay down," Sarah said.

"Thanks, Ma," Abe limped to the pump where two mummy wrapped siblings stood. "What happened to you two?"

"That's a story for later," Sarah said picking up Hathaway and guiding Zeke as he waddled to the house. Calling over her shoulder she said, "Abe, just to clarify, you couldn't promise to not get into another scrap with Ernie so I might have to insist on knowing the reason for today's conflict. Your injuries look like more than just a couple of rowdy boys scuffling. I need to think on it some."

Sarah took some time to think about how to tell the family about the needed cut-backs in a way that would make it palatable. She decided she'd serve up the news about money saving alongside a bountiful meal.

\*\*\*

That evening when the family sat down for supper, Josh was the first to comment. "Wow! Pork chops; mashed potatoes and gravy, green beans, and hot yeast rolls. My favorite meal."

Sarah poured glasses of milk for the children and served Sam a cup of coffee from a freshly brewed pot before she took her seat at the table. "We have apple cobbler with cream for dessert."

"Abe," Zeke said, "are you ready to say why you was fightin' Ernie Brown?"

Josh and Luke responded in unison. "Hush your mouth and mind your own business!"

"Boys! It was rude of Zeke to pry into Abe's business," Sarah said, "but there's no reason to be mean-spirited in pointing it out."

Sarah cut her eyes to Sam. His head was bent with his hand shielding his peripheral vision on her side. *The man's certainly intent on avoiding eye contact with me.* She looked over at Abe and caught him looking at Sam. *Well…isn't this something! Sam's demeanor and the quick retort from Luke and Josh tells me they all three know why Abe fought Ernie Brown. Besides Zeke and Hathaway, I'm the only one sitting at this table who hasn't been told. This will never…*

Sarah's thoughts were cut short by Luke. "Ma, what's holdin' up the prayer? Them taters are gonna get cold."

"Well we don't want that to happen," Sarah smiled at Luke. "Son, you say the prayer for us tonight."

Luke gave a perfunctory prayer, something he knew by rote. Sarah didn't take notice, her mind was elsewhere. *Abe probably confided in Sam when they did chores together. Luke and Josh would have had firsthand knowledge since the fight was at school. There's no two ways about it, I will find out. I'll give Sam until morning, but if he doesn't tell me, I'll have a big decision to make. I won't have my hired hand keeping a confidence with my children behind my back.*

"Ma, Ma!" Josh raised his voice an octave.

"Wh…what son?" Sarah shook her head.

"I said, would you please pass me some more taters," Josh repeated.

"Yes, certainly. Would anyone like another pork chop?"

Finding no takers, Sarah decided to get her 'speech' over and done with. "Please listen up everyone. We've got to cut back on expenses, and food is one area we can control. We won't be having meat for every meal for a while."

"No meat! Does that mean no bacon for breakfast? I can't face my day without bacon for breakfast," Zeke had tears in his eyes when he spoke.

"I believe you'll be able to hold body and soul together on oatmeal, biscuits and jam. I'll fix bacon for breakfast, just not every morning.

"We have plenty of canned vegetables to eat. There'll be fresh corn on the cob, tomatoes and squash come summer. No one will go hungry," Sarah said. "Sam, sorry but we'll be cutting back on coffee. I'll continue to make two pots a day, fresh in the morning, doctored to stretch in the evening."

"I expect that'll do me just fine, Ma'am. Won't be any harder on me than you," Sam replied.

"Ma, are we poor now 'cause we got sick chickens?" Luke looked as if he was going to cry.

"No, son, we aren't poor. We're short on cash money, but we're rich in the things in life that it can't buy, like family and friends and the love of God," Sarah reassured him.

"It's kinda hard to fry up a pan of God's love don't you think, Ma?" Abe said.

Sarah laid down her fork, picked up her napkin and blotted her lips. "Abe, I'll choose to assume you intended that to be a joke. You'll see that I'm not laughing. I'll not tolerate anyone making light of God's love for this family. I suggest that in the future you practice measuring your words before you let them escape your mouth."

"Sorry, Ma. I'm just feelin' worried, what with the chickens dying off and all," Abe said with his head hung low.

"I don't want anyone to be worrying about money. We'll be just fine. It isn't going to hurt us to tighten up a bit on our spending."

Oblivious to the table's conversation Hathaway held up her plate and said, "Mo, peze."

Sarah dished out another serving of mashed potatoes to the baby who was sitting between her and Sam. Sarah felt a ping at her heart stings when Sam reached over and brushed a straggling strand of hair from the child's face.

*Sam, please do the right thing and tell me about Abe's fight.*

# Chapter 27

The next day Sarah was making bread when Sam knocked lightly on the kitchen's door. Without altering the rhythm of her kneading she called out, "come in." Just moments before she'd glanced at the clock. It was ten o'clock and she was anticipating Sam's arrival for his mid-morning coffee.

In keeping with their morning routine Sarah had set out a mug for Sam. He fetched it and poured himself a cup of rich brew. As he was placing the coffee pot on the stove's back burner he breathed in the aroma of the bread Sarah already had baking in the oven. "Ma'am, when you announced that as part of the cost cut-back you'd be switching to sour dough instead of yeast bread, I'll admit I felt a twinge of sadness. But you know, I haven't missed it a bit. That bread you've got bakin' smells mighty fine."

"Your timing's perfect. Those loaves are due to come out and I've got three more ready to put in. Scoot out from in front of the stove so I can make the exchange."

With quick strides Sam made his way to the table and took a seat. "Ma'am, I don't want to interrupt your mornin's work, but I've got myself a dilemma that I need to discuss with you."

Sarah placed a saucer holding a steaming hot slab of bread in front of Sam and laid a knife alongside. She took a seat and pushed the crock of butter from center table toward him. "Tell me about your dilemma, I've got time to listen."

Sam generously slathered butter on the bread. "Last night when Abe and I were milkin' he told me in confidence about his fight. He needed to talk about it, but he didn't want to burden you."

Sarah leaned back in her chair and crossed her arms. "Abe told me he was sent home from school early yesterday because he got in a scrap with Ernie Brown. From the look of his injuries, I'd say it was an all-out fisticuffs rather than a scrap."

"Yes, Ma'am, I'll give you that."

"How about you give me the entire story."

"Ma'am, I hate to break the boy's trust in me."

"Sam, you're right, you do have a dilemma. You can break Abe's trust and tell me, or you can hold his confidence and loose mine."

Sam's brows knit as he sat taller, making his back ram-rod straight. "If you're gonna put it that way, *Sarah*, I guess I've got no choice but to tell you. But I want you to know that it grieves me to break the boy's confidence."

"If it helps any, I won't let him know that you told me."

"I'd be much obliged," Sam's face relaxed as he leaned in toward Sarah. "The truth is they were fighting about you."

"I suspected as much. Go on, tell me the rest."

"Ma'am, it's kind of a delicate issue. I don't want to offend your…uh, feminine side."

Sarah matched Sam's posture by leaning in and placing clasped hands on the table. "Sam, I appreciate you wanting to be discreet, but I need to hear it all. Just spit it out, we've both got chores to get to."

"The Brown boy said he overheard his parent's talkin' about you. They were sayin' that you were stupid for lettin' your husband back in your bed and gettin' you pregnant. Apparently they said that you already have enough children to care for without addin' another one to the bunch."

"Well, that's about as delicate as it gets."

"Yes, Ma'am it is. My apologies if I embarrassed you with the tellin'."

"No apology needed, Sam, I asked you to tell me. I owe you an apology for pulling you into the situation. You didn't hire on to be in the middle of such as this."

"No, Ma'am, reckon I didn't."

Sarah shook her head. "I'm so sorry Ernie heard his parents discussing my business. He's still a boy and needs sheltering from such talk just as much as my Abe does. I'm not surprised that Ernie spread the gossip, nor that Abe felt he needed to defend me. I'll have to figure out a way to broach the subject with Abe. There'll likely be more gossip and I can't have him taking on the whole town."

"What about the Browns? Aren't you gonna go give them 'what for' over them talkin' about you like that?"

"Sam, they were talking in the privacy of their own home. Besides, if I took on trying to still every wagging tongue, I'd die under the weight of the burden. People who want to talk, will talk. Not much I can do about it. Abe needs to come to that realization too. Living life can bring many opportunities for battle. A wise person learns to pick and choose, 'cause you can't fight them all."

"Ma'am, don't it hurt you to know folks are talking about your personal business?"

"I don't like it, that's a fact. It can't hurt me unless I let it get under my skin where it can fester. I won't let that happen. The Bible tells us to turn the other cheek when we're wronged. I can do that in this instance. God's word, Luke 6:28 also tells us to 'Bless them that curse you, and pray for them which despitefully use you.' I can do that too. I'll pray for Ernie and his parents."

"Ma'am, I don't reckon I've ever met anyone quite like you. I just don't see how you can take all that's happened to you without giving up hope."

"The Bible, Lamentations 3:23, says 'Great is His faithfulness; His mercies begin afresh each morning'. Because I believe that scripture and have faith, I can end each day with hope for a brighter tomorrow. I learned a long time ago to trust in God's faithfulness."

Sam ran his hand through his hair and shook his head. "Ma'am, I guess I don't understand the meaning of faith. When folks say, *I've got faith, or you need to have faith,* it comes off to me as something high and mighty they're spouting and has no practical meaning in life."

Sarah grabbed a kitchen towel and took the last batch of bread out of the oven.

"For me, faith means that when circumstances require me to hop off of my comfortable perch, and leap into the unknown, I'm going to sprout wings and fly, or God's going to catch my fall. Either way, I'm in His care."

Sam rose and fetched his hat and jacket that he'd hung by the door. "I'd like to have faith like that."

Sarah dumped the loaves from their baking pans on to her wooden work table. "The faith is there just for the accepting, Sam. If you'd like, I could share some more scriptures with you and we could pray together."

"Much obliged, Ma'am, but I got me some dead chickens to bury and some fence mendin' to do."

"Perhaps another time. What's the count stand at now? Any sign that we're finished with the spread of the infection?"

"Yes, Ma'am, I think the worst is over. I haven't found any newly

177

infected pullets for several days now. The number of dead each morning has continued to drop. Only two today. I'm thinkin' we might make it through with near two-thirds or a little less of the flock intact. That's better than I feared when they first started dying off."

"What do we do next?"

"Once we go three days runnin' without any more dead and no signs of the sickness, we'll empty the chicken house, clean and disinfect it. After that we'll pull the flock together again and go on about our business. With luck we might have us some layers in another eight to ten weeks."

"I sure hope your predictions come true. That bank payment at the end of the year is looming heavy over my head. God's got his hands full seeing us through this rough spot. Like I said, I've got faith all will be well but my spirits would lift considerably knowing how it's going to work out."

\*\*\*

A couple of weeks had passed since Abe's fight with Ernie Brown. During her morning quiet time Sarah reflected on the talk she'd had with her son about picking his battles. Remembering Abe's response brought a smile to her face. *"Ma, you don't want me to turn into a lily livered yellow belly do you?"* Sarah realized that with his pa gone, he likely considered himself the family's protector.

When she knelt in prayer she lifted her lingering concern about the conflict between her son and his school mate. *Dear Lord, please help Abe with his temper. He's a proud boy and he won't shy away from what he feels is his responsibility. I ask that you fill him with the wisdom he needs to make good decisions. And Lord…as an added precaution, please help the Brown's keep their mouths shut when it comes to our family's business.* Her advice aside, Sarah doubted Abe would take any more lip from Ernie Brown. She hoped her prayers for both of the boys would intercede and prevent further violence.

As Sarah rose from her kneeling position the methodic ticking of the Regulator hanging on her bedroom wall caught her attention. *It's nearly eight-thirty. I'd best get a hurry on.*

It was a Thursday morning and the women at the Methodist Church were gathering at ten o'clock. The wife of a missionary couple who'd recently returned from Africa was scheduled to give a talk. Sarah was eager to hear how God was using this couple for His work in a place so far away and different from her own culture.

It was a warm spring morning and Sarah selected a maternity frock with lavender flowers on a cream background. It had been her favorite when she carried Hathaway. Pregnancy suited Sarah and the contrast of the dress's fabric against her auburn hair gave her an enviable radiance.

The pies Sarah had baked early that morning, two apple and one peach, cooled in the pie safe. She'd take one of the apple pies to share at the luncheon. The peach and the other apple pie would be for their supper that night.

Since she wouldn't be at the farm to prepare dinner for Sam she placed two large pieces of fatback between slabs of bread on a plate, covered it with a kitchen towel and set it on the table. Feeling a tad guilty about the meager provision of sustenance for her hired hand, she cut a double size piece of their supper's apple pie and left it alongside the meat sandwich.

Zeke clutched his prized miniature wagon and Hathaway had her rag doll tucked under her chubby arm when Sarah lifted them into the wagon. The church kept a box with wooden blocks and various and sundry toys for children's distraction at such events. Other mothers would be bringing their children who were too young for school. Sarah hoped the toys and playmates would be enough to keep her two entertained while the missionary spoke. Her mother was also attending and would help keep them corralled if needed.

Sarah arrived at the church just as her mother's rig pulled in. They hitched their horses side by side, making sure there was enough slack in their tethers to allow them to drink from the water trough.

Mother and daughter entered a nearly filled room. A place was arranged in one corner for young children to play. Sarah instructed Zeke to keep an eye on his sister, share his wagon and keep as quiet as possible.

While Sarah got the children situated, Mary scouted out two side by side seats. She gave her daughter an 'I'm sorry' look when she motioned for Sarah to come take the second row from the front, third in seat next to her. A good seat, except for one thing. Sarah would be sitting with her mother on one side and Ernestine Brown, Ernie Brown's mother, on the other.

Ernestine was a dour looking woman, thin beyond what was becoming.

She had stringy mouse brown hair and eyes that were set close together. Her mouth most often formed a frown that coupled with her sour disposition left her sorely lacking in beauty.

*Dear Lord in Heaven, give me strength.* Sarah whispered in her head as she took her seat and settled her hands across her much protruding lap. "Good morning, Ernestine," Sarah proffered as a greeting she hoped was warmer than she felt.

With a pious smile on her pinched face, Ernestine whispered a venomous response intended to lay Sarah low. "You've got some nerve showing yourself here today. After what your son did to mine, and in your condition, you'd think you'd have the decency to stay home with that brood of yours."

Deciding not to acknowledge what Ernestine said, Sarah sat quietly. *Ok Lord, I just took it on the other cheek and the first blow still smarts. Enough…please!*

Ernestine struck again, "are you too ashamed of yourself to respond to me or is it that you lack the common decency to be civil?"

Ernestine's comments had been overheard by Mary. Among the Riley clan, Mary was affectionately referred to as the family's little spit-fire. One slap on the cheek of anyone in her family was her limit. She subscribed to the notion that turning the other cheek simply left one with a red face. "Sarah dear, would you please exchange seats with me."

"Ma, don't make it worse," Sarah said as she complied while thinking, *Ernestine, oh Ernestine, did you have to give a malicious encore?*

Now seated next to Ernestine, Mary whispered in the woman's ear. "Ernestine, I don't recall any of us making snide comments to you when, long before Jasper Brown put a ring on your finger, you came to worship Sunday after Sunday with your belly growing faster than Jack's bean stalk."

"Well I never!" Ernestine gasped.

"Ohhhh, yes you did! My Tom and I were traveling down Hog's Back road and happened on to you in Jasper's wagon. It was rockin' and your mouse brown head of hair was bobbin'." Mary patted Ernestine's hand, "It would serve you well to brush up on the Golden Rule principle, my dear."

"Welcome, ladies," greeted the Women's Society President. "We're happy to have all of you here today. Before we invite the missionary up to talk, let's all turn to page eighty-nine in the hymnal and sing *Jesus, Savior, Pilot Me.*"

"Ernestine," Mary said with a smile as she held up her hymnal to share with the now chagrinned, speechless woman who stood at her side.

# Chapter 28

Doc Adams escorted his last patient of the day to the door. "Trust me, Mrs. Pilgrim, in a day or two this fussing and crying will stop. Little Ruthie will reward you with one of her sweet smiles and she'll be sporting her first tooth."

"I surely hope you're right, Doc I don't recall my other babies havin' such a rough time cuttin' their teeth. My mister and my other two youngins' said if you couldn't cure her from this cryin' I should just leave her with you until she's in better spirits."

"It's the first tooth that seems to give the most misery to child as well as parent. As I said, in a day or two this trouble will pass. In the meantime just let her have one of your wooden cooking spoons to chew on. It'll help that tooth cut through the gum. Once that happens her pain will ease."

"Thanks, Doc Adams. How much do I owe ya?"

"No charge today. Go on home and tell your husband I said he should tend to the baby for a couple of hours and let you get some rest. You look like you're about to drop with fatigue."

"I don't expect there's much chance of that happenin'. Reckon I can hang in there a couple more days. This can't be no picnic for my little one either." Molly Pilgrim gave the baby a kiss on the top of her fuzz-covered head.

As Ben stood at his window watching mother carry child down the walk to their waiting horse and buggy, he saw Marshal Carter ride past on his horse. Ben had been waiting all week for Jeb Carter to get back from his trip to Howard County. Jeb's in-laws lived in a small town near Kokomo and he and Mrs. Carter had gone there to tend to her ailing parents. While they were there, Jeb promised Doc he'd do some checking in Kokomo to see if he could get more detailed information about Sam Hartman's past. Jeb had told Ben that at Sarah's request, he had made cursory inquiries about Sam by telephone before she hired him. Nothing untoward had surfaced. With Ben and Jeb both having nettling reservations about Sam, the pair decided an attempt to dig deeper into his past was needed.

The doctor knew his own motives weren't entirely honorable. He did worry about Sarah and the children and their safety. Sam Hartman hadn't shared much at all about his past when Doc was introduced to him. Why would he? They weren't friends.

On an intellectual level he realized that what he was feeling was jealousy more than real concern. He was jealous over Sam's accessibility to Sarah while he slept in her parlor. On an emotional level Ben couldn't help feeling threatened by Sam's good looks and farming abilities.

Emotions trumped intellect. Ben grabbed his coat and hightailed it to the Marshal's office. By the time Ben reached his destination he had reasoned that as Sarah's friend he might actually have a responsibility to find out if Sam had a skeleton or two hidden in his closet. And Jeb, well wasn't Jeb Carter best friends with Henry Whitcome before he became ill? Add all of that up and some might consider Jeb and him derelict in their duty if they didn't check on Sam's past.

Marshal Carter was standing in the threshold of his office reading several messages he'd found tacked on the door. He flinched when Ben tapped him on the back. "Jumpin' Jehoshaphat, Doc, ya scared the daylights out of me. I just rode in to town and was fixin' to come to your place once I got a fire built in the stove and read my messages." The Marshal swatted his left palm with the papers he held in his right hand. "Got me several complaints about a black dog killin' chickens. Some say they've spotted a black Labrador that appears to be a stray. Likely it's the culprit."

"I saw you ride by my office," Ben said, "I'm anxious to hear if you found out anything about Sam Hartman when you went to Kokomo."

Jeb rested his back on the door jam and folded his arms. "Sam's well liked around those parts. The town's law was as mum as a deaf mute when it came to Sam's business. They knew him well enough but said they didn't feel obliged to talk about the man behind his back. They asked if I had any official provocation behind my inquiry and I had to be truthful that I didn't. Sam hasn't broken any laws here in LaFontaine or Wabash County for that matter. I explained my relationship to the woman Hartman works for, but that wasn't enough to prime the pump for any meaningful flow of information.

Ben threw his arms open wide, "so you're telling me you didn't find out anything?"

"Hold your scalpel, Doc, I'm gettin' to it. It took some doin'. I finally got the Howard County Sheriff to give me the truth about Sam's past."

"Don't leave me in suspense, man, what did you find out?"

Jeb dropped his relaxed stance and walked back into his office, closing the door after Ben entered. "It's big. You best sit yourself down for the tellin'."

Ben took a seat in the chair directly in front of the Marshal's desk. Jeb stoked the stove's fire then went about making a pot of coffee. "I've been on the road all day and my tail's a draggin'. I got to have me a cup of coffee. You want one?"

"Forget the coffee! What did you find out?"

"Doc, I *said* I'd get to it!" Jeb filled the coffee pot with water, added grounds then set it on the top of the stove. "In his early twenties, Sam Hartman spent three years in Pendleton State prison for manslaughter."

Ben leaped from his seat. "Are you telling me that Sarah's hired hand killed someone?"

Jeb motioned for Doc to sit back down. "He was convicted of involuntary manslaughter. He didn't intend to kill the man, it was an accident."

"What do you mean by accident…like a logging accident or horse race gone bad? What?"

"It was a fist fight. The man that was killed had a reputation for being a troublemaker. He was drunk and it seems he was making unwanted advances to a young woman who had just come out of the general store. Sam rode up and was tethering his horse when the exchange between the hooligan and the woman took place. Sam stepped in to defend the woman's honor, the drunk wouldn't back off and Sam slugged him. The man fell backwards, cracked his head on the water trough and died."

"It sounds like an accident pure and simple." Ben scratched his head, "How did Sam end up in prison when he was just trying to do something honorable?"

"The guy he hit was the mayor's son. The mayor got some of his cronies to testify that Sam caught his son off guard and didn't give him a chance to step down from the fight, let alone defend himself. There was testimony to support Sam's side of the story but when it was brought to light that the woman Sam defended was a barmaid at the local tavern, the jury voted to convict Sam of manslaughter. The mayor pulled in some favors with the judge and Sam got the maximum sentence, three years."

Ben shook his head, "It might well have been an accident but Sarah needs to know what you've found out. What about her pa? Don't you think we ought to tell him, too?" Ben jumped up from the chair. "Jeb, your tail might be dragging, but this can't wait until tomorrow."

*** 

Sam was walking from the barn to the house when he saw Elmo Jones coming up the lane with the day's mail delivery. The hired hand was ready for a coffee break so he decided to intercept Elmo and hand carry the mail to the house.

"Howdy. How's it goin'?" Elmo greeted. "Looks like ya got yourself some mail today Sam. I got a piece or two for Mrs. Whitcome too."

"I'll take it to her, I was just going in for a cup of coffee."

"I'm catchin' me a whiff of fresh baked apple pie a comin' out that kitchen winder over yonder. I was thinkin' I might make me a special delivery today, see if I can snag me some pie."

Sam knew full well it wasn't pie Elmo was hoping to snag. He'd watched Elmo make many flirtatious overtures toward Sarah in the couple of months he'd been working on the Whitcome farm. Sam suspected that Sarah found the quirky little mailman somewhat annoying. Elmo was completely oblivious to the fact. Why wouldn't he be? Sarah was always kind, cheerful and polite to everyone. Habitually on guard with her himself, Sam made a study of the subtle nuances that sometimes belied her hospitable manner. He'd come to know when something or someone grated on her and Elmo Jones was clearly someone who rubbed her the wrong way.

When the two reached the house Sam called out through the screen door to Sarah who was working in the kitchen. "Elmo's here with the mail. Mind if I get a cup of coffee to take outside? A letter came for me. I thought I'd read it while I take a short break."

"Help yourself, Sam. The coffee pot's on the back of the stove and should still be hot."

"Howdy, Mrs. Whitcome, got a special delivery for ya today." The stubble faced mail carrier spit a stream of tobacco over his left shoulder and followed Sam through the screen door.

"Yoder's Seed Catalogue and the Poultry Monthly," Sarah said as she took the two pieces of mail from the short little man. "Where's the special delivery, Elmo?"

"They's all special deliveries when I bring them to your door, Ma'am."

"Thank you, but you could have left them in the mailbox or sent them in with Sam."

"I heard a slice of that hot apple pie callin' my name and I just couldn't resist bringin' the mail to the door my own self."

Sarah smiled, "Elmo, my pies are good, but I've never heard them talk. Sit down and I'll cut you a piece. I can't visit long. I've got a lot of work to do before this day ends."

Sam took his cup of coffee and sat under the shade of the maple tree to read his letter. It was from his old employer, Clem Hargrove.

> "Dear Sam,
>
> It troubles me to write this letter to you. The last time you wrote me it sounded like you was doing quite well there on the Whitcome farm. The Mrs. and I so hoped you had found a place where you would be happy.
>
> I'll get right to it. The LaFontaine Town Marshal was here in Kokomo yesterday asking a lot of questions about your past. No one to my knowledge told him anything but good about you. The problem is, he told Leonard Sheline he was going to stop by the County Sheriff's office before he left town. Sheriff Townsend is an all business kind of man. He might have told your Marshal about your past troubles.
>
> Hope it don't cause you no difficulties with the woman you're working for. If you haven't told her about your time in prison, now might be a good time to do that. Best she hears it from you rather than from your town's Marshal.
>
> God's Blessing on you Sam.
>
> > Your friend,
> > Clem Hargove

Sam folded the letter and put it in his pocket. Since the postmark on the letter from Clem, Sarah hadn't been to town and Jeb Carter hadn't been to the farm. *There's a chance Carter didn't find out anything about me while he was in Kokomo. If he did, he hasn't had a chance to tell Sarah unless he got back on Saturday and told her at Sunday service yesterday.*

Sam knew that his intentions had been good when he defended the woman's honor that day. Trouble was, all the good intentions in the world wouldn't bring the man he killed back to life. Having Sarah find out he had spent time in prison was going to be hard to bear. Having her find out he had killed another human being was near intolerable.

*I've never been able to forgive myself for what happened. How can I expect Sarah to accept that she has a killer working on her farm? I don't relish having to leave here. Sarah and the children have become like family to me. This farm gives me hope. If I work hard I might make a difference and in a small way atone for my past. How can I face her? How do I tell her?* Sam cradled his head in his hands. *The only thing worse would be having her find out from Marshal Carter.*

The postman was gone, the boys weren't home from school so now was as good a time as any for him to tell Sarah.

With the weight of his heavy burden bearing down, Sam rose from the shade of the maple tree, brushed off the back of his pants and walked to the kitchen door.

"Mrs. Whitcome, I'd like to have a word with you if you've got a minute."

"I do if we can talk while I knead this bread. Come on in and pour yourself another cup of coffee. Tell me, what's on your mind."

"Mrs. Whitcome…"

"Sam, you're scaring me with the *Mrs. Whitcome* formality. We've long past moved on to first name use. If it's bad news you're about to give me, make it quick. I can't stand the suspense.

In a flood of non-stop words Sam told Sarah about his conviction for manslaughter and his three years incarceration at Pendleton State prison. When he was done he said, "If you want me to pack up and leave, I'll understand."

"Sam Hartman, do you think I would give a strange man living quarters in my parlor without checking out his background first? I knew all about your trouble with the law before I hired you."

Sam's knees threatened to buckle, he pulled a chair from the table and sat down. "How, how did you know?"

"I asked Jeb Carter to find out about you when you applied for my hired hand position. He made some telephone inquiries, spoke to the Kokomo Town Marshal, and didn't hear anything but good. With the children to protect and me being alone here on the farm I took it a step further and asked my pastor, Ed Sloan, to inquire about you, too. He wrote to Byron Alcorn, the minister at the Free Will Baptist Church in Kokomo. You mentioned in your application letter that you had attended church there. Pastor Alcorn was reluctant, but did tell my minister about your past. Given the gravity of the news, Pastor Sloan told me."

"I'm surprised you hired me after finding out."

"Pastor Sloan explained the circumstances related to your conviction. He said most folks felt you weren't treated fairly and that your sentence was much too harsh considering what had occurred. He told me that you had attended church every Sunday until you got sent to prison. He said after you got out you seemed bitter and drifted away from attending church."

"Prison was hard. It changes a man," Sam said.

"I figured as much, Sam. After praying about it I felt comfortable with applying God's grace to your situation and hire you."

"I'm sure your minister didn't agree with that decision."

"Actually he was in full support. A pastor isn't worth much if he preaches forgiveness and grace from the pulpit, but doesn't practice it."

"I've exchanged howdy doo's with preacher Sloan several times when I've passed him in town. He never so much as gave a hint he knew about me."

"He and I have held the details of your past in confidence. We agreed it was your story to tell, if and when you felt the need."

"Ma'am, I can't tell you how relieved that makes me feel. I wish I had told you from the beginning about my scrape with the law. It would have saved me from many a sleepless night."

"Sam, the skills and background you wrote about in your application letter were what I needed. You've been true to your word and reputation on that score. I've been and continue to be pleased with our working relationship."

"Thanks, Ma'am,…uh, Sarah. I really like working here on your farm."

"Good. Now that we've got this all out in the open do you think you might try getting a good night's sleep without drinking from that jug you keep hidden in your room?"

Sam's face turned three shades of red, each darker than the one before. "How did you know?"

"I didn't know until you just now told me. I did have my suspicions. Sour mash has a distinctive odor. I've occasionally detected the scent of it when passing by your door."

"I know you don't hold with drinking ma'am."

"No, I don't like what liquor does to a man and I told you I wouldn't tolerate drinking when you hired on."

"Why haven't you said anything about it?"

"By the time I suspected you likely were taking a nip now and then you'd already proved to be a great asset to the farm. I prayed about it and God and I decided we'd just keep a close eye on you. If the drinking started to interfere with your work or if you ever seemed under the influence of alcohol we'd have to let you go. Thankfully that hasn't happened."

"Ma'am, have you ever made a decision without first discussing it with God?"

"I haven't for a very long time. I can't even fathom tying to carry the load of the family and the farm without His help. God is faithful and true and that applies not just to me, but also to anyone who calls on Him. I'm praying for you Sam Hartman. I'm praying that you will be able to let go of the bitterness you hold against God for being incarcerated. God didn't let you down, Sam, man did."

"I know you believe that, Ma'am, but it's hard for me to agree with you. Why would God allow me to be left with this never ending pain from taking another human's life?"

"Sam, you've saddled yourself with that pain, not God. God forgives and in the forgiving He forgets it even happened."

"How can you believe that?"

"I believe because the scripture tells me so. Psalms 103:3 says, *He forgives all my sins.* Verse 12 says, *As far as the east is from the west, so far hath He removed our transgressions from us.*"

The sound of horses galloping up the lane interrupted their conversation.

They looked out the window to see Jeb Carter accompanied by Sarah's pa and Ben Adams dismounting and tethering their horses.

"Ma'am, I think I know why you're getting' company. I got a letter today from my old employer and he said that Marshal Carter was in Kokomo a few days ago asking questions about my past. I'm guessing with him bringing along Doc Adams and your pa, he found out."

Sarah sighed and pushed an errant strand of hair off of her brow with the back of her hand. "I suspect you're right, Sam." She used her apron to wipe both hands free of flour before extending one to Sam in a gesture of solidarity. "Don't worry, I'll handle them."

Sam reached out his hand and the two shook. His eyes were moist when he said,

"I'd best get back to my work, Ma'am."

"Yes, that would be a good idea. I'll do the same once I get shed of this latest group of visitors."

# Chapter 29

*Sarah opened the kitchen door to greet her entourage of guests. Sam quickly scooted past her and out the door before the trio reached the stoop. He gave a curt greeting to the men and made his way toward the barn.*

"To what do I owe the pleasure of this visit, gentlemen?" Sarah said as she welcomed her pa with a hug and the others with a smile. "Sit down. Could I interest you in a cup of coffee and a piece of warm apple pie?"

Tom put his arm around his daughter. "Sarah, dear, we haven't come to pay a social call."

Jeb held his hat and fidgeted with the brim. "We've got some worrisome information for you, Sarah, and we thought it best if we came together to give it to you."

Ben took a step toward Sarah, caught himself and stopped. "Sarah, we're here out of concern for your welfare and the children's."

Sarah pulled her shoulders back and put her hands on her hips. "Well you best get to sharing this worrisome information then because I had no inkling that my family's welfare was at risk."

Jeb was the first to take a seat at Sarah's kitchen table. "It's about your hired hand's past."

Sarah folded her arms over her protruding mound and stood as tall as her condition would allow. "If you've come to tell me that Sam spent three years in prison for involuntary manslaughter, you could have saved yourselves the trip. I know that. I knew it when I hired him."

Doc and Tom stared at her, eyes and mouths opened wide. Jeb reared back so hard his chair almost toppled backward as he spoke. "How did you know when I didn't? The first time I checked on Sam, nothing turned up. This week I did some further investigating and that's when I found out."

Sarah's father stammered, "Gi...Girl, do you mean to tell us that you knew and still hired him?"

"Yes, Pa, that's right. Sam was just in here confessing his past to me. When I told him I already knew, he said almost the same thing, couldn't believe I hired him."

Jeb righted his chair, "So how did you find out, Sarah?"

"Jeb, it was shared to me in confidence. Suffice it to say, it came from a trustworthy source. After hearing the circumstances behind Sam's troubles and given that he had long since paid his debt to society, I didn't feel his past was cause for concern. I prayed about the situation. I felt God was leading me to take a step in faith and hire him."

"Sarah, why didn't you tell your ma and me? You must know that we worry about you," Tom said.

"I do know you worry, Pa. That's exactly the reason I didn't tell you. I didn't feel there was cause for concern and I didn't want you and Ma taking on the burden of worrying about who I hired."

Tom Riley ran his hands roughly across his face and through his hair. "You said Sam was just in here confessing to you. What prompted him to do that at this late date?"

"He got a letter today from his old employer telling him that Jeb was in Kokomo making inquiries about Sam's past. The man felt that their town folks would be discreet about what they told to an outsider, but that the County Sheriff wouldn't if Jeb made contact with him. Clem wrote Sam to encourage him to tell me before someone else did."

Sarah set about serving coffee and pie to the three men and then took a seat herself. "Let's look at the good side of this situation. Sam has worked hard since coming to the farm. We've started the egg production business. With his help we've made it through a difficult infestation of Roup and it looks like what's left of the flock is going to thrive. He's held up his end of this employment bargain and I don't feel I owe any explanation for my decision to hire him."

Jeb reached for the sugar bowl. "So you're not going to tell us who told you about Sam's past?"

"No, Jeb. I was told in confidence and that's where it will stay. As I said, Sam's paid his debt to society and he no longer has any issues with the law."

With a grimace Ben Adams shook his head. "So does this mean that Sam's going to go right on living here in your house with you and the children?"

"Yes," Sarah replied. "This living arrangement will continue until I have funds to build a proper bunkhouse."

Sarah's father reached over and took her hand in his. "Sarah sometimes I think you're so heavenly minded that you ignore earthly woes."

"Don't worry, Pa. With God's help I feel confident I've got a handle on things. I truly do appreciate the concern from all of you. I pray you each will respect my walk in faith when it comes to Sam and that you will also accept him as a man who has much to contribute. God has forgiven Sam. But Sam is on a path searching for the courage to forgive himself and to accept God's grace. That won't happen if he feels condemnation from this community. If others find out about Sam's past, let's let him be the one who does the telling."

As the three men rose to take their leave Marshal Carter said, "On another issue, Sarah, be on the lookout for a large black Labrador. A stray one's been seen around lately. There's been a couple of instances of chickens being killed and that dog is my prime suspect. If you see him lurking about, let me know."

"Thanks for the warning, Jeb," Sarah said. "I'll tell the children and Sam. The last thing I need is the loss of more chickens."

***

Supper that night for the Whitcome crew was a light repast, compared to the bounty Sarah usually served. A modest portion of beef stew with mostly potatoes and carrots accompanied by a slice of bread was it. In truth it was enough to provide sustenance, but that didn't stop complaints.

"Ma, when are we gonna stop bein' poor?" Zeke said with his mouth stuffed full of bread.

"Zeke, I know you're only four years old, but that don't make your complainin' any less rude," Abe said. "It's Tuesday and Ma always serves apple pie. You can eat a big slice of that and get filled to the brim."

When Sarah served only middling sized portions of pie the griping started up again.

"Ma, this slice of pie ain't big enough to fill a bird's belly. Why are ya serving us such small pieces?" Zeke whined.

"What with serving a piece to the postman, and then to your grandpa Riley, Marshal Carter and Doc Adams, there just wasn't enough pie left for usual sized portions." Sarah licked pie filling off her fingers, the only taste of the fruit of her labors she allowed herself.

"Why was Grandpa Riley and them here today?" Josh asked.

Sarah cut a look at Sam who sat expectantly waiting for her response.

"Marshal Carter wanted us to know about a stray dog that he thinks is moving among the farms killing chickens. He said he suspects it's a black Labrador. He wants us to let him know if we see one."

"If I see me a dog I'm keepin' it for a pet," Zeke said as he picked up his plate and licked it clean of every trace of apple pie.

"Me too!" Josh chimed in. "We been wantin' us a dog for a long time, Ma. I hear tell Labradors are smart. We could train it to fetch and teach it to stay away from our chickens."

Sam folded his napkin and laid it across his empty plate. "Josh, once a dog takes to killin' chickens it's likely he won't stop. They get a taste for the meat and it becomes more than they can resist. Sadly when that happens the dog usually needs to be put down."

"Ya mean it has to be kilt?" Zeke asked in a dubious tone.

"Yeah, dummy, 'put down' means killed," Josh spat out, punching Zeke on the shoulder.

Sarah poured Sam a refill of weak coffee. "Josh, don't speak that way to your brother and keep your hands to yourself."

Josh folded his arms and hung his head so low his chin touched his chest.

"Sorry, Ma. Sorry, Zeke. It just makes me mad to hear about killin' dogs when we need us one."

\*\*\*

At school the next day Josh was caught talking when he was supposed to be doing his ciphering. The punishment for the nine year old was to stay after school and wash down the blackboard.

The sun hung low as he made his way home. Alone in his walk he kept thinking about that stray black Labrador that Marshal Carter was looking for. He imagined what it would be like to have a dog. He pictured the animal lying at his feet while the family ate their meals. He'd train the dog not to beg for food. Of course he'd slip it a bite or two, not enough to be noticed. He'd teach it to fetch and do other tricks. He felt sure that if he loved the dog enough and explained to it that the chickens were to be left alone, the dog would comply. A Labrador would be different than other dogs that got themselves a taste of chicken.

A patch of black in his peripheral vision caught Josh's attention. He turned to see a slow paced movement through the tall reeds of prairie grass not far from where he stood. Instinctively Josh knew it was the sought after Labrador. The dog changed pace to a crawl and then stopped.

Josh cautiously reached in his lunch pail and extracted a crust of bread left from his lunch. He knelt down and calmed his breathing so his body made only a whisper of movement. Holding the offering in the palm of his hand he reached out to the animal.

"Come here, boy. I got somethin' for ya."

The dog didn't move. Josh continued to softly coo and coax. The animal stood and began to whine. Saliva fell from its mouth in droplets on the dry grass. The Labrador began a slow creep toward the food.

The dog reached the kneeling boy and stood snout to nose with him. The canine extended his large pink tongue and consumed the bread in one seamless motion then stared at his benefactor with pleading eyes.

"You're really hungry ain't ya, big fellow. Come with me."

Josh guided the dog toward the farm and a dilapidated shed on the outer perimeter of their large garden plot. The building lay on the northwest side of the farmstead, a far view from the house. The dog was big, nearly waist high next to the boy. As they walked, Josh occasionally reached down and stroked the animal's coat. He could feel the ripple of its muscles beneath the thick black fur. The dog reciprocated by nudging the boy's hip with his large head.

The shed's side boarding was rotting but the door's latch still worked. Josh opened the door and the pair entered. The boy knelt down, encircled the animal's neck with his arms, buried his face in its coat and whispered. "You stay here and keep quiet. I'll be back directly with some food."

Josh bent low as he approached the house then crouched beneath the kitchen window. He slowly rose and peeked in to see if anyone was in the room. Finding it empty he snuck through the door. Using his shirt as a sling he filled it with remnants of the noonday meal left on the sideboard, a slab of fatback and a hunk of cornbread.

He stopped by Zeke's dirt pile and confiscated his bucket. Josh primed the pump one handed. He gave the vessel a quick rinse and filled it with water. Still crouched low, he duck walked back to the shed and the waiting dog.

The animal gobbled the food and drank his fill from the pail of water. Josh stayed by its side as long as he dared. His chores were waiting for him. If he didn't get to them, someone would come looking for him. He gave the dog a parting hug. "Now you've been fed and you've got plenty of water. Don't be a thinkin' about gettin' out of here and goin' after chickens."

***

The discussion at supper that night was the elusive black Labrador. Sam had made a trip into town for fencing supplies. Continued attacks on chickens, perpetrated by a large black dog, was a hotly discussed topic. Sam shared the news with the Whitcomes. "That *dad-burned* dog has killed so many chickens some of the farmers got together and put a bounty on his head."

The expletive caused Sarah to cut a look at Sam.

"Sorry, Ma'am. Guess I got carried away with the excitement over the rogue dog. Us having chickens and all."

Before Sarah could respond Zeke blurted out. "Luke, pass me some more of them *dad-burned* potatoes and make it quick."

Sarah threw up her hands. "Zeke, that wasn't a polite request and don't say dad-burned. It's means damn and that's cussing, which you know I won't tolerate."

"Gee, Mom. Sam just done said it."

Sarah nodded toward Sam. "Yes he did and he apologized."

"I truly am sorry, Ma'am," Sam said, looking at Sarah with puppy-dog eyes. "Do I still get a piece of that rhubarb pie I smelled when I came to the table?"

Sarah covered her mouth with her napkin to hide her grin. "Yes, since you apologized you may have a piece, a small piece."

Abe reached for a slab of bread. "How much is the bounty? Will it pay dead or alive?"

Sam laid his fork on his plate and leaned in, elbows on the table. "They're offerin' two dollars, dead or alive with proof of it bein' the right dog."

With eyes as big as saucers Josh said, "None of ya ain't seen no black dogs around here have ya?"

Abe slathered jam on his bread. "Not yet, but you can bet I'll be lookin'. I could put that bounty money to good use."

In an uncharacteristic gesture, Josh offered to help his mother clear the table. The boy diligently collected every morsel of unconsumed food the totality of which didn't much more than fill a coffee cup. When Sarah wasn't looking he hid it down in his left boot. The pair were on the floor by the back door. "Ma, could we have us some popcorn before bed and maybe a slice or two of bread with jam?"

"Josh, didn't you get enough to eat at supper tonight?"

"Well, Ma, I am a growin' boy. I 'spect I might get hungry before bed time."

Sarah wiped her hands on her apron. "I guess I was forgetting how much a growing boy eats. By the way, were you the one who cleaned up the leftover food from today's dinner? I found the plate on the sideboard empty."

"Yes, Ma'am. I took the food."

"Son, please ask me first before taking food I have laid out. I might have been planning on using those leftovers to go with other food prepared for supper tonight."

"Sorry, Ma. What about popcorn, can we have us some tonight?"

Sarah ruffled her son's hair. "That's a nice idea, we'd all enjoy some popcorn later. Even the chickens will benefit. We can scatter any that's left over for them to find."

*Forget those 'dad-burned' chickens. I got me other plans for the left over popcorn.* Josh thought as he gave his mother a hug.

# Chapter 30

The overcast sky, void of moon and stars, shrouded the creature's dark coat to near total obscurity. Tall reeds of yellow foxtail made a faint whishing sound as the animal crept through, crossing the field that led to the chicken house. The beckoning scent grew stronger as the predator moved closer to the structure. The animal was consumed with desire, his need so intense he began to salivate.

The creature reached the building and circled twice looking for an opening. Finding none he began to dig at the earth near the foundation. As it dug it whined with anticipation over the treasure that lay within. As if sensing the danger, the chickens began to squawk and flap their wings. Rather than deterring, the racket excited the animal and he dug faster.

Abe was the first to be awakened by the ruckus. Groggy with sleep it took him a bit to realize where it came from and what the sound was. He quickly pulled on his pants and boots and ran down the stairs and out to the chicken house. The animal heard him coming and made his exit, but not quickly enough to avoid being spotted.

Sam, followed by Sarah, arrived on the scene just moments behind Abe. "What's got the chickens all excited? They're making enough noise to wake the dead," Sarah said, as she struggled to close her robe across her bulging belly.

"I don't know for sure. It might have been that black Lab. I saw a dark animal running away," Abe said.

Sam hoisted the lantern to shoulder height, casting a glow of light that illuminated a large section of the chicken house. "We best check the perimeter of the building and see if any damage has been done."

When the three walked to the backside of the chicken house they discovered the hole at the base of the building's foundation.

"Whew!" Sam exclaimed. "Whatever it was, it nearly breached the foundation with its diggin'".

Sarah put her arm around Abe. "Looks like you got here just in time, son."

The dark of the night disguised the blush on the boy's cheeks. "What're we gonna do? Can't leave a hole like this open," Abe said.

Sam pulled his left suspender up over his shoulder. In his rush to get dressed he'd left it dangling to the side of his pants. "You two go on back to bed and try to get a few more hours of sleep. I'll fill in this hole, build a fire and keep watch. Tomorrow I'll pack bales of hay around the foundation."

Sarah rubbed at the ache in the small of her back. She'd done laundry all day and her body needed more rest. "Bless you, Sam. Son, you go on back to bed now. You've got school tomorrow. See you both at breakfast in the morning."

Abe watched his mother walk back to the farmhouse, then said to Sam. "Wonder why the animal didn't go after the free-range hens instead of trying to dig into the chicken house?"

"The smell of all the chickens housed together likely caught the critter's attention over the free-rangers scattered hither and yon. This ain't done yet. Come dawn, we might find us a dead hen or two layin' around the farm."

"Why would the dog leave the chicken where it was killed?" Abe asked. "Looks like it would drag it off and eat it."

"When I said that a dog gets a 'taste' for killin' chickens, I wasn't referring to hunger. The taste is for just plain killin'. They never seem to get their fill. That's why there's no stoppin' them."

Abe, kicked a dirt clod and set it sailing. "If it has to nab any chickens, I hope it gets Luke's worthless, no good pet hens."

"Now, Abe, you don't really mean that. You know your brother would be heartbroken if Butterball or Buttercup were killed."

"Yeah, I guess you're right. It's just pitiful that a brother of mine has two chickens for pets. A snake or a lizard ain't snuggly but they make more sense. At least they're manly pets.

The boy started toward the house then stopped and turned. "Hey, Sam, thanks for keeping watch and lettin' me get some more shuteye."

"Glad to do it, boy. See you at mornin' chores."

***

The Labrador was restless as he tried to sleep in the drafty structure the boy had put him in. The sideboards to the building were loose. Using his snout he could easily push one of the planks to the side to allow exit and then re-entry. He was hungry. The mere pittance of food he'd been given late that afternoon had long since passed through his system leaving him empty and longing for something to eat. He'd been out once that night in search of sustenance without success. He laid down and tried to sleep. If hunger got the best of him, he'd go on the hunt again.

\*\*\*

As Abe approached the barn for morning chores he could see Sam off in the distance at the edge of the woods, west of the farmstead. He appeared to be digging. Abe jogged over to where Sam worked. "Good mornin', Sam. How'd it go last night? Why are you diggin'...?"

The boy's words trailed off. No explanation was needed when his eyes fell on the pile of dead chickens.

Sam raised his hand, palm out. "The new flock's safe and sound. These dead ones are free-range hens. They were roostin' last night on the backside of the barn. I heard the attack. By the time I got there these three were dead and I saw an animal chasing a fourth one off into that stand of trees yonder."

"Was it the black Labrador?"

"It had a dark coat and it looked like a dog to me. It could have been a coyote, but my money's on the black Lab. I'll go into town later this morning and tell the Marshal about the raid. I'd appreciate it if you'd get started on the milkin' while I finish buryin' these hens, then I'll come join ya."

"Sure thing, Sam. These old hens all pretty much look alike to me, but I don't believe any of these three dead ones are Luke's pets. Wonder if it was either Butterball or Buttercup that the animal chased off into the trees?"

"No, I'm happy to report that both were settin' just fine on their fat feathered rumps over by the privy when I used it this morning."

"Well I have to admit I'm happy to hear that. Losin' one of his pets would hit Luke hard and Ma don't need no cryin' boy to tend to on top of us dealin' with a chicken killin' varmint."

At Sarah's request no mention of the raid on their chickens the night before was made at breakfast. She thought it best to save discussion until supper when there would be time to talk it through. She wanted to dispel any fears the little ones might have over a dangerous animal lurking about. Sam was going into town and would report the incident to Jeb.

Until the culprit was caught she'd suggested to Sam that they round up the free-range hens and secure them in the makeshift chicken house used during the Roup contagion. Fencing would be needed to give the hens outside roaming space or they'd likely stop laying altogether. Sarah half chuckled to herself when she thought about all the time wasted each day walking the barn lot looking for eggs. Most of the free-range hens picked a roost and stayed with it for a week or so then moved to another spot. Not an intolerable job to find their eggs, but certainly not as efficient as keeping them confined to a chicken coop. There was enough fencing on hand but nails were in short supply. Sam would have to stop by the store while in town and buy some. The hens needed penned before dark fell.

Sam made a detour by the Town Marshal's office before going to purchase nails. He told Jeb what had taken place out at the farm the night before.

Jeb took off his hat, scratched his head and put it back on pulling the crown down snug. "Sorry you folks had trouble last night. Dog, coyote, whatever the dad blame critter is, it's a persistent devil. You scared it off last night and then it returned and attacked.

"Yours isn't the first report of chicken killin' from that neck of the woods, as you know. The Climmers, three farms over, was hit the night before last and Elmo Jones reported finding his best layer dead three nights ago. The scoundrel does its damage at night. Makes it hard to catch it in the act. If it takes to striking during daylight the chances of catching it or puttin' it down are more likely."

"Thanks, Marshal. We'll step up the watch and let you know if we see the animal again."

"Much obliged," Jeb said, taking a hands on his hips stance. "Hartman, I'm warmin' up to you, but just so you know, I'm still keepin' an eye on you."

Sam gave the Marshal a measured look, tipped his hat and moved on to Parker's General Store.

He purchased a pound of nails, half fourpenny and half sixpenny. As he was leaving the store, he saw the clerk who worked at the telegraph office nailing a flyer to the post in front of the building. Sam stopped to read it.

REWARD $50.00
for
*Missing Black Labrador Hunting Dog*
Suspected jumped from boxcar at LaFontaine
while being transported to Kansas. Dog answers
to Sir Lancelot. Telephone or Telegraph:
J.P. Garfield Attorney-at-Law, Fort Wayne, Indiana

\*\*\*

*"Hungie, me hungie." Hathaway fussed as she tugged at her mamma's skirt.*

Sarah broke off a piece of biscuit and handed it to the toddler. "I know you are sweetie. I'm hurrying as fast as I can to get supper on the table."

Standing with his chubby hands fisted at his waist, elbows sticking out, Zeke looked like an angry Bantam Rooster. "Hathaway, ain't the only one about to starve to death. I need me a biscuit to hold me off 'til supper."

Sarah made a failed attempt to smooth down the shock of hair protruding from the crown of her youngest son's head. "I really don't think you're going to starve, Zeke. Supper will be on the table in ten minutes. I think you can "hold off" until then. How about you go ring the bell to call Sam and the boys in from the barn. Get yourself washed up and take your seat at the table."

Sarah's parents had come by earlier that day and brought a large blade pot-roast from a recently butchered steer. Sarah thought it was just about the prettiest thing she'd seen in a long time. The marbling of fat in the cut of meat was so evenly distributed that it near guaranteed it would be tender and juicy. Early afternoon Sarah seared the roast on both sides, covered it with water and put it in the oven to slow roast. About an hour before suppertime she loaded the roaster to the top with potato and onion wedges and sliced carrots. After removing the cooked meat and vegetables from the roaster she used the drippings to make brown gravy. A peach pie, instead of their customary apple pie, was hiding in the cupboard.

*It's been nearly a month since I felt pride in a meal I served my family. Tonight's supper will be a much welcomed mouth-watering experience. If Josh's appetite doesn't perk up over this meal, I might need to take him to see Doc. He's been picking at his food, consuming hardly anything at mealtimes the past few days. Claimed he wasn't hungry. Yet, earlier in the week he admitted to taking leftovers from the cupboard shelf. Said he couldn't get his fill. I didn't see him eat more than a piece of bacon and half a biscuit at breakfast this morning. When I cleared the table his plate didn't have a thing left on it, looked like it'd been licked clean. I need to find out what's going on with that boy.*

"Supper's ready. Set yourselves down." Sarah placed a jar of raspberry jam on the table and realized no one was talking. As she looked from one child to another then to Sam she saw beaming, smiling faces. "What?"

Luke was the first to respond. "It's a feast, Ma. You done cooked up a feast!"

"Compared to recent suppers, it does indeed look like a feast," Sarah said. "Your Grandpa and Grandma Riley brought the meat to us today. I thought no use cooking a good piece of beef without the trimmings."

Sam closed his eyes and took a deep draw from the plethora of aromas. "Ma'am, my thanks to you and your folks."

Zeke raised his arms as high as he could and shouted. "Thank you, Grandpa and Grandma and thank you Jesus! Now let's eat."

"Zeke Whitcome! I think we can do better than that at giving thanks to the Lord for our blessings," Sarah chided. "You're old enough to take a turn at saying a proper grace. Everyone, please, bow your heads."

The tyke placed his small hands steeple style and gave a heart-felt prayer. "Dear Jesus, thank you for the beef. Since I'm doin' the prayin', could I have the biggest piece? Amen."

Once the food was passed and portions were taken, the table, but for the sound of eating utensils scraping against plates, was silent. Children and adults alike nestled in to that blissful state that comes when one's palate is not just satisfied but rather transported to a place so exquisite, no words this side of Glory can adequately describe it. Second helpings were called for and plates replenished with a mere nod or gesture. No words were needed. For that moment in time they were one in the spirit. All worries were set aside and they just enjoyed.

Sarah was the first to break the silence. "We've got peach pie for dessert. How about we sit, talk and let our tummies settle a bit before I serve it."

"Peach Pie, Boy Howdy!" Josh and Luke hollered in unison.

"Jinx, jinx and double jinx," quipped Abe.

"Hey, that ain't fair. Ma, tell him to take the jinx off," Josh whined.

"Don't make me no never mind, 'cause I got my fingers crossed," Zeke boasted as he proudly held up his right hand, pointer and middle finger intertwined and gooey with raspberry jam.

"Stop it," Sarah scolded. "All of you know I don't hold with casting jinx spells. All jinx are off. Everyone gets a piece of pie."

"Ma, when I got home from school I noticed that all the free-range chickens are fenced in around the old hen house. Why?" Luke said.

Before an explanation could be given Zeke boasted. "I helped Sam chase them birds all afternoon. Luke, those two pets of yours are the dumbest of 'em all. They wouldn't go into the pen 'til I put out a trail of corn. They ate their way in, one piece at a time and we had 'em captured."

"Don't be callin' Butterball and Buttercup dumb. They's smart enough to get some extry food off of ya before gettin' penned, wasn't they?" Luke said in defense.

Sarah called out, "Settle down, children."

"We're getting off track here," Sam said. "The point of this talk is to let you know that we have a varmint of some sort that's made a raid on the chickens. Last night it attempted to dig into the big chicken house. Abe heard the ruckus and scared it off. It came back later and killed three of the free-range hens and chased off a fourth. Other farms in the area have had similar attacks. Until we can capture or kill the culprit, we need to keep all the chickens corralled."

"Do you think it's the same animal Marshal Carter is looking for?" Josh asked.

"Yes, Josh, we think it's the same animal," Abe said. "The one I scared off from diggin' under the big chicken house was dark and looked like a black dog to me. Later Sam saw a similar looking critter chasing one of the free-range hens into the woods."

"I've got some other news that makes this thing even more interesting," Sam said as he got up from the table, grabbed the coffee pot and filled his and Sarah's cups. "When I was in town today I read a notice the telegraph office posted. Seems there's a man in Fort Wayne, a lawyer, who's offerin' a fifty dollar reward to anyone who finds his missing black Labrador retriever huntin' dog. A week back, the dog was being transported by rail through LaFontaine, en route to a sportin' event in Kansas. They speculate the dog jumped from the train when it stopped here in town to take on water. You'll think I'm making this up, but I'm just tellin' you what was on the notice. The dog's name is Sir Lancelot."

Everyone at the table either giggled or right out laughed at the hearing of the dog's name. Everyone that is, except for Josh. Josh just sat with his head hung low. Half of his portion of meat remained on his plate. He tried to be discreet, but Sarah saw him reach for another biscuit and place it and the meat under the table, then wipe tears away with his shirt sleeve.

*Why is Josh hiding food? Is he stashing it to eat later? The news about the lost dog seemed to upset him...I think he's crying.*

Sarah rose, fetched the peach pie and brought it to the table. "Abe, would you please serve the pie for me?" Reaching out a hand she said, "Josh, come with me. We need to talk."

Sarah grabbed her shawl and threw it around her shoulders and lifted Josh's jacket off of the hook. She took Josh's hand in hers and called over her shoulder as they went out the door. "Be sure to save a big piece of that pie for Josh and a small one for me. We'll be back directly."

Sarah led the now sobbing boy just far enough from the house to be out of hearing range. After helping her son put on his jacket she pulled him close and gave him a long and powerful hug. She held him until the sobs that wracked his small frame began to quiet. She placed her hand under his chin, lifted his face and used her apron to wipe it dry.

"You've been carrying a very big burden all by yourself haven't you, Son?"

"Ye...yes, Ma."

"I want to help. Where are you keeping the black Labrador?"

The boy withdrew. With his eyes as big as saucers he said, "How did you know?"

"When I saw you hide your meat and a biscuit under the table I wondered why. I knew you hadn't been eating much lately and that some of your leftover food had gone missing. It just came to me that you might have the missing dog and were feeding it."

"I didn't take the dog, Ma, I found it when I was walkin' home from school."

"I'm sure it was very exciting to find a dog. But, Son, we now know after Sam found that advertisement that someone is looking for their missing pet. That person loves that dog so much that they've offered a large reward to anyone who finds it."

The boy's lower lip trembled when he spoke. "Finders keepers. He's mine now."

"If you were the person who lost the dog, wouldn't you want the boy who found it to do the right thing and return him? Besides that, if this dog is the one killing chickens, something has to be done about it."

"I didn't know about no one losin' no dog. I hid the dog 'cause I didn't want no one to kill it. Ma, I don't believe it is the one killin' chickens. I've been feeding it and I told it to leave our chickens alone. He's a good dog. He wouldn't kill chickens."

"Josh, from what little I know about hunting dogs, especially retrievers, I expect you might be right about this dog. Retrievers fetch killed game and are taught to not eat it. Whether that turns out to be the case or not, we have to notify Marshal Carter and get word to the man in Fort Wayne that we've found a black Labrador that might be his. Now where do you have the dog?"

\*\*\*

Before entering, Sarah peeked in through the kitchen window. Her crew was still sitting at the supper table, laughing and talking. She opened the door and let Josh and the dog walk in first.

"Holy Moses!" Sam exclaimed.

Zeke and Luke squealed, Hathaway screamed. Abe was mute as he picked up his crying baby sister.

"Settle down, everyone," Sarah said. "Josh and I believe this might be the black Labrador hunting dog that man from Fort Wayne is looking for."

Josh bowed and with a sweeping hand motion said, "Everyone, meet Sir Lancelot."

Abe blurted, "what if it turns out this dog is the one that's been killin' chickens. Then what?"

"The dog seems gentle to me. He may not be the one that's been attacking chickens." Sarah said with more conviction in her voice than she actually felt. "Josh has spent quite a bit of time with it over the past few days and he says the dog's loving and gentle."

"Ma'am, like I said the other night, once a dog gets a taste of killin' chickens…there's no turning it away from the wantin'," Sam said.

"Yes, that's a fact. Josh and I have a plan. We're going to feed the dog and give it a bowl of water. You all can play with him until bedtime. The dog will sleep in the house tonight in my room. That way we'll know he can't get out to get to ours, or anyone else's chickens. Tomorrow Josh and I will go tell Marshal Carter we have the dog and we'll send a telegram to the gentleman in Fort Wayne."

Sam stood. With his thumbs tucked in the waist of his pants he said, "Ma'am, I'd appreciate it if you'd let the dog sleep in my quarters tonight. If he needs out in the night to relieve himself, I best be the one to take him. He's a big fellow and could jerk you right off your feet if he had a mind to take off runnin'. I'd be much obliged, Ma'am, 'cause I won't sleep a wink for worrin' if you don't let me take him."

"Thank you, Sam. He would be a lot for me to handle if he resisted the leash," Sarah responded.

"Ma, is Josh's gonna get fifty dollars reward for findin' this dog?" Abe asked.

"If it is the missing Labrador it will be for Josh to decide if he claims the reward," Sarah said.

Josh stroked the large dogs back. "Fifty dollars. I'd be rich." The boy got down on one knee and talked softly in the dog's ear. "What do ya think, feller? Should I take the reward ifin it's offered to me?"

Josh buried his face in the fur on the large animal's neck. "If you was my dog and I lost you, I wouldn't have me fifty dollars to offer a reward to get you back." The nine-year-old shook his head. "Nope, it just wouldn't seem right to take the money."

Sarah stepped to her son's side and put her arm around his shoulder. "If chickens get killed while we've got the dog locked up in the house we'll know that most likely he hasn't been involved. If there aren't any chickens killed anywhere in our area tonight then this dog's still a suspect. In that case, we'll turn him over to Jeb Carter and let him work it out with the dog's owner."

Zeke jumped off of his chair. "Times a wastin'! At least for tonight we got us a dog to play with. Where's a ball? Let's see if ole Sir Lancelot can play fetch."

# Chapter 31

"Don't worry big feller, breakfast is a comin'," Josh said, stroking the dog's fur as it lay at his feet. The Lab returned the affection by licking the child's hand and nuzzling his ankles.

"Josh, Sir Lancelot is welcome to the breakfast leftovers. Don't be feeding him directly from the table," Sarah instructed as she removed the browned-to-perfection biscuits from the oven. "Please help Hathaway get into her high chair..." Her words trailed off when she turned to see her eighteen-month-old already seated in her high chair, spoon in hand.

"Me ready eat," the baby said with a big smile on her face.

"Ma, Hathaway done climbed up in her chair all by herself," Zeke shared with pride. "I learnt her to climb and do lots of new stuff. Yesterday I showed her how to drag a chair over to the cupboard and climb up on it. She catched on real good, but even when she stands on her tippy toes she still ain't big enough to reach the cookie jar. I told her I'd have to keep fetchin' our cookie snacks for us til she grows a bit more. I hope that's soon. I'm tired of doin' all the work around here."

"I see. So you and Hathaway just get yourselves a cookie whenever you feel like it. Is that what you're telling me?" Sarah asked as she set a plate of bacon on the table.

"Yeah, Ma. Ain't you proud of us for not botherin' you ever time we need us a cookie?"

Sarah rubbed at the small of her back. It was early morning, the day had just begun and already she felt a slight ache. *I'm only six months along and already having backaches. Look at the size of my stomach.* Sarah ran her hand over the bulge at her waistline and then up her arm. *My arms don't seem any bigger. My face doesn't look any fuller to me. I've tried not to gain more than baby weight. I never remember being this large at just six months pregnant. How big am I going to get?*

*I didn't realize Zeke and Hathaway were sneaking extra cookie snacks. Not that it really matters except I wonder what other mischief they're into. Hathaway will only be twenty-two months old when this new one is born. She'll still be just a baby herself. I wonder if I'm going to be able to handle all of this work without help.*

*It's May already. Sam hasn't finished plowing my garden plot. I need to make it bigger this year. How am I going to get it planted with this aching back? I need to get Sam started on spring crop planting.*

*This new flock of chickens, the Roupe contagion, it has all taken a lot of time and the pullets are just now approaching the age for egg laying. The demanding work of the farm took Henry's health. How can I expect a hired hand to put in the hours needed to get everything done with just the promise of profit sharing?*

*Heavenly Father, fill me with your spirit of calm. Right now I don't feel up to the task of putting a simple breakfast on the table for my family, let alone running a farm.*

The sight of Abe coming through the kitchen door, followed by Sam, brought Sarah out of her daydreaming and prayer. The tall boy stood with his right hand behind his back and a smile on his face so big it nearly touched ear to ear. "Ma, I got a present for you."

"A present?" Sarah put a smile on her face and wiped her hands on her apron in readiness to receive the gift.

Cautiously the boy brought his hand from behind his back, reached out arm's length, and offered the gift that nestled gently in his palm. "Our first egg from the new flock."

Tears welled up in Sarah's eyes. Cupping her hands to use them as a receptacle, she offered them to Abe and received the light brown-shelled oval. "A brown egg. It's beautiful. Who would have guessed that the Barred Plymouth Rocks would be the first to lay?"

"Not me since three fourths of the flock we purchased are white egg layin' Rhode Island Reds," Sam quipped as he too gazed at the egg. "I hope they get to doin' their business soon and earnin' their keep. In a month we'll need to replenish the flock's feed supply."

Josh and Luke shoved and elbowed at one another as they crowded in to get a closer look at the new commodity, one which represented the hopes and dreams of the Whitcome family. Zeke, still a lot shorter than his brothers, had been closed out from view. The tyke used his body as a battering ram to penetrate the inner circle. Once he broke through he couldn't stop his momentum and he accidentally head butted his mother's hands. The egg went airborne. All eyes watched as it made its ascent then landing, smack-dab in the middle of Hathaway's high chair tray.

The impact crushed the shell just enough to stop the egg from rolling, but not enough to crack it fully open. The spectators watched in horror as the baby took her spoon and without hesitation, brought it down with all of her might on the egg, smashing it to smithereens. The room fell silent except for the sound of Hathaway's spoon as it continued to bang away at the pulverized egg.

All except for Hathaway held their breath, waiting to see what Sarah's response would be. She calmly picked up an empty pie tin and used her hand to slide the broken egg residue from the child's eating surface. Then she began cleaning the baby's gooey hands with a wet kitchen towel. "Well, the yoke was a nice rich yellow," she said as she worked.

Man and boys exhaled and took their seats at the table. The loss had been accepted. There would be plenty more eggs to come.

"So, Sam, how'd the night go sleepin' with Sir Lancelot in your quarters?" Josh asked.

"The dog was no problem at all," Sam said as he buttered a biscuit. "I took him outside to relieve himself one last time before I went to bed. He curled up on the rug and I didn't hear a peep out of him all night. This morning, I had to nudge him to get up so I could take him out to do his business before I started chores. On my way to the barn I dropped him off for your ma to watch."

"Ma, did you hear that?" Josh's eyes threatened to leak their brimming liquid as he reached over and squeezed his mother's hand. "I told you Ma, Sir Lancelot ain't the dog that's been a killin' chickens."

"I hope you're right, son." Sarah pulled the child's hand to her mouth and tenderly caressed it with her lips. "Josh, we don't know yet what occurred last night in our area or even here on our farm, for that matter.

"Sam, did we lose any more free range hens last night?"

It took a beat for Sam to respond and his voice was thick with emotion over the sweet exchange between mother and son that he'd just witnessed. "Nary a one as far as I can tell. Nary a one."

"That's good news." Sarah said as she passed the fried potatoes to Sam. "We still need to go to town and let Jeb know we have the dog. He can tell us if there were any reports of killed chickens elsewhere last night. If there were, that might mean Sir Lancelot isn't guilty. If there weren't any, then he could still be involved. Either way, we need to telegraph the dog's owner that we have him."

"Here ya go, Lancy, ol' boy," Zeke said as he handed the Lab a piece of bacon. "That's for bein' such a good dog."

"Ezekiel Whitcome! I said no feeding the dog from the table. He gets the left over food and that's all. Now you heard me say that."

"I heard ya say that to Josh, but ya weren't talkin' ta me." The four year old flipped back so quickly that particles of food spewed from his mouth.

Sarah slowly and deliberately lowered her fork to rest on her plate. She tucked in an errant strand of hair, then laid both hands in her lap. Abe, Josh and Luke all laid down their eating utensils and sat up straighter in their seats. Sam who had also noticed Sarah's reaction followed suit, righting his spine to be perpendicular with the back of his chair. Even baby Hathaway noticed the tone in her momma's voice. She paused mid-air with a piece of bacon fisted in her chubby hand and looked at Sarah.

Zeke, in a state of oblivion, commenced shoving a biscuit, slathered in strawberry jam, into his mouth.

"Zeke." Sarah tugged down on her bodice pulling it taut to her waist. "After we're finished eating, you will clear the breakfast dishes from the table. Then you will help me wash and dry them. While we work we will have a talk about the perils of sassing."

"Pearls? Pearls is for girls." The boy said with his cheeks pouched out like a chipmunk's. "Wash dishes? Men don't wash dishes!" Zeke studied his jam sticky hand, then began licking his fingers one at a time, pausing between digits to put a final nail in his coffin. "Sassin'? What's sassin'?"

"Oh, don't worry, Son. I'll be teaching you about sassing," Sarah said.

The frozen tone of his mother's voice caused the boy to divert his attention from licking his fingers to looking first at Sarah's stern face, then at the solemn look on the faces of the others sitting at the table. "What?"

A knock on their kitchen door provided a welcome distraction. Abe jumped up and opened it. Jeb Carter was standing at the threshold, hat in hand. "Marshal Carter, come in."

"Good morning, Jeb," Sarah said standing to greet their long time friend. "What brings you out this way so early in the morning?"

"I'm bringin' good news. I got that chicken killin' varmint last night.

He was a big black cuss of a dog. Caught him right in the act of killin' some of my own chickens."

"Boy Howdy!" Josh shouted.

When Jeb turned toward the excited boy he saw the large black Labrador lying at Josh's feet. "A black Lab! When? Is that…?"

"Come sit down, Jeb. We've got our own story to tell," Sarah said as she pulled another chair up to the table. Before we start, let me grab you a cup of coffee."

The reality that he was going to have to wash the breakfast dishes finally sank in to Zeke's obstinate little head. The boy jumped up and snatched his mother's empty coffee cup. "No sense gettin' another cup dirty when we already got us an empty one not bein' used."

# Chapter 32

Early Monday morning the town Marshal sent a telegram to J.P. Garfield to notify him that his hunting dog had been found. The lawyer's response came before noon. He was sending a courier the next day to retrieve the Labrador. Jeb caught Elmo Jones on his way out of town with the day's mail and asked him to deliver the news to Sarah.

Sarah responded to the knock at her kitchen door just as Elmo spat a stream of tobacco that landed near the children's digging pile. She flinched and made a mental note to use Zeke's shovel to toss it clear of the play area. "Hello, Elmo, what brings you to the door today?"

"Marshal Carter said ta tell ya someone's a comin' on the noon train tomorry to fetch that dog your youngin' found."

The Labrador had come to stand by Sarah's side. "Oh my, tomorrow! That's a really quick response."

"'Spect you'll be glad ta be shed of it. It'd take a powerful lot of food to fill up a dog that big," Elmo said gesturing toward the animal.

Sarah put her hand on the dog's head and pulled him close. "Yes, he's eaten a lot in the few days he's been here, but he's a gentle fellow. I'm surprised to hear myself say it, I think I'll miss him as much as the children will." Sarah reached out and took her mail that Elmo was holding. The news that the dog was leaving left her a bit sad and she didn't feel up to making small talk. "Thanks for delivering the message," Sarah said, closing the kitchen door before the mailman had an opportunity to invite himself in for pie and coffee.

\*\*\*

That afternoon when the boys came home from school, Sarah called Josh aside. "Sir Lancelot's owner is sending someone on the noon train tomorrow to pick him up."

"Oh, Ma, I wasn't expectin' him to be leavin' so soon."

"Neither was I. If you want to, you can stay home from school tomorrow to spend the morning with the dog and be here to tell him goodbye."

Josh looked out the window and watched as Luke and Zeke played catch with the Lab. "I'd like that, Ma. It's gonna be hard to see him go."

Despite Sarah's assurance that it would be appropriate to take the offered reward for finding the dog, Josh remained adamant that he wouldn't feel right about accepting it. Sarah was proud of the boy for sticking to his principles, but at the same time, she wondered if he grasped the enormity of fifty dollars cash money.

*If I had fifty dollars handed to me I'd use the majority of the money for family needs. Sam's working for profit share at harvest time. I'd give him some cash for pocket money, Lord knows he deserves it.* Sarah ran her hand across her baby bulge. *I'd also purchase some gingham yardage and make myself a new dress to wear after this baby comes in August.* Sarah looked over at Hathaway who was playing with blocks in the corner of the kitchen and said, "Sweet one, I think I'd buy an extra half yard and make you a matching dress. Would you like to have a dress that looks the same as Momma's?"

The baby responded with a big smile.

\*\*\*

Sarah delayed supper until after the sun was fully set so the boys could play outside with the dog. Sarah and Hathaway went out to watch. Sarah found it pure joy to hear her sons giggle and laugh as time after time they threw a stick or ball and the Labrador tirelessly fetched and returned it to whomever had made the toss.

Hathaway had been quietly standing at her mother's side watching the activity. She began to clap her tiny hands and call, "here me, here me." Sir Lancelot lumbered toward her full speed. Saliva spewed from the large animal's mouth and sprayed on the baby's cheek as he skidded to a stop, just inches from where she stood. The dog dropped the ball at her feet. The Lab was half a head taller than the child who stood frozen in place. Using his snout the animal nudged the ball toward the toddler. Hathaway was trembling when she bent down, picked up the ball, and gave it a toss. As she did, warm liquid trickled down her chubby legs and made a dark spot on the soil around her bare feet. The pitch was short, the dog quickly retrieved the ball, again dropping it at baby's feet.

Sarah bent down to pick up the ball just as the baby in her womb decided to turn. "Uhhh." The dog waited patiently while she took a deep breath then placed Hathaway's hand on the back of hers. "Here, honey, let mommy help you throw the ball this time."

Together they made an under-handed toss that sent the ball sailing. Sarah called out, "Boys, it's almost dark. Ten more minutes, then you all get washed up and come in to supper." Sarah took Hathaway's hand and led her toward the house. "Let's get you some dry britches."

***

The next morning Josh stayed in the kitchen with the dog and anxiously waited. He knew it was going to be painful to say goodbye. *I hope this ain't as hurtful as when Pa got his stroke and never knew us again. That made my chest ache somethin' fearful. I thought the feelin' would never go away and then one day it did.* Josh knelt and buried his face in the Lab's thick coat. "Guess if I can stop hurtin' over losin' my Pa, I can get over you leavin', Sir Lancelot. One thing for sure, I ain't never gonna forget how good you smell ol' boy."

The sight of a horse drawn wagon coming up their lane, with McVicker Livery Stable printed on the side, caught Josh's attention. "Ma, Ma, I need you, Ma. It's time, Ma."

Josh checked to make sure the rope they were using as a leash was secure, then led the dog out the door. Zeke, Sarah, and Hathaway, who was holding her mamma's hand, followed close behind. Pleasantries were exchanged and the reward offered and declined. "Are you sure you don't want to take the money, Boy?" the courier asked a second time. "Mr. Carter instructed me to make sure you were properly rewarded for finding Sir Lancelot."

"No, Sir, my reward will be knowin' he gets back safe ta his family."

Tipping his hat, the courier said, "Ma'am, much obliged for the invitation for coffee and pie, but I need to take my leave."

Josh knelt and whispered in the dog's ear. "Now it's gonna be a long ride ta your home boy. Relax and sleep. Afore you know it, you'll be back with your family. Think of me sometimes. I'll be thinkin' a lot about you." The boy walked the dog to the wagon and helped load and securely tether him.

Sarah put Hathaway down and the baby and Zeke ran to the dirt pile to dig. Josh clasped his mother's hand. Together they watched the wagon travel down their lane and turn onto the road to town.

Sarah released her hand and smoothed down her son's ruffled hair. "Josh, would you like to have a piece of pie and a glass of milk?"

"No, thanks, Ma. I need me some time by my lonesome." Using his shirtsleeve he swiped at the tears that were gaining momentum.

\*\*\*

It was Saturday morning, nearly a week since the Labrador left the farm. Spirits were low, despite the week's end signaling the beginning of summer break from school. The children were moping around with proverbial dragging tails. Sarah knew that getting them a dog of their own would make them happy. The practicality of feeding a dog, when barely a cup full of scraps could be gleaned from a meal at their table, held her back.

Truth be told there was just too much work to be done that day to spend any more time thinking about other than how to get it all done. It was May 28th, getting late for spring planting. Sarah's father-in-law, Jonas, had finished plowing her last year's pumpkin patch a few days before. Instead of pumpkins, the acre plot would be dedicated to planting a huge vegetable garden in support of Sarah's plan to sell produce at the Wabash Farmer's Market in summer.

Sarah, Josh, and Luke were getting ready to plant onions, potatoes, cabbage, carrots, and green beans. Mary Riley, Sarah's mother, was coming to help. Sam and Abe had already headed out to the fields to continue planting corn.

"Zeke, please gather up your bucket, shovel and any other things you might need for digging. You and Hathaway will be working in the garden patch dirt with the rest of us today," Sarah said as she packed a basket with a jar of water, cookies and an extra diaper.

Zeke headed for his dirt pile but was back almost before the door closed. "We got us some company. Doc Adams just drove up."

"Doc Adams!" Sarah repositioned a couple of hair pins to shore up her drooping coiffure. She looked down at the mound protruding from her waistline, dropped her hands and shook her head. "Wonder what brings him out here so early on a Saturday morning?"

Ben stepped up to knock on the door just as Zeke opened it wide. "Hello, Zeke. Is your mother home?"

"Yeah, she's here, but she ain't got time to visit. We got us a powerful lot of diggin' to get to." The boy pushed past Doc and called over his shoulder. "Ma, I'll get my tools gathered up."

"Good morning, Ben. Come in. Everything alright?" Sarah asked.

"Hello, Sarah. I've come with some concerning news. Is there somewhere we can talk in private?"

"Not since we gave up our parlor to Sam. Let's take a walk." Although the sun was shining, it hadn't yet burned off the morning chill. Sarah grabbed a shawl and called over her shoulder. "Josh, please look after Hathaway while I take a walk with Doc Adams. We'll be back shortly."

Sarah stayed quiet until they reached the smokehouse. She grabbed Ben's arm. "What's happened? Is it something about Henry?"

"I'm afraid it is. The mental hospital telephoned this morning. Henry's had a bad cold for a couple of weeks. The cold moved to his chest, fever set in and he has advanced pneumonia."

"Are you saying he's seriously ill?"

"Henry's doctor said his condition is grave. He thinks the family should come. He asked me to notify you and Henry's parents. I came here first."

"I must go to be with him." Sarah turned and started for the house.

Ben took hold of her arm. "Sarah, you're six and a half months pregnant. It isn't the best idea for you to travel in your condition."

Sarah pulled her arm free. "I'm going! Today!"

Ben held up his arms in surrender. "If you insist on going, I'll take you."

"That's kind of you, Ben. I'm sure Jonas and Emma will want to go. I can travel with them. You don't have to make the trip."

"Sarah, Henry was one of my closest friends. I want to go."

Sarah sent Josh to pull Sam and Abe in from the fields. Sam was sent to the elder Whitcome farm to notify them about Henry's condition. Sarah sent a hand written note suggesting they meet her and Doc Adams at the train station for an afternoon departure to Logansport.

Sarah called her children together. "Doc Adams has brought news from the hospital that your father is seriously ill with pneumonia. I'll be traveling by train this afternoon with Grandma and Grandpa Whitcome and Doc to go be with him."

"Is he going to die?" Abe asked.

Sarah opened her arms and gathered her boys into a collective hug. "We don't know. Often people don't survive pneumonia."

Sarah's mother arrived. It was decided she would take the three youngest children home with her. Abe and Josh would stay on the farm with Sam to feed the livestock and chickens and continue with the spring planting. The vegetable garden would have to wait.

Sarah stood in her bedroom looking in her mirror. The dress she wore for traveling was an old maternity dress from when she carried Hathaway. It was neither stylish nor flattering. The best that could be said for it was that it covered her bulging tummy and she had room to breathe. The trip would be tiring. Comfort was important. Little else in the realm of appearance mattered under the circumstances.

With trembling hands Sarah used her treasured hatpin, a gift from Henry, to secure her traveling hat. In the process she pricked her finger and cried out. "Henry, sweet Henry, don't leave me." Tears streamed down Sarah's cheeks as she sucked her wound to stop the bleeding.

Mary Riley's lavender scent announced her presence before her arms encircled her daughter from behind. "My darling. Henry was taken from you when he suffered the heat stroke last August. The body that lies ill at the mental hospital is only the shell of the man that you loved. Henry's long been gone."

"Ma, in my heart I know you are right. Until hearing this news today that he was gravely ill, I didn't realize that I was still harboring hope that he might recover and perhaps one day come home to us."

Sarah's children, one at a time, hugged her goodbye. Abe, the last to do so, held her hands in his. "Ma, we boys talked. We want you to tell Pa we love him and remember how special he is. Tell him we'll never forget him."

Sarah, too choked with emotion to speak, kissed her son's forehead. Ben helped Sarah up into his buggy. When she turned to wave goodbye she saw that Sam was holding Hathaway and patting her back as the baby nestled her face at his neck. Abe held Josh and Luke protectively, one under each of his arms. Zeke's face was hidden in his grandmother's skirt, her arm wrapped around his small shoulders comforting him as he cried.

Between sobs Zeke said, "My Pa already done died when he got stroked. If Ma had to go see that other man, then I should be goin' too. I ain't had me a train ride in ever."

***

It was 5:30 p.m. when Sarah, Henry's parents, and Doc Adams arrived at the Logansport Mental Hospital. Sarah, Emma and Jonas were immediately taken to Henry's bedside. Ben took a moment to confer with the doctor. "How is he? Any improvement in his condition?"

"I'm afraid not," the facility's doctor replied. "Henry's been feverish for the past two days. About noon today he slipped into a coma. I'm glad you were able to get his family here. From the looks of things, he's going to go quick."

When Sarah, Jonas and Emma entered the room, they found Henry lying unresponsive. A nurse was bathing his upper torso with cool water to keep his temperature down.

Sarah touched the nurse's arm. "I'm his wife. May I do that please?"

The family set up a vigil with Sarah on one side of the bed bathing Henry. Emma and Jonas stood on the other side, Emma held her son's hand and Jonas held Emma's hand.

Doc entered the room and broke the news that Henry wasn't expected to survive the night. Then he took up vigil at the foot of the bed.

Sarah bathed her sleeping husband's face. *How can this be happening? Could this all be a terrible dream?* Sarah felt a stirring within her when she started to bathe Henry's chest and arms. She longed to slide under the covers and cuddle in close to her husband's side and soak in the warmth of his body. *Dear Lord, might I pretend, just for a moment, that he will wake up and whisper my name and smother me with kisses.*

Ben saw that Sarah's face was flushed. "Sarah, are you alright? Can I get you some water?"

Doc's words felt like an abrasive intrusion to her private thoughts. Sarah wanted to lash out at Ben and everyone else in the room but instead screamed in her mind. *Leave me alone. Leave me to comfort my husband in private.* Sarah drew in a deep breath and slowly exhaled. "I'm fine Ben. Water isn't what I need."

Words came hard for Jonas and Emma. Jonas took a seat on the edge of the bed and placed his big calloused hand on his son's knee. A chair for Emma's comfort was brought bedside. She never let go of her son's hand while changing position. From time to time, she leaned over and kissed her child's feverish brow.

Sarah sympathized with a mother's longing to do something more for her dying child. "Emma, would you take a turn at bathing Henry for while?"

The women switched positions. Sarah took Henry's hand and began to talk to him. She told her husband about the farm and their progress with spring planting. She talked about their egg production venture and finding the Sir Lancelot. She told him she was considering letting the children get a dog, if she could figure out how to feed it. She told him about the children, how good they were doing, some of the funny things they'd said and done. She gave him the message of love that his boys had sent to him.

After a time, Henry's breathing became labored. Sarah asked if she might have some time alone with him. Not waiting for a response, the facility's nurse ushered all but Sarah from the room.

Sarah placed Henry's hand on the swell at her waist. "Feel that. It's your baby kicking. I promise you that this child will be told about the loving, wonderful father it missed."

In a whispered tone that lovers use, Sarah shared memories from the beautiful years she and Henry had spent as husband and wife, friends and soul mates. She repeatedly kissed his face and hands and told him how much he meant to her, of the joy he brought to her life and how special it was to have loved him and been loved by him in return. When she was spent and exhausted she laid her arm across his waist, her head on his chest and wept softly.

With much effort Henry lifted his hand and rested it at the nape of his wife's neck. Whether his gesture had intention mattered not to Sarah. It was her husband's hand, a touch she had longed for.

For a time they lay together like that, Sarah feeling the rise and fall and rise again of Henry's chest. Then the moment came. Her love's chest fell and never rose again.

# Chapter 33

Henry Whitcome died at nine-thirty in the evening on Saturday, May twenty-eight, Nineteen Hundred and four. He was thirty-six years old. The following morning the facility provided his family with a plain pine box for transporting his body home.

Before leaving Logansport, Doc sent a telegraph to Clyde Cutter of Cutter Brother's Undertaking and Embalming, requesting that a hearse be waiting for their scheduled May twenty-ninth noon arrival at the LaFontaine train station. He also sent a second telegram to Jeb Carter asking him to relay the news of Henry's death to Sarah's family.

\*\*\*

The adults in Sarah's family, along with Ed Sloan, Sarah's minister; and Jeb Carter huddled by the train station. They talked in murmured tones. Hathaway had the sniffles and was cranky. Her grandfather held her, patting her on the back, while she rested her head on his shoulder. The baby nodded off, her drool made a damp spot on the collar of Tom's shirt.

The children, except for Zeke, milled about quietly as they waited for the train to arrive. Zeke had spotted Cutter Brother's hearse, tethered at the side of the Depot. He was near chomping at the bit to get a closer look at the curious wagon. He'd ask twice if he could go explore the thing and his grandpa had told him no both times.

Zeke tried easing himself closer, inch by inch, to the wagon. Tom spotted him, approached, and drew a line in the dirt with his boot. "See this line, Zeke, don't cross it."

The four-year-old paced back and forth on the fringe of his line of demarcation. He was getting ready to breech the boundary when the train blasted its whistle announcing its arrival. Black smoke belched from the smokestack as its wheels ground to a stop.

Sarah and her traveling companions emerged from the train into the arms of fellow mourners. There were hugs of comfort, reassuring words, and tears. Their collective grief was so enormous it was palpable to onlookers.

Zeke's eyes were glued to the hearse as it backed up to the train's freight car. *Them fellers is unloadin' a crate off the train and puttin' it in that funny wagon.* The boy, just like a cat, felt himself being pulled by a force of curiosity so strong he was willing to risk life in pursuit. *If I could get just a bit closer, I might see me what's in that box....*

"Zeke! You're mighty close to crossin' that line. Get yourself over here, now," Tom said pointing to the ground at his side.

Doc Adams walked over to the boy. "Zeke, if I give you a dime will you take your brothers and cousins over to Parker's store and treat them to a stick of candy?"

Zeke snatched the dime from the palm of Ben's hand. "Boy Howdy! Ya don't gotta tell me nothin' twiced."

Abe volunteered to take responsibility for the shopping distraction. The Whitcome brothers and Riley cousins headed toward the general store with Zeke taking the lead.

Clyde Cutter sent his assistant to the funeral parlor with Henry's body, then joined Sarah and her family to discuss necessary arrangements. "Mrs. Whitcome, I'd like to offer my funeral parlor as a gathering place for your late husband's wake. There'd be an additional fee of course, but we're set up to handle a goodly-sized group of folks."

"Oh. I haven't given any thought to a gathering place," Sarah said. "My parlor isn't available right now. You say there'd be an additional cost?"

Mary Riley spoke up. "Sarah dear, your father and I would be honored to hold Henry's wake in our parlor."

"Ma, Pa, that's generous of you." Looking from her parents to Henry's parents she asked, "Jonas, Emma, would that be alright with the two of you?"

Jonas responded in a tone that reflected relief. "Sarah, your parent's home would be fine with me and Emma. We wish we could offer to hold the wake at our house, but our farm is a far piece from town and, truth be told, we're plum tuckered out."

Clyde Cutter, a bit prickly over losing the additional funeral parlor fee, responded, "Mrs. Whitcome, if you'll come this afternoon and pick out a casket, I can have the body prepared and delivered to your folks house for viewing by four o'clock in the afternoon tomorrow. I'm willing to make the personal sacrifice and work on the Sabbath, which is also Decoration Day, if that's what suits you best."

"That's kind of you, Mr. Cutter. Yes, I can come over now and pick out a casket," Sarah said. "I'd appreciate it if the funeral could be held on Monday. Pastor Sloan, would that be alright with you?"

With Pastor Sloan's concurrence the funeral was set for Monday afternoon, May thirtieth, at two o'clock, graveside at the LaFontaine IOOF Cemetery. Tom and Mary offered to take their grandchildren home with them so their daughter could get some rest. Sarah declined.

"We'll be fine," Sarah said. "It won't take me long to pick out the casket. We'll be home by early afternoon. Hathaway and I can take a nap before time to fix supper. I think the children and I need to be together tonight."

It was decided that Jack's wife and children would ride with Tom and Mary and be dropped off at their farm. Jack would take Sarah and her brood out to Sarah's farm.

Jonas and Emma would go on to their home for much needed rest and to make arrangements to have needs of their farm covered for the next couple of days.

Sarah kissed her in-laws goodbye and thanked Doc for traveling with them to and from Logansport. Jeb helped Sarah climb up on the seat of Jack's wagon. She gave his hand a tight squeeze in farewell.

The children rode in the bed of the wagon. Hathaway fell asleep in Abe's arms as they bumped along. Sarah leaned in and rested her head on Jack's shoulder. He responded by putting an arm across her shoulders and pulling her close. Sarah tried to hold back her tears but several made their escape. "Jacky, it hurts so bad."

Jack kissed his sister's brow. "I'm sure it does, Sis. I wish I could carry some of the pain for you."

It was two-thirty in the afternoon when they arrived at the farm. On the way up the lane they noticed that Sam was in the adjacent field planting. Once at the house Sarah insisted that Jack go home. "Thanks, big brother. Go home to your family. It'll be time for your evening chores soon enough."

Abe carried his still-sleeping sister to her crib, then joined the others in the kitchen. "Ma, should I go out and help Sam?"

"Honey, it'll be fine for you to take the afternoon off. Do whatever feels best for you."

"What about the rest of us, Ma? What's we supposed to do?" Josh asked, his voice full of emotion.

Sarah opened her arms wide. "You can come here and give me a great big hug."

Abe, Josh, Luke, and Zeke, gathered around their mother for a collective hug. Sarah said, "I'm so fortunate to have strong men like the four of you to give me comfort."

Sarah's body ached from the train ride and her eyes were heavy with fatigue. "Aside from evening chores, you boys rest or play. Likely some of our friends and neighbors will drop by to pay their respects and give their condolences. I'm going to join Hathaway for a nap. If they come while I'm resting, please be cordial to them."

"Give us some corndollies?" puzzled Zeke. "Is that some kind of cake or pie? 'Cause I could use me somethin' sweet to eat about now."

"No son. Condolence is an expression of understanding someone's sadness when a loved one dies. Sometimes the condolence is expressed in words, or it might be expressed with a hug and a kiss on the cheek. Some folks do both." Sarah started toward her bedroom, then paused. "Zeke, didn't you just finish eating a whole stick of candy on the ride home?"

"Ma, I cain't answer that right now. I got to figure me a plan to dodge them hugs and kisses that's comin' my way."

Sarah drew in a deep breath, then exhaled. "Oh, Zeke, do please try and be polite to any visitors that stop by."

Abe put Zeke in a head lock and gave him a knuckle rub. "Ma, go to your room and get some rest. I'll rub any developing plans out of this lunkhead's mind."

Sarah was exhausted and fell asleep instantly. She woke at four thirty in the afternoon to a house filled with a plethora of delectable aromas. She looked towards Hathaway's crib and saw that it was empty. Sarah tugged on and laced her shoes before heading to the kitchen.

Sarah found Hathaway, Zeke and Luke playing quietly with blocks. Josh was lying on the horsehair sofa, which had been moved into the kitchen, reading *The Adventures of Huckleberry Finn*. The boy looked up from his book. "Hi, Ma. Did you have a good rest?"

"Yes I did. Thank you so much for looking after things while I slept." Sarah gestured toward the pies, bread and other food on their kitchen table and cabinet. "What's all of this?"

"The neighbors has been a bringin' food all afternoon," Luke reported.

"How thoughtful. Can you tell me who brought what, so I can send thank you notes and return their pans?"

"Sure, but we already thanked 'em," Josh said. "It was Julib Carter that dropped off the pot of beef and noodles his ma made. William Johnson stopped by with them two sugar cream pies. Said to tell you that his sister Myra sends best wishes and will come to the wake. Elmo delivered the loaves of bread and the pound cake. The bread's from Pastor Sloan's wife and the cake from Mrs. Simon."

"Mrs. Frank Simon, the blacksmith's wife, or Mrs. Nobel Simon, the barber's wife?"

Josh scratched his head. "I ain't sure which, Ma. They both have notes attached to 'em."

Their conversation was interrupted by the sound of a wagon pulling up. Sarah opened the door and saw that it had Parker's General Store printed on the side.

"Howdy, Ma'am." The driver said, tipping his hat to Sarah. "I got a delivery here for you."

"I haven't ordered anything," Sarah responded.

"It was bought and paid for by Hickory Ramsey this mornin'. He told Mr. Parker to make sure it was delivered to you today, Ma'am."

"That looks like a really big delivery," Sarah said. *Hick, even though I know you can well afford it, this is too much. Guess this is your way of sending a condolence.* "Josh, Luke, would you please help unload the wagon."

When they were finished a twenty-pound sack of sugar and a twenty-pound sack of flour sat on the kitchen floor. A five-pound tin of coffee and a large sack of Horehound candy had been added to the other items that graced the table top.

Zeke was beside himself with excitement when he realized a sack of candy had been delivered. "Candy, I been needin' me some more candy. I can taste it now, sweet and meltin' on my tongue." The tyke popped a piece in his mouth. "Yuck!" Zeke spit the sticky chunk into the palm of his hand. "This ain't candy, it tastes like medicine!"

"Zeke, don't be ungrateful," Sarah scolded. "It is candy, it's called Horehound. Mr. Ramsey is an elderly gentleman and he likely thinks it tastes good. A lot of older folks appreciate Horehound's combination of mint, licorice and root beer." Sarah popped a piece in her mouth. "If you get a sore throat, you'll find sucking on this a soothing remedy."

"You can give my share back to Mr. Ramsey and tell him I said he can suck it." Zeke shook his hand over the garbage bucket and relieved himself of the unwanted sticky lump. "Yuck and double yuck!"

\*\*\*

Upon hearing the bell signaling supper was ready, Sam and Abe quickly finished with evening chores and came to the house. Both stripped to the waist and stood bare-chested at the pump as they washed up. Sam finished first, grabbed the communal towel and dried off, then passed it to Abe. "Abe, thanks for comin' out and helpin' me finish puttin' the corn in the ground this afternoon. It sure feels good to end the day knowin' we have that piece of spring plantin' done. I hope it wasn't too hard on you, circumstances and all."

Abe rubbed his face, chest and arms dry. "I appreciated the work, kept my mind from broodin' about Pa. His stroke took him from us several months ago, still it's a hard knock knowin' he's dead."

Sam nodded toward the house. "Wonder how your Ma's holding up?"

"Ma, she'll be fine, she's strong. Come to think of it, she's pert near the strongest person I know. Look at all she's been through recently. Still, every day when I wake up, she greets me with that big, beautiful smile of hers."

"I gotta agree with you there boy, she surely is a strong woman."

Abe tossed the towel over the pump handle and put his shirt on. "Ma says it's her faith in God that sees her through the hard times. I don't understand God like she does. But, I'm glad He works for her, because she makes everything work for the rest of us."

Sam followed Abe in to the kitchen. He felt awkward, this being the first he'd seen or had a chance to speak to Sarah since her husband died. With his hat still in his hands, Sam softly called out, "Sarah."

Sarah looked his way. "What, Sam?"

"Sarah," he paused, tried to clear his throat, but the words still came out thick with emotion, "I'm so sorry for your loss."

Sarah was touched by Sam's humble words and her tears threatened to spill. *God in heaven, help me hold these tears until I'm alone.* Sarah started to respond with a thank you, but was cut short by Zeke.

"Gee, Sam, don't you know nothin' about givin' corndollies to a person. You's apposta give her a hug and a kiss on the cheek when you say them things."

Sarah's need to chastise Zeke snapped her out of her vulnerable moment. "Ezekiel Whitcome, mind your manners! You will not speak to your elders in such a tone and you will not correct someone who is being polite and showing kindness."

Sam lowered his head in an attempt to hide the grin on his face. "No harm done, Ma'am. Truth be told, I've never been very good at expressin' my 'corndollies.'"

Sarah quickly pulled her apron up over her mouth. With only her eyes showing she looked at Sam, then Zeke, and shaking her head, looked back at Sam again. Sarah let her apron fall back into place and placed her hands on her hips. The big smile she'd hidden with her apron was gone, but a grin tickled at the corners of her mouth when she spoke. "It's the thought that counts. We can't all be good at everything. Now please, take your seat Sam. Supper's ready."

After they had eaten their fill of beef and noodles, Sarah said she wanted to talk to them about what had occurred that day and what to expect in the days to follow.

Sam folded his napkin and scooted back his chair. "Ma'am, would you like to be alone with the children?"

"Not at all, Sam. I'd be much obliged if you stayed," Sarah replied. "You need to know what's happening over the next couple of days."

"Please, let me help in any way you think I can be useful." Sam settled back in his chair and crossed his legs, knee over thigh.

"I have a scripture I want to share with all of you." Sarah picked her Bible up from beside her plate. The book's cover was worn and frayed on the edges. Many of the tissue thin pages were crinkled due to moistened digits used to thumb through the text. Others were marked for later reference with a curl of baby fine hair, or a pressed flower. Some passages, like the one she was about to read, fell open without effort, the bible's spine having been creased to that location multiple times.

"I'll be reading to you from John 3:16. *For God so loved the world, that he gave his only begotten Son, that whosoever believeth in him should not perish, but have everlasting life.* Sarah laid the Bible down on the table.

"Your pa trusted his life to God and accepted this scripture that I just read as truth. The soul of the man that was your father left us when he had the stroke last summer. An altered spirit remained in his body. Your father's body stopped functioning early this morning. Now your father is completely at peace. But as the scripture told us, he did not perish. Your pa is in heaven with his heavenly father, God. If we trust and accept what it says in John 3:16, we will join him one day when our time on this earth is finished.

"Tomorrow evening there will be what's called a wake for your father. It will be at Grandma and Grandpa Riley's house. Your father's body will be there and folks will come and look at it and say good bye to him. The day after tomorrow we will bury your father's body at the town cemetery.

"I don't want any of you to feel worried, or afraid. Life for us will go on. Our greatest sorrow occurred when your father had his heat stroke and no longer knew us.

"We've been sad, but gradually, because we had to move on, that hurting has been easier to handle, not as fierce as it was at first. We've been able to find joy and happiness. That's good, that's how life works. Now that we have to bury your pa's body, we're reminded of that first, fierce hurt, and for some of us it's a terrible painful hurt again, not just a dull ache in our hearts."

The family had remained silent, except for Hathaway who'd stayed content by gnawing on a tough piece of beef as she softly mewed. The baby grew weary of her efforts, threw the grizzle on the floor and reached out for her mamma. Sarah wiped Hathaway's face on the tail of her apron and pulled her out of the highchair and onto her lap.

Abe broke the silence. "Was Pa's body in the box they unloaded from the train into Mr. Cutter's hearse this mornin'?"

"Yes, son," Sarah answered.

Zeke had been in a state of oblivion during Sarah's talk. At the mention of a box being unloaded from the train, he perked up. "I saw that box. I wanted to get me a closer look at it."

Luke sat twisting his napkin, as if he were nervous. "Fatty Brubaker said when his grandma died he had to go to her wake and they made him kiss her right on the mouth. Are you gonna make us kiss Pa?"

Zeke sat up straight, his eyes open wide. "Pa, what about Pa?"

Josh who was sitting next to Zeke, finger flipped his brother's head. "Gee willikers Zeke, weren't you listenin'. Ma's been tellin' us about Pa dyin' and that his body will be at Grandma and Grandpa Riley's house tomorrow. It'll be laid out for folks to look at and say goodbye. Luke was a sayin' that some folks give the dead body a kiss when they say their goodbyes."

"Josh," Sarah's voice was stern. "You know I don't like for you to use slang like gee…"

Zeke jumped off of his chair and shouted. "I ain't never seen a dead body and I sure ain't gonna' kiss me one on the mouth. Ain't no one gonna make me neither." The boy started to sob, holding his arms out to his mother for comfort.

"Your Ma's arms are full with Hathaway," Sam said, holding his open wide. "Come here, I'll hold you."

Zeke ran to Sam and he pulled the boy onto his lap and wrapped his arms around his small quivering frame. Zeke snuggled in close.

Sarah mouthed thank you to Sam. "No one has to kiss your pa at the wake unless they want to," Sarah said reassuringly. "None of you are obliged to kiss anyone at any time, or let them kiss you, unless it feels like the right thing to do."

Hathaway raised her head from her mother's shoulder and softly kissed her Mamma's cheek.

Sarah smiled down at her daughter and returned the gesture. "I do expect you to be as quiet as possible during the wake and at the funeral. Also, please try to stay clean. But, the most important is to be polite." Sarah paused and looked at each of her children. "Does anyone have a question?"

Josh raised his hand.

"My goodness son, you don't need to raise your hand. What is it dear?"

"Can we have us some sugar cream pie now, Ma?"

# Chapter 34

Sarah had chosen a simple casket made from white oak. It was unadorned except for the necessary handles, two per side. Clyde Cutter considered it a modest upgrade from pine, insisting he had finer woods from which to choose. The coffin was lined with tufted, sky blue taffeta fabric. A small cushion was added as a head rest.

Henry was laid out in his Sunday white shirt with the collar, absent a tie, fully buttoned. He'd hated wearing a tie and Sarah saw no reason to put one on his body just for show. Clyde Cutter strongly advocated for posing and burying Henry with his bible on his chest, hands crossed atop. To his consternation, Sarah adamantly refused.

The leather cover on Henry's bible was worn from frequent handling. He'd held and read it so often it carried an imprint of his fingers and palm. Henry's habit, if he wanted a bookmark, was to extract leavings from the day's work that were captured in the cuff of his pants, a piece of straw, or a blade of grass.

Sarah longed for quiet time alone, to hold Henry's bible. She wanted to place her hand over his imprint and read the passages that had spoken to him with clarity and power, enough so, he wanted to be able to readily find them again.

Sarah requested that nothing be placed in Henry's hands. She didn't want attention drawn to how pale and soft they'd become during the six months he'd been gone from home. She'd always felt proud of her husband's tanned, work weathered, hands. Their appearance had been a testimony to his commitment to the farm and to providing for his family. The touch of Henry's calloused hands during the intimate times they'd shared had brought her pleasure and provided solace. Those were the hands she wanted to remember.

Clyde Cutter and his assistant set up two sawhorses in the Riley's parlor. On top of them they laid wide pine planks to form a platform. They spread a black cloth over the platform that cascaded to the floor on the sides and ends, forming a skirt. Henry's coffin was centered on top, leaving a three inch lip around its perimeter.

The lid to the coffin was removed and slid under the platform where the skirting hid it from view. Clyde had shown Sarah coffins with hinged lids, available in his upgraded line. The convenient feature had been ineffective in luring Sarah from the less expensive, plain white oak model.

The bumpy transport of the coffin, from town to the farm, had caused some shifting. Clyde took a few moments to reposition Henry's body and make adjustments to his clothing. He then called the family to come into the parlor for a private viewing.

Sarah, Hathaway, Abe, Josh, Luke, and an apprehensive Zeke, entered the room first. Jack, his wife, and their children, followed with Henry's parents and Tom Riley close behind.

In his undertaker tone Clyde said, "thank you all for gathering. I believe this is everyone…oh, it seems that Mary hasn't joined us."

Tom looked to his right, then left, then turned full circle. "She needed to step out back. I just assumed she'd returned to the house."

Clyde arched his brows as he pulled his watch from his vest pocket. Holding it in the palm of his hand he thumb flicked the cover open, took a quick glance, and then flipped it closed, the clink resonating in the quiet room. "I'm afraid we're getting close to the scheduled viewing time. Guests will be arriving."

"Please go ahead with the family's viewing," Tom said. "I'll fetch Mary."

Tom made a beeline outside to their privy. As he approached he could hear his wife crying. Tom knocked. "Mary, the undertaker has gathered the family for a private viewing. Can you come in the house now? It's getting close to time when guests will be arriving."

Mary opened the door and stumbled out to her husband. "The…the day Henry atta…attacked Sarah, aft…after Jeb and Jonas took him back to the mental asylum, I pra…prayed and asked God to release Sarah from her marriage."

Tom took his handkerchief from his inside vest pocket and wiped at his wife's tears. "Mary, take a deep breath…now another one."

Mary's sobs turned to weeping. "I knew Sarah would never divorce Henry. I realized I was praying for him to die. God knew that's what I was asking. My prayer was answered and Henry's dead."

Tom pulled his wife into his arms. "My dear, sweet, Mary, God knew the intent of your heart when you spoke that prayer. Henry's death has nothing to do with your words lifted up that day. When the stress of the wake and the funeral are both behind us, you'll sort it all out in your mind." Tom patted his wife's back. "God listens to our prayers, but he doesn't do our bidding." Tom handed his handkerchief to his wife. "Let's get in the house. Sarah needs us."

Sarah stood by the casket with Hathaway straddling her hip. The baby had flowers, tied with a pink bow, clutched in her hand. Sarah's and Henry's four sons were in a line at her side. Abe was positioned between Luke and Josh, a comforting arm around each. Luke completed the brothers' link with his arm around Zeke, who stood stiff as a board at his side.

Sarah leaned forward and helped her daughter place the small lily of the valley bouquet in the casket. Sarah spoke in a voice that was soft, but held conviction. "Henry Whitcome, you've left a fine legacy on this earth. I'm sure by now, you've heard God tell you, 'Well done, my good and faithful servant.'"

Extended family and many friends from miles around came to pay their respects. Gathering together was a healing experience. When Henry had his stroke his personality was abruptly changed. The man everyone had known and loved was gone, but not dead. No one had been given a chance to mourn his loss.

The wake provided an opportunity to exchange stories that spoke to the essence of Henry Whitcome and what he had meant to his family, friends, and community. Sarah watched as her three oldest son's chests puffed with pride as they listened to story after story about their father's generosity and kindness. She joined in their laughter when tales were told that spoke to Henry's love for humor and playing practical jokes.

Sarah surveyed the room. It was filled with close and casual acquaintances, some relationships spanning years. *Thank you Lord. This day is a blessings to my sons and to me. This is a celebration of a life well lived. The bittersweet remembering helps start the healing. Wish we didn't have to have a funeral tomorrow. What comfort can come from burying Henry's body?*

Early twilight had fallen on the day. Sarah glanced around the room. *Where's Zeke?* She looked out the parlor's window. *There he is sitting on the grass. Looks like he's digging.*

Sarah went outside for a breath of fresh air and to check up on her little loose cannon. *I expected Zeke's mouth to be the bane of my existence today, but he hasn't fired it off a single time. Wonder if he's coping alright.*

Sarah lowered her bulk to the grass and sat down next to her son. He acknowledged her presence with a nod, but didn't speak. Neither did Sarah.

It had rained a few days before and the top soil was still moist. Zeke tossed a fair-sized clod of dirt off to the side. A fat worm popped its head out and started trying to wiggle free.

Sarah watched as a robin flew down and stopped about two yards from the soil clump. The bird paced, back and forth, but didn't approach. *You want that juicy morsel don't you Miss Robin. I'll bet you've got a nest of hungry hatchlings waiting for you to bring their supper.*

Sarah plucked a long blade of grass, stuck the stem in her mouth and let it dangle. *My Henry's dead. Life goes on and it seems I'm not the only one with hungry babies to feed.* Sarah took the piece of grass out of her mouth and flicked it toward the robin. *Go hunting somewhere else, little mamma. My boy found this worm, it's his.*

Sarah initiated conversation with Zeke. "What are you digging?"

"A hole."

"What's that you're digging with?"

"A spoon."

"Where'd you get the spoon?"

"It was left over after I et me a bowl of custard."

"Oh. You feeling alright?"

"Yup."

"Ok, try not to bend the spoon. It belongs to your grandmother's set of good silver." *I suppose I should rescue the spoon but, all things considered, if it does get destroyed it couldn't be for a more noble cause. I'll just replace it with one from my matching pattern.*

Sarah got up. When she brushed off the back of her dress, she felt a large damp spot. *Oh my. I should have known better than to sit on the grass. Wonder if the spot shows? Of course it does. Do I care? No, not today.*

\*\*\*

May thirty-first dawned bright and sunny with temperatures in the mid sixty degrees. The graveside funeral scheduled for two o'clock in the afternoon at the LaFontaine Cemetery started on time with Pastor Edward Sloan conducting the service.

Preacher Sloan had a reputation for being long-winded and it didn't appear he'd be making any exceptions with Henry Whitcome's service. "Brother Whitcome was a loving husband and father and a God-fearing man. We don't always understand God's will. We don't know why he chose to call this fine man home at such an early age. Death is not ours to question..."

Sarah took a deep breath and blew it out, then inhaled and exhaled again. *Hogwash, Ed Sloan. My Henry being taken from us doesn't have a thing to do with God's will. Henry died because he caught pneumonia in a hospital when he was in a weakened state of health. His health was poorly because he had the heatstroke last summer.*

*Henry had a heatstroke because he was driven to get his crops harvested and the day was simply too hot for prolonged exposure, doing heavy work. Henry's stroke, his dying, aren't punishments either. These things just happened, Ed. It's called living life. I don't blame Henry, but truth is, he was stubborn that day and didn't heed to common sense, nor did I. I could have called him aside and made a stronger objection to him returning to the field when the sun was at its hottest, I didn't.*

Zeke tugged on his mother's arm. She leaned her head to the side so he could whisper in her ear. "Hathaway an me is real tired of sittin' here. Can me and her take us a walk? Pleasseee!"

Sarah turned her attention to preacher Sloan. It didn't appear he was even close to wrapping up his talk. *I never thought the service would be this long. It's gone beyond reason to expect the two to stay quiet.* She glanced down at her daughter who, several minutes before, had wiggled down from her lap and was now sitting at her feet, pulling grass.

Sarah whispered in Zeke's ear. "Ok, you may go for a walk. Promise to keep hold of Hathaway's hand. Don't walk beyond the road where the teams are waiting and you stay clear of the horses."

Zeke and Hathaway walked at a respectful pace, hand in hand, to the back of the crowd standing graveside. Zeke leaned down and whispered to his sister, "come on, Hathaway, let's you and me go explorin'."

Zeke took off walking at a pace so fast the baby's chubby legs couldn't keep up. He slowed when he realized he was dragging his sister, rather than leading her. What had him in hot pursuit was Cutter Brother's hearse. A team of horses remained hitched to the enclosed buggy and were tethered to a cast iron anchor placed directly in front of them.

Zeke led Hathaway away from the horses, to the rear of the hearse. He took a moment to assess the situation. It was clear that reaching the door handle was a challenge. He'd have to elicit cooperation from his sister Zeke tugged on Hathaway's arm to get her attention. "Up here, Hathaway, look up here."

Hathaway was bent over picking a dandelion with her free hand, Zeke jerked her arm. "Stop pickin' them dern flowers, Hathaway, you need to pay attention."

When she stood up Zeke took her face in his hands and tilted her head up. "See that there handle? Now look at them two steps. You climb up on that top step. I'll get on the step behind you and lift you up so you can reach the handle. When you reach it, pull down real hard so it'll open."

After Zeke had introduced her to climbing a few weeks before, Hathaway had taken it on as a sport, delighting in any opportunity that was presented. The baby smiled and nodded her head. She climbed up two steps and Zeke one. Positioned behind his sister he wrapped his arms around her waist and hoisted her as high as he could. The baby grasped hold of the levered handle, but wasn't strong enough to pull it down.

"Try harder, Hathaway, you's gettin' heavy..." Zeke's muscles failed him, he lost his hold and tumbled backward. Hathaway held fast, her body dangling off the lever. Her weight caused the lever to release and the door swung open slowly, pinning her up against the hearse. Her padded bottom made first contact and cushioned the bump. Her eyes got big, but she stayed mute and held fast.

Standing on the ground, Zeke was able to reach high enough to wrap his arms around Hathaway's legs and lower her to the ground.

Brother and sister paused just a beat, smiled at one another, then moved forward with their invasion. Hathaway eagerly climbed up again to the second step, which brought her chest high with the floor of the hearse. She stretched her arms out trying to find something to grab on to. Zeke, now on the step behind her, wrapped his arms around her legs and lifted her enough for her to be waist high with the floor. She bent forward and with a butt push from her brother, slid in.

Zeke jumped down, grabbed the bottom of the door and walked it over to the steps. He managed to maintain a hold on the door while he climbed inside the hearse. Placing his hand on the interior door handle, he pulled it closed and with a final jerk, heard the latch click.

"Boy Howdy," Zeke whispered, rubbing his hands together.

Hathaway jumped up and down. "Howdy, howdy."

"Quiet, Hathaway, we'se a hidin' in here."

The pair decided that the bed next to the large glass window looked inviting. They laid down on it and found it uncomfortable. Then they jumped on it. It wouldn't bounce.

"See them people out there, Hathaway. Directly they'll be burrin' that big box we was settin' in front of."

Hathaway elbowed for a better vantage position. "Me see."

When her face got close to the glass her breath formed a foggy spot. She used her finger and drew a line though it, giggling at the serendipitous discovery.

Zeke joined in and together they mastered the art of forcing air from their open mouths to create large fog canvases, on which to finger draw.

Sam arrived at the cemetery late and was surprised to find the Methodist minister still giving his graveside sermon. He didn't want to intrude so he found a place against a maple tree, a fair distance back from the collection of mourners. Looking to his left, he saw Clyde Cutter leaning up against a tree that was in line, but approximately ten yards, from his. Sam assumed he was waiting to oversee the internment and thought he appeared engrossed in what Preacher Sloan was saying.

Sam had noticed the hearse when he walked up, but didn't give it any thought. As his eyes tracked from Clyde back to the crowd, a movement in the hearse's window caught Sam's attention. The rig was positioned, on the backside of the tree where the undertaker stood, totally out of Cutter's view. Sam did a double take.

Zeke and Hathaway had their faces up against the window, hands splayed beside their cheeks, palms open. Their noses were flattened, their mouths were wide open with lips suctioned against the glass and their tongues were licking at the pane.

Distorted as the two mugs were, Sam recognized the interlopers immediately. Moving quickly, while trying not to draw Clyde Cutter's attention, Sam circled out and then up to the back of the hearse.

He opened the door with ease, not wanting to startle the marauders. When the siblings turned and looked, Sam placed his finger up against his lips in a shush gesture. He motioned for the pair to come to him. When they were both within reaching distance he wrapped his arm around Hathaway's waist and gently lifted her out. He reached to Zeke's side, latched on to the waist band of his pants and jerked him out. Without pausing to close the door, Sam circled back around and into the shade of the large maple tree. He kept his captives occupied by telling them stories until he heard the mourners sing, *When the Roll is Called up Yonder,* and the last Amen was pronounced.

After sending Zeke and Hathaway to find their mother, Sam walked through the disbursing mourners and gave his sympathies to the elder Whitcomes, then the Riley family. He looked around for Doc Adams. When he saw that Ben was standing graveside, obviously crying, he steered clear of him. He squeezed Abe, Josh, and Luke on their shoulders as he passed by them.

Sarah, now holding Hathaway, softly called out, "Sam, so nice of you to have come. Thank you."

"Ma'am," Sam gestured in a tipping motion with the hat he held. "I felt like I should come and give my sympathies to the family. Sorry I didn't get finished with my afternoon work in time to come for the whole service."

Sarah reached out and patted Sam's arm. "I know the work is a lot to keep up. That makes the effort you made to come all the more meaningful."

Sarah looked down at her youngest son who had just then sidled up beside her. "And you, Mister," she ruffled Zeke's hair, "thank you for being such a good big brother and looking after your baby sister."

"It weren't nothin', Ma." Zeke crossed his arms over his puffed out chest. "You can count on me anytime."

\*\*\*

It was past four in the afternoon when Jack Riley drove his team and wagon up to Sarah's door to deliver her and the children home after the funeral. They were climbing down when a buggy, with McVicker Livery Stable written on the side, came up their lane. Sarah and Josh recognized the driver as the courier that J.P. Garfield had sent a few days before to pick up the black Labrador.

Josh ran up to the wagon and blurted out, "Is there something wrong with Sir Lancelot?"

"He's doing just fine."

"Whew," Josh swiped his shirt sleeve across his eyes. "Hello, Sir, sorry I don't remember your name."

"Hello. The name's Crawford. Charles Crawford," the man said tipping his hat to the boy and to Sarah who had walked over to the wagon and was standing with her hand on Josh's shoulder.

Sarah looked up, her hand shielding her eyes from the sun. "Nice to see you again. Mr. Crawford, would you like to come in for some refreshments and tell us what's brought you back to our farm?"

Jack Riley stepped to his sister's side and put an arm protectively around her shoulders. "I'm sure you aren't aware that we've just come from the cemetery. We buried Mrs. Whitcome's husband today and she really needs to get in the house and lay down for a rest. Perhaps I can help you."

"Oh, Ma'am, I'm so sorry for your loss. My goodness, I had no idea you folks were in mourning. If I had, I would have picked another day to make my delivery."

"Delivery, what kind of delivery?" Josh asked.

"It's a gift for you, Josh, from Mr. Garfield. He was impressed that you wouldn't take the reward money for finding Sir Lancelot and he wanted you to have a token of his appreciation."

"A gift?"

"Yes, a gift." The courier raised the cover of a wicker basket setting on the seat beside him, reached in and lifted out a black Labrador puppy. He handed it down to Josh.

Josh gushed, "A puppy! A puppy for me?"

"Oh my goodness, Mr. Crawford, this is quite a surprise," Sarah said.

He pulled an envelope from his the inside jacket pocket. "Ma'am, this envelope contains the pup's pedigree certificate and a note from Mr. Garfield." Crawford turned in the wagon seat and gestured to the bags in the back of the wagon. "I've also brought a six-month supply of Kibble to leave for the pup's food."

"Kibble?" Luke approached and stood next to his uncle. "We don't grow Kibble around these parts. What do you make out of it?"

With one hand over her protruding mound and the other at the small of her back, Sarah interrupted, "Is it in a meal-type form, something that could be used for baking?"

"No, Ma'am. It's just for canines. Kibble is the recommended food for the Labrador and other breeds with pedigree," Crawford responded. "If you'll tell me where you'd like the feed put, I'll get it unloaded and be on my way."

Abe stepped forward. "Let's put it in the woodshed until we get this situation sorted out."

Jack helped Abe unload the Kibble. Charles Crawford expressed sympathy again, exchanged goodbyes, and headed back to town.

Josh sat down on the grass with the puppy in his arms. Luke, Zeke, and Hathaway crowded in, elbowing one another for closest proximity, squabbling over who would get first turn at holding the welcome newcomer.

Abe took control. "Josh, he's just a pup, a baby really. We can't let him run near the livestock. He could get hurt. Let's take him inside. You all can take turns holding the pup and if he gets loose, at least he'll be safe. Later tonight I'll help you figure out how to keep him corralled."

Taking his mother by the arm Abe said, "Ma, we need to get you off your feet for a rest. Josh, I'll go help Sam with the chores if you'll see to settin' out some leftovers for our supper. Uncle Jack, it's okay for you to leave. We'll be just fine and I know you need to get on home to your own chores."

Sarah looked at her oldest son, then over at her other children who were laughing and playing with the pup. "Yes, I think we're going to be just fine."

# Chapter 35

Ben Adams got out of bed. He'd spent the last hour tossing and turning. His mind wouldn't rest and sleep eluded him despite his fatigue from the day. Henry Whitcome's funeral had been a drain on his body and spirit. Ben lit the kitchen kerosene lamp and fixed a cup of chamomile tea. He often recommended the herbal remedy for his patients who had complaints of insomnia, anxiety, or muscle cramps. *My whole body aches. 'Rode hard and put up wet' fits me about right. I cried so much at Henry's graveside my eyes still feel puffy and irritated.*

With the lamp in one hand and his cup of tea in the other, Ben shuffled in sock covered feet to his rocking chair in the sitting room. He set the lamp and cup on the small adjacent table and plopped his weary frame down. Pulling the crocheted afghan from the back of the chair he wrapped in it to ward off the chill in the room.

*Henry, dead at thirty-six. Been the same as dead since the heatstroke last August, at least as far as the person he was. I miss his friendship. Why does it still hurt so much after all these months? Made a spectacle of myself, crying like that.* Ben picked up his cup and blew on the hot liquid to cool it a bit. As the steam rose he closed his eyes so his chapped lids could benefit from the soothing vapor.

*Hartman, yeah, he's a thorn in my side…sitting under that tree holding Hathaway, his arm around Zeke. According to Elmo, pulled the pair from doing mischief in Cutter Brother's hearse. Wasn't his place. Acting like he belonged…should have stayed at the farm and worked like he's hired to do.*

*Why'd I cry like that? I've had months to grieve the loss of Henry's friendship. I cried as hard at his graveside as I did at…Beth's…and the baby's.* Vivid memories of the day a few years prior, when he'd buried his wife Beth and their stillborn baby flashed in his mind. A tightness clenched at this chest and his breathing became rapid. *Maybe I wasn't crying only for Henry.* Ben's wife and baby lay at rest just a few gravesites over from where he'd stood earlier that afternoon.

Ben rubbed at his chest. *Need to stop this…they're gone, I've been though this, it doesn't help.* Gut wrenching emotions were surfacing. *Is Sarah's heart hurting? Can't stand to think of her alone and grieving. Wish we could hold and comfort one another. Hartman! Lying in bed in the room next to Sarah, I expect he'd like to hold her too.* Ben felt tortured over the thought that only a thin wall separated the hired hand's quarters from Sarah's bedroom.

*Sarah it isn't right! Having the hired hand live in your house hasn't been seemly from the get go. There was no talking sense to you when you hired Sam or even when you found out he had a criminal past. You're such a guileless, faith filled person. You seem to live a life so heavenly guided that sometimes, sometimes I don't think you show enough earthly sense. I love you and I can't tell you. I love you and you don't see it. I'm afraid your growing dependence on Sam's help will block you from ever seeing it and build a wedge that will prevent me from ever telling you.* Ben could feel the tears threatening to come again.

When Beth died it was Henry who befriended Ben. Now, Henry was dead and Ben didn't have anyone close enough with whom to share his deep personal thoughts. *I need a friend or someone to talk to...Henry why did you have to die?*

*What a perverse twisted soul I've become. Sitting here feeling sorry for myself because my best friend is dead and I don't have anyone to talk to about the woman I love. Except if Henry were alive, I couldn't talk to him anyway because it's his wife I'm in love with.*

Ben picked up the bible that lay on the table next to the rocker. He blew away a thin layer of dust and ran his hand across the book's cover. *I wonder, is it possible to have a faith and trust in God that's strong enough to see a person through these dark times? If I started reading the bible would I come to understand as my wife did, as Sarah does?*

The dust on the Bible was a reminder that the next day was Wednesday. Mrs. Hardacker would come to clean and cook for him. Ben half smiled to himself when he thought about the fresh smelling house and the home cooked meal he could look forward to the next evening. *Ben, you're living a lack-luster life when the thought of a visit from the housekeeper sparks a bright spot in your week.*

Ben held his cup in his left hand as he used his right hand to open Beth's bible to the page saved by her cross-shaped bookmark. Alongside the crocheted marker was a folded piece of paper. He laid both on his knee. The marked passage in the Bible was the twenty-third Psalm. Ben sipped at his hot tea as he read. "The Lord is my shepherd; I shall not want. He maketh me to lie down in green pastures: He leadeth me beside the still waters. He restoreth my soul: He leadeth me in the paths of righteousness for His name's sake. Yea, though I walk through the valley of the shadow of death, I will fear no evil: for Thou art with me; Thy rod and Thy staff they comfort me. Thou …"

When he'd finished reading, he picked up the cross and folded paper, placed them in the Bible's spine and closed it. He started to place the Text back on the table, then changed his mind. He opened the Bible again and took out the folded paper. *It's Beth's handwriting.* Unexpectedly finding the personal reminder of her, took him over the brink. Ben began to sob tears of grief for Beth and the baby that he thought had long since been wrung from him.

Gaining his composure he wiped his eyes so he could see clearly. Ben leaned in to the light of the lamp. He'd always found Beth's cursive difficult to decipher. "Death frightens us because we feel helpless in its presence. It isn't like a formidable enemy that we can face and fight. It isn't even like pain, suffering, disease or injury. We can't muster up enough strength and courage to overcome death. When we are separated from life on this earth, that portion of our journey is final. God, manifested as our Lord and Savior, is the only source of strength that can walk those of us left behind through the grief that shrouds us in darkness. Only He can steer us to the light on the other side of the pain. Our, Heavenly Father is the perfect shepherd. He promises to guide and protect us throughout our lives. He will keep us on the path toward light to bring us home to His house in heaven, if only we trust and believe in Him."

*Beth, my sweet Beth. Sometimes I'm able to picture you and our child in a glow of light, not shrouded in darkness. I'm not against believing. I just don't know how to make that happen.* Ben closed the bible and put it back on the table.

He got up and tossed the afghan over the back of the rocker, picked up the lamp and cup, then padded into the kitchen. After placing the lamp on the table, he turned the wick down extinguishing the flame and went back to bed. The bisabolol oil from the tea leaves had brought on the anticipated mellowing effect and he could feel sleep coming. Just before he let it claim him, a thought occurred. *Leave a treasure unguarded and someone's sure to take it. If I worry about Sam moving in too close to Sarah and do nothing, then I've got no one but myself to blame. Starting next week I'm going to visit her and the children on a regular basis. I'll keep going until she realizes I love her or she tells me I'm no longer welcome.*

\*\*\*

It was near nine o'clock the night of the funeral before Sarah got Hathaway to sleep and the other children sent off to bed. Exhausted, she lay in her bed listening to noise coming from the upstairs bedrooms. The boys were scuffling and giggling. The puppy's paws made a clicking sound as it ran about. She hoped the commotion wasn't bothering Sam too much. She'd give her sons a few more minutes and then make them hush if they didn't do it on their own accord. The happy sounds were a welcome respite. *A puppy. Now that's the last thing in this world I thought we'd be dealing with at the end of this day. Delivered right to our door, with a supply of food…the courier called it kibble. A dog with its own food to eat, not scraps from the table, something made especially for him. I never heard of such.*

*I doubt it's the puppy keeping the boys awake. It's tiny and must be tuckered out from traveling all day. Likely it's the other way around and the boys won't let it be so it can sleep.*

About ten minutes later the noise overhead ceased. *They must have all finally worn out.* Sarah knew that she too needed sleep. As was her nightly routine she lifted her thoughts in prayer. *Thank you, Lord, for the balmy weather and the beauty of this day. I felt your presence and I was comforted by the warmth of your touch through the sunshine on my shoulders.*

Sarah wiped at tears that seeped and ran down her cheeks. *Thank you for the peace that comes from knowing that Henry is in heaven with you. I trust you for the courage to carry on, until I too come to be with you in heaven and Henry and I are together again. Thank you for my children, my family and friends. They are all a blessing to me. I treasure the time I have left with them on this earthly plain. I give you praise for the joys Your Word promises are yet to come. Heavenly Father, use me as an instrument of Thy will and mold me and make me an example of your love and grace. Amen.* Sarah pulled the covers up around her shoulders, snuggled in and let sleep overtake her.

After about an hour of sleep the baby in Sarah's womb began to stir with such force that it woke her. She gently massaged her abdomen as a calming effort. *Hey little one, I'm trying to sleep. It feels like you're punching me with your fists and kicking me with your feet all at the same time.*

Sarah tossed back her covers. Moonbeams streaming through her bedroom's window bathed her protruding mound in a glow of soft light. *Good grief, it looks like a litter of kittens rolling around in there.* Now fully awake, Sarah turned her thoughts to her children. *This new one will never experience Henry's fatherly love. The other five did, but needed more of him. I hope they'll cling to special memories. Luke and Zeke's recollection of living with their father will fade quickly. I need to make a special effort to tell and re-tell family stories, which include him, Henry deserves to be remembered. Sweet little Hathaway likely won't remember her pa at all…*

The enormity of the loss, to her children and to her, swept over Sarah. Burrowing her face in her pillow to muffle the sound, she sobbed. As she cried she thought about the funeral and those who had attended. Sarah pictured each person as they stood graveside. Her mind's eye passed by Ben Adams, stopped, then went back and focused in on his face. *Ben cried the hardest of anyone at the funeral. He and Henry were close, but…*

With a jolt she lifted the pillow from her face and sat up. *Beth and the baby's graves were just a few yards from where we stood this afternoon. Ohhh, Ben, ohhh…* The reality of her friend's pain swept over Sarah and she was consumed with Ben's sorrow as well as her own. A loud ear-piercing groan from deep within her escaped before she got it stifled with her pillow.

"Sarah, are you alright?" The voice came through the wall that separated her bedroom from the hired hand's quarters. "Do you need anything?"

"I..I..I'll be fine. S..s..sorry to have disturbed you."

"I could make coffee and we can talk, if that would be of comfort."

"N..no." Sarah took a deep breath and gained her composure. "No thank you, Sam. Goodnight."

Sarah reached heavenward for comfort. *Father in heaven, please take the awareness of Ben's pain from me for tonight. His grief along with my own is just too much to handle. Bring Ben comfort, Father. I know he's hurting. Soften his heart so that he might be open and receptive to You. I ask You to send someone into Ben's life that will lead him to an understanding of Your love and grace, so that he can come to a belief and trust in You. A belief that will develop into a personal relationship with You, through which he can draw comfort.*

Sarah felt a familiar nudging, almost an urging as she silently prayed her request. Most often when this occurred she recognized it as God calling her to be involved in the answer to a prayer she'd just lifted up. *Heavenly Father, I really don't think the person to reach out to Ben right now is me. We've been close friends for years. Henry and I both often discussed our faith with him. I don't know what more I could say, he'd likely be more receptive to someone else...*

Sarah stopped praying as a scripture popped into her mind. Proverbs 3: 5-6 "Trust in the Lord with all thine heart; and lean not unto thine own understanding. In all thy ways acknowledge Him, and He shall direct thy paths."

*Lord, if I'm to be the one to talk to Ben about having a closer relationship with You, then please make it clear by providing me with an opportunity that won't seem awkward.*

To Sarah's relief the baby stopped moving about. Her tears had been cathartic and calming. She fell asleep, not waking until morning.

\*\*\*

Supper at the Whitcome farm the night of the funeral had consisted of leftovers. By Sam's assessment the food brought by friends and neighbors was fair to middling the first go around. It wasn't up to Sarah's quality of cooking, but passable. As a second offering, the food left Sam wanting. He cringed just thinking about it. *A dab of beef and noodles, not enough to go full circle around the table. The green beans were plentiful, but limp and tasteless. Now I have to say, that fried chicken was tasty, but shy on pieces. Three wings and one thigh, I could have eaten them all and not got satisfied. The children seemed content with filling up on bread and jam.*

*I don't have a pick about the leftovers being served. Under the circumstance, I didn't expect Sarah to cook. Still, I got up from that supper table feeling hungry. I felt a bit sheepish asking Sarah if she minded if I went into town. I wasn't asking her permission to go, just wanted to know if she'd be alright left alone with the children after the stress of the day.*

Sam had excused himself after supper and high-tailed it into town for a plate of beef stew in the LaFontaine Hotel's dining room. After the meal he'd stopped by the tavern and picked up a couple of bottles of beer for later.

These days he preferred to drink alone, just for relaxation. Drinking in taverns had brought trouble for him in the past. Once that was behind him, he'd vowed to steer clear of socializing in those type of establishments.

It was now about eight o'clock and Sam was nestled in his quarters. He was worn out from witnessing the emotions of the day and needed solitude. He was alone with two of his favorite companions, a bottle of Falstaff and a book. He got comfortable in his rocker. Reverently he smoothed his hand over the cover of his copy of Jack London's *The Call of the Wild*.

*I've been longing to read this since I first heard about it. ...been pert near a year since it was published. When I saw the clerk at Parker's fixin' to put it on the shelf, I snatched it right out of his hand.*

*I've got my solitude, guess I'll have to wait for the quiet to come. Sounds like the children and that new pup are going to be playing for a while.*

*A purebred Labrador arriving special delivery, with a supply of food. My, what a surprise. Spratt's kibble, I've seen it advertised in Forest and Stream. Personally though, I've never known a dog that ate other than scraps from the table.* Sam chuckled. *Kibble's a good thing for this new pup. He for sure would be left wanting if he depended on scraps from Sarah's table. With her hungry brood, even crumbs are in short supply.* Sitting in nothing but his union suit, Sam felt a bit of a chill. Rather than light the wood in his fireplace, he got up and grabbed the quilt off of his bed, wrapped it around his shoulders and snuggled in his rocker to read.

\*\*\*

Buck, snatched from his beautiful ranch in California, was deep in his brutal life as a sled dog in the Yukon when Sam decided to give his eyes a rest. *The house is quiet. Guess everyone finally fell asleep. I was so involved in the book I didn't even notice when the noise stopped.* He glanced at the mantel clock. *Quarter to ten. I've been sittin' here so long I think I need to step outside and get a breath of fresh air.*

The night sky was bright with stars. A three-quarter moon helped illuminate the yard. Sam stepped off of the front porch and instinctively glanced toward the chicken house and barn. All seemed well. He raised his left arm high alongside his head and grasped it with his right hand just below the elbow. He stretched upward causing a gentle tugging on his spine. He heard a faint popping as his vertebra aligned.

An owl in the sycamore tree to the left of where Sam stood was perched on an outer branch with little foliage and was easily seen. It called down *whoo, whoo.*

Sam returned the greeting with a whisper. "It's none of your business, that's who." Sam bent at the waist and let his arms dangle down, relaxing the muscles across the top of his shoulders while stretching those in his lower back. *It was a nice funeral, if a funeral can be called that. Henry Whitcome had a lot of friends and family that come to mourn him. Doc Adams was real tore up. Don't think I ever saw a man cry so hard. Wonder if he'll be comin' around more now that Sarah's a widow. Don't think he much likes me…might be he just sees me as a threat. Sarah held up well, awful tired though.*

The cool breeze of the spring night sent a shiver down his spine. Sam scurried back to the comfort of his quarters. *I hate to leave Buck stranded in the Yukon, but I'd better get some sleep.* Just as he was climbing into his bed he heard a deep groan followed by sobbing coming through the wall adjoining Sarah's bedroom.

"Sarah, are you all right? Do you need anything?"

"I..I..I'll ..be fine. S..s..sorry to have disturbed you."

"I could make coffee and we can talk. Would that be of comfort?"

"N..no. No thank you, Sam. Goodnight."

Sarah's crying now sounded muffled to Sam, as if she might have her face burrowed in her pillow. Sam stood in the middle of his room, not sure what to do. He felt embarrassed for both himself and Sarah. Her private moment had unwittingly been shared. *I'm so sorry for your loss Sarah. I wish I could bring your husband back for you. I love working here on the farm and being around you and the children. I'd gladly leave, if your family could be whole again. Since that can't happen I intend to stay.*

*After the new baby comes and after a time, I hope you'll want the love of a man again. I'll be here and I hope you'll see me as more than just your hired hand. I expect Doc Adams might try to court you. Ben has schooling, I have a lot to offer too.*

Sam spread the quilt out over his feather tic and crawled in bed. He lay with his head on his pillow, the ends folded up over his ears. He'd do what he could to give Sarah her privacy. *Hartman, who are you tryin' to convince that you have something to offer, Sarah, or you? It's obvious that God is extremely important in the woman's life. She more than just believes in God, she talks to Him, all the time. Can you offer to share that with her? Just where do you stand on the issue of letting God guide your life?* The question remained on Sam's mind when sleep staked its claim.

# Chapter 36

Sarah's mind wandered as she kneaded dough to make bread. *Two weeks since we buried Henry. I'm grieving his death, but not the loss of his daily presence. He'd been at the Logansport Asylum for six months and I've passed through much of that pain.*

*Truth is, I feel as if a heavy burden has been lifted. While Henry was in the hospital, hardly a day went by that I didn't think about him and how he was doing. After the heat stroke, he didn't know me or the children. I often wondered if he might be lonely or sad. It grieved me that I didn't know how to comfort him.*

*Somehow I now feel free. Free to think about the future beyond Henry's conventional, narrow approach to farming. Till, plant, harvest, then repeat the cycle. That was about it for him besides a dab of livestock to support our own needs. Henry made the success of this farm primarily dependent on the sweat of his brow and that cost him. There must be an easier way besides backbreaking tilling of the soil to make a living. I'm confident that the selling of eggs will bring in income, but that alone can't sustain us.*

A light scraping noise caught Sarah's attention. She turned to see the gnarly fingers on a slender branch scratching against the windowpane. When the breeze picked up, a section of the branch lush with new tender leaves, alternated between patting and slapping at the glass. *Looks as if the maple's new growth is touching the house. I need to ask Sam to pare it back some.*

Sarah smoothed her hand across the mound at her waist and the baby moved. That drew her attention to her children that were outside playing. Sarah walked to the screen door and took a peek. Josh and Luke were in the yard playing fetch with Lancy. The pup had been so named in honor of his father, Sir Lancelot. The two littlest were playing under the maple tree.

Zeke, as per his usual, was digging and loading his toy wagon with dirt. Hathaway, who could be heard barking orders, was directing his hauling efforts. "Ze, here." The small girl was sitting astraddle a mound of soil she'd already amassed and was motioning for her brother to add more. Zeke complied.

Sarah watched as her daughter aggressively pounded the dirt in place leaving tiny hand imprints in her wake. When Hathaway was done she scurried to Sarah's flower bed and plucked a bedraggled geranium. Back at the dirt pile she laid the limp flower at the pentacle of her creation. She leaned down and sniffed the bloom, then clapped her hands. With a mother's smile on her face Sarah returned to her bread making and ruminating about the farm.

*What if my boys have a hunger for growing crops like their pa did? I don't own enough acreage to divide among them for their start in life. Henry and I had thought we'd buy more land, but now I don't see how I'll ever be able to afford...*

Sarah's thoughts were interrupted when Abe rushed into the kitchen letting the screen door bang closed behind him. "Ma, look at the size of these eggs." Abe set a basket on the table that was mounded to overflowing with the day's collection of eggs from the new flock.

"My goodness those are large. Looks to be about two dozen."

"Ya got a good eye, Ma. I counted twenty-six in all. I think we got us enough pullets that's a layin' to start takin' eggs to market."

"I agree. Parker's said they would take up to three-dozen a day from us." Sarah glanced up at the kitchen clock. "It's only 9:00 a.m. If you hurry you could get two dozen in to the store before noon. Go get an apple crate, fill it with straw and bring it back." Sarah grabbed a damp cloth and began wiping the eggs clean.

Abe returned quickly with the crate and straw. "Thanks, Son, I'll pack the eggs for traveling, while you hitch the team."

Sarah had the crate of eggs in hand and was headed outside when Abe pulled up with the wagon. "Ma," Abe said, "that's too heavy for you to carry in your condition. Give it to me."

Sarah handed over the load and gave the boy a peck on the cheek. "You're a good son to look out for your mamma."

Abe loaded the eggs in the bed of the wagon while Sarah dispensed last minute instructions. "Drive the team at a steady pace and steer clear of the ruts as much as you can. Tell Mr. Parker we'll deliver at least two dozen and up to three dozen eggs Monday through Saturday from now on. Offer a selling price of eleven cents per dozen, but don't take less than nine. Tell him if he's agreeable, we can both keep track and settle up at the end of each month." Sarah pulled her son in to her arms and hugged him tightly as she whispered in his ear. "This is a proud day."

With a smile that spread ear to ear, Abe climbed up on the wagon seat, took the reins and gave the command to walk. The horses responded at a steady even pace. The boy's smile never waned as he drove the team down the Whitcome's lane to the main road that would take him to LaFontaine and his first of many planned egg deliveries.

*** 

"Zeke," Sarah hollered through the screen door, "please ring the dinner bell. Abe's not back yet but its noon and I need to get all of you fed. He should be home directly."

Zeke climbed up on the apple crate and was reaching for the bell's rope when he saw Abe turn in from the main road. "Abe's a comin' lickety-split up the lane."

Abe unhitched the team and led them to the watering trough. After both horses had their fill he quickly wiped them down then put them in their stalls. He hightailed it to the house and found the others already gathered at the table waiting for him.

"Ma, Ma, you ain't never gonna believe the news I have." Abe jerked his chair out from the table and sat down with so much force that it tilted back on its two hind legs. His arms started flailing in an attempt to gain his balance.

Sam jumped up and caught the back of the chair. "Whoa there, boy. If you fall on your head and knock yourself silly your ma will never get to hear the news."

"Thanks, Sam." Abe took a deep breath and started again. "I delivered the eggs to Mr. Parker like ya told me to."

"How much did you get per dozen?" Sarah asked.

"I bargained with him and got us ten cents per dozen. But that's not the news I have to tell ya. While I was talkin' to Mr. Parker a man by the name of Brockie was a standin' at the counter listenin' in."

Luke reached for a biscuit. "That sounds kinda rude. Did ya tell him ta mind his own beeswax?"

Sarah's arms flew out over the spread of food. "Hold on a minute.

We're all so excited to hear the news that we're forgetting to thank the Lord for our blessings. Luke, put that biscuit on your plate and you can say the prayer for us."

"Yes, Ma'am." The boy bowed his head and folded his hands. "Thank you, Jesus, for this good food we are about to eat and for the excitin' news Abe has brought us from town. If that news is that Mr. Parker sent us some peppermint sticks then a double Amen to ya."

Abe picked up the bowl of fried potatoes and spooned out a large serving. "This news is way better than peppermint candy. Like I said, the man's name was Brockie, Joe Brockie. He runs the Peabody Brother's Saw Mill at Woods Land, west of town. He said that if we were willing to deliver fresh eggs out to them every day, he'd pay us thirteen cents a dozen."

Sam took the bowl of potatoes passed on by Abe. "Thirteen cents a dozen. That's a really good price. How many dozen does he want?"

Abe pocketed his mouth full of food in the side of his cheek so he could respond. "That's the best part. He wants six dozen a day."

Sarah was quick to do the math. "We've got one hundred and fifty pullets. That's a potential of twelve dozen eggs or there about per day. We've promised Parker's General Store up to three dozen and the LaFontaine Hotel the same amount. Well praise the Lord. Those three customers alone will use up our daily supply."

Sam split open a biscuit and slathered it with butter. "What's nice about it is that the deliveries are all fairly close together. A mile into town to deliver to Parkers and the hotel and then a mile on west of town and you're at the Woods Land. Five miles round trip and you're done delivering."

"What about Sunday, Ma?" Luke asked. "Does Abe get to miss church so he can deliver eggs?"

Sam interjected. "The general store is closed on Sundays, but not the hotel dining room. The saw mill will still need to feed their crew. I could make the Sunday runs so it won't interfere with the boy attending worship."

"Eggs a day or two old are still fine for eating and cooking," Sarah said. "Maybe with using the free range egg collection and cutting back on our own use, we could get ahead a few dozen. Enough to cover Sunday's needs when we deliver on Saturday, then everyone would be free to go to church."

Sam picked up on the hint, but said nothing. For a time the only sound at the table was the clicking and scraping of eating utensils against plates.

Sarah hadn't eaten much. She sat looking out the window as she pondered Abe's news and sipped at her coffee. Her attention snapped back to the table when Josh yelled.

"Hathaway, give me back my pork chop. Ma, Ma, that ain't fair, that's my meat, she done already ett hers."

"Oh my goodness," Sarah said. "Here, Josh, you can have mine." She transferred her meat to her son's plate. "And you, Missy, if you want to sit up at the table with all of us then keep your hands off your brother's plate. If you don't, I'll push your highchair away and put the tray back on it."

The small girl was unaffected by the scolding. She picked up the stolen pork chop and began gnawing on it. Sarah took it from her and started cutting it in small pieces. "I wonder if we could market our fresh produce as well as the eggs to the saw mill. That would be easier than hauling it to the farmer's market in Wabash each week. I checked this morning and it looks as if we'll have green beans and onions ready to pick in about a week, carrots look to be close behind. We'll have corn, yellow squash and watermelon by mid-July. Potatoes will be ready to dig up by late August."

"Ma, that's a great idea," Abe said. "I told Mr. Brockie I'd make his first egg delivery a week from tomorrow. If you'll make out a list of the vegetables you're offerin' for sale and prices, I'll talk to him about it then."

Sarah laid her fork down and wiped her mouth with her napkin. "I'll make out the list, but I want to go with you."

Abe took a big gulp of milk then responded, "No need, Ma, I can do it."

"I'm sure you can, Abe," Sarah said smiling. "It's just that I've never had an opportunity to price dicker and I'd like to give it a try."

\*\*\*

A week later Sam set up a work area to teach Luke and Josh how to clean and pack eggs. He equipped each boy with a piece of cloth and he centrally located a bucket of water and the day's gathering of eggs. He also had a crate and straw ready for layering and packing at the ready.

Sam demonstrated as he talked. "Dip your rag in the pan and wring it out leaving it damp, but not dripping wet. Pick up an egg and hold it with one end resting on your thumb and the other end against your pointer and middle finger. In this position you can apply enough pressure to hold the egg securely and not worry about crushing it. Gently wipe the shell clean, then rotate it to make sure you've removed all of the excrement."

Josh's eyes flew open wide and his mouth went slack-jawed. "Sam, you know Ma don't hold with cussin' around here. If you're tryin' to tell us to wipe this here brown stuff off the eggs, it'd be best if you just called it what it is...chicken shit."

Sam was struggling to hide a grin on his face when he spotted Elmo Jones coming up the lane. His rig was leaving a trail of dust that kept on traveling toward the house after he'd pulled his horse to a stop. "Sam, got a telegram for ya."

Sam walked to the buggy. "A telegram. For me?"

Elmo spit a stream of tobacco over his shoulder. "It done come in a little whilst ago from Kokomo. Sent by a preacher name of Alcorn. Careful when you open it. The telegraph office done sealed that sucker tighter than a canned jar of tomato juice."

Sam reached up and took the telegram. "Thanks, Elmo."

"No need, deliverin' is my job," Elmo said as he sniffed the air. "I'm catchin' a whiff of apple pie. Think I'll go see if Mrs. Whitcome is in a givin' mood."

"Boys, you can go play. I need a minute to read this telegram," Sam said as he walked to the shade of the large maple tree. He placed his back against the massive trunk and slid to the ground.

JUNE 22, 1904
CLEM HARGROVE DIED 8:00 A.M. TODAY
FUNERAL JUNE 24, 10:00 A.M.
FAMILY REQUESTS YOU COME
PASTOR BYRON ALCORN, FREE WILL BAPTIST CHURCH

Sam let the telegram fall to the ground. He covered his face with his hands and wept. Sam had worked for Clem Hargrove for several years up to the time Clem decided to turn his farm land over to his sons and retire. That had been just prior to Sam coming to work for Sarah. Clem had been like a father to Sam. He'd been close to Clem's wife and his sons as well. He wanted to go pay his respects and say good-bye to his friend.

Sam sat rubbing at his chest while tears trickled down his cheeks. After a time he dried his eyes, folded the telegram and put it in his pocket, then went to tell Sarah that he needed to leave as soon as possible. He'd carry the burden of grief for the loss of Clem as well as the worry over leaving Sarah with the farm to manage alone until he returned.

# Chapter 37

Sam leaned back in his seat, closed his eyes, and listened to the clickity-clack of the train's wheels on the track. He needed to relax, the rhythmic sound helped. Sam was struggling with the reality that his former employer and long time friend Clem Hargrove was gone. For the past couple of months Sam had wished for a chance to go to Kokomo to visit Clem, the timing for such a trip just hadn't worked out. Now instead of sharing the burden of his unrequited love for Sarah with Clem and asking his advice as he'd hoped to do, he'd be attending his funeral.

Sam patted the tote filled with food that was resting on the seat next to him and his thoughts turned to Sarah. *Sarah is a wonder. She never even hesitated when I told her I needed to leave. All of her concerns were selfless and directed toward my well-being and the Hargrove family. She even took time to pack food for me.*

Clem Hargrove's face flitted into Sam's consciousness and he refocused on the tasks that lay ahead. Before getting on the train Sam had sent a telegram to Pastor Alcorn. In it Sam detailed his plan to arrive by rail in Kokomo at six o'clock that evening and that he'd rent a horse and ride out to the Hargrove farm the next morning.

The train started to reduce speed. Sam glanced out the window just as they passed the Kokomo city limit sign. With the long blast of the engine's whistle the train pulled into the station.

The first person Sam saw when he climbed down from the train was Byron Alcorn. His former preacher greeted him with an outstretched hand. "Welcome back my friend."

Sam grasped the pastor's hand. "Byron! Hello. I didn't expect anyone to meet me at the train station."

"I got your telegram saying you were coming in at six o'clock this evening. I figured the news of Clem's passing would be hard for you. I wanted to greet you when you arrived."

"Yes, it is hard. I still can't believe he's really gone. Had he been ill? The telegram didn't give particulars."

"They think it was his heart, Sam. He'd done his morning chores. Ate a big breakfast according to Clara and then sat down in his rocker to read his bible. She thought he'd fallen asleep. She didn't realize he'd passed until she called him to come for lunch. When he didn't respond she went to check on him and found him in a peaceful pose with his bible resting on his lap."

"What a shock that must have been for Clara," Sam said.

"It was a terrible shock. Thankfully their oldest, Roman, happened to stop by shortly after she found Clem. I doubt Clara could have hitched a team, or rode a horse to go for help. Having their boy stop by was a Godsend."

"The Hargroves are a close family. I'm so glad Clara has all of them to comfort her at this time. Of course you know Clem's retirement from farming and keeping only a handful of livestock was why I left his employment. With his sons taking over his acreage, there wasn't work for me."

"Yes, I'd heard that," Byron responded.

Sam motioned forward with the satchel he was holding. "Appears we're standing in the path of those wanting to board the train. Let's move on. We can talk while we walk."

"Certainly," Byron said. "Clem had a reputation for being a hard worker."

"That he was." Sam switched the satchel he was carrying to his left hand to make walking with Byron on his right side easier. "Clem worked harder than two men. He come nigh to puttin' me to shame more than once. Sounds as if his body just wore out on him."

"Could be," Byron responded. "Clem was past seventy. He had a long and prosperous life. He'll be remembered fondly by this town and sorely missed by his friends and family."

"I know I'm sure gonna miss him," Sam said. "If Clem could have planned his passing I don't think he would have changed a thing. He loved reading his bible. I've heard him referred to as a God-fearing man. I'd describe Clem more like a God-loving man."

"Amen to that brother," Byron said. "Come on with me to the parsonage and we'll get you settled in. Would a thick steak at the Steer's Inn whet your appetite?"

"A steak sounds inviting. But I couldn't put you and the missus out by staying at the parsonage. I'll get a room at the hotel."

"Nonsense. Millie is out of town visiting her sister and I'd love to have the company. I've got the guest room all set up. We'll drop your things off, then head on over for that steak."

The pair reached the parsonage. Sam stuck the tote containing food in the parsonage's icebox. Seeing Byron's curious look he said, "It's food that was sent along with me for the train ride, biscuits with thick slabs of ham. Add some hot coffee and our breakfast tomorrow morning will be covered."

"Sounds perfect for a couple of men without a woman to cook for them," Byron responded.

***

As they walked from the restaurant to the parsonage it was dark except for the glow from street lanterns and kerosene lamps that shown from the windows in houses they passed. Murmurs of conversations could be heard coming from porches or through screen doors. Both men were sated from the huge steak and generous side dishes they'd eaten. It was a balmy evening and the stroll was peaceful.

"How's your flock doing Byron?" Sam asked tipping his hat when a man and woman passed them.

"I'm guessing you're referring to the one at Free-Will Baptist and not those six scrawny 'mix-matched' hens we've got penned in the parsonage's backyard," Byron quipped as he likewise tipped his hat to the passing couple.

"Yes, your congregation. When I left town it seemed to be thriving."

"The Lord has blessed our church. We're growing, Sam. We're up to an average of eighty to ninety on some Sunday mornings. We've got forty to forty-five faithful who come to Sunday night worship and the number attending Thursday prayer meeting is on a steady rise."

"That's good news. I'm happy for you, Byron."

"What about you, Sam, you attending church anywhere?"

"No. Not that I don't have choices. LaFontaine, the town near the farm where I work, has a plenty. There's a Methodist, Christian, Church of Christ, and a Primitive Baptist."

"Well since you don't have a Free-Will Baptist in your town, I can't be accused of proselytizing if I give you my opinion. I'd steer clear of the

Primitive Baptist. They don't refer to them as "Hard Shell" for no reason. All choices considered, I'd recommend the Methodist Church. They're evangelical, believe in missions, and preach that we're saved by grace. As I recall the woman you work for goes to the Methodist church."

"Yes. She's a Methodist. She attends regularly with her children. Her parents and brother and his family who live in the area attend there as well."

"Has she ever invited you to go with the family?"

"Oh yes. I know I'm welcome to go with them. I'd feel comfortable attending by myself as far as that goes. I just haven't done it. I attended your church when I lived on Clem's farm because he expected it of me. I really didn't mind. If I hadn't attended I wouldn't have gotten to know you. Your friendship made it worthwhile, if nothing else."

With tongue in cheek Byron said, "Gee thanks, Sam. I'd hoped my sermons made at least a bit of an impression on you."

"Oh they did, Byron. I didn't mean to sound rude. You're a good preacher. It's just, well…this woman, Sarah Whitcome, the one I work for…she has a faith and belief that goes way beyond just going to Sunday and weekday services. Not meaning any disrespect to you but I've never known anyone who seems to be so Godly and near perfect as her."

"No offense taken. Tell me about Sarah's Godly ways."

"She's kind and loving, not just to her children and family but to everyone, even the grizzly old cuss that delivers the mail. She has a wisdom that I don't understand and she prays about everything. I mean everything, Byron. She prayed about what kind of chickens to buy and how many. They caught the Roup and she prayed they'd get well. Did you ever hear of someone praying for chickens? She talks about things I don't understand like seeking God's will and following where He leads."

"She sounds like a lovely woman."

"Oh, she is. She's lovely in every way. Did I mention that her husband was in a mental institution since last fall, but died a couple of weeks back?"

"No you didn't. So she's now a widow."

"Yes, she's free now."

"Free? That's an odd way to describe someone whose husband very recently died. Has something unseemly happened between the two of you? Are you interested in courting her?

"No, nothing has transpired between us. But, yes, I'd like to court her when the time is right. But I don't think she even notices me."

"Good grief man, pull in the reins. Your heart has you running way ahead of where she's capable of being at this time. Does she have any children?"

"Well, yes. She has four boys and a baby girl not yet two. Oh...and she's expecting another baby in about two months."

"Expecting a baby! I thought you said her husband had been away in a mental institution?"

"He was. He had a heat stroke, went crazy, got violent, beat her up and raped her. That's why he ended up in a mental institution."

"Sam, you haven't just lost your heart, you've lost your head!"

"I can't help it, Byron. I'm in love with her. I love her children too. I'm willing to wait while she grieves her husband's death. None of that worries me. What worries me is her faith in God. I believe in God, but I don't understand this need, this relationship where she passes by Him every decision she makes. I have the sense that God is the most important thing in her life. How can I ever expect to get close to a woman like that? How can I come to know God like she does?"

The pair had reached the parsonage when Byron responded. "There is a way for you to come to know God like that, Sam. However the relationship can never come from you wanting it as a leg up to capturing Sarah's heart. It can only come through your sincere surrendering of your will and inviting the Holy Spirit to fill the void thus created. Living a spirit-filled life and letting God lead, means seeking His will for you, not your own. His will very likely could be in keeping with your hope for a life with Sarah Whitcome. Or, it might not. That's where the surrender part gets sticky. Your love for God and being in His will has to come first. It's really the only place we can find true acceptance and happiness."

Sam shook his head, "Byron, you know I've made some mistakes that can't be fixed. I'm not so sure God would welcome me in to his...uh, fold."

Byron clasped Sam on the shoulder. "Sam, God invites us in to His family just as we are. He doesn't require that we change or clean up our lives first. He just wraps His arms around us and says, welcome. The beauty is that once we let His love in to our hearts, our wants become compatible with His will. There's no two ways about it, it takes a leap of faith. We're welcomed through His grace. God's grace is free; we just have to accept it."

Byron opened the door and gestured for Sam to enter. "I'll put on a pot of coffee and we can talk some more."

"Thanks, Byron, I'd like that."

# Chapter 38

Sarah started clearing the breakfast dishes from the table. She was a little later getting the task done than usual. She'd taken time immediately after they ate to supervise the loading of the day's egg delivery. She wanted to make sure the cargo was secure. The road into town was fairly smooth, but the delivery on out to the lumber mill required travel on a rutted and rough stretch.

Abe was in charge of making the daily deliveries. Sarah was sending Josh along to train as his back up. The boy had turned ten in May and had matured a lot over the previous six month period. Josh was smart and she knew he would catch on quickly to the business side of the delivery process. It was the handling of the team and wagon by himself that concerned her. Abe had been bigger and stronger at age ten. Josh was eager and willing and Sarah knew a mother couldn't ask for more.

They'd settled in to a routine of gathering eggs mid-morning and packing them for the next morning's delivery. This was a comfortable routine during the summer months and avoided last minute rushing. Come fall, when the boys were back in school, a different schedule would be required. Sarah was thankful she didn't have to think about that just now.

Luke had gone to the chicken house to collect the pullets' offering for the day. When Abe and Josh got back from their delivery route, Sarah planned to use the day's collection to finish training them and Luke how to wash and pack for delivery. Sam had started to teach them the day before and got interrupted when Elmo Jones brought him the telegram with the news that his former employer, Clem Hargrove, had died. Sam left immediately to catch a train to Kokomo and wasn't expected back until sometime on Sunday.

As she cleared the table Sarah felt a sense of emptiness. Sam's place at the end of the table opposite hers didn't require the clearing of dirty dishes. No one had sat there for breakfast that morning or supper the night before. *Sam left yesterday afternoon and already I notice his absence, it feels lonely. Is it Sam I miss, or is it that I miss the familiarity of another adult sitting at the opposite end of the table? Hmm...you best take stock and get that figured…"Ouch!"* The baby did a double kick-punch so hard that Sarah had to sit down.

\*\*\*

Luke set a basket full of eggs down on the washing worktable near the pump. He picked up an empty one and was headed back to the chicken house when he saw a horse and buggy coming up the lane. The boy waved as he called out, "Hi, Doc Adams. Nice day ain't it."

"It certainly is, Luke. How's the egg business?" Ben called out as he reined his horse to a slow walk.

"Great. Them chickens is a layin' eggs like they's been paid ta do it," the boy yelled back then opened the chicken house door and went in to continue his gathering.

Sarah heard the exchange of conversation but couldn't make out what was said. She got up and went to the screen door to see who had arrived. When she saw that it was Ben she hurried to her room and took off her soiled apron. She put on a clean, freshly ironed and starched replacement and tidied her hair. When she returned to the kitchen Ben still hadn't come to the door. Sarah went outside and found him sitting with Zeke and Hathaway in the digging pile, loading dirt in one of her son's closely guarded, miniature toy wagons. Seeing him such was so out of character that she couldn't resist teasing. "Hey, Mister, our dirt doesn't come cheap. That'll cost you a dollar a load."

Ben looked up at the freshly groomed Sarah and was thoroughly smitten. "I'm sure it's worth every penny." A bit embarrassed by the playful bantering he got to his feet and brushed off his pants.

"What brings you out here so early on a Thursday morning?" Sarah asked.

"Well, I've got a bit of interesting area news. I thought it would be nice to tell you before Elmo Jones for once," Ben said as he took the screen door handle from Sarah and gestured for her to enter the kitchen ahead of him.

"Hey, Ma!" Zeke barked in an angry voice. "Why you makin' him go in already? He ain't even dirty yet. Besides that ain't fair. Doc was diggin' with me and Hathaway first. Can't you wait and play with him later?"

Hathaway had never been allowed the honor of using one of Zeke's wagons for dirt filling, instead being relegated to using a wooden bowl. Seizing her opportunity she quickly commandeered the half-filled wagon that Doc had abandoned and started adding more dirt.

Catching her movement in his peripheral vision Zeke turned to see what she was doing. "My wagon. Ain't no girl gonna use my wagon. Give it back!" His fists were clenched and his face turned red. "Give it back now!"

Hathaway preferred action to words. She picked up the wagon, toddled over to Zeke and dumped the dirt out on his head then tossed the wagon at his feet.

Zeke screamed and then he cried. The tears made trails that turned to little mudslides down his face.

Hathaway brushed her hands together then walked to her mama who was standing speechless half in and half out of the kitchen door. "Me firsty me hungry." The babe toddled past her into the kitchen.

"Remind me to stay on her good side," Ben said. "Go on and tend to her. I'll get Zeke cleaned up."

Sarah put her toddler in her highchair and gave her a cup of milk and a cookie.

Ben came back to the kitchen and reported that all was well at the dirt pile. "I washed Zeke's face and helped him clean the dirt out of his shirt and hair. I got him a drink of water from the pump. He's digging and happy again."

Sarah put two cups of coffee on the table, sat down and rubbed at her bulging stomach. "They do play nice together most of the time. Another year and Hathaway hopefully will learn better 'dirt pile digging' manners. Thanks for helping, Ben."

"Don't mention it." Ben furrowed his brows at Sarah. "Everything okay?"

"I think so. This baby sure is a kicker. Sometimes it near knocks me off my feet. Hey, what's the news you have to share?"

Ben pulled an advertisement out of his jacket pocket. "These were scattered about town this morning. I thought you might find it interesting." He handed it over to Sarah.

---

### Tent Revival
**Wabash Court House Lawn**
**Wabash, IN**
**Thu - Sat, June 24, 25, & 26, 1904, 6PM**
**Evangelist, Wm (Billy) Ashley Sunday**
**An old-fashioned preacher**
**of old-time religion**

---

Sarah read it then looked at Ben. "I've heard of this preacher. For a lot of years he worked and traveled with evangelist J. Wilbur Chapman. Billy Sunday went out on his own when Wilbur Chapman left the traveling circuit. I thought he preached mostly in Illinois. I'm surprised to see he's come to our neck of the woods."

"How is it that you know so much about a traveling evangelist?" Ben asked good- naturedly.

"You've probably forgotten, but Henry has a cousin who lives in Chicago. Her name's Maybel Logan…Henry's mother's sister married a Logan. Anyway she wrote us about going to hear Billy Sunday preach."

"The talk is that he doesn't just preach, he entertains," Ben interjected.

"Yes, Maybel wrote that he's a 'thumper and a jumper'."

"What's a 'thumper and a jumper'?"

"It's a man who moves and hops about a lot when he preaches, carries his bible and whacks on it from time to time."

"Whacks on the bible! Well I've never." Ben looked at Sarah and saw the laughter in her eyes. "Oh, you're just pulling my leg, Sarah."

"No, really, Maybel says Billy Sunday is quite the showman."

"You mean he's just putting on a show? He's not sincere?" Ben asked.

"I wouldn't go so far as saying that Ben. Maybel said what he preached was bible based. The man might be very sincere. I'd have to reserve my opinion until after I heard him."

Ben took a gulp of his coffee. "I wondered if you would like to go with me to hear him preach on Saturday night."

"You mean travel to Wabash?" Sarah picked up the advertisement. "Just to hear this man preach?"

"We could invite your parents to go too. Pack a picnic and take the early afternoon train. We could have supper on the court house lawn and then come six o'clock we'll get a seat in the tent."

"I don't know, Ben. I'd have to take the children. That's a long afternoon and evening for Hathaway and Zeke." The prayer she'd lifted on Ben's behalf that night after they buried Henry popped in to her mind. She'd prayed that an opportunity would be made and a door would be opened for a discussion on faith. *Lord, are you at work in this idea…to get a whole bunch together and go hear an evangelist? Is this a step toward Ben coming to know you personally or for him and me to be able to comfortably discuss the subject?*

"Well, perhaps it's too much for you in your condition," Ben said taking the advertisement from Sarah's hand.

"Hold on." Sarah reached out and grabbed the flyer back. "It would be an experience for us all, that's for sure. We haven't done anything for pure enjoyment since I don't remember when. We could take a couple of blankets. If we get seats on the outer aisle by the tent's side or back flap we could spread them out for the little ones to rest on during the preaching. Likely they'd fall asleep." Sarah surprised herself with her growing excitement about the prospect of going.

"So is that a yes? Will you go?" Ben asked.

"Ma and Pa are coming over tonight for supper. I'll discuss it with them. If they agree to go then, yes the children and I will go too. I'll send word back to you through Pa." Sarah drank the remains of her coffee and stood up. "Now scoot on out of here Ben. I've got work to do and I'm sure you have sick people lining up at your office."

"Yes, Ma'am. I expect I do." Ben went out the door and closed it. "Sarah," When she looked toward the door he had his face pressed up close to the screen with a big smile on it. "Goodbye."

"Goodbye, Ben." Sarah, not oblivious to his lovesick puppy look, smiled back. But she was thinking, *Ben, this idea to go hear preaching sounds a bit like an invitation to go courting. I'm not sure I think that's seemly in my condition and so soon after Henry's death.*

Sarah silently prayed. *Lord, no point in trying to hide my feelings from you. The idea of companionship again does feel tempting. Father, may the meditations of my heart be pleasing to you.*

Sarah looked at the seat at the opposite end of the table from hers. She tried to picture Ben sitting there but Sam's face wouldn't move aside.

# Chapter 39

Thursday morning Sam woke anxious to get out to the farm to see Clara and offer his comfort. He'd come to Kokomo for that purpose and he'd steeled himself to handle the emotions. What he hadn't been prepared for was the talk about faith with Byron the night before. Up to that time Sam hadn't admitted that he had a longing to know God in a personal way.

For the first time Sam wondered if his tremendous attraction to Sarah might be due to her faith in God. *Sarah tried to explain her faith to me, but I never really understood. It could be that I never really listened, at least not like I did last night when Byron explained faith to me.*

*Do I want to be with Sarah the woman, or am I attracted to her because I admire her depth of faith? Sarah has a personal relationship with God. It's intimate, it's hers. I know now that becoming Sarah's partner in life won't bring me faith. I have to find it on my own.*

Sam picked the Bible Byron had given him up from the bedside table and turned to John 14:6. Byron had read the scripture aloud to him, then marked it for Sam's future reference. Sam read it again. "Jesus said unto him, I am the way the truth and the life: no man cometh unto the Father, but by me."

*I reminded Byron that I'd been in prison and why. He explained that God invites us into His family just as we are, regardless of our past. I asked him what if I surrendered to the Lord and invited Him in to my heart but still had a longing for things that don't meet His approval...Sarah included. Byron said it takes a leap of faith...once we let God's love into our heart, our desires, our will become compatible with His. Do I want to surrender my will? Do I have the courage to take that leap of faith?*

Sam finished dressing and made up the bed he'd slept in. After he and Byron ate a quick breakfast they left together to go to the Hargroves' farm. Byron had funeral arrangements to finalize with the family and going together saved Sam the need to get a horse from the livery stable. When they arrived, Clem and Clara's sons gave them both a warm greeting.

When Clara saw Sam enter the parlor she rushed toward him with her arms outstretched. "Sam, you came. I'm glad to see you." Clara was so short that Sam had to lean over and she had to stand on her tiptoes for them to hug.

"I'm so sorry for your loss, Clara," Sam said as he embraced, then released the plump woman.

Clara pulled an embroidered handkerchief from her pocket and dabbed at her eyes. "Come on over and sit with me. We've got a lot of catchin' up to do."

Lightly touching Byron Alcorn on his arm, she said, "Hello, Pastor. Thanks for comin'. My sons know my wishes for songs, scripture and such at the funeral. They've got all the details wrote down for you. You knew my Clem. I 'spect you know what last words he'd like said over his grave."

The preacher replied, "Yes, Clara, Clem was a good friend. You go on and visit with Sam. I'll meet with your sons and then talk with you before I leave."

A young woman, who looked to be in her early twenties, maybe eight or nine years younger than Sam, entered the room. She had raven black hair that hung to her waist. The sides were pulled off her face and clasped at the back of her head with a tortoiseshell comb. She was wearing high-heeled boots, but even with the height advantage didn't look to be more than five foot three inches tall. Her eyes were large and expressive, their shade of blue accentuated by the aqua in the blossoms on her dress's dainty floral pattern.

When she spoke, her tone was muted. "Cousin Clara, could I get your guest some refreshments?"

"That would be nice, Wilhelmina." Clara reached out a hand to the woman. "First come here dear, I want to introduce you to Sam."

Clara looked up at Sam then turned to Wilhelmina. "Sam, this is my cousin's granddaughter, Wilhelmina Reed. Cousin Wilhelmina, this is Sam Hartman. He's the young man I've told you about that used to work and live on the farm with Clem and me."

"Pleased to meet you, Mr. Hartman." Wilhelmina offered her hand to Sam. "I've heard a lot of good things about you."

Sam shook the young woman's hand. "The pleasure's mine, Miss Reed. Do you live near Kokomo?"

"No, my family lives over in Blackford County, near Hartford City. I arrived late last night."

"I'm sure Clara is grateful to have your companionship," Sam said.

Wilhelmina replied, "I've offered to stay with her for the summer."

Clara squeezed Wilhelmina's hand. "And, I've taken her up on the offer. Wilhelmina teaches school. Come fall I hope a position will open here in Kokomo so she won't have to leave."

Sam was sincere when he said, "That's wonderful, Clara. I'll find it a comfort to know you won't be alone."

Wilhelmina smiled at Sam. "Will you be staying in town long, Mr. Hartman?"

"Please, call me Sam. No I can't stay long. I work on a farm over in Wabash County and I need to be back by Sunday." Turning to Clara he said, "I could come out and do some chores here on Saturday if that would be of help."

Clara took Sam's hand in hers. "You're such a sweet man to offer. My neighbors have got that covered for me through the weekend. My sons will get something figured out for the daily chores that can't be handled by Wilhelmina and me after that. But Sam, we do want you here at the farm on Saturday. Please come out in the morning about ten o'clock. We'll be reading Clem's Last Will and Testament and I want you to be present."

Sam gave Clara a puzzled look. "I'll be here if you want, Clara."

\*\*\*

Sam had accepted an invitation from Byron to go to prayer meeting with him that evening. When he walked into the church with the preacher, several folks greeted him. Many knew Sam from when he'd lived in the area.

Sam saw an unknown face at the pump organ. The man was small with a shiny bald head. Despite his diminutive size, he had the billows filled to capacity and they were belching out, *Shall We Gather at the River*. While people continued to arrive and settle in, he played two other hymns that Sam knew well, *In the Sweet By and By, and Bringing In the Sheaves*.

Sam watched Byron as he walked to the pulpit to convene the prayer meeting. *Byron's a good man. He's made bringing in the sheaves his life's work. Sorry old friend, this sheave isn't ready to leave the field just yet.*

After a time of sharing concerns for one another, their neighbors and town folks, the group began to take turns praying. They prayed for the healing of ailments, the courage to face hardships and a plethora of other concerns. The Hargrove family as well as a family whose barn had burned received an extra measure of prayer.

Just when Sam thought the service was over the craggy voice of an old gentleman rang out, "The Lord has laid it on my heart that there is among us one who is considering making a profession of faith. I'd hate to see this service end without giving an opportunity for that person to come forward and accept the Lord as his Savior. Pastor Alcorn, could we sing a couple of verses of *Just As I Am?*"

Byron said, "Certainly, brother" as he moved to a position center front and instructed the congregation to stand and turn to page thirty-five in the hymnal.

By this time, the baldheaded organist had already taken to the bench and was selecting the appropriate stops. The billows filled with air, the pipes whined to life, and the prayer warriors commenced singing verse one. "Just as I am, without one plea, but that thy blood was shed for me, and that thou bidst me come to thee, O Lamb of God, I come, I come!"

Sam rose to his feet but didn't sing. *Was that old cuss referring to me? How does he know I've been thinking about taking the leap of faith? What if I ask God into my heart and He doesn't respond?* Sam was frozen in place by a combination of his own will and just plain fear. *I'm not ready. I need more time to think this through. No, not tonight.*

Showing no mercy the small congregation moved on to verse two, and then verse three and four, then five. "Just as I am, Thou wilt receive, wilt welcome, pardon, cleanse, relieve; because Thy promise I believe, O Lamb of God, I come, I come."

Sam's knuckles were turning white from gripping the back of the pew in front of him when a comforting breeze whispered at the nape of his neck. The breeze seemed to be nudging him and Sam stepped out into the aisle and made his way to the front of the church.

When Sam knelt at the Altar, Byron knelt beside him. "If you'll have me, Lord," Sam prayed, "I'm Yours. I invite You into my life as my Savior and guide." Instantly a spirit of complete peace washed over Sam and he knew he had been accepted into the Family of God.

# Chapter 40

By the time Saturday rolled around, the entourage for the excursion to hear Billy Sunday preach had grown considerably. In addition to Sarah, her five children, and Ben Adams, there were Sarah's parents, Tom and Mary Riley, Sarah's brother and sister-in-law, Jack and Rebecca Riley, their two children, and Elmo Jones. Elmo had weaseled himself an invitation from Sarah when he'd heard through his grapevine that the trip was in the planning.

The little man had been crestfallen to find out he wasn't the first to bring Sarah the news of the traveling evangelist holding a tent revival in their area. He claimed he desperately wanted to hear God's word extolled by the renowned clergyman. Problem was he hated to travel alone, him being so socially shy. He wondered since they'd be on the same train anyway, would she mind if he sat in the coach with her, Doc, and the Rileys. Then he asked her if she minded if he joined them in their picnic supper. He'd of course bring his own food, a piece of fatback and a cold biscuit. As was his plan, Sarah offered to pack enough food for everyone and told him not to worry about bringing anything to contribute.

The train ride from LaFontaine to Wabash was an adventure for the Whitcome children and their cousins. They were given the freedom to find seats to themselves a few rows away from where their parents sat. The children giggled and laughed and sang silly songs as the scenery flew by at a speed that astounded them. All too soon for them the whistle blew and the train pulled into the Wabash station. The party disembarked and divided up the baskets of food, blankets and totes for the two-block walk to the courthouse lawn. Hathaway insisted on walking, but about a half a block toward their destination it was obvious that she couldn't keep up. Doc gave the basket he was carrying over to Elmo and hoisted the toddler up for a piggyback ride.

Sarah, walking at his side leaned in and whispered, "She's still not fully potty trained. This is a lot of excitement for her."

The child kicked her chubby legs and giggled. Ben held her little hands securely. Kissing the back of the left one he said, "I'll take the risk."

The town was alive with activity. There were street vendors selling apples, fruit tarts and lemonade. There was a huckster with harnesses and tools, and a cooper with shiny cooking pots and bolts of hair ribbon and lace. They passed a man cranking out music from a box that hung around his neck. A monkey dressed in a red jacket and hat was tethered to a leash looped over his wrist. The organ grinder was hawking peanuts from a bag slung over his shoulder. "Peanuts. Fresh roasted peanuts. Get 'em here, a nickel a sack." The monkey randomly dispensed free samples.

Hathaway, screamed at the sight of the long tailed creature. Remembering Sarah's caution about the baby getting excited, Ben quickly pulled her from his shoulders and held her close.

Zeke, took an offered nut from the primate. "Thank you kindly, little feller. You sure are ugly, but your red jacket looks right sporty."

The carnival atmosphere continued along the walk to the courthouse square where an enormous tent had been erected. All around the tent's perimeter families staked out their space to picnic and bide time until the preaching began. Sarah and the group found a cool spot under the shade of a large maple tree.

When Sarah bent to deposit the basket she was carrying the baby kicked so hard her knees buckled and she went down.

Ben saw it happen and rushed to her. "Sarah, what is it. Are you in pain?"

"I'm fine. Baby kicked hard. Need to catch my breath."

"Maybe this trip is too tiring for you, Sarah," Ben said.

"The baby kicked. That's what they do. Now don't fuss over me or you'll spoil my fun."

\*\*\*

The group enjoyed a bountiful picnic. Sarah brought ham, thick slices of bread to make sandwiches, a jar of pickles and deviled eggs. Mary contributed two apple pies and a big batch of Saratoga Chips, fried to a crisp perfection. Becky, Sarah's sister-in-law, brought potato salad, fried chicken and chocolate cake. White linen table cloths were spread atop their blanketed patch of lawn and the picnic feast was laid out.

The children were so excited they had to be coaxed to eat. Mary and Becky nibbled with the minimalism required for the corseted female physique. Sarah, unencumbered by the restrictive undergarment due to her pregnancy, ate with abandon.

Sarah glanced at Elmo. *The little man was eating voraciously. He's having a nice day. I'm ashamed I didn't really want him tagging along. Including him has taken such a small effort on our part. Even quirky little mail carriers need a picnic with friends now and again. Heavenly Father, thank you for loving us just as we are and for creating a world big enough for all of us to have a place.*

After they'd eaten, the children were allowed to run and play while staying within eyesight and earshot. The adults settled in for a time of relaxation and lazy chatter.

Elmo used his pocketknife to hack a cheek-sized hunk of Bull Durham from the plug he carried in his back pants pocket. After strategically placing it in his cheek he stretched out on the grass. "They say Billy Sunday was a professional baseball player afore he took to the kerosene circuit and commenced ta preachin'."

Jack was leaning back on his elbows with his legs stretched out in front of him. "That's right. He was an outfielder in the National League during the eighties. Played for the Chicago White Stockings, then in ninety was sold to the Pittsburgh Allegheny team. Had a short stint with the Phillies before leaving baseball altogether for preaching."

Mary was sitting with her back to the tree trunk, fanning herself. "I thought professional baseball players were paid a good amount. Must have been hard to give up the income and go into preaching."

Tom chuckled, "don't feel too sorry for him, dear. I expect they'll be passing the collection bucket around today. With this size crowd he's likely to rake in a sizeable sum."

Becky took off her large brimmed straw hat and adjusted a few loose hairpins in her upsweep. "Elmo, you said Billy Sunday went on a Kerosene Circuit. What did you mean by that?"

"I was referrin' to his preachin' in rural communities like ours that still light with kerosene lamps. Ones that don't have electricity like them big towns such as Chicagie, Illinois." Nothing seemed to please Elmo more than being the one with the answer. His grin was so big his chaw was exposed.

Sarah's boys took turns watching after Hathaway while she ran and played with them. When her drawers were soggy and hanging low, they brought her back to her momma. After changing the child Sarah snuggled with her on the blanket, to get her to take a nap. The comfort of nature and the security of family and friends to look after her children allowed Sarah to thoroughly relax. She, as well as Hathaway, fell asleep.

The comb holding Sarah's Gibson Girl upsweep slipped loose. Her hair fell free, cascading down over her shoulder and breast, as Hathaway lay nestled in the crook of her arm. Ben found it difficult to keep his eyes off of the pair. His breath caught when he saw a stirring beneath the protruding folds of Sarah's skirt. Time was growing close. Another four to six weeks and a new life would enter this world. He hoped to win Sarah's heart before that time came. Ben wished for the courage to share his thoughts with her. *I want to marry you, Sarah. I want to be more to you than your friend and doctor when the baby is born. I'll love it like it's my own. Just as I'll love each of your other five if you'll give me the chance.*

\*\*\*

Ben gently picked up Hathaway and stroked Sarah's arm to awaken her. They needed to join the others who had already gone to the tent to secure seats. It was near time for the service to start.

The seating in the tent was arranged in five sections, five rows each, twenty chairs to a row for a total seating capacity of five hundred. An approximate four-foot aisle separated each section. The outside groupings had a three-foot space between the last chair and the side of the tent. Sarah, her children, Ben, and Elmo, took the back row in the far left section when facing the front. Sarah, took the end seat and spread the blanket out between her chair and the tent side. Ben laid the still sleeping toddler down and took a seat next to Sarah. Sarah's parents, Jack, Becky, and their two children, sat in the row just in front of them.

A stage stretched across the front of the tent covering nearly the entire expanse. A pulpit stood dead center. Folks from the area formed a choir that occupied a grouping of chairs stage left. There was a pump organ far stage right. Its billows were filled to capacity and it was belching out hymns as the people flowed into the tent in a seemingly never-ending trail.

At six o'clock all seats were filled and latecomers were being turned away. The organist ceased playing the medley and began changing stops.

Homer Rodeheaver, Billy Sunday's front man, walked center stage and signaled for the choir to rise. He gave the organist a cue, got the crowd to stand, and led all in the singing of We're Marching to Zion.

Mid way through the song, Rodeheaver exited the stage and Billy Sunday made his signature entrance. Preacher Sunday marched, rather than walked, on to the stage. His left arm was crooked and his hand was resting on his hip. In his right hand he held his Bible, arm lifted to the heavens. He used the Bible to punctuate his high stepping, much like a drum major uses a baton to lead a marching band. Sunday, sang at the top of his lungs as he moved back and forth across the stage.

The audience fed off of the evangelist's enthusiasm and Billy Sunday spurred them on, encouraging them to lift their voices louder and louder with each verse. When the final refrain was sung there was a burst of applause as loud as thunder. There were amens, hallelujahs and praise the Lords from every section of the tent. Elmo, who was sitting at the opposite end of the row from Sarah, was among the loudest.

Sarah sang along but was taken aback, rather than being caught up in the spirit. Wondering what Ben was thinking, she looked in his direction. He was turned facing her with his eyes wide open and his eyebrows raised. Sarah smiled at him and crossed her eyes. The shared sense of incredulousness was palpable between them.

Both Ben and Sarah cut a look at Elmo. The little guy was clapping wildly, his spit can locked firmly between his booted feet.

Eventually the fanfare died down and Sunday began his sermon. "If you're here tonight and you don't know the way to Zion, brothers and sisters, then you're headed down the pathway to perdition."

The heart of the evangelist's message was biblically based on Romans 6:23, For the wages of sin is death; but the gift of God is eternal life through Jesus Christ our Lord.

He pointed to the crowd and shouted, "There are adulterers, thieves and vipers among us here tonight. I'm an old-fashioned preacher of the old-time religion. I'm here to tell you that you've got to come to a personal relationship with God."

True to Maybel's accounting, Sunday thumped his bible, jumped and gyrated about mesmerizing and astounding the crowd. His sermon climaxed when he cried out, "Brothers and Sisters, you've got to come home to Jesus," and he dove headfirst across the stage, as if sliding into home plate.

The organ started playing *Softly and Tenderly Jesus is Calling*. Homer Rodeheaver, took to the stage to lead the singing and the crowd took to their feet. Simultaneously multiple collection buckets began passing down the rows of chairs.

Billy Sunday moved center stage and gave an altar call. He invited anyone who wanted to accept Jesus as their Savior and dedicate their life to serving God, to come forward as a sign of commitment. Person after person, some walking slowly, some running, men, women, and children, went forward that night.

Sarah glanced up at Ben just as he swiped his handkerchief across his eyes. When she looked down the row, she saw that Zeke and Luke were asleep. Josh was standing with his head bowed. Elmo looked as if he was under conviction and was standing with half his body in the aisle and half still in front of his chair. You could see the bulge in his cheek moving as if in time with the music. Abe pushed past Elmo to the aisle. Instead of heading down to the front, the boy ran out the exit at the back of the tent.

Sarah's attention was diverted from Abe's abrupt departure to Ben when he griped her arm and blurted out, "Sarah, I want a personal relationship with God. Could we talk about it, just the two of us?"

Sarah patted the back of Ben's hand, "Certainly. Perhaps later tonight."

Tom Riley turned in his seat and faced Sarah. "Did you know Abe left the tent? He looked troubled."

"Yes, I saw."

"Do you want me to go to him?"

"No, Pa. You go to Elmo, he looks like he might need someone to pray with him. Ben, please watch the children. I'll go check on Abe."

# Chapter 41

Sarah found Abe sitting under the tree where they'd eaten their picnic supper. Head down, knees drawn up waist high, he was plucking at the grass around him, tossing it in the wind as if to rid himself of something unwanted.

Sarah sat down next to him. "Son, you looked upset when you left the tent."

"Yeah."

"What upset you?"

"The whole darn show upset me."

"Show?"

"Tonight was more like a circus act than a church service. Billy Sunday don't seem like no preacher. His slide across the stage, I think he called it goin' home to Jesus, was the slickest part. He should 'a stuck to playin' baseball."

"What did you think about folk's response to his Altar call?"

"That's when I had to get out of there. I couldn't stomach watchin' all those people goin' up front like they really believed what he was sayin'."

"Well, Son, there is such a thing as coming under conviction. That's when God tugs at our heart strings in a way that pulls our thoughts away from things of this world toward Him. God sometimes works through people like Billy Sunday to reach out and touch us through word and song. I think for many that happened tonight."

"So you hold with Preacher Sunday puttin' on a show, like it was the same as goin' to church?"

"It may have appeared to be entertainment to you, but for some it was worship. As for me, no, that's not my preference in worship style. I do however respect that it did touch others. I believe Elmo was among those who were blessed by Reverend Sunday's message."

"Ma, I ain't sure I'd call it bein' blessed. Elmo was a standin' next to me shiverin'. It seemed more like he was excited."

"Elmo may have gotten excited but that doesn't mean he didn't experience a blessing. It is however important to realize that the excitement and high emotions will fade away. If we really let God touch our hearts, that feeling will linger."

"Well, if Elmo really got touched tonight then I'll expect to see him stop his gospin' ways."

"Sometimes when we turn to God we know immediately what needs to change in our lives. More often it takes time to develop a relationship with Him that's deep enough to discern His will for us."

"How do you develop a deep relationship?"

"By getting acquainted with God. Developing a relationship with God isn't that different from making a new friend. You have to talk and listen to get familiar."

"I understand that prayer is talking to God, but how does He talk back to us so we know what He's thinking or what His opinion might be?"

"Reading the Bible helps us to gain an understanding of God. When we believe that the scriptures are God's word, then the truths that are revealed to us when we read them can be interpreted as God speaking back to us."

"Pa had a relationship with God. It didn't do him much good."

"Oh, Abe, it brought your father tremendous joy to serve the Lord. Heartache happens son, you'd best learn how to deal with it without laying blame."

Sarah held her hand out. "Help me get up. Here comes the rest of our group. It's time we get on over to the station to catch our train back to LaFontaine."

When Abe pulled Sarah to her feet, she pulled him into a hug. The boy surrendered to the love of his mother's embrace.

The travelers had nearly two blocks to walk to their point of departure. Elmo took the lead and it was clear that the faith smitten mailman was soaring from his tent meeting experience. He was stepping high and singing *Marching to Zion* at the top of his lungs.

The entourage walked ahead while Elmo stopped at the open door to O'Flaherty's Pub to sing a few extra choruses of the hymn. Someone within yelled "put a sock in it". Elmo saluted and scurried to catch up with his companions but his jubilance never faltered. He continued to march and sing until they reached the train station.

\*\*\*

Weary from the day's excitement, the rhythmic clickity clack of the train's wheels lulled Sarah and her companions to sleep not long after they departed Wabash. Less than an hour later all but Zeke and Hathaway woke when the locomotive blasted its whistle signaling their arrival at LaFontaine.

Abe carried Zeke off the train and Doc carried Hathaway. Motioning for Josh to take a seat on a nearby bench, Ben passed the sleeping baby to the boy and went to fetch his rig. Doc had insisted he be the one to take Sarah and the children home since the day's excursion had been his invitation.

It was a balmy summer night with a full moon that provided good light for their short trip. The moonbeams shining through the canopy of leaf laden tree branches along their route cast shadows that seemed to dance before them as they made their way to the farm.

Sarah took off her shawl and wrapped it around Hathaway. She wanted the child to stay snuggly in her brother's arms in hopes she would make the transition from buggy to bed without waking up. As for Zeke, she wasn't concerned. He was already sawing his boy sized logs, which for him meant he was in a deep stage of sleep. Sarah knew her littlest son wouldn't rally until he smelled bacon cooking the next morning.

Sarah leaned in and whispered to Ben, "Do you want to come in and talk when we get to the house?"

Ben looked down at Sarah's tired face, aglow in the lunar light. "I do want to talk to you, but not tonight. I heard the clock at the train station strike ten o'clock just after we got into town. I know you must be tired."

"Yes, I'll admit I am tuckered out."

"Sarah, thanks for going. I enjoyed the day with everyone and I really did want to hear Billy Sunday preach."

"Thanks for inviting us to go. I'd never have made the attempt on my own, Ben, and it would have been a shame to have missed the event."

Ben looked deep into Sarah's eyes. "The pleasure was truly mine, Sarah. What if I came out tomorrow afternoon? Would you be up to talking about faith then?"

"Tomorrow's good," Sarah said. "Let's make it more toward evening, about five o'clock. You could have supper with us."

"I accept," Ben answered without hesitation. "Will I see you at church in the morning?"

"No, I'm thinking I'll let the boys sleep in a bit since we're getting home so late tonight. With Sam gone, Abe and Josh are handling the chores alone. Sam's due back by midafternoon tomorrow and things will get back to normal around here," Sarah said.

Ben forced a smile but inside he cringed. *Hartman coming back will get things back to normal! Oh, Sarah, that sounds as if you're getting really dependent on him. I need to do something to turn that around.* "Tomorrow evening sounds good. See you then."

# Chapter 42

Sarah stood at the threshold to the room watching her two oldest sleep. She patted her bulging tummy. *Oh, little one, there'll be a lot of years between you and these big brothers of yours. I hope you can come to appreciate all that they do to help out on the farm.*

"Josh, Abe, wake up," Sarah softly called. Getting no response, she walked to the room's window and raised it. A cool morning breeze blew in bringing with it the freshness of a new day. A honeysuckle shrub directly beneath the window graced that side of the house. Although late June, it still sported several trumpet-shaped blooms making it a choice source of sustenance for hummingbirds.

One of the miniature wonders darted into the room. It hovered over the bed flapping its delicate wings, sprinkling sweet fragrance down on the sleeping boys, before making its exit.

"Get up, sleepy heads. The eggs need to be gathered and the cows are bawling to be milked."

Abe woke with a start and sat partially up, leaning his torso on his elbows. "Wha...what time is it?"

"It's seven o'clock," Sarah responded.

"Abe jumped out of bed and stumbled across the room to where his work clothes hung. "Ma, why'd you let us sleep so late? We'll never get the chores done before time for church."

"We're skipping church today," Sarah said. "It was late when we got home from the tent preaching last night. I thought you needed to sleep in a bit."

Josh, awake but still nestled under the bedcovers, yelled, "No church, boy howdy!"

Abe started to pull on his bib overalls, then stopped. "Ma, turn your back please."

Sarah complied, but couldn't keep from smiling.

"You can turn around now, Ma," Abe said.

Sarah clapped her hands, "Let's get to it. When you're done we can have a leisurely breakfast."

Looking longingly at his mother Abe said, "Ma, could we maybe have pancakes?"

Sarah rubbed her chin with her hand and stared at the ceiling. A few seconds passed before she smiled. "Let's have the whole kit and caboodle; pancakes, fried potatoes, eggs, bacon, biscuits and gravy."

The boy's face broke out in a grin as wide as the Mississippi. In a seamless stream of movements Abe pulled the covers off of Josh, kissed his mother on the cheek, and ran down the stairs and out the door.

\*\*\*

It was one o'clock when Sam boarded the train at Kokomo for his trip back to LaFontaine and Sarah's farm. The rail car had few occupants. He could enjoy some solitude which he sorely craved. Recent days had been hectic. Sam wanted time to reflect on what had transpired.

He placed his travel satchel in the overhead storage, took a seat and nestled his tote bag by his side. It contained a sandwich, an apple and a large piece of cake that Clara had insisted he take along for his trip.

Sam stretched out his long legs, placed his hat over his face and folded his arms across his chest. *Gone only four days and so much has happened. My talk with Byron about faith, my decision to invite Christ into my life, Clem's funeral, the reading of his will. It's a lot to think about.*

Sam ran his hand across his shirt pocket where he carried a letter written by his dear departed friend. He'd first learned of the letter's contents after the funeral. The lawyer who handled Clem's Last Will and Testament read it to the Hargrove family and Sam.

Sam put his hat on and sat up in his seat. He couldn't resist taking the folded paper out and reading it again. How many times would this make? He'd lost count.

Dear Sam,

If you're hearing this letter it means I've gone on to glory. Don't mourn me long. If I'd had a choice I would have stayed. I hate the thought of leaving Clara, my sons and family and you, but when the Lord calls you home, you go. I'll be at peace up yonder; I've no doubt about that.

Sam, I've loved you near like one of my own sons. You always did us proud when you worked on our farm and I wish you all of the best life has to offer.

Clara and I discussed this with our boys and we have their blessing as we make this decision and set this to writing. Sam, we're giving you the twenty-acre farm over by Tolliver Creek. As you know, I was able to buy it cheap a few years back. We just never had the manpower to farm it, what with it being so far from our other land. It's got an old farmhouse that needs fixing up. With your carpentry skills I expect you can make it right comfortable to live in. The soil is rich and should bring you a good crop yield. I'd go for soybeans the first year then rotate over to corn.

If you decide you don't want to live in these parts again, sell it. Farmland has appreciated in value. It ought to fetch a good price per acre. Get yourself some land somewhere, find a good woman and set to growing roots.

We also want you to have three hundred dollars in cash. God loves you, Sam, and so do us Hargrove's.

Your friend,
Clem Hargrove

The farm Sam had inherited was located about five miles north of Kokomo. That morning he'd rented a horse and rode out at the crack of dawn to survey the land and assess the condition of the house and out buildings.

*I don't know when the fields were last planted. I expect they've laid fallow for five to six years at least. Plenty of time for the soil to replenish nutrients and rejuvenate. That clump of ground I held in my hand…don't reckon I've ever smelled any richer. I'd do just what Clem suggested in his letter. I'd plant soybeans the first year, see how that goes then rotate over to corn.*

*Tolliver Creek runs through the parcel where the barn and house are situated. Sittin' on the house's front porch steps I could see the stream and hear it gurglin' and babblin'. Sounded like it was talkin' to me.*

*The barn is in satisfactory condition but the farmhouse needs attention, that's for sure. Nice big kitchen with an indoor pump that works. I never expected to find that. The cook stove looked like it was missin' some parts, but nothin' too major. Two other rooms downstairs and two fair sized bedrooms upstairs.*

*Repair the roof, patch the walls, chase out the varmints and a fellow would have himself a right comfortable home. Comfortable, but lonely, compared to living at Sarah's place.*

Sam's newfound relationship with God flicked into his mind. *Lonely… but not alone.* Sam caught a glimpse of a windmill in his peripheral vison as the train passed by. With his attention drawn to the present, he took out his pocket watch. *Two o'clock. We'll pull into LaFontaine in another half an hour. There'll be chores to tackle when I get out to the farm. I best eat the food I brought. I need something to tide me over until supper.*

\*\*\*

Ben Adams paced the floor in his parlor. He was anxious to go out to Sarah's place. She'd invited him for supper at five o'clock. He'd checked the mantel clock a dozen times. It was only a little past noon. His trying to wear a hole in his carpet hadn't made the hands move any faster.

On Sundays, Doc knew the train came through LaFontaine at two-thirty in the afternoon and on it would be Sam Hartman. His thoughts tortured him. *Sam will pick up his horse at the livery as soon as he gets off of*

*the train. He could be out to Sarah's place by as early as three o'clock. Knowing
Sarah, she'll invite him in for a cup of coffee. She'll ask about his trip and the
two will have a cozy chat.*

*Jumpin' to Jericho and back, that's a whole two hours before I get out there.
Why, after all of this time of him living in her house, does it bother me so much?*

***

It was about a quarter after three in the afternoon when Sam arrived
at Sarah's farm. He watered his horse and put it in the barn before he
hightailed it to the house and knocked on the kitchen's screen door.

Hathaway saw him first, "He here, he here." When Sam opened the
door and stepped in, she ran to him and wrapped her arms around his leg.

Lancy, who was in the corner chewing on a wooden block, started
yipping. The puppy ran to Sam, sunk his teeth into Sam's free pant leg and
started pulling and growling. Sam chuckled and made a show of turning
in a circle, mopping the floor with the pup and the baby who both clung
tight.

Sarah was sitting at the table peeling potatoes. "Welcome home. How
was your trip?"

Sam picked up Hathaway. "It was…it was…uh, eventful."

"Well I'm anxious to hear about everything. How is Mrs. Hargrove
holding up?"

"She's grieving, but she has a lot of family and friends. Clara will be
fine."

"Do you want a cup of coffee? We can talk and catch up."

"No, I think the boys and me best get to the chores. When I was ridin'
up I noticed some storm clouds movin' in." Sam kissed Hathaway on her
cheek and put her down. "It would be nice to get finished before we get a
downpour. I'd enjoy catchin' up later though."

Sarah walked to the window and looked out. "My goodness. Those are
some black clouds to the west."

Luke came bursting through the kitchen door. "Ma, Ma, it looks like
it's about ta rain cats and dogs. Abe told me and Zeke ta come fill up your
wood box. Josh and him went to the barn to start chores."

Sam rubbed Luke's head. "I'll go join them."

A gust of wind grabbed the screen door and wrenched it out of Sam's hand. It swung all the way back and banged against the side of the house. Sarah felt a sense of foreboding and looked out the window to check the dark clouds again. They were still off in the distance but moving closer.

Zeke was standing out in the open, arms raised high. The sun, partially blocked by clouds, caused the boy's body to be silhouetted, accentuating his cowlick that jutted to the sky.

Sarah called out, "Zeke, come in the house."

"In a minute, I'm gettin' ready to catch me a lightin' strike."

"You need to stop." A shiver ran down Sarah's spine. "Come in the house, Zeke, now!" She turned to Luke. "Don't worry about bringing in firewood. I want both of you boys to stay in the house.

Zeke came into the kitchen, head hung low, slapping his bare feet on the linoleum, each step more exaggerated than the one previous. "I was havin' me some fun. There ain't nothin' to do here in the house."

"I don't like the looks of the weather. I want you to stay in the house. Play with your blocks for a while," Sarah said as she put Hathaway in the highchair and gave her a biscuit to chew.

Sarah moved her chair next to the window. She sat down with the bowl on her already full lap, peeled potatoes and watched the clouds. *Wonder if Sam and the boys are tracking these clouds? Wish they'd put a hold on the chores and come to the house. I'd feel a lot better if we were all together until this thing passes over.*

The sky had a greenish hue and Sarah worried that a particular cloud she'd been watching looked ominous. *Did that thing start to dip down, or are my eyes playing tricks on me?*

Sarah had never liked storms, especially during Indiana tornado season from spring through early summer. When a child, there was a school yard rhyme that gave her the willies. Remembering it unnerved her still. "Green sky prepare to die." *It's late June. Likely we're getting a severe thunderstorm, nothing more.*

The eerie feeling didn't pass and Sarah jumped up. "Luke, Zeke, go get the quilts off of your beds and bring them to me. I'm going to show you how to make bed rolls."

In addition to the bedding Sarah put a change of britches for Hathaway, a jar of water and a loaf of bread in a basket. After placing the things at the ready by the kitchen door she resumed her vigil of cloud watching.

Sarah had seen the aftermath of destruction from a tornado, but had never witnessed one. Whether a Godsend or just an inclination, all at once Sarah knew she needed to get her children to safety.

She removed pots of cooking food from the stove to the dry sink. She grabbed a handful of matches from the holder that hung beside the stove and shoved them into her apron pocket.

Sarah told Zeke to pick up the puppy, Luke to carry the bed rolls, and she snatched Hathaway out of her highchair. Sarah looped her arm through the handle on the basket containing provisions and led her boys out the door, around the side of the house to the cellar.

Working against a now fierce wind, Sarah pinned Hathaway between her legs and opened the cellar door. "Zeke, get down the steps. Luke, throw those bedrolls down, pick up Hathaway and you and her go down too."

In unison the boys screamed, "It's dark down there."

"I'll light the lantern and follow right behind you."

Luke threw the bedrolls and picked up his sister as instructed but he and Zeke refused to descend more than a couple of steps.

With her right hand Sarah grabbed the lantern that hung at the top of the cellar steps while with her left hand she pulled the door closed. They were enveloped in total darkness. The children screamed and the pup yelped. Sarah took a match from her pocket and struck it. Using the flame's glow to guide her, she lit the lantern.

By reassuring and coaxing she got the children down the steps to the dark, dank cavern and the crying and yelping subsided. Sarah hung the lantern from a nail in a rafter and told Zeke to spread out the bedrolls. She took Luke firmly by the shoulders. "You're in charge while I run and get your brothers."

"I'm scared, Ma. Please don't leave us," Luke whimpered.

"Be brave, I'll be back."

At the top of the stairs Sarah used the muscles in her back to force the cellar door open. Once on top of the ground she let it bang shut and took off for the barn as fast as her cumbersome body would allow.

As she rounded the corner of the house she saw Abe, Josh, and Sam running her direction. Sarah yelled at the top of her lungs. "We're in the cellar."

Sam cupped his hands and called back. "Get down there. We're coming right behind you."

As Sarah turned to go back she saw a funnel cloud. It was still off in the distance, but closing in. She grabbed the handle to the cellar door and managed to pull it open. Unwilling to enter until her boys reached the safe haven, she stood struggling against the wind to keep the door from closing.

Wind tore away her hairpins, her long mane blew untethered whipping at her face. Warm liquid gushed and ran down her legs as she felt herself being lifted in the air.

# Chapter 43

Sam, Abe and Josh were at an all-out run when they rounded the house. A few feet shy of reaching the cellar, Josh let out a blood curdling scream and Sam saw. Sarah was being lifted in the air by a vortex of wind. Her hold on the long metal bar that served as the cellar door's handle was all that kept her from being sucked away. Sam sprinted, grabbed her around her midriff and placed his hand on the bar next to hers. "Praise God, I've got you."

Abe and Josh bolted down the cellar steps. Sam yelled, "Sarah, pull your hand free. I'll keep the door open while I swing you around and down on the first step."

Sarah followed instructions and hurried down the stairs. Sam jumped down on the top step and using both hands struggled against the wind to close the door. Just before it surrendered, Sam saw the tail of the tornado lick the ground and gobble up the woodshed.

The action of closing the door caused a vacuum to form. Sam, Sarah, Josh, and Abe grabbed at their ears. Luke, Zeke, and Hathaway screamed and didn't notice.

Sarah turned up the lantern's wick, throwing more light into the space. The three little ones ran to their momma. The pup saw Josh, ratcheted up his yelping, and leapt into the boy's open arms.

Josh cradled and crooned to the pup, "It's alright, little buddy, I've got ya now."

Sarah comforted her three youngest. "Calm down, you're safe." As she tried to reassure them the whine of the air being sucked through the cracks around the cellar door reached an ear piercing pitch. The children resumed their screaming and Sarah prayed. *Father in heaven, I ask for a spirit of calm for my children. I ask for protection…*

Sarah's unspoken prayer was interrupted by a loud crack followed with a thud. The impact was forceful enough to be felt underfoot. Hathaway was knocked off her feet while the others staggered to maintain balance. Sam picked up Hathaway. Abe pulled Josh into a bear hug and Sarah grabbed Zeke and Luke by the hand.

Sarah was the first to speak. "What was that?"

"It sounded like somethin' big fell on, or near the house." Sam responded. "Maybe a tree." He cupped his hand around his ear. "Listen, the wind's stopped howlin'."

"I'm going up top," Abe said, "I need to see if the chicken house is ok."

"Not yet, Abe," Sarah cautioned. "We want to make sure that the storm's passed over. Wait a bit longer."

"Gosh, Ma, how'd your skirt get so wet?" Josh said pointing. "It was a blowin' wind more than it was rainin'."

"It'll dry," Sarah said dodging her son's question as she motioned for Sam to step aside with her.

"What is it?" Sam said.

"My water broke while I was struggling to hold the cellar door open."

"Your water?"

Sarah laid her hand on her stomach. "The water that surrounds the baby."

"What does that mean?"

"It means that labor pains will start fairly soon. I've already got a lower back ache. Could be that's from struggling to hold the door open. Time will tell."

"How long does your labor usually last once it starts?"

"It's gotten shorter and shorter with each child. Hathaway was born within two hours of my first labor painnnn...." Sarah doubled over grabbing her stomach.

"Oh no, oh no," Sam ran his hand through his hair. "Ok, ok, we can do this. Abe, move one of those quilts over here to the corner of the room. We need to make a place for your Ma to lie down."

Sam took Sarah's arm and helped her lower to the floor, then knelt beside her. He patted her hand as he whispered, "Sarah, please try to get real still, maybe you won't have any more labor pains."

"Sam, hoping no more pains come won't stop them. If labor doesn't start fairly soon the baby will be in danger since my water has already broken.

"I usually give birth easily enough but I'm six weeks from my delivery date. That can be a problem under good conditions. Here in the cellar it might be a real concern."

"What kind of concern?" Sam asked.

"Babies that are born too soon sometimes are extremely underweight and have breathing problems. They need to be kept extra warm and away from dampness. That will be hard to do here in the cellar."

Hathaway started to cry, "Mama, want Mama." She ran to where Sarah lay and sat down on the blanket beside her.

Sarah patted her daughter's chubby leg. "Hush now, everything is just fine. I bet with all of this excitement your britches are wet. Abe, you'll find a change for her in that basket. Would you ooh, ooh, oooh," Sarah clutched the blanket.

"Another pain?" Sam asked.

"Yes."

Sam's voice went up an octave. "Sarah, not even five minutes has passed since your first pain."

Sarah was panting and didn't respond. Sam took charge. "We need to make some privacy for your mother. Luke, spread the other blanket over yonder by the stairs. Josh, take Hathaway and Zeke, go join Luke. I'm puttin' you in charge of keepin' them quiet."

"What's wrong with Ma?" Josh asked. "Why's she makin' noises? Is she sick?"

"Your Ma isn't sick. The new baby has picked now to be born," Sam said.

"Ma," Abe said with his eyes as big as two full moons. "You can't have it down here in the cellar. I'll go up and see if we can safely get in the house."

"Hold up, Abe," Sam said, as he bounded up the steps. He held his ear to the door. "I can't hear any wind, just a gentle rain. I'm going to peek out." Sam tried pushing up on the door. "It won't open." He put his back to the task, still no movement. "The door won't budge, must be blocked."

Abe ran up the stairs. "Slide over so I can get to the top step. If we put our backs to pushin' together, we might move what's blockin' it."

Sam stepped to the side. Abe got into position and said, "On the count of three."

Man and boy counted in unison then pushed. Nothing. They counted again, pushed and groaned. Still their efforts were futile. Sam said, "Whatever fell when we heard that big thud must have landed across the door."

Luke whined, "You mean we're trapped like rats?"

"We aren't trapped." Sarah said firmly. "Now that the storm is over someone will be coming to check on us and whoever it is will take care of getting the door unblocked. We just need to settle in and be pa...tienttttt." Sarah buried her mouth in the crook of her elbow, but couldn't entirely muffle her pain cry.

Sam ran to her and knelt. "Are the pains gettin' stronger?"

"Yes. I couldn't stop myself from pushing with that one. I felt the baby move significantly. I don't think we have much time." Sarah placed her hand over Sam's. "We need to get ready for this baby to be born."

"I have no experience in birthin' humans," Sam said. "I'll need instructions."

"The baby will come out head first," Sarah said. "If it doesn't immediately take a breath on its own, turn it face down and give it a light pat on the back.

"Have a string, a boot lace will work, at the ready to tie off the cord. Make a knot that will hold, then use your pocketknife to cut the cord below the knot.

We'll need something to wrap the baby in to keep it warm. Bundle it right away, mustn't let it get chilled."

Sam nodded, "Ok, I understand so far."

Sarah continued with instructions. "The cut end of the cord will remain attached to the birth lining that's still inside me. You'll need to push on my stomach so the lining comes out. Once that's done, it's over. Any questions?"

Sam couldn't look at Sarah when he asked, "don't we have to uh, uh, make a clear way for the baby to come out?"

"Yes," Sarah responded. "I'll take care of that while you find a string and explain the situation to the children. Abe will worry the most. Tell him I'll have a job for him."

Sam went to the children and explained as best he could what was about to happen. Turning to Josh he said, "Go ahead and change Hathaway. If she's dry, she'll be more comfortable and apt to stay quiet."

In her supine position, Sarah slipped her undergarments down and off. Then, in order to maintain some semblance of modesty, she pulled her long skirt down over her bent knees and let its hem puddle at her feet.

She instructed Abe to take her petticoat and tear it in half. One of the half sized pieces would be used as swaddling for the baby. She told him to tear the other half in to wide strips and fold them. She wanted something ready to use for padding or packing as needed after the delivery.

Abe reached into his pocket for his knife. He needed to cut through the decorative tatting around the hem of the garment so the fabric would tear. After finding both pockets empty, he concluded it must have fallen out. He turned to Josh. "Hey buddy, could I borrow your pocket knife, I need to cut up Ma's petticoat to use for the baby that's comin'?"

"Sure thing," the boy said, proudly handing his double blade Hukill Hunter to Abe.

Josh's task of keeping his younger siblings entertained was proving to be difficult. Zeke hollered. "Ma, I'm gettin' hungry."

Abe barked at Josh. "Can't you keep him quiet? I saw a loaf of bread in that basket, give that to him if he's hungry."

"We already done ett that," Zeke yelled back.

"Well I'll be hog tied," Abe said, shaking his head. "We haven't even been down here an hour."

Josh tried to regain control. "Luke, do you have your harmonica in your pocket? Some tunes might take Zeke's mind off of food."

"No, thank ya," Zeke replied with his head down. "Bein' hungry is bad enough."

"Try singing some hymns," Sam said. "That would be of comfort to all of us."

"I can't think of any hymns," Josh responded.

"How about *Marching to Zion?*" Sam suggested.

"No," Abe blurted out. "Any hymn but that one."

"Let's sing *Jesus Loves* Me," Luke offered. "We all know it."

Just as the children finished with the song, footsteps and a muffled voice yelling out Sarah's name could be heard overhead. Abe, Josh, Luke, and Zeke, started yelling, "Down here, we're down here in the cellar."

A second muted voice called, "I think I heard yellin'. Let's check the cellar."

As the voices neared the cellar door, both were recognizable. Ben Adams and Jeb Carter had come to the rescue. Abe ran up the stairs, put his mouth next to the cellar door and yelled. "The door's blocked. We can't get it open. Ma's havin' the baby. Get us out."

Another labor pain hit and Sarah pushed. Sam called out, "I see the head, I see the head."

Jeb yelled downward. "There's a huge limb blockin' the door. Stand clear boy while we try to get the thing moved."

Grunts and groans were audible. "Doc, stop tryin'," Jeb, out of breath, puffed. "It's too darned heavy. I'll go for help."

"That'll take too long," Ben's voice was frantic. "Sarah's in labor, she needs me. We could try leverage to pry it up."

"Good idea…use the slant of the door, roll it off." Jeb turned in a circle searching the strewn debris with his eyes.

In the dank cavern, another pain with simultaneous push and Sam hollered, "The head's out."

Jeb sprinted to where the woodshed had once stood. "Found some two by fours," he yelled over his shoulder.

Sam supported the baby's neck. Sarah bore down, pushed and a new Whitcome emerged. Sam was jubilant, "It's out, it's out."

Sarah's energy was spent and her voice weak, "Hurry, cut the cord, wrap it up. Can't let the baby get chilled."

A yell from above, "Just a little higher and I think she'll roll."

The newborn sucked in air and forced it out with a strong cry. Sam laid the baby up on Sarah's abdomen, tied and cut the cord. He grabbed the petticoat remnant, wrapped the baby in it and handed the bundle to Sarah.

The cellar door flew open. Dust mites scurried and swirled about in the sudden intrusion of light. Ben frantically called out. "Sarah, Sarah, I'm here, I'm coming." The children jumped up and down and yelled. In double step strides, Ben bounded down the stairs and knelt at Sarah's side.

Sarah's eyes were welled with tears, she grabbed Ben's hand, "I knew you'd come."

Ben cupped Sarah's cheek in his hand and with his thumb wiped away a trickling tear. "Always Sarah, always."

Sam cleared his throat, "Uh, the baby's out, that's as far as I got."

Ben's eyes stayed on Sarah when he spoke, "Sam, I'm glad you were here to help. Sarah, we need to deliver the afterbirth now."

"I'm ready when you are," Sarah responded.

Doc pushed on Sarah's abdomen and the afterbirth slid out. He pushed again to assure the womb was clear. "Dear Lord in heaven," he cried out. "There's another baby and it's sideways."

"Another baby!" Sarah raised up on her elbows. "Sideways, how do you know?"

"A fist popped out."

Sam looked, "I see it too, a tiny fist."

Sarah's voice quivered, "Can it be born that direction?"

"No," Ben said, as he ripped off his jacket and rolled up his shirt sleeves. "I'll have to use my hand to reach in and push the baby upward so I can turn it to get the head in a downward position." Doc squeezed Sarah's hand, "Trust me."

"I do," Sarah whispered.

"Sarah, let Sam hold the baby," Ben commanded. "Do you have any vinegar stored down here? I need something to clean my hand before I do this."

"That large bee sting crock," Sarah pointed. "It still has some of last summer's pickled cucumbers in it. The brine contains vinegar."

Sam took the baby from Sarah. He held it in his right arm. With his left hand he unbuttoned his shirt. He placed the baby against his bare chest and closed the shirt's flaps.

"It'll have to do," Ben said. "We've got to move fast before the uterus starts contractions to close itself."

Ben ran to the crock and took off the wooden lid. He plunged both of his arms in the brine. While he used his left hand to briskly scrub his right hand and forearm he called out. "Abe, I need one of your bootlaces."

Abe frantically unlaced his boot and yelled, "Doc, catch."

"Got it. Jeb, get the children out of here."

Jeb picked up Hathaway and he and the four little ones scrambled up the stairs.

Abe took a determined stand and said, "I'm stayin' with Ma."

Ben and Sam said in unison, "No."

Sarah ordered, "Abe, you need you to go see to the chickens. Go!"

Abe ran up the stairs.

Ben slid his hand alongside the baby's fist, up its hidden side, cupped its buttock and pushed upward.

Sarah groaned.

Doc removed his hand. "It's turned, the head is down."

Almost immediately Sarah felt a cramping that came in waves cresting to a full labor pain. She pushed and the head came out. Another pain followed, a big push and a lifeless body emerged.

Ben laid it on his coat, tied and cut the cord. He swept up the limp body and flipped it face down. With the palm of his hand he rapped its back. No response.

His second rap was firmer, no response. On the third rap the miniature mouth opened and sucked air. A whisper of breath mewed back.

"Is it alright?" Sarah asked.

Ben used his jacket as swaddling, then cradled the baby in his arms. "It's small and seems weak, but breathing's steady."

Sarah propped herself up on her elbows. "What is it...uh, they, boy or girl? The first one, is it alright?"

"Mine's a boy," Sam said. "I can feel his tiny heart beatin' strong."

"Mine's a girl," Ben said. "I didn't get a good look but I know she's beautiful."

Sarah looked from Ben to Sam, then back at Ben. Her eyes lingered holding him in a firm embrace. "Praise the Lord."

Printed in the United States
By Bookmasters